I0824996

THE GAME OF OATHS

THE GAME OF OATHS

S. C. BANDREDDI

CANDLEWICK PRESS

First edition 2026

Library of Congress Control Number: pending
ISBN 978-1-5362-5263-7

26 27 28 29 30 31 SHD 10 9 8 7 6 5 4 3 2 1

Printed in Chelsea, MI, USA

This book was typeset in Adobe Garamond Pro.

Candlewick Press
99 Dover Street
Somerville, Massachusetts 02144

www.candlewick.com

EU Authorized Representative: HackettFlynn Ltd,
36 Cloch Choirneal, Balrothery,Co. Dublin, K32 C942, Ireland.
EU@walkerpublishinggroup.com

To the younger sisters who have felt lost, afraid, or full of rage
—or all of the above.

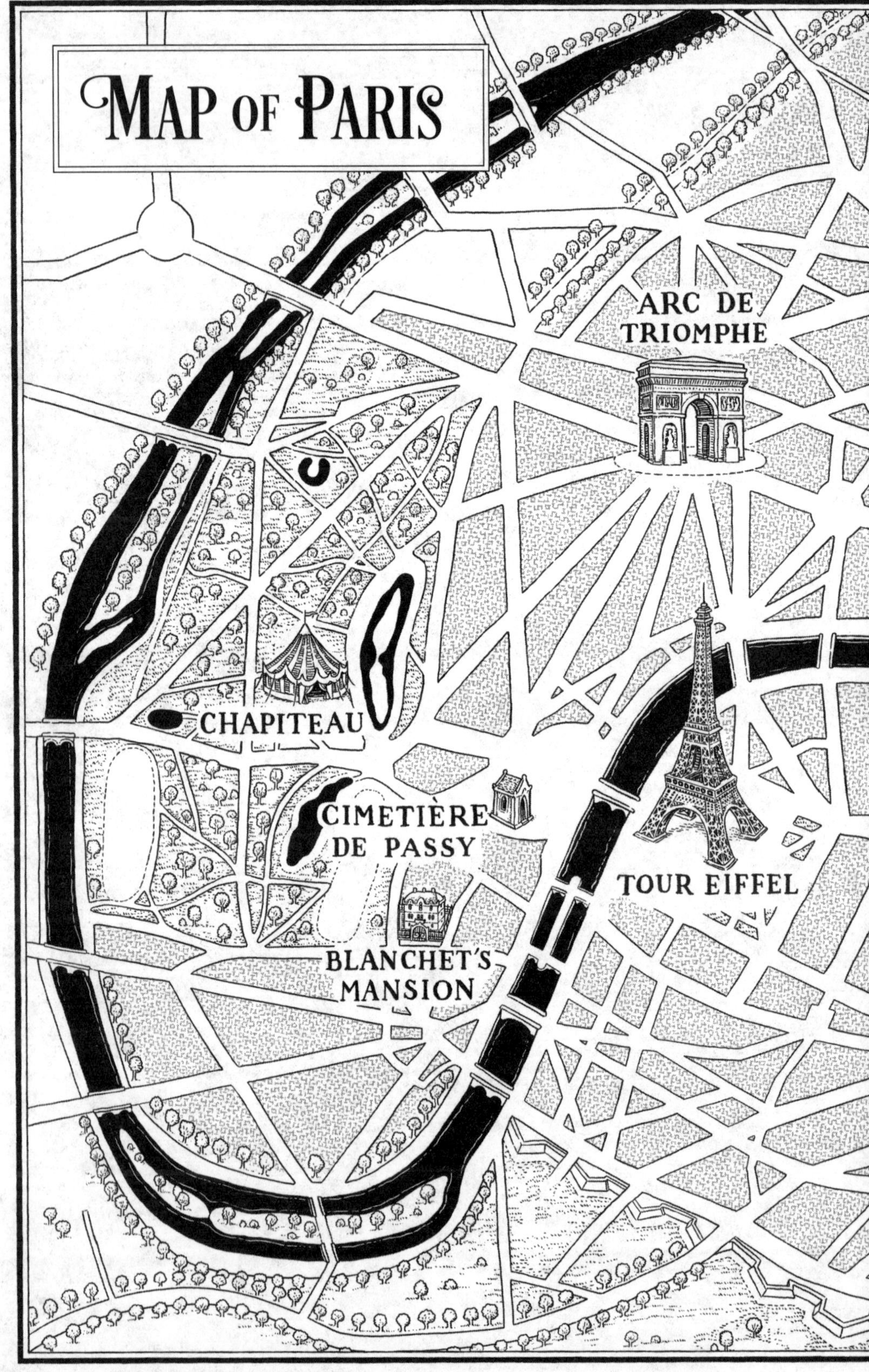
MAP OF PARIS
ARC DE TRIOMPHE
CHAPITEAU
CIMETIÈRE DE PASSY
TOUR EIFFEL
BLANCHET'S MANSION

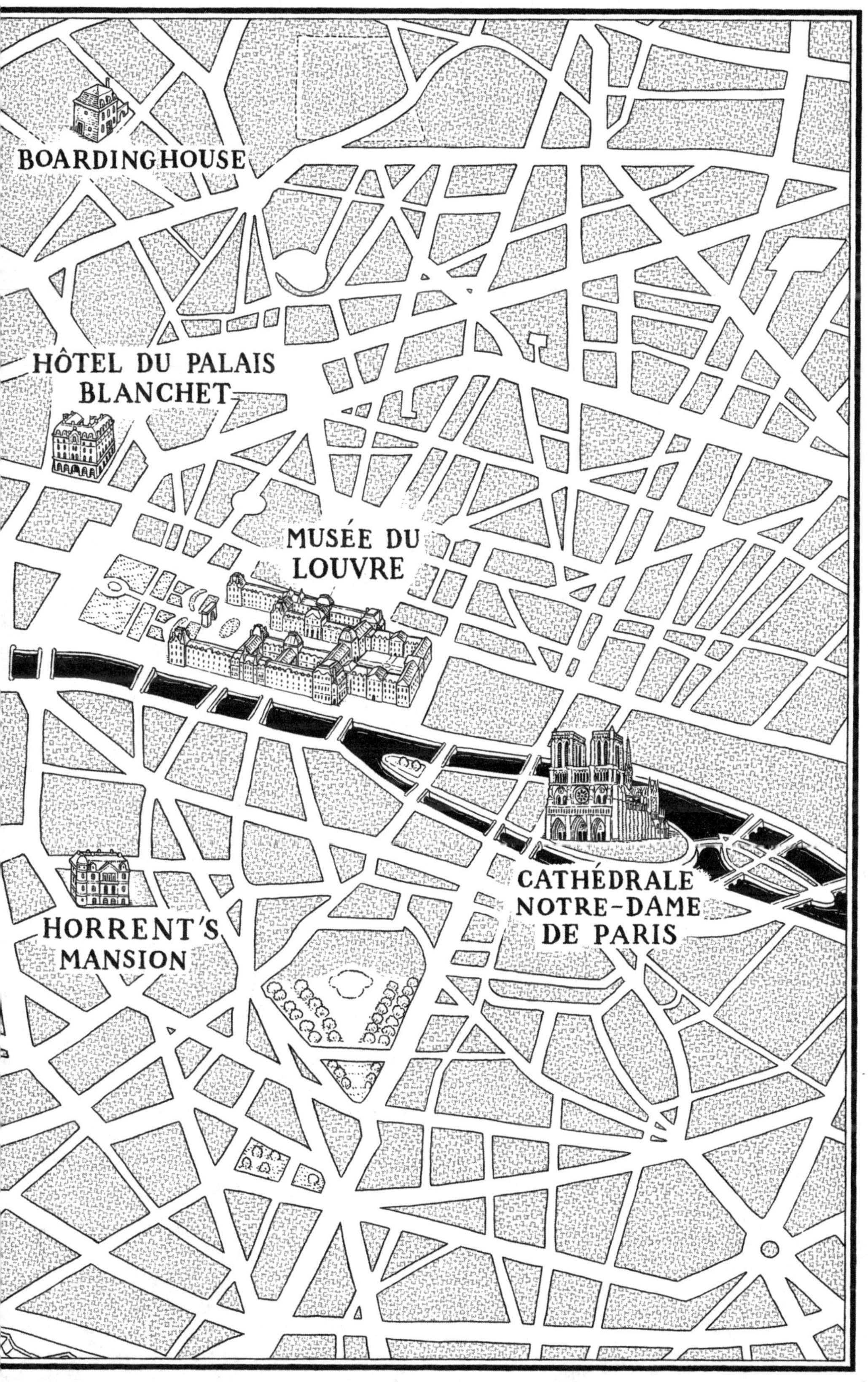
BOARDINGHOUSE
HÔTEL DU PALAIS BLANCHET
MUSÉE DU LOUVRE
HORRENT'S MANSION
CATHÉDRALE NOTRE-DAME DE PARIS

AUPARAVANT

The arena is packed tonight.

The normally empty hotel understory, made of stone and silence, is alive. A spiral of red and white has magically appeared overhead and cascaded down the walls; the audience feels like they're in a genuine tent, rather than the bottom story of a towering hotel.

The ringmaster can just make out his beloved spectators through the darkness. He practices the dapper tipping of his black top hat; adjusts his red coat, although it already lies straight on his broad shoulders; checks his gold pocket watch despite knowing exactly when to start.

11:58. Two minutes to showtime.

He feels the different bonds he has with each performer shifting as they rush around him, puppets on their strings hurrying to their starting positions. The spectators can't see them yet, the preparations taking place around them made invisible by a shroud of darkness over the arena.

They can feel the anticipation, however. The echoes of harried footsteps pattering around them, the pumping of their hearts, the excited whispers fluttering among them like delicate butterfly wings, the *crackle-pop* of a piece of candied popcorn, the creak of bodies settling into their seats.

The performers, however, feel quite a different set of emotions. They smooth down their costumes, touch their faces to ensure their makeup is flawless, ready themselves to fly, dance, dodge, twirl, bend at the ringmaster's will. All second nature, but the nerves have never disappeared. Some performers await with eagerness, craving the temporary euphoria they will feel once they step into the spotlight. Others are disgusted at themselves for the pull; the stage beckons them regardless.

One performer, a trapeze artist waiting in the wings high above, feels nothing at all.

At the stroke of midnight, a series of lights suddenly rise to the ceiling of the arena, emitting a collective gasp from the crowd. Then a single light shines down on the stage, illuminating the ringmaster. The crowd's gasps turn to cheers, and the ringmaster basks in their glory.

"Welcome!" His voice booms around the room—the tent. "Welcome, all, to le Cirque des Ombres!"

The tent is an illusion. The lights above him are an illusion.

But the crowd's admiration is not. Although all of his puppets are waiting, ready at his beck and call, the ringmaster is the only true performer here. Without him, there would be no Cirque des Ombres. And all of his unfortunate puppets would be left to the glittering depths of Paris—the city would eat them alive.

The audience never fails to be dazzled by the spectacle before them, but its true nature is the same as everything else in le Cirque des Ombres.

An illusion.

PART I

The Reckoning

"The government allots certificates for trusted Enchanteurs who use magic with care, men who will not harm our superior society. To let anybody inferior use such abilities freely is a thought I can neither fathom nor support."

—*Guillaume Gallien's Origins of the Arcane*;
Ch. 1, p. 18 (1868)

I

November 6, 1896

FALAN SUNKARA HAS NEVER GAMBLED IN A GRAVEyard before.

In her three years of scamming cercle patrons, her marks have usually insisted on meeting in underground bars, bouillons, even alleyways. But to be gambling in a place of old ghosts is a strange feeling; the prickle of the icy November air across her skin gives her the chilling sensation of being watched.

Nevertheless, le Cimetière de Passy is a clever choice for a covert game of poker. It's closed off from the curious eyes of stray passersby, yet open enough to flee at a moment's notice if the authorities arrive. The tombstones scattered about the cemetery are dusted with a light layer of snow, just barely starting to melt in the winter dawn. It's beautiful, in its own morbid, sorrowful way. But Falan's eyes are fixed on her targets for the day, two occasional cercle gamblers named Clément and Dumas. They sit between the arches of a crypt on low stone slabs, using one as a makeshift table.

"It's your turn," says Dumas, looking toward the fourth player.

Falan raises her eyebrows at Meera Kumar, otherwise known as Claude to the targets. Her roommate grins back, a devilish smirk Falan has come to know far too well over the years. "It's a rather weighty decision," Meera says with a sigh, taking her time. "After all, it will determine the game."

Clément and Dumas fidget beneath their thick coats and hats, expressions gritted with thinly strung patience. Meera's smirk grows, and Falan knows their aggravation has just delighted her into taking a few more minutes.

Falan resists an eye roll. She did not ask her roommate to come along on this grift—not after the last time, when they narrowly avoided a beating after Meera turned over the table in a fit of rage after losing and tried to steal back her stipend—but Meera tailed her to the graveyard, introduced herself as Falan's friend Claude, and sat down to play.

At least she had the sense to put on a good disguise. Falan herself is dressed in trousers and a loose shirt, her long black hair tucked up into a cap. She looks like a young peasant boy now, no more than fourteen, a good three years younger than her true age.

Most men will not gamble with a lady, but the idea of cheating a peasant boy out of his last few coins usually tickles them. Particularly if it's somebody they think doesn't belong in Paris. With their dusky complexions and thick, dark hair, Falan and Meera fall into that category.

"Hurry up!" Clément finally snaps. "Some of us have to work in a few hours."

Falan passes Meera a bored look over her own fan of cards. She knows that her roommate's hand is no good. Meera thumbs her deck when she's possessive of what she has. Her fingers have barely moved in the span of her turn.

But still, Meera says, "I call," and pushes forward the meager amount of coins in front of her.

Clément throws down his cards. "Bust."

"Flush," Dumas says with a satisfied smile.

"Bust for me too," Meera says, laying down her cards.

The two men shoot her puzzled looks. "But you called," Dumas says.

Falan lays her cards face up. "Straight flush. I win."

The men watch in shock as Falan scoops the francs into her bag.

"The two of you are working together!" Clément exclaims.

"Is that against the rules?" Meera asks languidly, flipping a stray coin in the air and catching it.

Clément scowls but says nothing.

"And where did you learn to play like this?" Dumas asks Falan skeptically.

Instead of answering, Falan tosses the strap of her bag over her shoulder.

"Better luck next time, gentlemen," Meera says as she stands to leave, but she accidentally trips over her stone slab, knocking into Falan.

Five cards spill from Falan's sleeve onto the ground—the same five cards she swapped out for a straight flush. She clenches her jaw. She could kill Meera, truly.

As Clément kneels to study the cards, Falan suddenly runs, Meera right behind her. She hears the men's angered shouts for them to stop but only quickens her pace. She makes for the exit of the graveyard, Clément and his curses chasing after them. Her shoes slap hard against the packed dirt as she weaves through the path of gravestones.

Falan wonders if ghosts feel it when somebody walks over their graves. As if to taunt her, a sudden shiver runs down her back, like if a specter's icy fingers had traced her spine.

"My mistake," Meera says as they reach the street. "But at least I didn't flip a table over this time."

"I should have made Ary tie you up so you couldn't follow me," Falan snaps.

"And disturb her sleep on this awful day?"

Across the road from Trocadéro Palace, Falan takes a second to glance back. Clément is rapidly catching up. In the growing light of the dawn, tailing them back to the boardinghouse would be all too easy. Quickly, Falan swaps her bag with Meera's. "Go right. If you're followed, bribe Erwin to lie for you. There are two cigarette packs in the bag."

"I thought you'd be more generous on Le Jour de L'Élu," Meera says critically. "Even the possibility of being chosen for death doesn't soften—"

"Your death will no longer be a possibility but a reality fulfilled by me if you don't *go*," Falan says coldly, and Meera finally runs.

Falan turns her attention to Clément, waiting for him to come closer. When he is mere feet away, she bolts down the left path, leading him deeper into the streets of downtown Paris. The city is still dreamy with slumber, lagging behind the breaking dawn. Its clouds look like they should belong to another morning, light and airy, and the glow from the arc lamps lining the path is soft against the pinkening sky.

The alley coming up on her right is a good spot to take to the roofs. But as Falan runs into the passage, a stray brick flies past her face and just barely misses her, crumbling against the opposing wall.

Clément stands at the far end of the alley, panting, a hand held out in front of him. How did he—

Falan swears. *He's an Enchanteur.*

But this is not the first time a grift has gone wrong. A few of her past marks who caught her cheating were also Enchanteurs, and she was able to handle them.

"You made a mistake," Falan says coolly. "Using magic without a cert? I could easily turn you in to the authorities."

This is when her past marks have usually faltered. Certificates aren't commonly given; only a handful of Enchanteurs are allotted the privilege of using their magic for public benefit, usually for entertainment or military purposes. Every other Enchanteur risks incarceration if discovered using magic without a cert.

So when Clément pulls something small and rectangular from his coat pocket, Falan tenses.

"Oh, but I *do* have a cert, mon cher." Sunlight plays over the wax seal on the card. "Try turning me in and see how that goes."

"You used magic to attack me," Falan says, taking a step back. "That can't be under your allowed usage."

"You're worried about laws when you're the one scamming me, you little thief?" Clément says.

He's right. Anybody could argue that using magic to catch a thief was necessary, even noble. If he turns *her* in, on the other hand, she'll be in much larger trouble for theft. It will be his word against hers.

Falan swivels and bolts back down the alley but manages only a few steps before something hard hits her in the back, sending her onto the ground. The cobblestones scrape her palms and knock the air out of her lungs. Before she can get her bearings, Clément has already caught up. He yanks her to her feet, his fingernails digging into her arm.

"Now give me back my money, or I will show you what magic can really do," he snarls. The fingers of his other hand curl, and the stones and debris in the alley start to rise around them.

In response, Falan yanks herself away. The cap on her head falls off, sending her long, black hair tumbling down her back.

"Mon dieu," Clément says with a gasp, so startled the debris drops to the ground once more. "Tu es une fille?"

His surprise gives her the few seconds she needs. Falan scoops up the cap and shoves her elbow into the man's face. He crumples back with a howl, clutching his bloody nose as she sprints for the alley wall, then grabs its protruding slabs of brick. By the time Clément's broken nose stops distracting him, she's halfway across the city, jumping from roof to roof, scaling buildings.

Fervor rushes through Falan's veins, pumped by the near capture. To soar between rooftops is more thrilling than any performance she has ever done at le Cirque des Ombres. On Paris's rooftops, the world changes around her in a smear of color; nobody is watching, nobody is waiting. Today, however, she's quicker than usual, eager to put distance between herself and Clément.

Falan eventually pauses atop one of the buildings on Avenue des Champs-Élysées to catch her breath, letting the breeze blow her unruly hair back as she settles on the roof's edge. Normally she would need to rush back to the boardinghouse and get to practice for the Cirque's performance that night. But not today. Today, Falan has a bit of extra time to gaze out at the cityscape, drinking in the sight of Paris rousing to life. Even at dawn, the city has no shortage of tourists, especially prevalent during this time of the year.

With the Game of Oaths rapidly approaching, every aristocrat is hungry for a coveted ticket.

The Game of Oaths has always been an open secret among the Parisian upper class, an annual underground tournament for their entertainment. However, when many from all over the world came to Paris for L'Exposition Universelle in 1889, aristocrats from beyond city borders were invited to view the Game. Over the past seven years, it has only increased in popularity, fueled by the rich's insatiable appetite for bloodshed.

Falan lingers on the rooftop for a bit longer, watching the sun rise higher in the sky. She's not quite ready to go back to the boardinghouse yet. But, even today, she can't stay out too long. With a flourish, she gets to her feet and runs.

On a normal day, the boardinghouse smells like stale bread and ash. The smothering scent of cigarettes seeps through every room of the building, day and night.

Today, however, the boardinghouse smells like nothing at all.

Falan descends the wall from the boardinghouse's roof into her tiny bedroom window. Swinging into the room and onto her bed, she finds Meera counting her money on the bottom of the opposite bunk.

Ary Chea, their other roommate, is watching her from the bed above but gasps softly, startled at Falan's entrance. "Falan."

"You look far too unhappy for somebody whose belly is going to be full for the next week," Meera says as a greeting.

Falan throws Meera's bag at her. "I didn't want you coming with me."

"That's rude. I am wonderful company," Meera says. She doesn't take her eyes off the pile of francs, her black hair falling in unruly waves over her hunched shoulders. "Besides, today's targets seemed to be bigger fools than usual."

"Not quite as foolish as you," Falan says cuttingly.

Meera laughs. They all know the cercle is abundant with the same overly indulgent, witless individuals as the Cirque's spectators. Owned by luxury hotel le Palais Blanchet, both the Cirque and the clandestine gambling club are two of the most frequented attractions in Paris. The cercle opens after sunset, and the Cirque's shows are held at midnight. While the Game of Oaths may be an underground spectacle, the Cirque is not. A government-issued certificate approves Jean-Pierre, the ringmaster, to use his magic for entertainment purposes.

Unfortunately, as Falan has come to know, life as a performer is not quite as magical as the shows they partake in. Their stipends are barely enough to pay for one meal a day, so finding other means of making money is essential. Public gambling is prohibited in Paris; due to their role at le Palais Blanchet, performers and cercle dealers alike are strictly forbidden to gamble at the hotel, so Falan holds her games outside with those who are greedy enough to disregard the law.

But, like this morning, grifts can sometimes entail a few snags.

"You got a rip there." Meera gestures carelessly to the scrape on Falan's knee, where her trousers tore.

"Does it hurt?" Ary asks. Her dark eyes, large and inquisitive, survey Falan's grazes.

"No," Falan says shortly, then asks Meera, "Were you followed?"

"Don't think so." Her nonchalance annoys Falan further. "I didn't bother to bribe Erwin, if that's what you're asking."

"Good," Falan says, resting on her back. She has a bunk all to herself, since the bottom bed has been empty this past year. "And fool or not, Clément nearly got me in the alley. The bastard was an Enchanteur with a cert."

Meera smiles, but nothing about it is humorous. "Imagine if we had that magic."

Falan shakes her head. "I'd rather not. We'd be worse off trying to hide it."

The Enchanteur population is a strange paradox of both rare and common—rare enough to be vastly outnumbered by non-magic individuals, but common enough to not be a mystery. Not that it matters; even if she were an Enchantresse, someone like her would not be given the privilege of a cert.

"At least if I were an Enchantresse, I'd stand a chance of ripping up Jean-Pierre's cert," Meera says.

"Meera, don't say things like that!" Ary whispers furiously.

"She's right. You never know who could be listening," Falan says, even though it's an unspoken rule among those who live in the boardinghouse not to leak information to Jean-Pierre.

Meera scoffs. "Let them listen. The bastard can't control what we say today."

She has a point, but Falan doesn't bother to respond as she leaps down from her bed, takes her bag back from Meera, and checks inside for the cigarette packs. Even though Meera didn't end up bribing Erwin, Falan still needs to give him his payoff.

"So, breakfast?" Meera says with a smile that's far too cheerful.

"I don't know if I have the stomach for it today," Ary says. Indeed, it looks like she might be sick.

"That's all right, Baby Bird. I'll eat your portion," Meera says good-naturedly.

Falan rolls her eyes. "I'm leaving in ten seconds. Make up your mind."

Ary leaps down from her bunk. Meera stands, slinging an arm around Ary's shoulders, and walks to the door with her. "Did you really mean that, about eating my food?" Ary asks Meera anxiously as they exit the room.

Falan throws her bag over her shoulder and follows them, slamming the door behind her. As she walks down the stairs, she brushes her hand against the pockmarked wall. The boardinghouse isn't the prettiest place—Falan has not once seen Erwin pick up a broom or cloth in the five years she's been here—but even if it were not mandatory for them to live here, Falan knows far too well that there are worse places to reside.

Their proprietor may be just like the building he runs—dirty, harsh, and in violation of many laws—but his penchant for accepting worthy bribes has allowed her to get away with far more than most do. For instance, two cigarette packs a week equals freedom; none of her unapproved trips are written in the logbook, where Erwin notes the name of each cercle dealer and Cirque performer and their reason each time they leave the building.

Meera opens the door to Erwin's office at the bottom of the stairs, and they walk in to find him slumped over his desk, indulging in a glass of some sort of liquor rather than his usual cigarette. The tiny room, cramped with only a bed to accompany the desk, reeks of spirits and stale ashtrays.

"Bonjour, Monsieur Erwin," Ary says politely while Meera's nose wrinkles at the smell.

Erwin tips his head in greeting.

"A drink that tastes of smog is no substitute for genuine smoke," Falan says pithily.

Erwin flashes a rare smile at her, deepening the wrinkles in his face. "I will not be indulging in smoking until after the Game of Oaths," he says.

An odd tradition of his, it's one Falan usually dreads. The scent of cigarette smoke indicates normality.

Meera and Ary leave after telling Erwin they're heading out for breakfast, which he notes in the logbook, but Falan stays behind. As soon as the door shuts, Falan pulls out the cigarette packs from her bag and tosses them on Erwin's desk. "Alcohol is easier to get," she says. "Perhaps you should stick with it."

Erwin leans back in his chair, which creaks tiredly. "I'll tell you what: If you are chosen tonight as a player, you can go wherever you want until you're taken into seclusion. No cigarettes needed."

"Feeling compassionate today?" Falan says with a ghost of a smile.

"You won't be picked anyway. People want to place their money on the strongest. Cunning as you appear to be, you're a tiny thing."

Falan's expression turns to stone. Perhaps before last year, she might have agreed with him. But with the specter of a familiar voice whispering in her mind, having haunted her for the past year, she's less inclined to believe the Game's usual patterns anymore.

"That's what people said about Lavanya," Falan finally says. "And look what happened to her."

Erwin falters for the briefest of moments. "You're right. I suppose at this point, one can't predict an outcome." He doesn't add anything more, but Falan remembers the pitiful remarks after last year's Game.

It's such a shame.

Lavanya didn't deserve this fate.

I'm so sorry.

Erwin says one can't predict an outcome, but for this year's Game of Oaths, Falan is sure of it. By the time the tournament is over, Jean-Pierre will find himself with nothing. And then Falan will finally do to the ringmaster exactly what he did to her sister.

Murder him.

II

November 6, 1896

UNTIL LAVANYA'S DEATH, FALAN ASSUMED THAT Jean-Pierre never intervened in the tournament's outcome. He brought to life the setting of each game using his magic, but remained omniscient like the shadowy figure of a story's narrator.

This belief shattered a year ago, when Falan watched Lavanya fall to her death during the first round of the tournament.

Three weeks before the Game of Oaths, Lavanya had told Falan she was plotting their escape from the Cirque. It was far too coincidental that she was chosen for the Game right after. Falan's mind has remained stuck since Lavanya died, continually replaying the scene of her sister's death. The first round of the tournament had involved players crossing a beam that was elevated to deadly heights. Lavanya had not fallen off the beam itself but from the top of the ladder down from it. She had not slipped; the rung broke beneath her feet. Mostly, Falan remembers Jean-Pierre's expression that night. Satisfied. He had clearly killed Lavanya out of spite, not even leaving her already slim fate to the chance of the Game.

In the dark of the sleepless nights that followed her sister's death, Falan plotted how to pick apart the ringmaster's defenses, how to leave him with nothing. Over the past year, she has been waiting. Watching.

Conspiring.

"Joue ta chance, Falan," Erwin says as she turns to leave his office.

Gamble your luck.

It's what performers often say around the Game of Oaths before the players are chosen—sometimes simply *chance* for short, as it's often said around the cercle. Rich with irony, for only a few have a solid amount of luck to gamble with.

The boardinghouse is a tram ride away from le Palais Blanchet, set in the heart of Quartier du Faubourg-du-Roule. Generally, the hotel is barren during the morning, as most of its excitement happens at night. Falan passes by the front of the hotel, the lobby visible through its glass doors. The pull in her chest is at ease, like a bind around her heart has slackened; Jean-Pierre must be inside. Although the thought of him being close by fills her with discomfort, being too far away affects her physically.

Even prior to coming to France, Falan had heard of contracting—an agreement between an Enchanteur and a non-magic individual that permits the Enchanteur's magic to imbue the other person—but only after arriving in Paris did she see how much the French utilize it, particularly Jean-Pierre. The Cirque's performers are each bound to the ringmaster by an unseen link; to Falan, it feels like shadows curled around her bones, like the coldest part of winter mingled with the blood in her veins.

Running is futile. She tried once, just to see how far she could go. With each step, Falan felt the strain grow stronger, like cuffs biting into her limbs. She finally collapsed at the outskirts of the fourteenth arrondissement, her shaking legs unable to take another step, her entire body in agony. It was only on her journey back that she felt relief, the restraints going slack.

The French call it le Lien. The Bond.

The only way to break a contract is to destroy the object that the magic is embedded into, which is what Lavanya planned to do in order to free them both. Although the magic can be kept in any object, it's traditionally imbued into physically signed contracts, which Jean-Pierre keeps locked away in the safe in his office at the hotel.

Falan looks up at the penultimate floor of le Palais Blanchet, wintery sunlight reflecting off the window of Jean-Pierre's office, before casting her gaze back at the lobby. On a normal day, performers would be rehearsing for shows at this time, but most are probably sleeping in or at the bouillon down the street for a meal; the place is accustomed to the dealers and performers, even friendly with them, offering meals at lower prices.

But today, most performers will buy expensive pastries and delicacies, as if to treat themselves before a night of terror. They always do on Le Jour de L'Élu—the Day of the Chosen, when twelve performers will be picked to compete in this year's Game of Oaths. The performers have plenty of nicknames for Le Jour de L'Élu, the most common one being the Reckoning. No matter what they call it, attendance tonight will be mandatory. There's no point in resisting.

Ary and Meera must already be halfway through their meals. But instead of going to join them, Falan walks inside the hotel. Unnoticed, she slips past the expensive marble floors and glass windows of the front lobby.

There are two doors in the farthest hallway behind the lobby, hidden by illusion, visible only to those who have permission to enter. To the ordinary eye, the doors are nonexistent, one with the smooth white wall. Through the first door lies the cercle, while the second leads to a staircase that descends beneath the hotel. The walls are draped in black like a silken shadow, the carpet underfoot a red velvet. At the end of a hall are the red-and-white canvas folds of a tent, blocking what is waiting inside—le Cirque des Ombres.

In the dark of the night, the arena comes alive. Falan is certain she will never see it again after tonight. The Game of Oaths is not held in the arena but in the Chapiteau, a large red-and-white tent that appears each year on a plot of land in Bois de Boulogne.

Falan walks down the steps to the arena, remembering all the performances and practices held here. Though she despises this place, a part of her longs to see it in a gloriously silent, undecorated, empty state, an echo of what it will become in the future. Just a spacious room ringed by lofted seats circling a pit of a stage, only made special by Jean-Pierre's magic.

Instead, Falan walks in to see her trapeze partner, Ronan Allaire.

Ronan is suspended high above the ground, a ribbon wrapped around his torso as he does a beautiful backflip in midair. His eyes are closed, relief softening his usually hard expression; it's like he's dancing weightlessly with invisible wings.

Irritation washes over Falan. Seeing Ronan on a regular practice day is already an annoyance. Seeing him now is even more vexing, especially knowing his thrill on the trapeze is a genuine one. Not only does Jean-Pierre's magic bind them to him, but it also enhances each performer's Affinity—their prime aptitude, their gift. It's something every person, non-magical or otherwise, has, and something only Enchanteurs can see. Jean-Pierre generally picks those with Affinities circling around physicality when offering contracts. They become unearthly; fire performers who dance effortlessly among flames, contortionists who can bend into any shape imaginable, knife throwers and dodgers with razor-sharp dexterity. And when their Affinities are activated as they perform, they experience a thrill that for many is the only modicum of happiness in their day-to-day lives.

A fresh wave of venom rushes through her veins as Falan watches Ronan, and she can't stop herself from interrupting his state of reverie. "Practicing for a canceled performance is a rather ineffective use of your time," she says.

Startled, Ronan drops through the air, but the ribbon tightens around his torso and breaks his fall mere yards from the floor. He flips back down and lands on his feet, the surprise on his face turning to contempt. "Falan." His blue eyes blaze with irritation at the sight of her. But it doesn't mask the ecstasy still rushing through his body. She sees it in the glow of his olive skin, damp with sweat, his relaxed muscles. "Any particular reason you're seeking me out?"

His forced diplomacy only aggravates her further. She'd rather he just be direct with his disdain, but he's always been like this, coldly polite with the strained, tortured manner of somebody getting a tooth pulled. "I wasn't seeking you out," she says.

Ronan raises an eyebrow. "Then why come here? As you said, practicing for a canceled performance is an ineffective use of one's time."

"I didn't come here to practice." Falan grabs one of the ribbons cascading from the trapeze bar above. "I knew the arena would be empty today, and I came to soak in the solitude." She casually flips up the ribbon before sliding back down, her trained muscles feeling no strain from the action. But she feels no thrill, no burst of euphoria. She aches to try another flip, just to chase a sensation she's never felt on the trapeze, one she still craves even after all these years.

Although Falan holds the same acrobatics Affinity that Lavanya did, she has never quite reached Lavanya's level of skill. Nor has she felt the thrum of ecstasy the other performers experience when activating their Affinities.

"Sorry to interrupt your solitude soak," Ronan says, not sounding sorry at all.

Before Falan can retort, footsteps from the stairwell echo behind her. "I see you're not the only one who came here to relieve stress," she says sarcastically.

But Ronan doesn't respond. He's fixed on whoever just came into the arena, his eyes filled with a shade of vigilance. It's a look Falan recognizes well, and she turns to see none other than Jean-Pierre.

Each time Falan sees the ringmaster, her lungs restrict like all the air inside them has been sucked out. It's a fear she cannot make herself unlearn, no matter how vengeful she is. Tall, with blond hair, fair skin, and an ever-youthful face, Jean-Pierre exudes an aura as mysteriously enticing as his circus. Falan has seen the way audience members look at him. How some women whisper to each other behind cupped hands.

"Sunkara, Allaire, what are you both doing here?" It appears as if he's feigning surprise, but many times Jean-Pierre's actions seem ungenuine.

"I couldn't sleep, so I came here to occupy myself," Ronan says smoothly.

Falan doesn't answer, but it's as if Jean-Pierre doesn't notice she's there, because he walks right past her to Ronan. "Save your energy. You have a big evening ahead of you, particularly if you have the honor of being chosen for the Game of Oaths."

"Yes, monsieur, an honor," Ronan says.

Falan starts to walk away, but the rope around her soul yanks, preventing her from going any farther. She turns to see Jean-Pierre looking over at her, his hand curled slightly. "Yes?" she says.

"You walked away in the middle of a conversation. That's quite rude, don't you think?" the ringmaster says lightly, but his eyes have that dangerous gleam that brings a shiver to Falan's bones once more. The pull tightens and Falan barely holds back a gasp for air.

"My apologies," she says, walking back over to them. "Is there anything I'm needed for? I was thinking of going to get a meal at the bouillon, if that's all right."

"I'll join you," Ronan says before Jean-Pierre can speak. "I'm feeling peckish myself."

There's no need for Ronan to go to the bouillon—if he's down in the arena practicing, he's already eaten. Jean-Pierre must know this, but strangely he doesn't call Ronan out on it. Instead, he says, "Very well. I will see you both tonight. Chance to you both."

"Merci." Ronan is already guiding Falan to the stairwell. "We'll see you tonight."

Falan can't bring herself to say anything. She tips her head in a parting gesture.

It's only once they're back in the lobby of the hotel that she can breathe again. Ronan gives her a long, knowing look, but she turns on her heel and walks off. She doesn't want to see the understanding in his eyes, even if it's something they share.

Warmth washes over Falan as she walks into the bouillon, which is packed with dealers and performers. Most performers have more than the usual bowl of stew in front of them, as she expected. Even Meera and Ary have splurged on two chaussons aux pommes.

"What's this?" Falan asks after getting her stew and joining them.

"We didn't get you one," Meera says with a smile as sugary as the apples in her pastry.

"I didn't expect you to." Falan sits beside Ary, who splits her pastry in half and holds a piece out to Falan. But she waves it off, keeping to her stew.

"Falan's not a large fan of sweets," Meera says. She's lying, but Falan doesn't refute her, knowing Ary would have kept trying to offer half the treat. An unspoken agreement has formed between Falan and Meera over the past seven months, often claiming they aren't hungry so Ary can have a bit more to eat.

Sure enough, when Meera finishes her stew, she pushes her pastry across to Ary. "I think I'm done. Do you want mine?"

Temptation flits across Ary's face, but she hesitates. "Are you sure?" When Meera nods, Ary eats half, but pushes the rest back over to Meera. Falan watches, nearly amused by the display. For months, Ary didn't question their generosity—when one is hungry, there's no room to question—but lately she's been shrewder to their claims of satiety.

Meera relents and picks up the chausson aux pommes, taking a bite. It looks like she's going to wolf down the rest of it, but Falan is surprised when she holds out the remainder to her. Powdered sugar rests atop the flaky pastry like light snow, pureed apples spilling from its crust, and Falan's mouth waters.

But she shakes her head, turning back to her stew. "I don't like sweets, remember?"

Ary and Meera exchange glances, catching the dark tone in her voice. The former opens her mouth to question Falan, but Meera is quicker to smile and say, "Whatever you want," before devouring the rest of the pastry.

Falan looks down at her stew. She won't take anything from Ary if she can help it.

But she certainly won't take anything from Meera either.

III

November 6, 1896

LE PALAIS BLANCHET'S STORAGE ROOM IS CRAMMED with a large variety of objects—shelves of linen towels, bins of unwashed bedclothes, rusted metal buckets, and boxes of unopened envelopes from businesses seeking partnerships. Adding to the cramped clutter in the room are the performers themselves, waiting to be called down to the arena one by one to be assessed.

Falan sits in a corner, her back pressed to the wall. The edge of a box juts into her shoulder. Although futile, she pulls the sheer silk garment of her trapeze costume tighter around herself. Even with so many people in the room, a chill wafts through the vents, matching the wintery night air outside.

It's much too cold for an outfit like this, but it's mandatory to dress as they would for a performance. Jean-Pierre says it makes them seem like caricatures to pick from, pleasing the panel. Falan wears a ruffled leotard of black and white shrouded in transparent silk. Her dark hair is done in her usual style, half of it up in two small buns while the rest is loose. Lavanya styled it best, despite her hair being thick and long, with a desire for getting as tangled as possible.

"All done, petite renarde," Lavanya used to say when she had finished.

Petite renarde. Little fox, due to the buns looking like fox ears.

Ronan trips over Falan's feet while passing by, stumbling before righting himself. "Watch yourself," he growls, then frowns in recognition as he turns to face her. "Oh. You."

In response, Falan sticks her legs out farther in his path. It's not a good time to make any enemies, but she's not about to start getting along with Ronan. To be gracious now would be futile, even a sign of fear. Just as she expects, Ronan bows an apology in that forced polite manner, then walks off stiffly, disappearing behind a shelf of linen towels.

"Charming as usual," says Meera, who is sitting next to her.

"Meera, not now," Ary, who is settled on her other side, says. Their outfits look similar, even if Meera is a dancer and Ary is a tightrope walker. Both wear black bustiers and silk red tutus, but Meera's bustier has sequins and Ary wears a cream-colored bodice on top.

"I was being genuine," Meera says. "Falan usually would have said something cutting."

Falan shoots her a flat glare. "Want to be a recipient of that?"

Meera laughs, and Falan waits for Ary to play peacemaker.

But she doesn't. Her large eyes are darting around the storage room, drinking in the sight of nervous performers. Most sit by themselves, staring into space as they wait for their fate. Some pace, like Ronan. A few have their hands pressed to their heads as they rock back and forth, incoherent mumbles dropping from their lips.

"Take it all in, Baby Bird," Meera says, patting Ary's back. "It's my fifth time and nothing has changed."

Alarm flashes in Ary's eyes, but it's to be expected. At fifteen, she's the youngest member of the Cirque and the newest, having joined about seven months ago. Sometimes Falan wonders how Ary ended up here, but there's an unspoken rule at the Cirque: Nobody talks about their pasts. Ary tried to tell her once, but Falan cut her off before she got any further than her arrival aboard a ship from Cambodia.

"She won't be picked," Meera says. "New performers rarely are."

"Not just them," Falan says. Her eyes stray to the loudest corner of the room, where a handful of performers are talking and laughing much too obnoxiously. "*They* seem to stay around forever."

Meera rolls her eyes. "But Ary isn't a Lily."

Ary actually laughs, a sharp chirp that bubbles shakily from her lips. "No kidding."

Lilies—the name started as an inside joke among those at the boardinghouse but turned to an unofficial dubbing. Although Lilies join the Cirque out of desperation like any other performer, they are the lucky few who don't live at the boardinghouse, instead getting a comfortable room to themselves at the hotel because they are favored and sponsored by particularly generous Cirque patrons.

Meera cups Ary's face in her hands, squishing her cheeks. "Doesn't matter. You're lovelier than any of them."

Ary smiles and averts her gaze, embarrassed. "Thanks."

"But you won't ever be one." Falan is still looking over at the Lilies, who occupy the only bench in the storage room. "You're stuck among the boarders."

From the moment she joined the Cirque, Falan understood that Lily favoritism could only be achieved by birth. The Lilies may be like most of the other Cirque performers in not having been born in France, but unlike the boarders, most have emigrated from other European nations. They usually have the features she never will, the milky complexion or small nose or light eyes and hair. Most boarders, no matter how much they strive to earn the consistent sponsorship of a patron, will never gain it.

"It doesn't matter," Falan says, ignoring Meera's disdainful look. "They may last longer, but they are all picked eventually, the same as us."

“Right, because the audience has got to have *somebody* to root for,” Meera mutters sarcastically. “We know how much they love a Lily winner.”

Neither of them mentions that the majority of the past Game of Oaths’ winners have been Lilies. The record for a continuous streak of Lily winners was nine years in a row, until it was finally broken last year by a boarder.

The door suddenly opens, and a hush falls over the storage room as all forty-two performers look to the entryway. Jean-Pierre walks inside, doubling the tension in the air. Some performers hunch themselves farther into a corner or against the wall. The ringmaster’s eyes flit to each potential player, as if sizing them up. When his gaze flickers to Falan, his lips turn up for a wisp of a moment, like he’s silently laughing at an inside joke.

“Salut,” Jean-Pierre finally says, tipping his top hat. “It is the day we have been waiting for all year. It’s time to select those who will be performing in this year’s Game of Oaths.”

Performing. The word choice is laughable. For the courtesy of the new performers, Jean-Pierre goes on to explain the history of the Game of Oaths and its rules.

Forty-five years ago, before the Enchanteur Certification Law of 1851 was passed, Paris was in a state of unrest due to the growing public use of Enchanteur abilities, the fear that those with magic would wield it dangerously—particularly those who were not men, those who were not French, and especially those who were not white. The unrest grew into what would be known as the Sortilège Riots. Twelve French citizens died, and the government responded by passing a new law that was intended to limit the use of Enchanteur abilities to those carefully selected recipients of a cert.

As Jean-Pierre tells it, on receiving his cert, he founded le Cirque des Ombres to show the masses the wonder magic could be used for. The Game of Oaths followed shortly afterward, to take place on the anniversary of the Sortilège Riots each year, supposedly established in good faith. According to Jean-Pierre, the oath taken by each performer when they are bound to the Cirque is supposed to represent a promise that magic will be reserved for the benefit of society, that an event like the Sortilège Riots would never happen again. The tournament takes place the second week of November, as remembrance for the riots, and is five days at maximum. It has never gone on for longer.

But what Jean-Pierre doesn't mention is that many suspect the government itself of requesting the tournament. That over time, the show of competition turned to deadlier feats. A one-night performance has turned into a series of rounds, new games were invented, and the exclusivity of the show increased. Performer deaths have gone from being rare to expected, now encouraged by the audience. Yet the government has never intervened to stop the show; some officials even attend it. Though there are whispers of other officials being concerned that Jean-Pierre's scope of power is too wide, they have been unable to do anything about it, especially since the Game's exposure during L'Exposition Universelle, when le Cirque des Ombres officially became part of the hotel le Palais Blanchet. The Game has become Paris's most open secret, and Jean-Pierre remains untouchable.

"You will come down one by one to the arena to be assessed," Jean-Pierre says after he's finished giving an overview. "The panel will decide whether you are to compete or whether you will remain a candidate for a future Game."

"What does he mean?" Ary asks softly.

"Have you not caught on yet?" Meera says, shaking her head. "You either walk out of the Cirque a winner of the Game, or you don't walk out at all."

"But our contracts are for seven years," Ary says, trembling. "That doesn't necessarily mean—"

"Do you really expect to not be picked for seven straight years?" Falan says.

It's always pitiful to see the truth dawn on a new performer. Falan watches Ary's face pale the same way hers must have during her first Reckoning. Realizing how Jean-Pierre offers contracts only to a specific archetype: adolescent and desperate. How no performer is over the age of twenty-five. Falan remembers how Jean-Pierre described the Game when she and Lavanya first met him on that cold winter night—a life-changing chance to win money and luxuries beyond one's wildest dreams. All part of his honeyed trap when coaxing desperate people to sign. He said nothing about the Game's deadly stakes.

"Don't worry. The damning realization happened to all of us," Meera says in her flippant way, patting Ary's back in sympathy. "Falan here nearly cried during her first Reckoning."

"I don't recall that," Falan says stiffly.

Ary doesn't answer. She's still trembling, her eyes far away. When she shifts, Meera instantly moves to grip her wrist. "Don't," she says, slow and soft. "Don't be the person who runs."

"I wasn't," Ary says, but Meera doesn't let her go.

Falan eyes the other performers as Jean-Pierre continues to speak about how they are bringing pride to the Cirque, to France. She knows somebody will run. Somebody always does.

Sure enough, seconds after Jean-Pierre finally finishes his speech, a performer suddenly sprints for the door, one who joined just a few months before Ary. A gymnast. He barely makes it to the threshold before he falls to his knees, hands gripping his chest.

Jean-Pierre stands a few feet away, his hand outstretched, yanking the performer by le Lien. The room suddenly seems to drop in temperature. He curls his fingers, tightening his hold, and the performer gasps. It must have coiled around his lungs, choking him, the smell of smoke rich in the air. It always smells like ashtrays when Jean-Pierre exerts le Lien, like cigarettes long gone sour.

It smells like death.

The ringmaster's face betrays no emotion, but his eyes have darkened. A shiver runs through Falan's veins. Next to her, Ary quivers, her shallow breaths uneven. Even Meera can't hide the terror in her eyes.

The coldest parts of winter, mingled in their bones.

Jean-Pierre steps over the performer, briefly leaning down to whisper in his ear, then releases his grip before walking down the hall. The performer stumbles to his feet and follows, still gasping for air.

"Think he'll be picked?" Meera asks.

Falan doesn't respond. After witnessing Lavanya's orchestrated death, she doesn't know the answer.

The storage room slowly drains of people, the tension growing with each performer gone. Falan still sits between Meera and Ary, waiting for the telltale tug of le Lien, the signal that it's her turn to go down to the arena. Talking is too painful now. Even Meera has ceased a conversation.

By the time Falan feels the tug, a jolt so powerful she physically coils forward, there are only five people left in the room, including Ary.

"Chance, Falan," Ary says as Falan gets to her feet.

Falan nods, about to leave without replying, but says "Chance" at the last minute before slipping out of the storage room.

The arena is barren tonight. The seats are all empty, except for five in the front row. The panel usually consists of Jean-Pierre, three of the Cirque's never-changing highest-paying patrons, and Monsieur Jacques Alain Blanchet, the owner of le Palais Blanchet and its cercle. Blanchet looks as extravagant as his hotel, dressed in a crisp white suit. His blond hair is coiffed, not a strand out of place.

But this time, there's somebody new. One of the usual patrons, an old white-haired man who leered creepily at each female performer, has been replaced by a boy Falan instantly recognizes.

It's Jules Devereux Blanchet, the son of Monsieur Blanchet.

Even after seeing him around the hotel for years, it's startling how different Jules is from his father, more so in personality but looks too. His hair is the color of dark wheat, hazel eyes framed with delicate gold spectacles. Thin, not so tall. Lean, angular face. Crooked nose. Tanned skin. Falan has heard whispers questioning Jules's parentage, suspicions that he's the illegitimate child of an affair between Blanchet and one of his servants, but nobody has the evidence or gall to directly accuse Blanchet, one of Paris's wealthiest men, of anything scandalous outright.

But Jean-Pierre isn't the only person Falan has been watching over the past year.

Falan knows Blanchet planned to introduce Jules to a proper role in the Game once he turned eighteen, so the defining birthday must have finally passed. But he doesn't seem particularly thrilled to be here. Jules keeps his gaze on the ground and clutches a satchel close to him.

"Salut, Sunkara," Jean-Pierre says, drawing her attention.

Falan nods politely in response, although her eyes keep sliding to Jules.

Monsieur Blanchet smiles. "I see you have taken notice of my son's presence."

"Yes, I have," Falan says.

"Enchanté, Mademoiselle Sunkara," Jules says quietly. His demeanor is polite but subdued, but that's how Jules is. He's always been nervy, nonconfrontational, the exact opposite of his father. The past year, Falan has noticed just how much he looks at the floor, how he clutches himself as if he has something to hide. Sometimes he frequents the cercle, but he has never had any luck.

"Allow me to reveal that you are quite a topic of discussion among the panel this evening," Jean-Pierre says.

"Oh?" Falan says evenly.

"You have gone fairly unnoticed during your past four Reckonings, which I found to be a shame," Monsieur Blanchet says.

This much conversation alone is already a change. Usually the panel takes one look before dismissing her. "Why is that?" Falan asks.

"After Lucien Trichet's win last year, it occurred to us to give the more overlooked performers their chance in the spotlight," one of the patrons says.

"Someone like you," Jean-Pierre adds. "We feel an acrobatics Affinity like yours has to be put to good use. After all, look at what happened with Lucien Trichet."

Lucien Trichet. Last year's winner and the boarder who finally broke the streak of Lily winners before they won ten Games in a row. Boarder winners are never well received, but Lucien's win caused more outrage among the spectators than usual. Generally, winners are invited to private parties hosted by wealthy patrons, showered in praises, and connected to many of the upper-class patrons. As far as Falan knows, Lucien has gotten none of that.

He has, however, received the standard prizes so far: five hundred thousand francs, a year of living in luxurious quarters at the hotel, and—perhaps the most coveted prize—freedom from his contract as soon as this year's tournament is over. It doesn't matter how many years are left on Lucien's contract; due to his win, it will be broken in a week's time. He will leave the Cirque for good, no longer bound by le Lien.

The panel's intention for this year's Game is clear: with more performers like Falan competing—boarders who are seen as weak or, in their words, overlooked—then one of the few Lilies chosen is more likely to win. No matter how they try to dress it, this is about gaining back their spectators, avoiding a second backlash.

And that is exactly what she was counting on.

"So we have made our decision," Jean-Pierre says calmly. "Falan Sunkara, you will be competing in this year's Game of Oaths as player number eleven. A sincere congratulations to you."

As the panel claps accordingly, their applause echoing throughout the arena, Falan only stares back impassively. She makes sure her face betrays no emotion, the numb reaction of a shocked performer realizing their gruesome fate. Jean-Pierre's eyes twinkle as he claps, a satisfied look on his face. Perhaps he's recalling the night he watched Lavanya die, imagining Falan's death in a similar manner. She's certain he has suspected her vengeful feelings toward him, and this is his way of solving the problem.

It's only when Falan turns away to leave that the ghost of a smile finally breezes across her lips. Jean-Pierre would never dream of her winning the tournament, let alone successfully enacting revenge on him. His guard is now down, as he thinks the problem is taken care of.

But over the past year, Falan has been watching. Waiting. Plotting. She knows exactly who to use to ensure her victory in both the Game and in getting her revenge. And Jean-Pierre has given her exactly what she wanted—a chance to play.

Welcome to the real game, Jean-Pierre, Falan thinks as she exits the arena. *May the best player win.*

IV

November 7, 1896

BELLAMY DURAND HAS NEVER HAD A DEAL FAIL HIM before.

He grits his teeth as another punch meets his face. Pain explodes across his cheek where the ring-covered knuckles smash against it, but Bellamy refuses to crumble. Instead, he tilts his head down and spits a gob of blood onto his attacker's shoes. Black locks of hair, damp with sweat, hang in his eyes, stick to his brown skin. Outside, the moon is bright over Paris, the faintest rays of pale light spilling into the otherwise dark study.

From the far side of the room, Monsieur Horrent waves a gloved hand, blue eyes gleaming behind his spectacles. "Again."

Horrent's associate, Cadieux, punches Bellamy once more, and Bellamy bites back a sound of agony. "Don't you think I've had enough, monsieur?" he says in a cool, ragged voice. "You have already taken away my good looks for at least a few months."

Horrent ignores him. "Again. Make sure the rings draw blood this time."

Bellamy can't stop the groan that escapes his throat as Cadieux's fist makes contact yet again, rings digging so deep into his skin it feels like they're scraping against his cheekbone. The gold ring on Cadieux's middle finger, the signature of Horrent's associates, is the sharpest.

"Again," Horrent says.

Bellamy coughs as Cadieux's fist slams into his stomach this time. His jobs have never gone wrong like this. It's a simple formula: Sign a contract with an Enchanteur among the haute bourgeoisie, find out where they keep their valuables, loot through them for items to resell in various underground markets, and break their contracts before his marks are aware of what is happening.

Bellamy has never held a contract for more than a week but knows most people don't have that luxury. Although he works as a dealer at le Palais Blanchet's cercle, he's lucky that Blanchet is no Enchanteur and therefore cannot bind his employees to him in the same way.

Over the past three years, ever since he snuck away from Marseille to Paris at the age of fifteen, he's successfully pilfered from a handful of the upper class as well as visiting aristocrats. Artful enough to ruffle feathers and avoid their attempts at catching him.

Monsieur Horrent, however, is a different story. As not only one of the most powerful members of the Parisian upper class but someone well rooted in Paris's lawless world, he was an ambitious mark. Too ambitious.

For the first time, Bellamy was caught sneaking back to break a contract. The statue that the contract magic was embedded in now lies in pieces a few feet away, but he was restrained before he could flee. Then, after confronting him regarding their newly discovered information about his cons, came the punches.

Somebody else enters the room, another one of Horrent's men.

"How much did he take?" Horrent asks.

"Too much. Three hundred thousand francs worth. Are they still in his possession?"

"Appears not," Horrent says with a heavy sigh, stroking his gray goatee. "What shall I do with him?"

"We could slit his throat right here. End the problem once and for all," Cadieux says.

"A rather rash choice." Bellamy stands up and straightens his clothes. "You think killing me will recover the items you've lost?"

"So you're telling me you haven't sold them?" Horrent says. "You can return them right now?"

"What if I told you I can do better than that?" Bellamy says. If he makes it out alive tonight, he has time to think of a plan. "What if I told you that rather than returning the items, I can get you the money's worth? All three hundred thousand francs in exchange for the items I have lost."

"Stolen," Horrent corrects him, but appears to be considering it. "And this money will be clean?"

"Does it matter?" Bellamy asks with a wry smile. He can't help himself.

"I don't want any more barbarians showing up at my doorstep thanks to you."

Bellamy is about to talk his way around it when Cadieux readies a fist once more. "All right, as you wish," he says calmly. "It will be untraceable."

"Clean."

"They're two sides of the same coin."

Horrent studies his face before snapping his fingers. Cadieux moves back, and Bellamy takes that as a cue to leave.

This was easy. Too easy.

Bellamy dares not take a breath of relief. Not yet. As he makes to climb out the window, Monsieur Horrent's steely voice stops him. "You have a week."

Bellamy turns to face him with a steady smile. "Of course."

"Hmm." The Enchanteur's eyes narrow. "It's a shame you have broken our contract. Your talent lies elsewhere than stealing from others."

Bellamy's smile grows crooked, and he vanishes out the window before Horrent can elaborate. When making contracts, Bellamy's one request is not to be told his Affinity. He doesn't want to know. He's seen how it takes hold of people once they feel that burst of euphoria; it's a drug, like a defense mechanism to cope with being chained to somebody, and Bellamy can't afford to get hooked.

Bellamy takes the rooftops back to the hotel. Usually when he travels this way, he enjoys how the world rushes past him as he jumps between buildings. But tonight the only thought Bellamy can focus on is Horrent's icy eyes on his back.

Horrent could have killed him. He *should* have killed him.

Either way, he will be watching, making sure Bellamy does not flee Paris. Now the issue is dredging up three hundred thousand francs. Certainly the money won't be clean, but Bellamy has gotten funds through untraceable sources before.

This, however, is an amount that will require a bargain in return.

When le Palais Blanchet appears, Bellamy takes to the streets, as the building is too high to scale. Although the hotel's lobby is unnervingly bare when he walks in, he creeps around to the staircase instead of taking the elevator, making his way to the roof. It's his place of solitude, a place he can calm himself. Bellamy breathes in the cool air as soon as he steps onto the rooftop, forgetting for a minute that he might not live past the next week. The tranquil moment is cut short when he notices somebody sitting on the raised ledge.

Falan Sunkara, one of the Cirque's trapeze artists. Also one of his most frequent associates.

It's not unusual to see Falan up on the hotel's roof, although he certainly wasn't expecting her tonight. This is where they usually rendezvous when making deals, whether to split spoils from a shared con or trade information about potential jobs or scams.

Most of the time, she only reaches out to him when she wants something, but Bellamy has done the same in return. Dealers and performers often feel like passing ships in the night, despite living in the same building and working at the same hotel. Their lives are owned by different people. The only perk to being a dealer is not having to compete in the Game of Oaths.

"Sunkara, I didn't expect to see you up here," Bellamy says, hoisting himself next to her.

She doesn't respond, but that doesn't surprise him. Falan is selective about when to spend her generally callous words. Still, there's something off about her demeanor tonight. Perhaps it's the distant look in her usually sharp eyes as she stares out at the city.

"I am aware tonight was Le Jour de L'Élu. Not to compare, but my night was nearly as exciting. I had a little run-in with a client," he says flippantly. "So who is part of the unlucky dozen?"

Something flickers in her eyes, darker than black ice. "Do you think any luck was spared for me tonight?" she finally asks.

Bellamy's gut sinks as it finally dawns on him. "You were chosen," he says slowly.

"Apparently, this year they're picking performers they think have been . . . overlooked."

Bellamy parts his lips, at a loss for words. Usually they come easily. But when Falan looks at him with such unnerving calm, he has no idea what to say. There's no point in wasting words of comfort on her. Falan will not believe any of them.

"You seem unbothered," he finally says.

Falan just shrugs. She's always impassive, but this calm of a reaction is extreme even for her. "What happened to your face?" she asks. "I've eaten apples with fewer bruises."

"Charming," he says with a scoff. "As I said, my client and I had a bit of a disagreement. Nothing that wasn't sorted out."

It's hard to tell whether she believes him or not, but all she says is, "I hope getting a beating was worth whatever goods you stole." There's the faintest trace of a smile on her face; most others wouldn't notice it, but after three years of working together, Bellamy has figured out how to catch it. The corners of her lips just barely tilt up, more subtle than a twitch, and there's a quick glint in her otherwise flat brown eyes, framed by those absurdly long lashes. If he doesn't watch carefully, he'll miss it, like the beauty of most magic tricks.

Bellamy takes out his deck of cards and absently shuffles them, a tick that keeps his hands busy while his mind runs. "So do you know who else was picked?"

She shakes her head.

Bellamy shoots her an incredulous look. "Have you been up here on the roof this whole time?"

"I knew you'd show up here eventually, so I waited for you."

He stops shuffling. "You waited for me?"

"I have a job offer for you. How would you like to make the most money you have ever made on a deal?"

Falan could not have known about his predicament with Horrent, so this has to be a lucky coincidence. Yet her offer seems too good to be true. Moreover, telling him of a job right after being selected for the Game of Oaths is strange. "Your priorities astonish me, Sunkara," Bellamy says playfully, but remains skeptical. "How much is the client offering?"

"How much do you want?" she asks.

Bellamy pauses. "If it were anybody but you, I'd assume you were joking. No client is that generous."

"I'm telling the truth," Falan says. "I know you can never resist a large payment, which makes you perfect for this job. Your connections, your knowledge, and your greed."

She tilts her face up to the cool rush of wind that passes by. Her eyes close; even in the darkness of the night, Bellamy once again notices those eyelashes of hers, how they flutter in the breeze, and a hazy memory flashes in his mind of the two of them on the rooftop. A night he was too drunk, too vulnerable, which shames him to think about even now.

Bellamy clears his throat, tucking his cards away. "What is the job?"

Falan opens her eyes, her cool gaze meeting his. "I want you to help me win the Game of Oaths."

If not for Horrent's threat, Bellamy would laugh. But now an impending sense of doom washes over him. It's as he thought—the deal is too good to be true. Falan must know her chances of winning are miniscule. The audience views performers like her as the ones who exist to die first, giving a bloody taste of what's to come.

"*You're* the client?" he finally says.

"It's a game, Durand. Just like everything else you've taught me to cheat."

She's right. It is a game. But it is not *just* a game. Bellamy raises an eyebrow at her. "To try to cheat the Game of Oaths is too large of a gamble."

"And I thought you proclaimed to know how to best any game," Falan says.

"The Game of Oaths is not just any game." Bellamy crosses his arms. "There's no way to ensure a win. In games like this, the house always wins."

"But upping my chances is a start toward a victory," Falan says. "Beginning with your involvement. You dealers turn into Jean-Pierre's assistants throughout the duration of the Game. You run around as his errand boys. No doubt you've gained a lot of information that could assist me. Am I correct?"

Bellamy gives her a long look. She's right. This will be his third year, and he knows by heart the ins and outs of how the process works. He has insider information that could be pivotal to the success of a player.

But what she's asking for is nearly impossible. A logical gambler would dismiss Falan at once.

Instead, Bellamy can't help thinking that if she does win, the wealth waiting for her is tremendous. Five hundred thousand francs. More than enough to cover the amount he needs to pay Monsieur Horrent back. And it is true that she stands little chance in the Game without help.

But what if she does have the help she's asking for?

She will be at a disadvantage in obvious points—smaller than most of the other competitors, less physically powerful—but if Bellamy were betting, he would not count Falan out so soon. Her acrobatics Affinity will still be of use. And, while smaller, she's fast and agile, both her body and her mind; Bellamy has seen her come up with strategies for grifts that have left him more than impressed. If he provides her with enough information, then she will do most of the thinking herself.

It's a gamble to trust her with such risky information, but perhaps it could pay off for him. All the way to fulfilling his debt.

"Three hundred thousand francs," Bellamy finally says. "That's my price." She doesn't need to know about the debt he owes. Information like that will only give her the upper hand.

"You want more than half of the winnings. Greedy, aren't you?"

"In exchange for helping you win, I think it's fair. And I won't see a coin unless you succeed, ensuring my loyalty." Bellamy stands up. "Wouldn't you say your life is worth three hundred thousand francs? Or do you think it's worth less?"

In response, Falan stands too, meeting his challenging gaze with her dark-eyed stare.

Bellamy grins roguishly. "I do adore that look on you, Sunkara. Makes you truly intimidating."

Falan continues to stare at him. For a moment, Bellamy thinks she's caught on that he's hiding something. But then she steps back, arms crossed like she's cradling a secret of her own, and says, "We have a deal."

Satisfied, Bellamy settles down on the roof's ledge again. The soft wind ruffles his dark locks of hair. "What do you want to know?"

"Tell me about what happens after we're taken into seclusion."

An easy enough start. "Sunday at dawn, you will be transported to the Aviary. It's an underground building beneath the Chapiteau where you'll stay between rounds. You will be confined to your room before the first round. Afterward, you can explore as you wish."

"Assuming I survive, that's risky," Falan points out. "If a competitor finds out which room I'm in and wants to harm me, they have the means to do so."

She's right. Since the gore is meant to take place in front of the watching audience, players are not allowed to kill each other outside of the rounds. But there are no rules against harming each other. It's not encouraged, but civility is not enforced either. Bellamy has seen it, how most players start out with the intention to keep to themselves, only to end up spiraling into paranoia-fueled madness.

"The layout might work in your favor," Bellamy says. "The rooms are decided depending on your starting bids. Most don't realize this until a few days into the competition." He pauses. "The exception to this rule are the Lilies. They are always placed on the second-highest floor."

"*Second*-highest?" Falan asks.

"Yes. The Aviary is made up of four floors, with four rooms on three of the floors. The top floor is the winner's hall. Last year's winner stays there for the Game's duration." Bellamy wonders if it will be the same this year, for it appears the Cirque wants to hide Lucien Trichet away like a shameful secret.

Falan nods, then suddenly asks, "Dealers are allowed to leave the Aviary, am I right?"

"Yes," he says, puzzled. "Myself and the other dealers will be doing hourly sweeps of the Aviary, so we'll be going in and out."

He waits for more questions about that, but she doesn't ask. Instead, she says, "So we will be taken to the Aviary after the Betting Party?"

The Game of Oaths officially starts on Monday at midnight, but Saturday night is when the Betting Party is held. Thrown in the hotel's ballrooms, it's an extravagant fête that the twelve players are required to attend. Here, the spectators will get their first glimpse of the competitors and place their initial bets, using bearer bonds to remain untraceable. The dealers are expected to be there as well, waiting on all the guests with flutes of champagne and trays of hors d'oeuvres.

It's a miserable affair for everybody except the audience. But it's the players who have the roughest time. Bellamy recalls them being questioned for hours on end, standing in place and attempting to charm bettors for any advantages they may receive, such as grants—gifts that spectators are allowed to buy for players to aid them during the tournament. The thought of Falan doing that is laughable.

"Yes," Bellamy says. "Be prepared to have an . . . overwhelming night." When her expression darkens, he can't help but grin. "You can't be walking around with that face at the Betting Party. Your eyes look like murder. Bettors aren't fans of that."

"They're only fans of murder when it happens on a stage to somebody else," she says.

She's right, of course. The audience doesn't care. They watch each round, then go home and sleep peacefully, unburdened by the fact that they relished in somebody's death.

"That doesn't matter," Bellamy says. It's a game, and she needs to pretend to play by the rules.

Or else they both lose before it even starts.

With a weary sigh, Falan settles down next to him. "We're not done. For three hundred thousand francs, you're answering every question I have."

"For three hundred thousand francs, ask away."

It's four in the morning by the time Bellamy fills Falan in on everything he knows, obliging all her questions. When they finish, they both walk downstairs and leave the hotel in silence.

After a long pause, Bellamy tells her he'll see her at the Betting Party. Falan nods back, and a look of understanding passes between them. It's a look they've shared many times at the start of a con. Then Bellamy disappears down the street, stealing away into the night as only a thief does.

V

November 7, 1896

JULES DEVEREUX BLANCHET HAS NEVER WORN A red tie with a white suit before.

Despite being in the midst of a panic-fueled haze, he can't help but look at himself in his bedroom mirror, scrutinizing the brilliant crimson against its background of white fabric. It looks like a bloody gash ripping down his chest. The contrast is garish, and Jules's mouth twists in disgust. But it is the traditional uniform for the panelists, and as their newest member, he had no choice but to don it.

Jules pulls off the tie and throws it on the wooden floor, although he knows what will happen if his father finds out how he treated such an expensive object. His hands curl around his dresser, fingernails clawing into the top drawer, leaving familiar crescent moons in the white paint. Bile rises in his throat.

Breathe. Breathe, he tells himself.

But no matter how many times he inhales, his lungs can never grasp enough air. The room feels like it's closing in, its slanted ceiling diving right at him. Something on top of his dresser shakes and Jules backs away with a gasp, wondering if he somehow made the object levitate.

No, it was just his quivering hands shaking the dresser. The discovery lowers the bile in his throat and calms his racing heart, but not entirely. Never entirely. Not even sleep can kill the illogical bouts of panic; they merely lie in wait until he wakes up the next morning.

Jules leans to pick up the tie, his gaze involuntarily skirting to one of the tiles making up his bedroom floor. With his father still at the hotel, he has the mansion to himself aside from the house's servants, who won't enter his room without permission. His fingers slide toward the tile; if his father knew it had come loose, he'd demand to get it repaired immediately. But Jules doesn't tell him. He only hopes his father doesn't one day step directly onto it.

He gently pulls the slate off, revealing the hollow below, and takes out the book inside. Jules looks over his shoulder at the door, then at the window, wary of prying eyes. Perhaps it means finding a better place for this book than the floorboards.

Jules dusts off the cover. *Guillaume Gallien's Origins of the Arcane*, the title reads. Acquiring this book without being caught was in itself a challenge, but with a few extra coins to a bookseller's assistant in the fifth arrondissement, one of the shop's copies was suddenly misplaced. The book itself is weathered despite its minimal use, some of the pages dog-eared and with a perpetual scent of dust no matter how much Jules brushes it.

Last time he opened it, he was on chapter five, but as he so often does, he returns to chapter one to reread the introduction to Enchanteur history, the journey of Enchanteur treatment from centuries ago to modern times. Inexplicably so, because the story itself is brutal.

The French call them Enchanteurs. Only centuries ago, they called them witches, Gallien says. *The world has different titles for these individuals now—Magicians, Conjurors—but the name Enchanteur took its hold in France around 1740, eventually replacing the term witchcraft after Enchanteur uses were proved beneficial to humanity.*

Enchanteurs can master control over physical objects and bring illusions of fantasies before human eyes; they can take one look at an ordinary individual and see their particular gift—untapped potential waiting to be discovered. And yet such arcane power always holds the danger of being misused. The bloody history laid out in this book is illustrative of the endless push and pull between honing such abilities for the good of man and ensuring these gifts are not abused.

After the Sortilège Riots in Paris in November 1851, the French government passed the Certification Law to allot certificates only to those Enchanteurs trusted to use magic with care and to contribute positively toward society. Furthermore, certified Enchanteurs are limited to members of aristocratic society—to allow anyone inferior to wield such power would undoubtedly end in disaster. Even the most powerful of Enchanteurs must remain under the control of the government—a balance to make sure the two are in harmony and the hierarchy never topples.

Jules is certain that he falls under "inferior" according to Gallien's terms. Not like Jean-Pierre. From witnessing the ringmaster's illusions, it's clear he's incredibly powerful. Most Enchanteurs do not have the ability to make such complex and long-lasting illusions. Nor do most Enchanteurs have the leeway that Jean-Pierre is allowed by the government. But Jules knows that the few officials who are opposed to Jean-Pierre's amount of power will not step in to stop him. The deaths of nearly a dozen people each year, particularly those who have little importance or value to France's society, seem to be a small price to pay to keep Jean-Pierre cooperative with the government. For all that Gallien says about Enchanteurs abiding by the law, Jules is in doubt about who's really in charge in Jean-Pierre's case.

Jules thought that he might get some practice in tonight. But with his father coming and going due to the Game of Oaths, perhaps not. After careful consideration, he puts the book back under the slate. He supposes he should use magic to seal up the floorboard; that way it would never rouse suspicion. But the thought of not being able to unseal it terrifies him.

Magic itself is a terrifying thing. To not be in control, to fear accidentally levitating or shattering or throwing an object without using his hands in public . . . it's agonizing.

The room feels too hot once more, too suffocating. Without changing out of his suit, Jules snuffs out the gas lantern, leaves his golden spectacles on his dresser, and collapses on his bed. He stares up at the ceiling as blue moonlight floods the room, illuminating all of its nooks and corners—the oak wood bookshelf on one side, the shine of the dresser's mirror.

Despite his nerves, Jules drifts off, grateful for the brief break in his anxiety. He suddenly wakes sometime later in the night in a state of delirium, the world swimming before his already blurry eyes. There's no reason he should have woken. And it's much darker.

It's then Jules realizes the curtains are closed.

Through his haze, it faintly concerns him, because he swears he remembers leaving them open. But the lull of sleep pulls him back, alluring with its promise of serenity, and then he doesn't care at all.

VI

November 7, 1896

THE BOARDINGHOUSE IS COMPLETELY DARK BY THE time Falan finally returns. Even the light in Erwin's room is off. In some sick irony, Falan remembers the bargain he offered her the previous morning.

To Falan's relief, both her roommates are fast asleep when she sneaks into their room. Neither of them stir as she hoists herself onto her bed. Sleep isn't an option, but even if it was, she would avoid it; far too often, her unconscious thoughts are plagued with rewatching Lavanya die. Instead, her mind roams back to her deal with Bellamy. Working with somebody so unscrupulous is a gamble, as flippant as he pretends to be. But his importance goes further than helping her win the Game, further than he knows—he can help her avenge Lavanya.

She didn't tell him of her true intentions beyond winning the Game; information is dangerous, especially in the hands of somebody who has the patience to use it during the most vital of moments. Since he can go in and out of the Aviary, Bellamy will unknowingly be her eyes and ears in the hotel. He will have no trouble cracking the safe in Jean-Pierre's office, even stealing everything inside for her. If he questions her, all she has to do is remind him of the money she's winning him.

For all his power, Jean-Pierre's control over the Cirque and its performers lies in something so simple yet untouchable—his contracts. If they are destroyed, his position will crumble. For there can be no Cirque without its performers. And if freed from their contracts, no performer will stick around to find out what happens next.

Falan gazes out the window, watching the glow of the rising sun start to wash out the pale sky. In about an hour, she will have to report to the hotel, where she and the eleven other players will be fitted by Anaïs, the Cirque's tailor, for the Betting Party tonight.

Falan remembers Lavanya's gown last year. She arrived breathless in their room, having somehow snuck away from the Betting Party with a profiterole for Falan. "Burnt umber" was what she called the color of the dress. Short sleeves, cinched at her waist, the skirts puffed out around her.

"Do I look good?" she asked, doing a twirl.

"Yes," Falan said, but that was an understatement. Lavanya's black hair curled down to her waist, gold accessories cascading through her dark locks. She wore matching silk shoes. Eyes bold, shining.

Falan clutches her sheets, shoving the image from her head. The dress is gone, as is Lavanya, like the last rays of sunlight succumbing to the night. "Le soleil et la lune" is what people at the Cirque used to call them: Lavanya, as bright as the sun; Falan, as mysterious as the moon.

But Falan has always been seen like that, even back when she lived in Yanaon, a town on the coast of southeastern India steeped in French rule. She heard the way the neighbors talked to her mother about her. An unemotional child. Unapproachable. Curt. Improper for a girl. Even her name was uncommon.

Her father, a translator fluent in English and French, had set off for England when Falan was eight years old, leaving her brother in charge. Falan was never close to her brother; he was nine years older than her and out of the house from dawn till nightfall. Her mother, who had wanted another boy, never made much time for her either.

Her life was unremarkable before the age of eleven. After that, the memories are hazy but sharp with fear. Coughing. Uncontrollable shivers. Weak calls for water. Her mother, unmoving, eventually taken away. Her brother carted out the same way. She later found out they died due to malaria—one day they were breathing, the next they weren't.

Falan expected to succumb as well, but she lived, cared for by her neighbors. Slowly, painfully, the feverish hazes dimmed. When she received the news about her mother's and brother's deaths, she simply went to sleep, refusing to talk about them when she woke. She supposes they loved her in their own way, and she loved them in hers. She missed the presence of somebody she could call family. And she supposes that's why, when she received a letter from her father a few months after her recovery asking her to join him in London, she agreed.

It's been more than five years since she received that letter. Sometimes, on mornings like this, Falan wonders about her father, whether he ever thinks about her. If he ever theorizes why she never made it to London.

Falan watches the sun climb higher in the sky, pushing the dawn farther aside. From the sudden tension in the room, it's evident Meera and Ary are awake.

"So," Meera finally says, breaking the silence. "I think it's time you both know I have to leave in a bit because . . . I'm player number ten in the Game of Oaths. I guess I was a little too close to the end of my contract for Jean-Pierre's comfort."

Falan turns to face them. "Unfortunately, I'll be coming along with you." She's hit with a strange burst of delirious amusement.

"It was my fourth Reckoning. I knew it would come eventually. If not this year, the next."

"I'll be coming too," Ary says in barely a whisper. Her eyes are red. "Player number twelve."

Falan oddly feels no surprise. Jean-Pierre not only picked her but picked her roommates as well. Falan doesn't have to look at Meera to know she must have been expecting it too, if Jean-Pierre gave her the same speech about overlooked players.

"It's not supposed to be this way, Baby Bird," Meera says. "It's not fair."

No, it's not, Falan thinks, remembering Lavanya. But the Game of Oaths never has been.

For the second time in the span of a day, Falan finds herself waiting in the hotel's storage room. Only this time, instead of forty-two people inside, there are eleven others, giving her the chance to study her competition. She watches them all as she sits alone in a corner, recalling the order in which each person was called down to the arena last night and matching their player numbers.

First is Sylvestre, one of the fire performers and a Lily who makes his hatred of boarders no secret. Tall, muscular, and perhaps with a gift for dexterity if he can manipulate fire. Next is Hugh, a man of pure muscle who can lift and crush anything. Then Cyril, an agile weapons dodger. Thomas, the knife thrower who replaced Lucien after his win. Eliot, an escapist and Lily.

Then there's Ronan, at number six. His presence admittedly surprises Falan; he was more well-liked by patrons than most, and everyone knew it. Following him is Arthur, an acrobatic balancer and Lily who goes to Jean-Pierre about every rumor he hears of a boarder breaking the rules. Collette, a Lily fire performer who is part of a double act with Sylvestre. Martin, a contortionist who can bend his limbs in practically every direction. Then Meera at number ten. Ary at number twelve.

The competition is steeper this year, with more Lilies than usual. But perhaps that's intentional on Jean-Pierre's part to ensure a Lily winner.

"I didn't expect to see you here," says a rough voice, breaking Falan out of her thoughts. She looks up to see Ronan towering over her.

"Nor I you," she admits.

Falan doesn't expect it when Ronan sits down next to her. A part of her wants him to go away so she can go back to observing the other players, yet she doesn't tell him to leave.

"It seems chance wasn't spared for either of us, was it?" he says.

Falan shoots him a sideways glance. Unlike his usual forced politeness, his now soft, almost remorseful, tone seems genuine.

"It never was for me," she finally says.

He laughs quietly, almost sounding amused. They continue to sit in silence, watching players exiting the room throughout the day and coming back in elegant attire, whether gowns or dress coats and trousers. She can't help glancing at Ronan occasionally, still puzzling over why he's sitting with her.

On the trapeze, Ronan is always there to catch her. He has never let her fall. On the ground, however, Falan wants nothing to do with him. It goes beyond the fact that she and Ronan have never gotten along, despite him being previously close to Lavanya. Ronan has done something practically unheard of for a boarder—he became a Lily. Within his first month at the Cirque, a wealthy patron took an immense liking to him for his "exotic looks." Like Falan, his roots go back to India; they share the same dark hair, but his skin is fair and his eyes are blue. Even in India, he would have been favored for his appearance.

Falan knows that if she had the same chance that Ronan did, she'd take it in a heartbeat. But it's still hard not to be bitter toward him, even though she's aware it's another way that the performers are controlled, pitted against one another. It's one thing to resent the Lilies who have never been shunned in France, the ones who will always be accepted. It's another to resent somebody who is still an outsider, even shares the same motherland, but is treated better nonetheless.

It's seven in the evening when Falan is finally called for her fitting. Everybody else in the room is dressed beautifully except for her and Ary. Meera has just returned from her fitting in a lavender gown with gossamer layers, like clouds against her brown skin. Her dark hair is swirled up in a bun. She looks stunning, but Meera always looks stunning. Falan can only hope Anaïs can make her look as appealing, but the tailor does not attempt to hide her distaste when Falan walks into the Cirque's designated dressing room.

"You're a bony little thing," Anaïs says as Falan warily strips off her clothes. "Easy enough to crush."

She continues to make aggravating comments as she measures every inch of Falan and ponders which color and style the dress should be—Falan is too small, her figure is too flat to cinch the waist of the dress, she'd look better in each color if her complexion was fairer, her hair is impossible to style properly. Falan's teeth grit tighter with each remark.

"All right, stand still and lift your arms," Anaïs finally says about forty minutes later. "I think I've figured out how to make you look somewhat presentable."

Falan does as she says. Anaïs raises her hands and her fingers curl. Fabric flies out from a nearby box, wrapping itself around Falan faster than she can comprehend. She feels it settling on her skin, smooth and silky, and her hair twisting without being touched.

When the fabric slows its spin and takes more form, Anaïs leads Falan in front of a mirror against the opposing wall. Falan stares, stunned at her own reflection. The dress itself is a silvery gray. Sheer sleeves are tight over her arms, like she's dusted in glittering moonlight, and fall off her shoulders just above the opaque bodice of the dress. Anaïs says she can't get it to cinch properly at the waist, but it doesn't matter because the skirt puffs out and sweeps around Falan in a cloud of layered fabric. Her hair has been done in some sort of updo with silvery accessories, with a select few waves cascading down her back. Silken white shoes adorn her feet.

Clair de lune herself, Falan imagines the others thinking.

After a final check, Falan is directed to go back to the storage room. The moment she walks in, the Lilies are looking at her. Collette leans close to Sylvestre, perfectly curled rose-brown hair spilling down her back, and whispers something to him. A smirk spreads across his face. Falan squares her shoulders and walks forward, resolute to remain unreactive. Even a stumble will show weakness.

Meera joins her, amusement already on her lips. "You look like you're walking on ice," she says. "Sylvestre and his friends are whispering about you, and not in a good manner."

"Like that's anything new," Falan says. This isn't the first time she's been the target of Sylvestre's remarks. But he sneers at every boarder, determined to make it clear how superior he views himself over them. As much as she despises him, it wouldn't be wise to confront him and put a target on herself before the first round. "Did Ary leave for her fitting?"

Meera nods.

Ary joins them half an hour later, donning a gown in puffy layers of light pink. Her dark hair has been left alone, short and straight, but there's something different in the sparkle of her eyes, the glow of her face.

"What do you think?" she asks, her cheeks matching the color of her dress. She can easily join Meera as a sunset cloud.

"It suits you, Channary," Meera says genuinely.

"You won't get to keep it after tonight," Falan says, looking at the door. Somebody should be coming to get them any minute now. "Anaïs will take it apart after the party to use for some other corpse next year."

Ary winces, and Meera rolls her eyes. "I suppose it would kill you to show a touch of sensitivity, wouldn't it?"

Before Falan can respond, the door opens and a dealer walks in. Not Bellamy, but Falan knows he will be wearing the same black dress coat and trousers and white shirt. The dealer beckons for them to walk in their chosen order, and Falan finds herself between Meera and Ary as they all line up.

They arrive at the ballroom, the doors purposefully shut for their entrances. The dealer starts to send the players in one at a time, allowing at least half a minute between each person. Falan's heartbeat begins to speed up, thinking of the crowd waiting inside.

They're not the ones you should be afraid of, she tells herself after Meera walks in. *They're the ones watching, not killing.*

The dealer opens the doors. Somebody calls out number eleven, not bothering with her name. Falan walks inside the large room. It's gold, from the walls to the floor, but that might be due to the glow from the crystal chandelier hanging from the ceiling. A large window spans the wall to her left, displaying the inky night and the glittering city lights. A long table sits at the back of the room, the platters of different confectionaries and pastries looking more for display than consumption.

Every head is turned her way as she continues down to the center of the room where the other players stand. It's tempting to pretend that each look from the guests is one of admiration. She can't see their expressions under the masks they wear. But Falan imagines scrutiny, scorn, dismissal, a few looks of feigned pity that mean nothing.

The masks themselves are startlingly creative. Falan recognizes many of them from prior Cirque performances. There's a peacock mask made of genuine feathers, a mosaic of teal and dark cyan and small dots of black. There's another mask put together like a jigsaw puzzle with cleverly fitted black-and-white puzzle pieces. And a diamond one where gems drip down the wearer's cheeks like tears.

The spectators feel more like entities than human beings, like beasts lured by glitter and wealth. But perhaps if they watch people killing one another for entertainment, they are closer to beasts than human beings.

Falan takes her place next to Meera, who mutters, "Try smiling if you want one of them to even consider you."

Smiling won't do anything. Falan knows her cool and sulky demeanor has already painted an image of herself. True, she doesn't come off as somebody naive or gullible. But she's small, scrawny, and has a dark-eyed, placid stare that makes her look more like an insolent child than anybody capable of winning a deadly competition.

Falan watches Ary walk down the room. She suspects there must be more pity than scorn among the spectators now, for Ary's shy demeanor might gain her some sympathy points. After she joins the rest of the players, they are finally free to move around. Players cannot talk to bettors. Instead, they must wait for someone to approach them. Falan moves to the refreshment table, knowing nobody will seek her out.

"Care for an hors d'oeuvre?"

She turns to see Bellamy carrying a plate topped with canapés. "What happened to the bruises on your face?" she asks, noticing the purple smudges are now gone.

He flashes that same satisfied smile that she's seen many times before. "The Cirque's physician had some secrets that I graciously agreed to keep. In turn, he agreed to heal my wounds before Blanchet caught sight of them."

"What secrets?"

"I wouldn't have a reputation if I spilled confidential information so readily, ma chérie."

Although he is dressed in the same clothes as the dealer who led them here, Bellamy holds her attention for longer. His dark hair is tousled, and his black dress coat rests neatly on his straight shoulders and lean figure.

"This is the first time I've seen you wear something adequate in three years," she says.

"Compliments tend to be more affectionate than that." His amused gaze flickers to her gown. "Such as, for you, tu es radieuse ce soir, mon cœur."

Falan rolls her eyes, ignoring the strange warmth in her chest. "I wasn't complimenting you. But, if you insist, you look . . . embellished."

"You are truly a champion of eloquence, Sunkara," Bellamy says dryly.

"We're not here to compliment each other. We're here to gain the help of some useful allies."

Starting with Blanchet's son—Jules Devereux Blanchet.

Falan pretends to be occupied with brushing dust off her sleeve. "Did you successfully do as I asked?"

Bellamy nods. "The Blanchet mansion, for all its glory, has abysmal security measures."

"And did you take care of his bag?"

"Do you really have to ask?" It's hard to tell whether he's teasing or is genuinely offended at her questioning his skill.

"It will be hard to talk to him if he stays by the other patrons all evening," Falan says, eyeing Jules. The nervy, dark-haired boy stands stiffly, fidgeting with his gold spectacles, a champagne flute raised to his lips that he hasn't taken a sip of. The opposite of his father, who is on his third glass of champagne and playing his part as a vibrant host.

"Don't worry about that," Bellamy says. "He'll make his own way outside soon enough."

Instead of asking what he means, Falan takes an hors d'oeuvre from Bellamy's platter. "Do these have meat in them?"

Bellamy shakes his head. "The cook used mushrooms for this one."

Falan pops the canapé in her mouth. The small piece of savory pastry is flaky, topped with some sort of mushroom and caper spread and a smidge of salty cheese. She wants another. But she restrains herself. She will indulge once she accomplishes what she must tonight—securing not just Jules's help but Lucien Trichet's too. Getting information about the rounds ahead of time means nothing without knowing how to prepare for them.

Cirque performers are not allowed to watch the Game of Oaths, as Jean-Pierre and Blanchet don't want future players to study the games, but many have dared to sneak in at least once.

Falan had snuck into the Chapiteau to watch last year for Lavanya's sake; she would have kept sneaking in if her sister had survived past the first round.

"Find me once you've talked to Jules," Falan says.

Before Bellamy can respond, she moves through the crowd, leaving him behind. Considering Lucien has been hidden away the past year, there's not a large chance he will be here tonight. However, since this event is in the hotel itself, Falan holds on to a bit of hope that he will show up. If not, she will need to find some other way to talk to him, perhaps sneaking up to his quarters.

Her eyes stray to the center of the room. Bettors surround the players she expects—Sylvestre, Eliot, Arthur. But a few talk to Meera and one even talks to Ary. Nearby, a dealer holds a platter with champagne flutes. It isn't wise to consume alcohol, but Falan considers that daintily sipping from a glass might add to her elegance.

She takes the last flute on the tray and is just raising it to her lips when somebody behind her says, "They're all out? A pity."

Falan turns around, looking right into the brown eyes of Lucien Trichet. So he has come after all; perhaps tradition was too important to dismiss, even for Jean-Pierre. She doesn't break his gaze as she holds out the champagne flute.

"Five minutes of your time and this is all yours."

VII

November 7, 1896

BELLAMY HATES PARTIES LIKE THIS ONE. THEY'RE just like the gatherings his grandfather used to make him attend: a bunch of wealthy socialites standing around drinking champagne, trying to outdo one another in who is the wealthiest.

He shudders. Memories of his grandfather are about as welcome as this party is.

At least this time he has something to do other than stand with a plate of hors d'oeuvres all night. He just needs to wait until Jules makes his way out, which will be soon enough. After watching him at the cercle, Bellamy has Jules Devereux Blanchet's habits memorized. The first time he gambled and lost, his face practically turned green before he fled. He did the same each time after each loss, a never-ending stream. Once or twice even in the middle of a tension-filled game. One thing is clear—Jules flees when anxious.

Judging from the look on his face, Jules is close to doing it sometime soon. Perhaps his first time on the panel is more overwhelming than he expected. Or perhaps it's a pressure that he never wanted at all.

Unfortunately for him, it's about to increase. People truly underestimate the power that a secret holds, some worth their weight in diamonds. Because, as Bellamy found out from his conversation with Falan last night, he's not the only one who's been observing Jules.

The Blanchet boy finally moves toward the door of the ballroom, impressively managing not to draw any attention. After a couple of seconds, Bellamy follows, still carrying his tray. Thankfully, the hotel's hallways are empty—this floor is closed to the general public tonight, so tracking the echo of Jules's footsteps is effortless.

To Bellamy's bemusement, Jules goes through the back exit of the hotel. Is he leaving the party entirely? Bellamy strides down the hallway and pushes the door open. The cool night air rushes over him, refreshing after the stuffiness of the hotel ballroom. In front of him, Jules is on his knees, vomiting.

Now is the time to put him to the test.

"Monsieur, are you all right?" Bellamy asks, shutting the door behind him and setting the tray down. The light from inside the hotel spills from its windows, creating patches of gold on the dark asphalt.

Jules whirls around, running the back of his hand across his mouth, careful not to stain the sleeve of his beige dress coat. "I—I'm fine, thank you," he stutters, alarm in his hazel eyes.

"Parties like this make me anxious as well," Bellamy says lightly. It's not a lie. His grandfather's words echo in his mind.

I'll make you a proper French boy.

"I'm fine," Jules says again.

"I'd be nervous too, if I were you," Bellamy says. "Gaining a position on the Game's panel is a large jump from lounging around the cercle. It means more interaction with the spectators, with Jean-Pierre, with your father."

Jules pauses, a wary expression on his face. "I don't see how that concerns you."

"Forgive me, I'm overstepping boundaries," Bellamy feigns apology. "But it just occurred to me that more interaction means a higher chance of any one of those influential figures learning your secret."

"What secret?"

"Oh, the one about you being an Enchanteur," Bellamy says casually.

Jules stiffens at once. He stares at Bellamy for a long moment, terror flashing in his eyes. His lips are parted, as if searching for the right words to say, but nothing comes out.

Before the previous night, Bellamy had no idea about Jules's abilities; he'd been surprised and rather annoyed that he hadn't noticed before, but secretly impressed that Falan did.

"Why would he cooperate with you?" Bellamy had asked Falan last night when she'd insisted on securing Jules's help.

"Simple. We know two things about him," Falan had said.

"Two things?"

"One, he's Blanchet's son."

"And the second thing?"

"That he's an Enchanteur."

Bellamy had blinked, startled. "How do you know this?"

"I've been watching him for a while, checking his things."

"His things?" He had paused. "You *broke* into the Blanchet mansion?"

"Jules has been careful, but I found a book hidden in his room: *Guillaume Gallien's Origins of the Arcane*," Falan had said, ignoring Bellamy's surprise. "A book used to learn and master the intricacies of magic. Of course, no Enchanteur would dare to even glance at the book without the protection of a cert."

"But that doesn't make sense," Bellamy had said. "Enchanteur abilities are hereditary. Blanchet isn't an Enchanteur. Nobody in his family is."

"Exactly. So why would Jules be reading a book like that in secret?"

The answer clicked. "The rumors about Jules being the illegitimate child of an affair. Does that mean . . ."

"It's undeniable proof."

The Blanchet family has managed to avoid or dismiss the whispers all these years, as nobody has been able to solidly prove or make a direct accusation that Jules is the child of an affair. But Jules's hidden Enchanteur abilities are clear evidence. If the truth got out, it would obliterate the Blanchet name, for Jules is slated to take over the hotel someday. It would destroy the hotel's reputation if people knew for sure that the future owner is not only the child of a servant but somebody who is not entirely white. Bellamy wonders if Blanchet himself has any idea of Jules's magic.

Either way, it's a secret Jules will do anything to keep hidden.

As he gazes at Jules, Bellamy wonders how long it will take him to crumble.

"You shouldn't be making such accusations," Jules finally says as he gets to his feet, his wobbly voice paper thin.

Bellamy scoffs. "Little tip: If you don't want to be found out, find a better place to hide Gallien's book."

"What are you talking—"

"Under the floorboards? That's quite unoriginal, Mr. Poe; you need to come up with another place for your Tell-Tale Heart," Bellamy says flippantly. "Anyway, your satchel was left in the cloakroom. Which makes it easy enough to . . . add things that might not have been there before."

Jules falters for a moment, but then he spits out, "I'll tell my father that you're tampering with the guests' items *and* that you've broken into our residence. You'll be incarcerated at once."

"You see, I thought you might say that. For good measure, I

used the wax stamp on your desk to add your family seal to the inner corner of the book. It is yours, after all, is it not?" Bellamy cocks his head with feigned cluelessness, wanting to irritate Jules further. "Why would I be accused of tampering with your bag if all that's found in there are your items?"

"Possession of a book doesn't mean anything," Jules says, trying to sound defiant. But his face is paler, his breathing quicker. "Perhaps I am just curious about Enchanteur abilities. It doesn't mean I have them."

Bellamy raises an eyebrow. "So you would be happy for me to openly reveal this information? You think the public will take kindly to this, especially with the rumors about your background?"

Jules says nothing.

"All right, then."

Bellamy turns to head back inside, but Jules blurts out, "Wait!"

"Yes?" Bellamy says nonchalantly, stopping. He recognizes the look on Jules's face. It's the expression of a player who has realized they've lost the game.

Jules pushes his hair back from his forehead, damp with sweat. "What do you want from me?"

"How quick of you to assume I want something," Bellamy says, his smile turning dangerously innocuous. "I could simply be a curious soul interested in the Blanchet background."

"So you *don't* want something?"

"No, I want something."

Jules presses his lips together, crossing his arms. Perhaps it's meant to be intimidating but it comes off as defensive instead. "What?"

"I've got a . . . friend competing in this year's Game of Oaths," Bellamy says. "I won't speak a word of your identity if you agree to supply us with information about the rounds ahead of time." He drops his voice. "If not, then I'll be glad to spread word of your secret."

"You're bluffing."

"So that's a confession, then?" Bellamy's smile widens. "It's too easy with you. No wonder you've never won a single game at the cercle. You give yourself away every time."

"I didn't confess anything!" Jules insists, but his clammy face and trembling body oppose this statement.

"Try to deny it, if you can. After all, rumors that hold no truth often die out fairly quickly, especially when refuted with proof. But the ones that are truthful, well, I can't say the same for." When Jules doesn't respond, Bellamy adds, "I'm fantastic at keeping secrets when it benefits me. All you need to do is agree to provide us with whatever information you know of the coming rounds."

Despite himself, Bellamy can't help but feel empathy for Jules. It's not easy to be around the scrutinizing, snobbish upper class when you are so different from them, to be pushed around by a domineering guardian who tries to mold you into their vision.

Bellamy knows this firsthand.

But he can't afford to feel sympathy for Jules. Not when Horrent's deadline is hanging over him like a guillotine's blade, waiting to have his head on the chopping block.

"I can't do what you're asking," Jules says, his voice hoarse. "I—I don't . . ."

"All of Paris will know about your background. Think about what that will do to you. You have no chance of getting a cert. Your father would never pull strings to get one for you because that would mean acknowledging that the rumors about an affair hold truth. He will distance himself from you. He won't use any connections to save you from imprisonment if you slip up and use magic. But that doesn't have to happen. Not if you provide us with the information we want." Bellamy pauses. "Do we have a deal?"

Jules's hazel eyes flicker with uncertainty, practically reflecting his thought process for Bellamy to read. The risk of revealing he is an Enchanteur is too much to gamble. Minds like Jules's can be easily shaped with the right words. Plant the correct seeds of doubt and they will bloom magnificently.

"All right." Jules is still trembling and clammy, slightly hunched like he might vomit again, but he nods as if trying to convince himself. "Deal. What do you want to know?"

"Tell me what the first game is," Bellamy says.

"The panel meets every morning, so it hasn't officially been agreed on. But unofficially the decided game is the Joker."

Bellamy grimaces. The Joker holds a high mortality rate compared to the spectrum of previous games. It's an audience favorite, to the point where it's been one of the rounds in every Game of Oaths he's been around to witness, and then some. It's a popular opening game, but sometimes it's saved for the middle of the tournament when the deaths aren't coming quickly enough for the audience.

To cheat through it seems like an impossible task. But Lucien's help could give Falan an advantage. Bellamy glances at the door, wondering how much progress she's made. He should return to the party; it's not wise to be gone for this long. "That's all for now," he says to Jules. "I'll be seeking you out again."

As Bellamy turns to go back inside, picking up his tray on the way, Jules says, "This friend of yours. Which player are they?"

Bellamy shoots him a wry smile. "Wait and see," he says before disappearing into the hotel.

VIII

November 7, 1896

THE LAST TIME FALAN TRULY LOOKED AT LUCIEN Trichet was the night of Lavanya's death, right when she tore her eyes away from Lavanya's corpse to look at the other players. Lucien's eyes, so very brown, glittered with shock and tears. For the first time in a year, she meets his gaze again.

In his gold and black dress coat and trousers, Lucien is dashing. He wears a button up white shirt inside, stark against his brown skin, and has a black top hat resting on his curls. Even now, he still has his belt of gleaming knives around his waist.

But his eyes are different. They used to twinkle around Lavanya, come to life. Now they are the eyes of a boy who does not care about anything. Her sister was friendly with nearly everyone at the Cirque, but perhaps the closest with Lucien.

It's all the more strange that Falan feels like she barely knows him. Unlike Jean-Pierre and Jules, she hasn't been able to observe Lucien this past year, for he barely stepped out of his luxurious quarters until tonight. And even though Lavanya was so close to him, Falan never spoke much to Lucien beyond civil greetings. But his relationship to Lavanya is all she truly needs.

"The only reason I agreed to this is because it will be at least five more minutes before they send out another batch of champagne," Lucien says as he stands next to the refreshments table with Falan.

"Very kind of you," Falan says snidely. "I'll be quick. I sought you out to ask you for your assistance in the Game."

"You want to cheat?" Lucien asks.

"I want to win," Falan says. "And your knowledge of how to survive will help me prepare for each round."

"First, there is no guarantee you will face the same set of games I did. I won't know ahead of time what you will be enduring." Lucien tilts the champagne flute up to take a sip. "And second, all the preparation and help in the world are no match for the intense will of the other competitors."

"So, without help, I'm damned, and with help, I'm still damned."

"Pick your poison." Lucien leans against his cane. "If you truly want a chance at survival, you should be trying to swindle spectators into buying grants for you, like all the other players are doing. And what makes you think I would choose to help you?"

"You were close to Lavanya," Falan says. "But more than that, you made it out of the Game when nobody thought you would."

During last year's tournament, Lucien fell from the high beam in the first round and landed badly on his leg. The audience pretty much considered him gone after that, but he proved them all wrong by taking the crown. However, his leg never set right after the fall. So when he won the tournament, Jean-Pierre gave Lucien a beautifully crafted cane of black and silver.

Lucien sets down the empty champagne flute. Five minutes have certainly gone but he hasn't moved. "In a week, I'll be free of my contract," he says. "Getting involved is a needless risk for me. Not to mention, the only way I can offer anything is if I have knowledge of the rounds beforehand, and I don't."

"Say you did," Falan says. "What would be worth taking this risk?"

Lucien studies her, and Falan knows what he's thinking just from his expression. It's the same way so many people looked at her after Lavanya's death. Their eyes would soften, as if pulled into a memory.

You look so much like your sister, they all said.

None of them knew the irony of that statement. In this case, however, Falan hopes he's reminiscing enough to sympathize and help her.

"There is one thing that might convince me to take the risk," Lucien says softly.

"What?"

Lucien takes a macaron from a nearby tray, rolling it between his fingers. "You're friends with Bellamy Durand, aren't you?"

"Business associate is more accurate," Falan says curtly.

"Whatever you call it, I've heard he's well connected. So here's my offer: If I tell you how to play each round—provided you know what the games are beforehand—then you convince him to use all the connections he has to find somebody for me. The deal isn't complete until we find the person I'm looking for." He pops the macaron in his mouth.

Convincing Bellamy won't be particularly hard, considering he himself struck a deal to help her win. Plus, this only gives Lucien more incentive to help keep her alive.

"That sounds reasonable," Falan says. "Who are you looking for?"

"How exactly do you plan to figure out the games before each round?" he asks, skipping over her question.

At that moment, Falan spots Bellamy slipping inside the room. The triumphant grin on his face tells her everything. "I've already done it," she says as Bellamy approaches them.

"The Joker," he says quietly. "That's the first round."

Falan curses under her breath. Jean-Pierre's choice of a first game with a reputation for a high death count sends a clear message for how this year's Game of Oaths will be.

"Should I ask how the two of you figured that out?" Lucien asks.

"We secured the help of a somewhat reliable source," Bellamy says with a wink. He and Lucien seem fairly friendly with each other. But then again, Bellamy is on good terms with pretty much everybody except the Lilies.

Falan glances around for Jules. She finds him in the corner of the room, once again holding a champagne flute to his lips and not drinking from it. But this time he's lost in thought.

"Blanchet's son," Lucien says, following Falan's gaze. "Just joined the panel, right? How did you get him to tell you?"

"That doesn't matter," Falan says. "What matters is that we have a way of knowing beforehand what each round will be. I agree to the terms of your deal. It's up to you now."

"So I declared," Lucien says with a little sigh. "We have a deal. Meet me at the bouillon after the party. It's not safe to talk about this here." With that, he walks to the nearest champagne platter and takes a flute from it.

Bellamy smiles crookedly. "Should I bother to ask what deal you made with him?"

"Not yet."

"Keeping me in suspense, I see. But he has a point," Bellamy says. "You shouldn't be talking to me either." Then, before she can respond, he walks off too, leaving her alone.

She still has more than two hours of this headache to get through. The dessert table beckons her, particularly the croquembouche. It's improper, but Falan plucks a profiterole off the tower and pops it into her mouth. The choux dough melts on her tongue, pastry cream flooding her senses.

Even after five years in France, Falan still finds herself comparing the meals here to the ones back in India. She has grown used to the daily stew at the bouillon, although she misses the ragi porridge she ate before. Figuring out which foods were considered impolite to eat using her hands took several months; it surprised her how much the French rely on utensils.

"You are supposed to use the knife, you know." Beside her, Ronan cleanly cuts a profiterole off the tower. "If you yank, it rips at the others."

"At the end of the night, it will all be eaten or thrown away. And there's nothing wrong with using your hands. That's why we have them," Falan says as she takes another. She isn't sure if she's more annoyed or skeptical that Ronan is talking to her.

Even now, after two years of knowing each other, Falan still isn't sure how to speak to him. Lavanya was the one who was close to him, having been his trapeze partner first. In fact, Falan was certain Lavanya was in love with Ronan. She wouldn't stop talking about him and would brush off the company of others to go spend time practicing with him. When with him, she would do things like giggle and toss her hair.

It irritated Falan immensely. She didn't see what was so appealing about Ronan beyond his looks.

Perhaps Ronan showed a softer side of himself to Lavanya. Falan remembers how Lavanya claimed one day to know Ronan's real name; often when Jean-Pierre takes in performers, he makes them change their name to something more familiar to a French audience. When Lavanya first signed with Jean-Pierre, she introduced both herself and

Falan under her birth surname, Sunkara, which Jean-Pierre gave his approval for. Even though Lavanya is gone, Falan still keeps Sunkara as her surname.

Falan is still unsure what quite passed between Lavanya and Ronan. To go against the Cirque's unspoken rule and speak about one's past would be a large feat, as would revealing something as personal as a birth name. But Ronan was clearly fond of her, even if he was more reserved about showing it. Not that he had any other friends. The other Lilies shun him due to his Indian heritage, and the other Cirque performers shun him for being a Lily.

It was shortly before Lavanya's death that Ronan suddenly stopped interacting with her altogether.

The only thing Lavanya said when Falan asked was that they'd had an argument. She didn't say what about, but the details don't matter in the end. Ronan's actions are reason enough for Falan to dislike him, just as she always has.

"I don't know what you're up to, but I can tell you it's not a good idea," Ronan says. "You've looked incredibly suspicious all night."

In response, Falan puts the entire profiterole in her mouth.

"Fine. Ignore me like a child, then," he says coldly, sounding more like the Ronan she's used to. "I'm telling you this for your benefit."

"You would not do anything for my benefit, especially now," Falan says through her mouthful. "By tomorrow night, we stand a good chance of killing each other."

"You completely disregarded the bettors and have only conversed with one of the dealers and Lucien Trichet," Ronan says. "It looks suspicious to anybody watching."

"So you admit you were watching me?" she says, reaching for a macaron this time. The crisp shell crunches between her teeth and dissolves to sugar on her tongue.

"No, I was not."

"But you just said it yourself," she remarks, still chewing. "You said I looked suspicious and listed off my conversation partners of the night."

"You only spoke to two people," Ronan says irritably, but—is she imagining it?—he looks a touch embarrassed. "And it's rude to talk with your mouth full."

"Are you going to eat your profiterole? You've been holding the same one for ages."

Ronan rolls his eyes, about to eat the pastry, when he suddenly says, "Anaïs gave you a good color." It sounds like the words are scraping painfully against his throat. "You look . . . beguiling."

Falan isn't sure if that is meant to be a compliment or an insult. But she eyes Ronan as she helps herself to another macaron. She saw him back in the storage room, but it's only up close that she notices how his blue dress coat and trousers match his eyes, and his black hair has been combed back. He looks even more handsome than usual, but she doesn't say it.

"It will all disappear in a few hours," Falan says instead, gazing around the large room. "All of it. One big dream. Or nightmare, depending on who you are."

Ronan's mouth twitches. "You're right," he says. "The Game has already begun."

Yes, it has. Falan glances at Jean-Pierre, busy talking with a cluster of socialites. *It began a year ago, and I've been playing ever since.*

IX

November 7, 1896

LUCIEN TRICHET HAS NEVER ATTENDED A BETTING Party twice.

Few people have had the so-called honor, but Lucien assumes the previous winners had a far better time at their second Betting Party than he is having. Previous winners, even if they were boarders, were presumably sought out by people. Then again, the thought of talking to spectators about the gory journey to his win is nauseating, so perhaps their evasion is a blessing.

Lucien gazes around the crowded room as he sips from another champagne flute, gauging this year's audience. There are more people than last year, more types of masks. None are identical to each other, which Lucien finds impressive on some level. Like last year, the majority of the spectators are gathered around the expectedly popular players—the Lilies—while the others are left to savor the glitter of the party.

Falan in particular is savoring the dessert table. Lucien watches as she pops a profiterole in her mouth, talking to her trapeze partner. The sight already sends a curdle of irritation through him. Although Falan has never favored Ronan the way her sister did, watching her talk to him now reminds Lucien of when Lavanya would talk nonstop about him. She would prioritize Ronan over everybody except Falan.

It made Lucien want to pulverize the bastard.

Lucien tips the rest of the champagne flute's contents into his mouth. He's no fool; he knows Falan came to him expecting him to say yes to helping her solely due to his connection to Lavanya. And he did say yes, for he loved Lavanya. Saying no would mean breaking the promise he made Lavanya right before her death.

Also, if it means getting one step closer to finding Fayette, he can't object.

Perhaps he should have told Falan who he's looking for. But Lucien is afraid to allow himself to hope. Hope is not only precarious but cruel too. The chances of Falan making it through the Game of Oaths are slim, and if she dies, his chances of finding his sister die with her.

The only thing Lucien hopes for at the moment is that wherever Fayette is, it's a lot better than where he is right now.

Too much. He drank too much. Lucien shakes his head to clear it, seated at a table with Falan and Bellamy. The walk to the bouillon is always difficult, even more so when drunk, but he made it. As one of the few places open in Paris after midnight, the bouillon is bustling on a chilly night like this. It is a blessing because their conversation will be drowned out among the others, but the ambience only makes Lucien sleepier, as does the steaming bowl of stew in front of him.

Falan and Bellamy, on the other hand, are rapidly gulping down their bowls. Even after a night of eating desserts, Falan is still ravenous. She's out of her silvery dress, now in a loose white shirt and trousers, similar clothes to Bellamy's. Lucien has no clue where she got ahold of men's clothing, but he doesn't ask.

"Not hungry?" Bellamy inquires, looking at Lucien's full bowl.

"I indulged myself at the Betting Party." Lucien forces himself to eat a chunk of meat floating in his stew and shifts his gaze to Falan.

"I noticed you left the party without Jean-Pierre's approval."

She shrugs in response.

"And your gown?"

"I dumped it in the dressing room." A wistful expression briefly crosses her face, gone as quickly as it appeared. Her expression was so uncannily similar to how Lavanya looked after last year's Betting Party that Lucien is stunned.

"I've never worn such a beautiful thing before," Lavanya had said after changing out of her orange dress, the one that looked like rays of the sun were sewn into the fabric itself. "And I doubt I ever will again."

Lucien regrets not telling her that she looked more beautiful than he'd ever seen her. That she always looked beautiful, no matter what she wore. He didn't even make a snide remark or joke as usual to cheer her up. He was too consumed with his own worries about the upcoming tournament.

"So," Falan says once she finishes her stew, "tell me how to win the Joker."

The Joker is a game of survival and deception. It takes place in any setting Jean-Pierre desires; last year it was the top story of an abandoned castle. It's all an illusion, but it looks real. It *feels* real. Everything is interactive—one can block, climb, move, throw, and do more with the objects around them. One of the twelve players is secretly the Joker, whose task is to hunt down and kill as many of the other players as possible. When the Joker claims their first victim, unofficially dubbed the Clockstarter, a countdown spanning one hour starts. The only way to cut the hour short is if someone manages to kill the Joker.

Protected by the noisy atmosphere, Lucien launches into the details of last year's game. He recalls how dark and dismal it was, how it seemed like lightning was truly flashing outside the castle and the corridor walls he sat against were made of stone. He remembers the hollow echo of his feet each time he took a step.

"In this game, being a fast runner is preferable to being a strong fighter," Lucien continues. "But that wasn't a choice for me."

"How did you do it, then?" Falan asks.

"I hid, which I recommend you do as well. Don't go looking for a fight." Lucien pauses. "There's a sense of hope once you know the hour timer has started; I didn't even have time to feel remorse for the fact that somebody was murdered."

"So I won't be able to tell who the Joker is?"

"To the audience, the Joker and players are clear," Lucien explains. "But for the competitors, the person who is the Joker has an illusion placed over them, making them look like the Joker character from a playing card. But if you figure out who they are and say their name, the illusion disappears and you have the ability to kill them."

"Does the Joker know their role in advance?"

Lucien shakes his head. "No. Jean-Pierre will tell you what weapon denotes the Joker before the round. If you wake up and find you're armed with it, you know your role. As for the other players, last year, weapons were hidden around the setting for us to find." A beat. "Unless, of course, you're given a weapon grant before the round starts. The Joker could have their starter weapon *and* a grant."

"What kind of weapons are hidden around the setting?"

"Last year it was mainly knives, which worked in my favor."

"That was lucky for you," Bellamy says.

Lucien nods absently. As one of the knife throwers at the Cirque, his Affinity weaponry gave him an advantage throughout the tournament. It was something the spectators initially thought would make him a watchful contender—until after the first round, when he severely injured his leg. Then the previously promised grants never came. He was left in a hopeless situation . . . and he'd lost Lavanya.

He was never supposed to win. No wonder there was so much backlash.

"Hold on," Falan says suddenly. "If grants are given before the round, I just need to pay attention to who is getting what. Then if the Joker has a grant, I'll know who they are."

Lucien shakes his head. "You'll be blindfolded," he says, and dismay crosses her face. "Grant distributions happen before and after each round, handed out by the Game's previous winner."

"Which is you," Bellamy adds.

The remark oddly strikes a nerve. "Yes, I have the utmost honor of handing people items that might save them from an untimely death," Lucien says sarcastically.

"I was merely pointing it out," Bellamy says placatingly, sipping his stew.

Lucien sighs heavily; he's finding it harder to stay focused. "The grants before rounds consist only of weaponry, and the grants after rounds consist of things such as food and medicine. The weapon grant distributions before rounds are always blindfolded so the other players can't prepare themselves."

The frustration on Falan's face is even more evident than her dismay, but Lucien isn't sure what she was expecting. It would have been far too easy otherwise.

"Did you figure out the Joker's identity in your round?" Bellamy asks curiously.

A memory flashes in Lucien's mind. Crouched on the icy ground of the stone castle, his strength draining from him, making one last desperate attempt for his life. "Yes," he says. "Rocque. I noticed the Joker holding his weapon with his left hand and I remembered Rocque was left-handed."

Rocque was the lead fire performer before Sylvestre, and an early favorite. None of the other performers liked him, not even the other Lilies. Once Lucien revealed him, he stood no chance.

"What if she figures out the Joker's identity and they still kill her?" Bellamy asks.

"If they kill her, she'll be dead. Not much she can do after that," Lucien says bluntly.

Falan has been quiet for a long time, Lucien realizes. She's staring into space, lost in thought. It's only after a minute that Lucien realizes she's thinking of an outcome she doesn't dare ask him about.

The one where *she* is the Joker.

"What happens if the Joker gets killed *before* they take their first victim?" Bellamy asks suddenly. "Suppose they attempt to kill the Clockstarter and they end up getting killed in self-defense?"

Lucien pauses, thinking back over the previous six years. The Joker has been a round in every single Game of Oaths, but there's never been an instance of the Joker getting killed first. "It's never happened in my time here."

And he knows why—Jean-Pierre makes such an outcome impossible.

"There's something odd about the Joker. Perhaps the reason nobody has ever slain one before the Clockstarter is killed," Lucien says, staring down at his stew. "I contributed to killing Rocque. I was lucky. I use knives as a long-distance weapon. But before I knew his identity . . ." He swallows. "I don't know if it was the magic, but everything suddenly felt . . . off."

"How do you mean?" Bellamy asks, riveted.

"With each step I took toward him, the strength left my body," Lucien says. "I couldn't even think straight. When I figured out it was him and called out his name, the strange feeling vanished along with the illusion on him. My strength came back, and my thinking was as clear as ever."

Falan finally speaks. "What are you saying?"

Lucien meets her eyes, hoping she sees the desperation in his. He can give all the advice in the world, but she won't know how horrific the Game is until it starts. And he can't afford to feel hopeful for anything—such as finding Fayette—in the face of such naiveté. "I'm saying there are two keys to survival. One, this tournament is all about loopholes: find one per round to exploit, and there's a higher chance of getting out alive. Two, stop thinking the tournament is a game, because it's not."

"But it is," Bellamy says. "Sick, twisted, deadly. But at its core, it's just a game."

"It isn't." Lucien finally smiles, somber and haunted. "For games are supposed to be fun, mon ami."

X

November 8, 1896

IT'S TWO IN THE MORNING BY THE TIME FALAN HAS finished talking with Lucien, getting all the information she needs to brace herself for the first round. When they finally exit the bouillon, Lucien stops her. For a moment, he looks as if he might embrace her, standing just a few inches away.

Instead, he leans down and whispers, "You better keep to our deal."

When she nods, he walks away in the direction of the hotel. Falan thinks about who Lucien could be looking for, remembering how he skipped over her question at the Betting Party. Is he seeking a sibling? A parent? A friend?

"What was that?" Bellamy asks.

After a moment, Falan says, "He wished me luck."

Bellamy looks like he doesn't quite believe her, but he says nothing as they start back to the boardinghouse together.

Paris is quite different deep into the night. The City of Light is now shrouded in darkness, broken only by the arc lamps illuminating their path. At dawn the city will start to rouse, gently nudged awake from its slumber. But in the dead of the night, everything is silent. The only sounds are their footsteps on the cobbled path below.

Falan watches Bellamy as they walk. He's uncharacteristically quiet. Usually all quick hands and sharp smiles, it's unnerving to see him so deeply lost in thought. She can't help noting how the dark of the night mutes the already faded freckles dusting his cheeks. It strengthens the shadows under his eyes, making him look older than eighteen years of age.

Walking with him in the dark takes her back to a sudden memory that she hasn't let herself dwell on in so long. Bellamy, drunk on the hotel roof in the middle of the night months ago. Bellamy, stumbling along the streets with her as she somehow managed to get him all the way back to the boardinghouse. Bellamy, with his sad gray eyes and sadder smile—

Falan stops herself. Bellamy never brought it up, so she's certain he's forgotten about it entirely. Or perhaps he was too drunk to remember in the first place.

"If you keep staring at me, Sunkara, you'll trip on a stone and hurt yourself before the Game even starts," Bellamy suddenly says. That goading, cheeky smirk is back on his face.

Falan quickly faces forward. She hadn't even noticed she was staring at him.

When they finally arrive at the boardinghouse, Bellamy makes his own way inside. He briefly pauses in the doorway and glances over his shoulder at her. "See you tomorrow."

"See you tomorrow," she says.

And then she's all alone. She should go inside too. But she doesn't.

Many players stay up all night before seclusion so that they are tired enough to sleep during the day, avoiding waiting the hours of nerve-chewing agony before the first round. Last year, Lavanya spent the night roof jumping, exploring Paris in the dark. Falan wanted to come, but Lavanya told her it was something she needed to do alone.

Tonight, Falan does what she wished for a year ago. She adores traveling the rooftops. It's the closest she will ever come to flying, higher than the trapeze, defying the sloped buildings and cobbled streets below.

Soleil et lune. Lavanya was the sun, destined to wilt away in the dark, only to bloom again in the morning. Falan is the moon, belonging to the night. She breathes in the rush of cold air, closing her eyes against the wind.

This city glitters, but not for us.

When Falan returns at dawn, she finds both Meera and Ary asleep. For a moment, it feels like a regular morning where she's just returned from a bout of gambling. But knowing what today holds erases the familiarity.

Erwin comes knocking on their door less than an hour later. All of them are awake by now, sitting in silence. None of them says a word as they follow Erwin out the back of the boardinghouse, where the other players are being ushered by dealers into private fiacres. Falan looks around for Bellamy but doesn't see him. He must be getting the Lily players at the hotel.

Falan is pushed into a fiacre of her own, where a dealer climbs in after her and hands her a flask. "Drink," he says.

"What is this?" Falan asks.

"Drink," he says again, a cross between impatient and bored.

Falan opens the flask and drinks.

Sleep is more welcome than Falan imagined, her exhaustion keeping her out long after the drug's effects wear off. She dreams. Mainly of Lavanya, as usual, but surprisingly not of the night she died. Instead, she experiences memories she's refused to let herself relive since her death. Exploring Paris together. Sipping a rare treat of hot chocolate.

The day they first met on the ship to Marseille.

After Falan's father sent for her, it took a few more months of preparation before she could embark on her journey to join him in England. He managed to get fare to her, as well as secure her a spot on a ship headed for Marseille through the Suez Canal. She would have to travel across France and take a ferry from Le Havre to England, where he would meet her.

Most of the people occupying the passenger ship were French, and therefore given priority. Falan, however, was put in the least sanitary of rooms, spiking her fear of contracting an illness once more. Not to mention the food options—lots of salted meat, which she avoided, sustaining herself on hardtack.

It was her third day into the journey when things changed.

Falan escaped to the deck whenever she could. She found little to enjoy about the early morning air, which was much too cold, but she preferred it over the cramped lower quarters. Usually the deck was empty at dawn, but not today. As she shivered in her thin clothes, Falan eyed the only other person around, a girl who stood dangerously close to the edge of the ship. She gazed out at the gray ocean, her black hair whipping behind her in the sea breeze.

Falan wrapped her arms around herself, continuing to shiver. The majority of the French passengers donned heavy overcoats the likes of which she had never owned. There was no need for such clothing in Yanaon's sweltering climate. Perhaps this girl was able to enjoy this weather because she too wore a thick coat.

She suddenly noticed Falan's presence and walked over. Falan tensed and took a step back, alarmed. She wasn't used to people so readily approaching her.

"You're looking at me like I plan to rob you," the girl said, speaking in Telugu. She appeared a couple of years older than Falan, with wavy black hair that fell over her shoulders, brown skin, and large brown eyes.

Falan said nothing. Generally, when people saw she wouldn't respond, they stopped trying to hold a conversation and walked away.

But the girl didn't. Instead, she pulled something from the pocket of her coat. "If you're hungry, you're welcome to share my breakfast. It's something fresh, not like that hardtack."

Falan's eyes flickered with interest, anticipative at the thought of good food.

The girl's smile brightened. "Aha, I knew you could understand! Are you from Cocanada?"

The smile on her face unnerved Falan more than irritated her. She didn't know why anybody would keep a smile for so long.

"Yanaon," Falan finally corrected her.

"Oh, so you *can* speak. Anyway, I stole this from a passenger's plate on the upper deck last night. Don't worry, she got a replacement. It's a . . . savory tart, one of the people called it."

Falan hesitantly took the slice handed to her. She studied its crumbling pastry stuffed with cheese and onions.

"No meat in it, if that's what you're checking for," the girl said, taking a bite of her own slice. She closed her eyes, sighing contentedly.

Falan dug in, suddenly aware of how hungry she was. While cold, the food was fresh, not stale like the hardtack she'd consumed for the past two days. The slice was gone in under a minute. Falan licked the pastry crumbs off her fingers, and the girl watched her with a little smile.

"Do you have more?" Falan asked.

"I do, but I want my next meal to be just as good, so I'm saving it." She paused before switching to English. "And you're no longer glaring at me, so I assume I've won your approval?"

Falan hesitated, but nodded.

"You speak English. French too?"

Another nod. Before he left, her father had made sure Falan and her brother were fluent in both English and French.

"I understand French well enough, but I can't speak it," the girl said.

"This ship is headed to Marseille," Falan pointed out.

The girl just smiled. "Then I'm in for a trying time, aren't I?" She settled against the ship's rail. "So why are you headed to Marseille, Chelli?"

Falan nearly recoiled. She didn't expect this stranger to address her so familiarly.

"Well, if you won't tell me why, then I'll tell you what I'm doing here," the girl said. She had quite a loquacious nature, Falan was starting to realize. It was irritating yet appreciated. "The Mirage Diamond."

Falan cocked her head, bemused.

"It's in Paris, in a museum called the Louvre," the girl continued. "It was originally mined in India—the Kollur Mine. I intend to see it."

"You paid for this trip?" Falan asked.

The girl's smile turned sheepish. "I may have . . . snuck aboard."

She's a fool, Falan thought warily. *Leaving India—sneaking aboard a ship, traveling all the way to Paris—just to catch a glimpse of some diamond. Who would do that? What about her family?*

"My father," Falan said. "I'm going to England to see him."

The girl raised her eyebrows in surprise. "So you're traveling across France?"

Falan nodded, finally allowing herself to step closer.

“Chelli, since we’re both traveling alone, we should go together, at least until we reach Paris,” the girl suddenly said. “France will be easier to navigate if there are two of us.”

Falan waited for a convincing argument as to why. It was clear the girl needed her; traveling through France without knowing how to speak French was unfathomable.

“You’re fluent in French, and I know how to get us some good food,” the girl added. She dug into her coat pocket again, holding out another wrapped slice of tart.

“You said you stole this?” Falan asked, taking it.

“I always steal from those who I know will get an immediate replacement.”

One bite of the tart and Falan already made up her mind. The ship’s journey would take months, and the thought of consuming hardtack for all those days sounded dreadful. Good food was worth putting up with this girl.

“My name is Lavanya.” The girl held out a hand.

Falan stared at it as she finished her food. Her gaze flickered up to Lavanya’s eyes, softer than she expected them to be. She didn’t take the hand but nodded in assent.

A sharp breeze rushed by, and Falan shuddered, hugging her arms around her slight frame. Lavanya immediately removed her thick overcoat and draped it around Falan’s shoulders. Falan looked on in surprise as Lavanya tugged it tightly around her.

“Wouldn’t want you catching a chill, would we?” she said.

Falan shrugged away from her grip. “Did you steal this too?”

“Most people say thank you when receiving a gift.”

Stolen or not, the coat was warm, and Falan pulled it tighter around her body. Lavanya’s smile turned pleased, and they settled to watch the gray waters together.

Falan holds on to the warmth of the coat, gradually becoming aware that Lavanya is not really here, that this is just a memory.

A dream.

She shakes herself awake, disoriented and heavy-headed. Her bleary eyes just barely flutter, lids weighed with slumber. She looks down to see her fingers curled around the folds of a thin, white blanket.

Still groggy, Falan pushes herself up, rubbing her eyes. She's lying on a low bed with plain sheets in a square, windowless room. The place is shrouded in darkness, barely lit by the lantern set upon a small desk in the corner. The only other items she can see are a bucket and a wooden chair, occupied by Bellamy.

"Welcome to the Aviary, Sunkara," he says quietly. "You're finally awake."

"What do you mean?" Falan asks, her mouth dry. "Are you supposed to be in here?"

"The drug wasn't meant to keep you out this long, which concerned the other dealers. I suspected it was merely your own exhaustion, so I volunteered to keep an eye on you." Bellamy frowns. "When was the last time you properly slept?"

Falan doesn't answer. She shifts to face him, her legs hanging over the edge of the bed. With the warmth of slumber quickly fading, nerves are already twisting her stomach. "Time?"

"It's nearly time to go," he says, standing up and handing her a package. "Get dressed. I'll be outside, so knock when you're ready."

"Hold on," Falan says. "If everybody is leaving at once, will we not see who comes out of what room?"

"Leavings are staggered randomly, and players will be blindfolded upon reaching Jean-Pierre," Bellamy says. He's uncharacteristically impassive, even detached. Odd. He exits the room, leaving her to open the package with her outfit inside.

The uniform is the same as last year, and Falan has a feeling it hasn't changed much over time. Perhaps it holds some nostalgia for the audience. Each person gets a red overcoat with gold buttons, a crisp white shirt, and black boots. But the women get a red-and-black bodice dress to wear over their shirts and sheer black stockings while the men have trousers. On the back of each coat is the number of the competitor, framed by the outline of a playing card. Stamped in gold on the back of Falan's is the number eleven.

It also has the symbols of whichever card suit they are assigned. Falan is the Queen of Hearts.

Falan does her hair as nicely as she can for Lavanya's sake. Half of it up in two little buns like fox ears, the rest flowing down her back.

All done, petite renarde.

Falan realizes her hands are trembling, and she forces herself to stop. She cannot afford for anybody to sense her fear. Biting down on her lip, she unlatches the lock on the inside of the door, a rusted metal sliding mechanism, and opens it.

Bellamy walks in, shutting the door behind him. "Ready?"

"The outfit's a bit big on me," Falan says snidely. "I have a few complaints about that."

"Anything else?" he asks.

"Why so somber, Durand? I didn't think you'd worry about me so much."

"I'm not, because you're not going to back out of our deal by dying. So quit acting as if you are."

Oddly enough, his aggravation calms her nerves. "I thought more of your appreciation for human life," she says. "But clearly you're worried merely about your three hundred thousand."

"Fine. You can't die, for if you do, I'll deeply miss your twisted remarks and callous behavior," Bellamy says dryly. "Does that satisfy you?"

"Very much."

A ghost of a smile breezes across Bellamy's lips. But he turns to the door and opens it without another word, leaving Falan to follow him into the hallway.

The Aviary's dingy interior makes the boardinghouse look extravagant. The stony gray walls in the tunnellike hallway are stained with patches of green, discolored from years of neglect. It would be pitch-dark were it not for the lanterns lining the walls. Falan's is the only room in this hallway, causing her to wonder if each room has its own corridor. At one end of the hall is a staircase leading to an upper story.

The other end opens into a wide space where several other players, now blindfolded, are lined up. Jean-Pierre stands in front of them, a row of dealers behind him. The layout of the Aviary is larger than Falan expected it to be—there must be four different hallways on this level, including hers. Each one is marked with a letter above the entrance: N, W, S, and E. The direction of each hall.

Jean-Pierre watches as she takes her place in the row of players. Seconds later, he snaps his fingers and a blindfold flies from his pocket and over Falan's eyes, tying itself.

Falan listens for more footsteps after Bellamy's die away. She hears people slowly trickling in from all four hallways. Bellamy was right—they stagger the arrivals. Nobody speaks either, so she has no clue who is coming from where.

Finally, the footsteps stop altogether, and Jean-Pierre's voice echoes around the Aviary. "Salut, my dear competitors. It is nearly time to start the first round in this year's Game of Oaths. But before we do, there is still the matter of grants. We will be having distributions before and after rounds. The grants given before rounds are weapons you will find helpful during the game, while grants given after rounds are items that will aid you during the waiting period."

Falan's stomach does a low turn. It's just as Lucien said.

"Here to distribute the grants is last year's winner, Lucien Trichet."

Falan listens carefully as Lucien walks down the row, his footsteps getting closer. He seems to be whispering something, though she can't catch what he's saying. He eventually stops in front of her and says, "My apologies, there are no grants for you at this time."

Once Lucien has finished, Jean-Pierre resumes talking. "The first round is almost upon us," he says. "Normally, I would surprise you along with the audience, but I cannot in this case. The first game of the tournament is the Joker." He goes on to explain the rules of the game to everyone, stating pretty much everything Lucien prepared her for. "The chosen weapon for this year's Joker is a tourné knife, which I have enlarged with magic. If you find yourself armed with it at the start of the round, it means that you are the Joker. Exciting, is it not?"

Nobody answers.

"With that, all I have left to say is, joue ta chance." Jean-Pierre snaps his fingers, and Falan hears the dealers hurrying forward.

One of them slides something smooth and cool into Falan's hands. A flask. "Drink up," says a low voice, and Falan recognizes it as Bellamy's.

Without hesitating, Falan brings the flask to her lips and drinks. The concoction is the same as this morning's, thick and sweet. Its effects are quick because Falan is already swaying by the time she lowers the flask. Bellamy catches her as she tips forward.

"Chance, Sunkara," he whispers in her ear. He says something else, but slumber washes out his words.

It feels like mere seconds have passed when the roar of a crowd and music bursts through her consciousness, fuzzy and overwhelming. Falan's eyes flutter open, the cacophony sharper. She blinks, staring up dizzily at a red-and-white open-topped tent. Her head pounds as she stands, brushing off the straw sticking to her outfit.

Straw?

Jean-Pierre's booming voice echoes around the Chapiteau, vibrating through her bones. "Ladies and gentlemen, if I could have your attention—it is finally time for the Game of Oaths to commence!"

PART II

The Joker

"Most Enchanteurs cannot achieve illusion to a complex level of reality, a state where they can make others see exactly what they want them to see, to sense what they want them to sense. It is hard to manipulate something that is there. It is much harder to manipulate something that is not there."

—*Guillaume Gallien's Origins of the Arcane*; Ch. 2, p. 37 (1868)

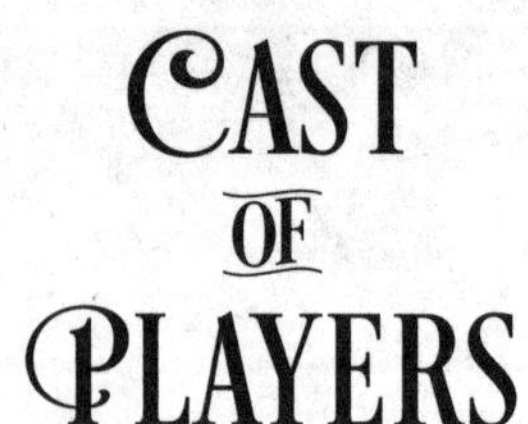

1. Sylvestre - FIRE PERFORMER - King of Spades

2. Hugh - STRONGMAN - King of Hearts

3. Cyril - WEAPON DODGER - King of Diamonds

4. Thomas - KNIFE THROWER - Jack of Diamonds

5. Eliot - ESCAPIST - Jack of Spades

6. Ronan - TRAPEZE ARTIST - King of Clubs

7. Arthur - ACROBATIC BALANCER - Jack of Hearts

8. Collette - FIRE PERFORMER - Queen of Spades

9. Martin - CONTORTIONIST - Jack of Clubs

10. Meera - DEATH DANCER - Queen of Clubs

11. Falan - TRAPEZE ARTIST - Queen of Hearts

12. Channary - TIGHTROPE WALKER - Queen of Diamonds

XI

November 9, 1896

IT'S A CIRCUS TENT.

Falan surveys the area from her spot as Jean-Pierre explains the rules of the game to the audience. She's the only one inside, thankfully. It looks like the type of tent used to train animals in a typical circus ground. Le Cirque des Ombres doesn't have any animal acts, but this tent has bales of straw stacked around her, and empty horse stables lie to her left. A few hoops are thrown carelessly in the corner.

She recognizes the music now too, which has only gotten louder—a carousel's melody.

It's both incredible and terrifying what Jean-Pierre accomplished. Her first year at the Cirque, Falan snuck into the Chapiteau with Meera to watch the opening round of the Game of Oaths. She remembers how the stage looked from the audience; it felt as if she were looking down at a large, clear globe, an entirely different world below her, more lifelike than any theater production. She could see every movement of each player, hear their voices clearly, particularly where the most action was taking place.

But here, on the stage itself, she can't see the crowd or Jean-Pierre. This illusion has become her world. She will be able to experience only what's on the ground.

Falan looks up to see a large, golden clock hanging in midair. Now it makes sense why the tent is open-topped. The clock's fingers are frozen on its face, both pointing up. Presumably it will remain that way until the first person is killed. The Clockstarter.

Falan runs her fingers over her outfit, checking to see if a tourné knife has been attached anywhere. Nothing. Nor is a knife lying on the ground nearby. So she's not the Joker. Tension quickly replaces the initial relief she feels. The Joker might be lingering right outside this tent, waiting to make their first move.

"When the bell sounds, it means the players will be able to move around the setting," she hears Jean-Pierre say. "Sit back, relax, and enjoy the show!"

Falan waits, breath catching with each inhale. Seconds later, a bell goes off, the deep toll a clock tower might make, and the sound of the applauding crowd and music is sucked away. Now it's replaced with something else . . . the eerie tinkle of a music box. Faint, but enough to raise the hairs on the back of her neck. A French lullaby, though the name of the song escapes her. For a moment, Falan is frozen with fear, quivering as she faces the pitch-black crack in the tent folds.

If she goes outside, she might be greeted with a tourné knife through her chest. But waiting in the tent means a greater chance of getting cornered.

She pauses, remembering how Lucien mentioned that weapons will be hidden all over the place. Falan doubts Jean-Pierre would put her in a tent with weapons from the start, but she takes the time to sift through the bales of straw as quietly as she can, ears pricked for any noises. Above her, the clock doesn't change. The Joker must be taking their time. If they were waiting outside the tent, they would have walked in by now.

To Falan's dismay, she finds no weapons in the straw stacks. But, staring at the straw itself, she has an idea. She leans down and eases off the rope binding one of the bales. When she finally succeeds, she grabs handfuls of straw and starts stuffing it into her clothing, filling the wrinkles until they puff out. Although it's not likely to completely stop a knife's blade, the straw padding may soften any wounds.

The small sense of security pushes Falan to the exit of the tent. Another desperate glance up at the clock reveals it still frozen. Nobody has been killed yet, even though it must have taken at least ten minutes to maneuver the rope off the bale. She steps out of the tent, arms raised to defend herself. There's nobody in sight, but the tinkling of the music box grows louder. So sweet. So chilling. The sound of a child's giggle briefly laces the music, and Falan shudders.

There are no children here.

It's cold outside the tent, like she's really stepping into the night air, and dewy grass lies underfoot. She's now grateful for her oversize clothes and the straw padding, both of which provide extra warmth. Her breath creates white clouds, and stars dot the velvet sky above her. It all looks so real; if she touches the tent, she can feel the rough canvas material against the pads of her fingers. Fog mists the red-and-white tents standing around her, leaving no room to see anybody coming.

A sharp bang in the distance freezes her. She listens, waiting. But nothing. Falan's heart slams against her ribs. Hearing nothing is worse than hearing something. It means somebody is trying to be quiet.

Lucien won his round by hiding, managing to play a cat-and-mouse game with the Joker before taking him down. But in this circus ground setting, hiding is risky. Too many places to be cornered, not enough to escape from.

Something brushes her shoulder. Falan looks behind her. Nothing.

To her far left is a carousel. Soundless, it spins in its lazy circle, weaving painted horses and lions that slowly bob up and down on their loop. The carousel will give her the best view of the setting if it continually spins. Falan holds her breath as she skitters among the tents, which blow in a gentle breeze even though there is no wind. The sweet scent of puffed corn fills the air, as if there's a popper meters away. Another smell curls around it too, something coppery like rust.

Or blood.

Falan quickens her pace to the carousel, whose lights shine in the darkness like a beacon. She's having second thoughts about whether it's wise to head there but decides the stark lights will be enough to deter anybody else.

It's as she reaches the silent carousel that she hears a footstep on the wet grass behind her. Falan whirls around to see Ronan holding a knife in front of him, the tip pointed at her. It's a regular blade, not the curved one of a tourné knife. So Jean-Pierre did hide other weapons around the setting, just as Lucien said.

And it also means Ronan is not the Joker, as he has no illusion over him either. Ronan, however, has clearly not garnered the same amount of sense.

"Are you the Joker?" he snarls.

"Do I look like one?" she snaps back.

"You truly want me to answer that?"

Falan crosses her arms, more irritated than wary. "You may not be the Joker, but you sure are acting like one."

Ronan glares, but confusion replaces his venom as he focuses on her outfit. "Why do your clothes look all lumpy?"

Falan glances down at herself. "Stuffed with straw."

"Why?"

"I wanted to be a scarecrow," she deadpans.

He scowls but finally lowers the knife. It's clear he's considering the same factors as her. They can part ways, not trusting each other. But on the other hand, it's unlikely they will be attacked if they stay together. The Joker will go for somebody alone, easy to pick off.

"Did you see anybody else?" he asks, taking a careful step toward her.

"No." She stares at the knife in his hand. "Where did you get that?"

"My tent, hidden under a platform." Ronan quickly adds, "It was the only one I could find."

"Where were you heading?"

"The same place as you."

They finally start to walk, falling in step with each other. "Afraid you'll get dizzy?" Falan asks as they step onto the spinning roundabout.

"Taunting somebody with a knife is tactless." Ronan sits down against the center of the carousel. "Stay close to the middle. The spinning has a lesser effect."

Falan doesn't listen, taking a seat atop one of the galloping horses. Something feels off, but she can't put her finger on it. She traces the curls etched in the painted wooden mane of the horse, a pale blond to match its white coat.

"The music is gone," she suddenly realizes.

"It's been silent the whole time," Ronan points out.

She shakes her head. "Not the carousel. The music box. There's no more music."

He looks at her blankly. "What music box?"

"The one playing earlier."

Ronan's wary look tells her he still has no clue what she's talking about, but Falan knows what she heard. It must mean something.

She leans forward on the horse, arms around its neck. The music box melody grew louder when she came out of the tent and when she heard something in the distance but is now gone.

It's almost like . . .

Falan tenses.

It's a warning. The louder the melody, the closer the Joker. Falan shudders, remembering how loud the music was when she first ventured out of her starting tent; had she taken the wrong turn, she might have come face-to-face with the Joker.

It's then she realizes Ronan is still staring at her, blue eyes startlingly dark under the shimmering lights of the carousel, an unreadable expression on his face.

"What?" she says, impatient.

"Nothing." He averts his eyes, jaw clenched. "You just . . . look like her in some ways."

Falan blinks, first caught off guard, then uncomfortable. She doesn't know what to say. Ronan is one of the few people who hasn't said that statement to her before. Until now.

But there's a tiny part of her that wonders in what way he thinks she and Lavanya look alike. It's ironic, because nobody at the Cirque knows they are not related by blood. And while it's true that she and Lavanya did share some similar features, they showed them differently. Brown eyes, but Lavanya's were expressive while Falan's have always been flat. Black hair, but Lavanya's was smooth while Falan's is rough. Slender faces, but Lavanya's features were softer than Falan's.

Le soleil et la lune. The sun and the moon. So alike. So different.

But she squashes the thought of asking. Now is not the time, nor is it important what Ronan thinks. It only makes Falan angrier at him for having the audacity. He's never talked about Lavanya to her before and made it clear he's never wanted to. She felt the same. Why would she want to discuss Lavanya with the person who treated her so disdainfully during her final weeks?

The faint tinkling of the music box causes Falan to stiffen, washing away any thoughts of Lavanya and her ire at Ronan.

The Joker.

Falan quietly slides off the carousel horse and inches closer to Ronan, who gives her a wide-eyed look of new understanding.

The music box melody only increases. So does the sound of running footsteps.

It's when she hears two pairs of footsteps that Ronan drags Falan to the floor of the carousel. In a moment of blind panic, she struggles in his grip and reaches for his knife, thinking she's been tricked, until he forces her to look at him and holds a finger to her lips. She roughly shrugs him off, huddling against the carousel's center.

A choked shout suddenly rises above the music box melody, which is louder than ever. It sounds like a male voice, but the words are unintelligible, a slurry of pained moans and weeping. The trill of a knife cutting through air scrapes the night, followed by the merciless squelches of its blade gutting through flesh.

Falan hardly dares to breathe. She doesn't look at Ronan, but in her peripheral vision he hangs his head low, gripping his knife so hard his knuckles are white.

The player's sobs give way to gurgling gasps. Falan tries not to think what must be going through his head, whether his fear has melted to futility. It's not a thought one can succeed in ignoring when the person is being stabbed to death mere meters away.

Then there are no more wheezing gasps. No more sobs. Just the hollowness only death can bring. The music box's song continues.

The footsteps pick up again and, to Falan's relief, fade away along with the melody. The night is silent once more, but only for a few seconds before a ticking sound fills the air. Falan dares to skirt to the edge of the carousel, Ronan on her heels, and looks up to see the hands on the hanging clock finally moving.

The countdown has started.

XII

November 9, 1896

FOR A FEW MINUTES, NEITHER FALAN NOR RONAN moves, making sure the Joker has gone for good. Falan is prepared to stay where she is, but Ronan walks off the carousel and toward the corpse, possessed by curiosity. Unable to stop him, Falan steps off the spinning platform and steadies herself on solid ground, the mushy grass wet under her boots.

Lying away from the carousel but close enough for its shadowy light to illuminate the corpse is Martin, the Jack of Clubs, staring lifelessly into the night. Blood has pooled around his body and out of his mouth, staining the grass below him, and his limbs are twisted in a sick display of irony to resemble one of his contortionist poses.

Falan has seen death before. Her mother and brother. In Paris, on the street corners when those without homes quietly went to sleep on frosted nights and never woke up. And most recently, Lavanya.

Death has embalmed her life, has shaped her experiences. Her desires. Her regrets.

But here, she has nothing to say. She knew Martin but didn't know him. She knew the basics, but Falan suddenly wonders what attributes define themselves as basic: name, age, profession.

Suddenly it's not Martin lying there, but Lavanya.

Falan tears her eyes away, but she doesn't dare show emotion, knowing the audience is watching. Instead, she looks to Ronan, who is still staring at Martin. She wonders if he knew him at all. She wonders if he's thinking of Lavanya too.

Falan tugs his coat sleeve, catching his attention, and he finally turns his back on the corpse. His expression is unreadable once more, except for a hint of sadness. But neither of them can afford it. She glances up at the clock overhead. “Fifty-five minutes,” she whispers, “and we make it out alive.”

“Of this round,” Ronan mutters under his breath, then realizes he spoke aloud. But she was thinking the same thing.

Her gaze falls on the knife in his hand. “I need a weapon.”

“*I* have one,” he says.

“That’s not the same thing,” she says. “I think we should check the tents for more.”

Ronan hesitates. “We might run right into trouble.”

“My chances of surviving the next fifty-four minutes are much slimmer without something to defend myself with,” Falan says. “Unless you are willing to give me yours, of course.”

Just as she thought, Ronan narrows his eyes and says, “No. Let’s check the other tents.”

They start for the farthest tent on the opposite side to where Falan awoke. They don’t see anybody on the way there, both relieving and worrying. It’s not a big setting, so the others must be hiding well.

A sound of agony suddenly echoes in the night.

The shout came from the other end of the grounds, giving them at least a few minutes lead on the Joker. This time, Falan understands Lucien. No time to feel remorse. She doesn’t know who is being killed nor is she forced to listen to the gory details.

Falan nudges Ronan, who’s still staring in the direction of the shout. “Let’s go.”

Ronan flinches, then glares at her as if she’s said something offensive before continuing to walk. By the time they reach the tent, there’s about forty-seven minutes to go on the clock. The sound of the music box is too faint for the Joker to be nearby, but Ronan enters first anyway, and Falan follows close behind.

Although it's clear the tent is empty, Falan doesn't relax. The only things inside are throwing targets—three of them, lining the back of the tent—all covered in dried blood, dripping over the swirling red-and-white bull's-eye patterns. Even the wrist and ankle restraints on the targets are flecked with crimson. The smell is pungent, coppery like coins and raw meat.

Falan strides to the targets to check for any weapons, but there's nothing behind them. She glances up through the open-topped tent. Forty-four minutes left on the clock. It's too risky to sneak around without something to protect herself with, even a makeshift weapon. Anything would be preferable to wandering around empty-handed.

Her gaze lands on the wooden structures holding up each target. Breaking one for a heavy piece of wood might work, but smashing it will make noise, alerting everybody to their location.

"Can we leave now?" Ronan asks, his face green. Not that she can take much more of the stench either. Besides, if they find a new tent, there might be weapons there.

"All right," she finally says. "Pick a different tent to look in." Falan lets Ronan lead the way, taking in a breath of fresh air as they exit. She keeps an ear out for the sound of the music box, but the melody is barely audible.

Ronan ducks into the tent opposite them, Falan close behind. It's empty, but they both stop at the sight of multiple small circular platforms below hoops hanging down from a beam horizontal to the tent top. An acrobats' tent, clearly. But it occurs to Falan that, as one of the only acrobats in the competition, the top of the beam has likely not been checked for weapons. Whether it's worth checking is the question.

"Go," Ronan says, making her decision for her.

Falan scurries to one of the platforms and hoists herself on the hoop to pull on the rope attached, which has been thrown over the beam to lift it. Generally when she performs on hoops, she has Ronan controlling the rope so she has the use of both hands. But this is a simple thing, child's play. She pulls herself high enough to reach the beam, then grabs onto it.

As soon as she does, Falan knows she's made a mistake. The beam is far too unstable, and she releases it just before it comes crashing down. Every trapeze artist masters how to fall, and Falan is no different. She lands with grace, unfortunately cut short when the heavy beam slams into her body and pins her awkwardly against the edge of the platform. The straw padding her clothes barely softens the blow. She chokes back a gasp of agony, pain racing across her abdomen where the beam struck her, the tent swimming before her eyes.

Thankfully Ronan is already lifting the beam off her, muttering strained curses under his breath. She's not sure what he's swearing for—the fact that she's hurt, or the fact that the beam's bang against the floor has made a noise loud enough for the entire grounds to hear.

"Can you stand?" he asks.

Falan shakes her head vaguely, implying she won't know unless she tries. Her abdomen is tender, throbbing with pain, and her knees buckle when she attempts to get to her feet. "Won't . . . work," she manages to gasp. She's half expecting Ronan to leave her now, but he doesn't. He's looking at the tent's entrance, worry etched across his face.

That's when she hears the tinkling sound of the music box, bone chillingly loud, and freezes.

The Joker.

She should have considered the danger of Jean-Pierre's manipulation, especially after seeing what happened to Lavanya. He made the beam break on purpose. Desperation forces Falan to her feet and she slumps against Ronan's shoulder.

The entrance of the tent flutters. A white-gloved hand reaches around the left canvas fold as a pointed black boot steps through. Then another, revealing a leg leading up to a tight bodysuit made of black-and-red-and-white stripes, splattered with blood. A masked face of white, a circle of red on each cheek connected by a sinister smile too wide to be human. Finally a hat, streaked with red and black and adorned with jingling bells. The curve of a tourné knife, enlarged to the size of a cleaver, flashes despite no moonlight inside the tent, still dripping with crimson from its last kill.

Ronan has frozen at the sight of this monstrosity. So has Falan, pain momentarily forgotten in her horror. This cannot be a competitor. Not this creature, even if it is an illusion. The aura of malice that radiates from them cannot be part of the apparition.

Then Falan remembers what Lucien told her. How disoriented he felt the closer he was to the Joker. She isn't sure if it's due to the beam's impact or the Joker's, but she suddenly feels lightheaded.

"What's happening?" Ronan says through gritted teeth.

"Knife," Falan chokes out.

Ronan takes the blade out, but his hand is quivering so badly that he can't possibly have the energy to drive it into somebody's heart. His legs shake like he's struggling to stand, and Falan collapses to her knees.

The Joker starts to approach. The figure doesn't run but walks at a steady pace, as if confident they have all the time in the world.

The thought of Bellamy and Lucien watching her grounds Falan for the briefest of moments. She looks up at the Joker, mere feet away. The knife drops from Ronan's hand, and Falan reaches out to grab it as he also collapses. She can't speak. Each time she tries, her tongue thickens in her mouth.

But the knife in her hand gives her a speck of strength. She may not be able to kill the Joker. But she can hurt them. Her arm screaming, she plunges the knife forward just as the Joker reaches them. The blade sinks into their shin, not stopping until it hits bone, and the Joker howls in pain.

The voice. Falan's breath catches. The illusion may hide the person's looks, but not their voice.

Even more, she recognizes it.

She grips the knife and twists it, prompting another roar of agony from the Joker. The knife slips from her grasp as they fall onto the ground. There it is, guttural and deep, the voice of a Lily she knows well. For all the times he's belittled boarders, dehumanized them.

"Sylvestre," she croaks through her thickening tongue. "I . . . I know it's you. Sylvestre."

The Joker makes a sound of rage and surprise. The mask starts to deteriorate like white mist, floating upward. The hat does the same, and the rest of the illusion follows. Recognizable features appear in its place: blond hair, pale skin, frosty blue eyes narrowed with rage. A tall and burly frame pieces itself before her eyes.

Strength leaks back into her bones, her muscles, just like Lucien said happened to him. The sound of the music box dies away, leaving only the sound of their breathing.

"You bitch," growls Sylvestre.

Ronan sits up, coughing like he's been choked. To both Falan's and Sylvestre's surprise, he moves in front of Falan as if to shield her.

"Allaire, what are you intending to do?" Sylvestre says. "Barter your life over hers?"

"No," Ronan says, voice hard. "But I don't intend to offer her up to be killed either."

A nasty grin slices across Sylvestre's face as he lunges forward with the tourné knife. Falan throws herself backward as Ronan's arm takes the brunt of the blade, slicing through his coat sleeve all the way to his elbow. An agonized sound of pain escapes his throat as Falan scrambles back, a hand still on her smarting abdomen.

He could have moved his arm. Why didn't he move?

Sylvestre is no longer smiling. He attempts to stab Ronan, this time through the heart, but Ronan catches his arm in time and sends his knee into his stomach. Sylvestre grunts, rolling to the side to recover. Falan's gaze goes to the beam lying on the platform. If she can lift it somehow and aim the blow at Sylvestre's head, it might be enough to kill him.

But Sylvestre is no longer focused on Ronan. His wild eyes are fixed on Falan, like a deranged hunter closing in on its mark. Falan stumbles to her feet, knowing she won't get far. In one movement, Sylvestre tackles her, pinning her squirming figure to the ground before bringing the knife down. He's aiming for her throat, but she manages to move so the blade scrapes across her cheek, the tip puncturing her ear. Sylvestre then tries to slit her throat, but Falan's hands shoot up to block it. The knife slices into her palms, now slick with blood. All she knows is the threat of death seconds away, kicking, squirming, fighting Sylvestre.

"Hold still," he snaps.

In response, Falan spits in Sylvestre's face. He growls a stream of expletives, but it's enough time for Ronan to grab his knife off the ground and shove it into Sylvestre's upper back. Sylvestre crumples off Falan, cursing louder. Before she can get her bearings, Ronan is pulling her to her feet and dragging her from the tent.

"His throat! You should have slit his throat!" she rasps. When he doesn't respond, she wrenches herself away. "Give me your knife. I'll kill him myself!"

"Have you lost your mind?" Ronan snarls. "You don't stand a chance against him. Going back alone would mean your death, because I'm not going with you." He looks up at the clock. "We have twenty-four minutes left. That's plenty of time for him to kill us if we don't move now."

Falan could murder Ronan, Joker or no Joker. How dare he take away her chance to rid the world of Sylvestre? But it occurs to her then that, despite the nature of the Game, Ronan doesn't want to end up killing anybody. The stab in Sylvestre's back was simply to inhibit him.

Still. He can be as noble as he wishes—if that's what he thinks of himself—but depriving her of her opportunity to kill Sylvestre is something she cannot overlook forever.

But she *can* overlook it for the next twenty-four minutes. With a flourish, Falan starts to walk, Ronan keeping after her. They no longer have the help of the music box; it ceased after she revealed Sylvestre as the Joker. But Falan suspects Sylvestre will no longer attempt to be quiet. They know he's coming after them, and he won't try to hide it. Knowing this, the best place to go is the carousel again. It will provide them with the widest view of the grounds, and its openness makes for an easy escape if needed.

The clock reads nineteen minutes left by the time they reach the carousel, now full of the melody it lacked beforehand. Although less chilling than the music box, it still makes Falan want to shudder.

As she steps onto the rotating platform, someone darts behind the center and she stiffens.

Ronan stops as well, his feet shifting as if ready to run. Falan, however, says, "You can come out," she says. "There's two of us. We're clearly not the Joker."

A few more seconds tick by. Then the hider steps out.

It's Meera.

XIII

November 9, 1896

THE HONOR BOX IS LUXURIOUS, A CRIMSON PARADISE made of red plush couches and fountains of alcoholic beverages. It signifies the elite, the guests of honor. Many would kill to sit here, as it has the best view of the stage with its high angle.

Not that many of the honorable guests are watching. The room smells strongly of liquor, and most patrons call over dealers for more servings of alcohol as they talk boisterously. One of them, a patron wearing a rather ugly green mask, has already consumed four glasses of wine.

Jules himself craves the soothing buzz of a drink; unlike his cheerful company, he feels like the room is suffocating him. But with his stomach gurgling with nerves, it's unwise to consume anything except water. He is the only person in the room other than the dealers and his father who is sober.

It's eerie to see his father so quiet. Rather than mingle with the other patrons, Monsieur Blanchet sits motionless in his chair, facing the stage. His cold blue eyes are narrowed in concentration, fixed on the game. It's as if he's studying the illusion for any discrepancies.

Jules's gaze strays from the stage to the audience. He wonders where Lucien Trichet is sitting, if he even came to watch at all. Normally last year's winner would be in the honor box. But Jules realized ten minutes into the round that Lucien was not with them.

When he brought it up, his father told him shortly, "I decided that Lucien's presence might upset our patrons, many of whom lost money because of his win last year."

Jules didn't push it. He knows not to question his father, and he knows what awaits him if he does. Although naive, Jules has prided himself on avoiding the delusion that his father has ever loved him. He was a mistake, never supposed to be born. His mother, originally from India, was brought to England before arriving in Paris, where she worked for Blanchet. All Jules knows about her is that she died giving birth to him, and Blanchet tried to hide the secret by taking Jules as the son of him and his now late wife.

And that she was an Enchantresse, something his father has thankfully never known.

So instead of saying anything, Jules sits beside Blanchet, watching the horrors happening below. So far, two players have already been killed. Martin, the contortionist, was not one the patrons were highly betting on. But a few groaned in dismay when the Joker shoved his blade into Thomas, one of the Cirque's knife throwers.

"That's what I get for not placing my money on the fire thrower," the patron with the ugly green mask said. "I thought the skill with knives would give *this one* an advantage."

Another laughed obnoxiously. "Have you learned nothing from the previous tournaments, mon ami?"

"After losing a considerable sum last year, I decided to go against my judgment." The patron shook his head, downing a gulp of wine. "Never again."

Jules listened to the conversation rather uncomfortably. The bettors acted like this boy's death was worth nothing, but even now, Jules realizes that Thomas is still alive. Barely, but he can just faintly see his body twitching. He certainly won't make it to the end of the round, but he'll be alive long enough to live his final moments in agony.

As he watches Thomas lying on the ground, Jules can't help but put himself in the player's shoes. He thinks of Thomas staring up at a false sky, bloodied, a prayer on his lips as he begs for death to come take him. Jules grips the armrests of his chair, willing himself not to vomit, hoping his father doesn't notice.

Breathe. Breathe. But air won't come, and he can't afford to take deep breaths like in his room.

"Monsieur." The voice cuts through Jules's panic, and he looks up to see Bellamy at his side, holding a wineglass and a bottle. "Would you like some wine?"

This is the fifth time Bellamy has come over to ask. Jules wants to slap the wineglass out of Bellamy's hand, remembering how Bellamy not only snuck into his room and stole his book but also blackmailed him about it. But the urge to settle his nerves is much stronger, even if it means his gurgling stomach will burn a bit more. He nods and Bellamy pours him a glass of wine, lingering a bit too long after handing it to him.

Jules notices he's looking out the honor box window at the game below once again. It's strange how every time Player Eleven took the audience's attention, Bellamy came forth to the window. Realization suddenly washes over Jules.

Player Eleven, Falan Sunkara, must be the one that Bellamy blackmailed him into helping.

Jules sizes the girl up. She's more vicious than he thought she'd be; she somehow managed to guess the Joker's identity and not only evade him but wound him.

"What are you doing standing here?" Monsieur Blanchet snaps, suddenly noticing Bellamy, who still hasn't moved from the window. "Make yourself scarce."

"It's all right," Jules cuts in before Bellamy can walk away. "I'm keeping him next to me in case I want another glass of wine."

Blanchet stares at Bellamy for several moments before turning back to the window, locked in concentration once more. Bellamy gives Jules the subtlest of nods. Jules doesn't acknowledge him but brings the wineglass to his lips. The sweet tartness of the drink turns sour when he looks back at Thomas, who is now completely motionless. Only his eyes are wide and unblinking, not having the time to close before death finally came and took him away.

XIV

November 9, 1896

"WELL I NEVER THOUGHT I'D SEE THE DAY THAT THE two of you ally," Meera says after a minute of silence, looking between Falan and Ronan.

Falan steps forward, then pauses when she notices one more person hiding behind the center pole. Fair skin, light brown hair. The back of his coat shows his face card: Jack of Hearts. It's Arthur. He's the Lily that, ironically, Meera has expressed the most hatred for out of Sylvestre's little pack.

"I could say the same for you," Falan says to Meera.

Meera eyes Falan's outfit stuffed with straw. But instead of commenting, she says, "We are not allies. I came to the carousel only moments before you did and he happened to be here."

Arthur grumbles something, but it's nothing Falan wants to hear anyway.

"The Joker is Sylvestre," Ronan says impatiently. He doesn't look too happy to see either Meera or Arthur. "We escaped from him about seven minutes ago. Barely."

"And now you've probably led him straight *here* to kill us," Meera snaps.

"We didn't think we'd run into anybody here," Falan says. "We nearly killed him, but then we fled."

"Where's the sense in that?" Meera says, irritated. "Why didn't you finish him off?"

"Not my decision. I wasn't the one with the knife." Falan knows she's pushing it. The last thing she needs is Ronan deciding to go off on his own, taking the only weapon they have and leaving her and Meera with somebody who would turn them over to Sylvestre.

Ronan's fingers wrap around the handle of his knife. If it's supposed to be a threat, Falan isn't fazed.

"What should we do with him?" she asks instead, finally acknowledging Arthur, who's glaring at all of them.

"I say we kill him now. Joker or no Joker, he's ready to hand us over," Meera says.

"No," Ronan says. "We are not killing anybody."

"You don't get to make that decision for all of us," Falan says.

"Or I could just kill all three of you," Arthur says, standing up.

Arthur may be able to overpower both Falan and Meera, but Ronan is the one with a knife in his hand. Arthur must suddenly realize this too because he shifts back a little. The three of them exchange glances, reaching an unspoken mutual agreement.

At the same time, they all leap for him. Falan drags Arthur's coat off, Ronan pushes him against one of the carousel's poles, and Meera slams her hand over his mouth. Arthur shouts obscenities into Meera's palm as Falan uses the coat to bind his hands together behind the pole.

"He's getting saliva all over my hand," Meera says in disgust.

"You need to keep your hand on his mouth unless you want to use your own coat as a gag," Falan says, yanking the knot tighter and holding it so he doesn't break free.

She suddenly stops talking. They're being too loud. They've been for the past few minutes, and the sound of the carousel is already enough to draw Sylvestre here. They all seem to realize at once, because nobody says a word now.

"Shit!" Meera hisses, yanking her hand away from Arthur's mouth for only a few seconds.

But it's enough time for him to yell, "Sylvestre! They're hiding here, by the caro—"

Meera slams her hand over his mouth as Falan snaps, "What did you do?"

"The bastard bit my hand!" Meera says.

Ronan tenses and drops down behind the center of the carousel. "Get over here; he's coming!" he whispers.

Falan knows it's futile. The second she and Meera let Arthur go, he will direct Sylvestre over to them. If they continue to restrain him, Sylvestre will find them anyway.

Meera seems to come to the same conclusion, for she punches Arthur's nose to subdue him and joins Ronan. Arthur curses her viciously, his face screwed up in pain.

"I know you're here!" Sylvestre shouts.

"Sylvestre, they're on this side!" Arthur says.

With a curse, Falan lets go of the coat tied around Arthur's hands, causing the bind to unravel instantly.

"Allaire, if you give her to me, I'll let you live this round," Sylvestre says, his voice nearer.

Falan peeks around the carousel's center. Sylvestre is walking slowly and is hunched over from the knife wound in his back. But the look in his eyes is as wild as it was in the tent. Vengeful, venomous.

She glances up at the clock. Ten minutes left.

By now, Arthur has rounded the bend of the carousel, shouting to Sylvestre where they are. Fleeing will do no good. It's open land around the carousel, and Sylvestre and Arthur will easily see which way they go. Sylvestre might not be able to run fast due to his wound, but Arthur can.

"Any suggestions?" Meera says impatiently. "I'd like them to *not* catch us."

"Give me your knife," Falan says to Ronan.

His expression turns to stone. "So *you* can attempt to kill him? I don't think so."

Sylvestre steps onto the carousel with a loud slam of his foot, and Meera flinches.

Falan has not turned away from Ronan. "If I want to take this chance to kill that bastard, then I will, and you are not the person to stop me."

"Even if it means your death?" Ronan says, surprisingly gentle. "Would it be worth it then?"

Without answering, Falan yanks the knife away from him and stands up. He rises with her. But Sylvestre has already come around and spotted them anyway.

"What's this? One more?" he says, noticing Meera.

Above, the clock shows eight minutes left.

Falan hesitates. Eight minutes is a long time. Enough time for him to kill them all. Her only option is to stall until the final minute on the clock, then make her move. He might be stronger than her, but she's faster and smaller, a harder target to strike. Sylvestre lunges at them and they back up. He inches closer to Falan, who wraps her hands around one of the carousel's poles and swings backward when he thrusts the knife toward her.

She suddenly realizes Arthur is nowhere in sight.

"Falan—" Meera starts to shout, but it's too late.

Somebody grabs her from behind, one arm pinning her wrists and the other around her throat after yanking the knife from her hand. "I got her now," says Arthur as Falan struggles in his grip.

"We should have killed you when we had the chance," Meera says, more disgusted than alarmed.

Arthur points the knife at her when she takes a step forward. "Stay back or I'll slice you up too."

Meera looks impressively bored. "Cretin. I bet if Sylvestre had found you before the clock started, that knife would be in your back right about now."

"Don't listen to them, Arthur," Sylvestre says. "They'd say anything to save themselves."

Falan's eyes flicker up to the clock. Six minutes.

"Enough wasting time," Sylvestre says. "I'll stab her chest and then you slit her throat."

In a panic, Falan kicks out at him with her unrestrained legs despite her aching abdomen, but Sylvestre dodges her. She doesn't look at Meera or Ronan, for she knows neither of them will jump in to help her. That's what the Game of Oaths does to people, even those who have been friends for ages. She may have known Meera for five years, but she also knows firsthand that Meera will put her own life first. As for Ronan, she expects nothing from him except his audience.

Arthur has about a foot in height on her and his arms are locked tightly around her body, too strong for her to break free. As Sylvestre raises the knife, a solution flashes in her mind. She sinks her teeth into the arm holding the knife at her throat, causing Arthur to release her with a howl of pain. Falan slips behind him, her small stature finally an asset. But she isn't finished yet.

Without waiting, Falan pushes Arthur forward—right into Sylvestre's blade.

Arthur chokes, going limp and dropping the knife. Meera's mouth is open in surprise. Ronan's eyes are wide. Even Sylvestre looks startled, seeing his friend's body on his outstretched knife, but Falan doesn't stop. She shoves Arthur farther up the knife's curved blade until it is embedded deep in his stomach. Blood spews from Arthur's mouth, dripping onto the carousel's pale yellow platform as his body convulses.

It's a wound he won't be coming back from. It's also a wound that will take at least a few minutes to extract the blade from, occupying Sylvestre. Falan lets Arthur go once he stops convulsing. His limbs sag, and he crumples farther forward onto the knife.

Snapping out of his surprise, Sylvestre pushes the body to the ground. Before he can roll Arthur over to take the weapon, Falan scoops up the knife Arthur dropped and kicks Sylvestre in the chest. The surprise works in her favor, for he falls back against the steps of the carousel with a grunt. She swings the knife down on him, but he's recovered and hits her in the stomach, right where the beam struck her earlier.

The pain is unimaginable, seeping through her brain, shaking her vision. Falan coughs, the air knocked from her lungs, fighting to get her bearings. Sylvestre staggers over to Arthur's body, rolling it over to take the tourné knife.

Somebody pulls Falan to her feet, causing her to blindly swing the knife out. But a hand fastens around her arm, and she's looking into Ronan's cold eyes. "Two minutes," he says in a low voice. He yanks her aside before the tourné knife swipes through where she was just standing.

Meera is nowhere in sight.

"You have no chance, Sylvestre," Ronan says. "There's only a minute left on the clock."

Falan realizes, with fury, that Ronan has taken the knife from her.

"Want to bet?" Sylvestre snarls. "I might not have time to cut her up, but fifty-five seconds is still plenty of time for me to burn her."

Falan backs up farther, but Ronan asks, "What are you talking about?"

With his free hand, Sylvestre pulls out an ornate box of matches from his pocket, a malicious grin spreading across his face. A grant.

He suddenly throws his tourné knife up high in the air; for Falan it feels like time has slowed as Sylvestre takes a match and strikes it, grabbing the fire in his hand as the knife tumbles back down. Falan darts forward to try to catch the handle, but Ronan's arm pushes her back.

Sylvestre laughs triumphantly as he catches the knife and pockets the box of matches. Tucking the knife under his arm, he uses both hands to control the flames. Seeing the fire dancing in both his palms, Falan backs up again. If she had the knife, she would have made one last attempt. But without it, trying is futile.

Forty-five seconds to go.

Sylvestre throws a fireball right at them, and in their haste to dodge, Falan jumps in a different direction than Ronan. Sylvestre grins, having her cornered, and throws a second flame at Ronan to distract him before lunging at Falan with the knife once more. Falan throws herself backward, doing a back handspring, then another when Sylvestre tries again with the knife. She can imagine the audience getting riled up as the clock ticks down, antsy for one of them to overpower the other.

The acrobat versus the flame thrower.

"Come on, Sylvestre," she says softly. "You're making a fool of yourself. You won't be able to kill me in fifteen seconds."

Fourteen seconds. Thirteen.

Sylvestre tries one last lunge with a clumsy swipe. Falan jumps, grabs the bar above her beneath the carousel's roof, and kicks Sylvestre. The bar's height helps her, and her feet hit him square in the chest and knock him down.

Ten seconds.

Something strange happens as Falan drops back down to the carousel's floor. The ticking of the clock gets louder with each second passing. So does the music of the carousel. The smells of caramel and butter and dew and blood intensify, mingling together. Everything is oversaturated, the lights too bright, the colors too strong.

Falan stumbles off the carousel, nearly losing her footing on the wet grass. She tastes hot chocolate, sweet and rich. She tastes blood, coppery and strong. Her head spins. Overwhelmed, she falls to her knees.

A bell tolls. By the time Falan looks up through the dizziness, the illusion is gone. No more carousel. No more tents. No more fog or wet grass or starry night. The straw stuffing her clothes has disappeared, leaving her garments loose once more over her injured stomach. The sound of a crowd washes back in her ears, faint at first, then a roar.

She doesn't have to look up to be aware of the spectators, some clapping, some jeering at their chosen player dying. The Chapiteau is bigger than she remembers; there must be thousands of people watching, surrounding the perimeter. It resembles the Cirque's arena in a lot of ways, save for the honor box at the top of the tent, where the panelists and a few patrons are seated.

The round is finally over. There are at least three dead bodies lying on the stage, one that she had a hand in killing.

Falan lifts her head to meet Ronan's eyes, still disoriented. However, when he sees her, they harden along with the rest of his expression. He's back to being cold, not the boy who saved her life in the game. Before he can move away, her hand wraps around his wrist, stopping him.

"If you ever take away my opportunity to kill him again, I'll make sure it's *you* I'm pushing in front of a knife," she says. "You self-righteous bastard."

XV

November 9, 1896

"WAS THAT NOT A FANTASTIC PERFORMANCE?" JEAN-Pierre asks as he walks out onto the stage, clapping loudly. The performers barely look up at him, all of them either wounded or still dazed from the sudden shift in reality. "What an exciting start to this year's Game of Oaths!"

The crowd shows its appreciation by applauding. It seems three casualties is enough bloodshed to satiate them tonight. Lucien, sitting in the very back row, does not applaud with them. If it were up to him, he would not have attended the round at all, but Jean-Pierre made it clear he was still to be present, despite not being allowed to sit in the honor box.

He watches as Jean-Pierre forces the surviving players into a final lineup, as if corpses aren't lying on the stage in full view. Dissatisfied noises sound from the spectators who betted on the fallen three. Lucien can't bear to look at Thomas, the knife thrower who replaced him. It's not as if Thomas was a friend, but he spent time training him. He wasn't at the Cirque for long either, about nine months.

The newest performer, a tightrope walker named Channary, seems to be holding her own, however. Her eyes are still blown with panic as she stands in the lineup, but there's a hard set to the line of her jaw. It's something desperate, the hunger for survival, but she looks wilder than the others in the lineup, who are doing a much better job of hiding their desire to win. They appear calm, steady.

Even Falan, despite her injuries. Lucien saw how hard the beam hit her when it came down; she must be a nudge away from collapsing.

"And now, it is time for our performers to retire for the night," Jean-Pierre continues. "My dear spectators, if you would wish to buy one of them a grant to aid in their conditions before the next round, please consult the tent on the other side of the grounds. Merci, and bon soir!"

Jean-Pierre claps his hands, and the audience gasps as a plume of smoke erupts on stage. When the smoke clears, he and the remaining performers are gone.

Excited whispers flutter throughout the crowd. Lucien watches them all, the only one maskless among a sea of facades. His thoughts have shifted to Falan. After her performance tonight, she's more likely to get grants. At the very least, several bettors will be keeping their eyes on her. However, she's wounded and has a target on her back after doing something nobody expected—she killed a Lily.

But she's alive. Lucien oddly feels no surprise. It's like Falan is so willful that her making it out of the round was meant to be. There's still much of the tournament to go, but he can't help but feel a smidge of hope. Suppose she wins . . . suppose the deal between them works out . . . suppose he finds Fayette?

But six years of separation is a long time, and Lucien feels his hope slipping once more. It's the same feeling he had the morning his father died; when, weeks after, he awoke and Fayette wasn't on the bed opposite him; when the man his father was indentured to declared Lucien an unnecessary expense and cast him onto the streets. Lucien welcomes the desolate feeling until it physically hurts, refusing to continue to wonder. Hope is a tall spire that he will not fall from again.

"Lucien." Bellamy is suddenly at his side, having found him in the crowd. "You need to come with me."

Lucien looks around to see the Chapiteau is nearly empty. It's time for him to go and obtain the grants to hand out to each performer. He gets to his feet, feeling the familiar ache in his leg as he stands. "Of course, the grants," he says.

Bellamy shakes his head. "There is something we need to do before that."

"We?"

Bellamy starts to walk, and Lucien follows so they don't attract suspicion. "We need to find out what the second round is," Bellamy says in a low voice.

"From Blanchet's son." Lucien remembers the Betting Party. He didn't speak to the boy directly, but Bellamy's and Falan's glances at him made it clear they'd somehow convinced him—or blackmailed him—to help.

The winter chill has settled over the air outside, but nobody seems to notice. Lucien is grateful for it. The cool breeze leaves kisses on his cheeks, and his heartbeat slows in comfort.

Illuminated by the sliver of moon in the otherwise dark sky, the grounds are packed with spectators, all busy talking about the events of the round. They stand in circles, absorbed in their conversations. Some are lined up in front of the grants tent. Some are buying souvenirs from another tent, objects like cards from a deck featuring the players. With so many people, Lucien doubts they will be able to find Blanchet's son, and unnoticed too.

But to Lucien's surprise, Bellamy starts walking around the perimeter of the Chapiteau. Curious, he follows until they reach the back of the large tent, the area empty except for one person. Blanchet's son is on his knees, throwing up on the grass.

“We have got to stop meeting like this, Jules,” Bellamy says with a sigh as they walk up behind him.

“Beat it!” Jules chokes out miserably. “I can’t be seen with you.”

“Is this when you introduce us?” Lucien asks, eyeing Jules with scrutiny. He can’t believe this nervy, vomiting boy is truly Blanchet’s son.

“Ah, yes, of course.” An amused smile tugs Bellamy’s lips upward. “Lucien, meet Jules Devereux Blanchet, our little informant. Jules, meet Lucien Trichet, last year’s winner.”

“Pleasure,” Lucien says coolly. He holds no fondness for anybody and anything related to Blanchet. “We’ll *beat it*, as you put it, as soon as you give us the information for round two.”

Jules sends him a flat glare. “It’s nice to meet you too.” He stands up, wiping his mouth. “And I don’t know anything yet. I’ll find out more tonight and tell you tomorrow.”

“That’s not going to work.” For the first time, concern traces Bellamy’s features. “We don’t have anywhere to meet where we’d remain unseen.”

For a minute, the three of them stand in silence.

Then finally, Jules swallows. His hazel eyes flicker. “I think I know a place.”

XVI

November 9, 1896

THE COOL NIGHT AIR IS A SLAP IN THE FACE, CHILLier than Jean-Pierre's circus ground illusion, but Falan breathes it in gratefully. It keeps her alert, wipes the fog from her mind. Pain quickly takes its place. Her abdomen is killing her. One side of her face and neck is covered in dried blood from when the tourné knife sliced her cheek and punctured her ear. Her palms are also slit.

At least she's in better shape than Sylvestre himself, who can barely walk. His eyes look like murder. Eliot and Collette glance over at her as they walk with him, whispering to each other, unfortunately unharmed.

Falan and the other performers slip through the grounds among the spectators, cloaked by Jean-Pierre's illusion abilities. The nearby black-and-white-striped medical tent, where Jean-Pierre has instructed the performers to stay until the crowd clears out, is also hidden by illusion.

Surprisingly, Falan finds herself walking alongside Ronan, although the two of them don't speak. Her gaze slides to Ary, who is with Meera. Seeing Ary unharmed unknots some of the nerves in Falan's stomach, although she will never admit it. Seeing Meera, however, sends a fresh wave of fury through her. It's just like Meera to leave her to die, but she expected that.

There is nothing much inside the medical tent, except for eleven chairs and an examination table behind a curtain where the Cirque's physician is waiting for them.

"Your examinations will begin shortly," the physician says after Jean-Pierre leaves the tent.

Silence as the performers occupy nine of the chairs. Then, quietly, Ary asks, "Why are we waiting?"

Everyone looks at her in surprise. Even the Lilies look startled that she dared to question something.

Even more shockingly, the physician answers. "Some of you may be receiving grants to aid with your injuries," he says. "Once I get my information, I can heal accordingly."

As he goes back behind the curtain, Meera whispers to Ary, "Why did you ask?"

A pause. Then Ary says, "Because he had no reason not to answer."

Falan wouldn't have expected such boldness from Ary. But looking at her, there's already a change to her demeanor. There is something harder, more determined about her. Falan spots a long scrape on her leg, cutting through the stockings, and wonders if she had an altercation with Sylvestre during the round too.

As she turns away, Falan suddenly feels Ronan's gaze from beside her. She waits for him to say something, but he just looks at her with furrowed brows and intense eyes. Seeing his thoughtful expression brings back what he said during the game: *You just . . . look like her in some ways.*

"How's your arm?" she asks, breaking the silence.

"Not as bad as it seems," he says. "How hurt are you?"

"Manageable," she says, although she's struggling not to keel over from the pain in her abdomen.

Ronan raises an eyebrow. He's not fooled. "Will you be all right during the night?"

For a moment, Falan thinks he's mocking her. But there's no

humor in Ronan's voice. Still, she says, "How does that matter to you?"

Ronan leans close and whispers, "I heard them talking on the way over here. Sylvestre. Eliot. Collette. They're going to be roaming the Aviary at night, tracking you down. Looks like you angered them enough for some special attention."

"Unsurprising," she mutters.

"If you feel unsafe, you can . . . stay in my room."

What a strange offer. Falan sees no reason to trust him. True, he saved her from Sylvestre at one point in the round, but when Arthur had her trapped, Ronan stepped in only after she had killed him. Perhaps he's using her, making her do the dirty work for him until the end so he can win.

On the other hand, if that's the case, then she can use him too. "Why are you offering this? Are you preparing to lead me into an ambush?"

Ronan frowns. "If that was the case, I would have let Sylvestre stab you during the round. If anything, it's *you* I should be worried about."

"I prefer to stab my enemies from the front," she says.

For a moment, something flickers in Ronan's blue eyes, too fleeting for her to grasp. But he says, "Are you accepting my invitation or not?"

A pause. Then, painfully, she nods.

The sounds of the crowd outside fade slowly as the next hour ticks by. Falan notices the other performers starting to fall asleep. Ary rests her head on Meera's shoulder. Even Ronan has dozed off beside her. The tendrils of sleep are creeping up on Falan as well, but with how Sylvestre is still looking over at her from time to time, she's wary to even blink around him.

Finally, a dealer steps through the entrance of the tent. He goes to the physician, and they talk for a few minutes in a low voice before he leaves. The physician walks out from behind the curtain and claps his hands once, startling everyone awake. From next to Falan, Ronan wakes with a small gasp, blinking rapidly.

"The examinations will now begin. We will go in order of your numbers," the physician says, and beckons to Sylvestre. Falan watches as he limps behind the curtain. It's too much to hope that he won't receive a medical grant for his injuries. Unfortunately, when he walks out from behind the curtain, he is fully healed sans a few bruises.

When it's finally Falan's turn, the physician looks her over quickly, declares she has no life-threatening injuries after wrapping gauze around her abdomen and hands, and dismisses her without healing anything, just as she expected.

Outside the tent, Falan is greeted by none other than Bellamy, who raises his eyebrows as he takes her in. "You've looked better."

"One often looks unsightly after an absence of medical grants," she says sardonically.

"Bad luck. And it seems after I agreed to check on you during your long slumber, I'm now the dealer officially designated to you," he says with a wry smile. "I'll be escorting you to lineups before rounds and back to the Aviary after." When he glances over at her once more, his expression sobers. "How badly are you injured?"

"No internal bleeding or broken bones, according to the physician," she says. "Just some intense muscle bruising."

A soft sigh escapes Bellamy's lips. It almost sounds like relief, but when she looks at him, his face is neutral.

There is no sign of the large Chapiteau now; the grounds are empty, as if the tent never existed. The crowd is long gone, and the night air is eerily silent. The only thing that remains is a small ticket booth, empty and abandoned. Bellamy leads her over to the booth, gesturing for her to go in first. Hesitantly, she steps inside; there's barely enough room for the two of them.

There's nothing here, but Falan isn't fooled. She watches as Bellamy closes the door behind him before kneeling, pulling something up from the grass. A perfect square of the ground suddenly lifts, revealing a flight of stairs leading down to the Aviary.

It's a door hidden by illusion, like the ones in the hotel for the cercle and the Cirque. Falan follows Bellamy down the steps, wincing with pain, and looks up as the door shuts. It instantly blends in with the smooth stone of the ceiling, like it was never there at all. Without a dealer, there's no chance a performer can leave the Aviary.

"Jean-Pierre certainly took precautions," Falan says quietly.

Bellamy waits at the foot of the stairs. "He's done this the past two years as well. Nothing new for this year."

Falan examines both ends of the tunnellike hallway after finally descending the staircase. On her right is a dead end, the wall bare. Down the other side is a set of mahogany double doors. In front of them are the only set of stairs leading to the floor below.

"The winner's hall?" Falan asks, and Bellamy nods. "Is it locked?"

He nods again. "Even I don't have access. Only Lucien and Jean-Pierre."

Falan eyes the keyhole on the doors. "The lock seems like something you could pick easily."

"It does." Bellamy smiles, and for a moment Falan thinks he is going to attempt it, but instead he says, "Come on. Let's go see if you received any grants after your performance tonight."

Falan is already dreading the walk down multiple stories. She steadies her body against the banister, bracing herself as she looks down the steps. She isn't sure if she can walk down all three flights.

One was already agonizing. Her hand curls around the railing, and her teeth sink into her lip as she slowly descends each step. Bellamy doesn't say anything, but he keeps looking over at her.

Just before they start down the last set of stairs, Bellamy suddenly grabs Falan by the wrist. She turns to look at him, surprised by the warmth of his fingers against her skin. Before she can ask what he wants, he leans forward and slips something into the pocket of her coat. A wave of body heat from his proximity gently brushes over Falan, and she finds her breath caught in her throat until Bellamy backs away. He gives her a subtle nod, an unspoken message passing between them, before continuing down the stairs and leaving her to follow. Falan slips a hand in her pocket to feel a small piece of paper. A note, perhaps.

Annoyance pricks her. A note is the most idiotic way to get them caught.

The other performers are already lined up when they reach the bottom, with Jean-Pierre and Lucien standing in front of them. From the echoing footsteps above, Ary isn't too far behind. Jean-Pierre raises his eyebrows as Bellamy walks Falan over to the lineup. "Was there a delay, Durand, Sunkara?"

"It's difficult to walk quickly with an array of injuries," Falan says before Bellamy can speak.

"Don't let it happen again." Jean-Pierre waves Bellamy off. "Durand, you're dismissed. Go see Monsieur Blanchet for your shift time."

Bellamy nods before walking away, leaving Falan to study the Aviary's layout while she waits. She tilts her head up and looks at the layers of floors above her, viewable since the center of each floor has been carved out. Each floor seems to be split into four hallways with four staircases, following the same pattern as her floor.

Once Ary joins the lineup and the last dealer leaves, Jean-Pierre smiles around at the nine remaining players. "Congratulations on an excellent performance tonight," he says. "Prior to the round, many of you were allotted weapons to help during the Game, but now many of you have been rewarded with grants to aid your living conditions here. After Lucien gives them out, you are free until the performance tomorrow night. Let me remind you that there will be hourly patrols to make sure you are saving your energy for the performances."

Falan knows what he is really saying. *If you're going to harm somebody, do it between patrols, but no killing.* Sylvestre could beat her within an inch of her life, and as long as she's still breathing, she would be deemed eligible to compete tomorrow.

Jean-Pierre claps his hands once more. "Now then, Lucien, the grants."

Lucien walks forward with a bag in his free hand, putting it down each time he pulls a grant from it. To Falan's dismay, everything except the water bottles are wrapped in parcels, making it impossible to tell what the other players are receiving. She doesn't expect to receive anything, but she's surprised when Lucien hands her a glass bottle of water. When he's finished, Jean-Pierre bids them good night before he and Lucien disappear in a plume of smoke.

An anxious tension suddenly pervades the area as they all glance at one another; it's as if they're seconds away from attacking one another. Falan doesn't dare look for too long at Sylvestre or the other Lilies, who have gathered to compare grants. This is her chance. She walks toward Ronan, who has a water bottle of his own along with a small parcel, but she doesn't stop when she reaches him and heads for the west staircase.

"Falan." Ronan quickly falls in step with her. "What—"

"Your room," she says in a low voice, "before they follow us."

XVII

November 9, 1896

RONAN'S ROOM IS IN THE EAST HALL ON THE FLOOR above, leaving Falan grateful that she has only one staircase to climb. Although it's strange because Falan remembers Bellamy telling her Lilies are always put on the second highest floor. Then again, there are four other Lilies, a higher number than usual. But Falan realizes this is most likely the case at the hotel too—Ronan always holds the lowest status among the Lilies.

When Ronan opens his door, the difference in quality from Falan's room is instantly apparent. His bed is much larger, enough to fit two people, with clean white sheets that are already half torn off. His desk is wider, and on top is a clock and a gas lantern. Rather than having a wooden chair, he has a comfortable beige chaise.

Most of all, his room has a lavatory connected to it. Falan stares, thinking of the pail in her room. "Generous," she says as he closes the door.

"I suppose so," he says, brushing past her to lock the door. "I imagine the upper floor's rooms are far more luxurious."

How much more luxurious can they get? Falan nearly says. Instead, she takes a seat on the chaise.

Ronan sits on the corner of the bed nearest to her and starts unwrapping his parcel, revealing half a baguette in the folds of brown paper. His gaze flickers to her. Falan expects him to say some condolence that will irritate her, but instead he tears the bread in half and holds out a piece to her.

When she stares at him, not quite trusting the offer, he impatiently says, "Take it."

Normally she would make a quip in return, but she hasn't eaten since the night of the Betting Party. The sharp hunger in her stomach wins out and she takes the bread, sinking her teeth into it. Even after sitting in its parcel, it's fresh and soft. The bite makes her mouth water, and she ravenously digs in.

Ronan watches her as she eats. His expression is the same as when they were at the carousel, his blue eyes bright. Falan wonders if he's thinking of Lavanya again.

"Why are you doing all this?" she asks quietly after taking a much-needed drink from her bottle of water. "You protected me, you invited me here, you shared your grant with me . . . What do you want?"

"I don't want anything," Ronan says, suddenly uneasy. His gaze drifts to the gas lantern, its glow sending flickering shadows across his face as he toys with the piece of bread in his hands. "But we were partners on the trapeze. So we know each other well. I know your strengths and your weaknesses, and you do mine. We'd make good allies."

Falan senses from Ronan's continued fidgeting that this isn't the only reason. "Is this guilt?" she asks plainly. "For Lavanya?"

Ronan blinks, startled. "What?"

"For how you treated her before her death. You suddenly stopped speaking to her and she died a few weeks later, and now you feel guilty because you're facing me in the Game, so you decided to help me?"

For a long minute, Ronan stares at Falan. "I feel guilt," he finally says quietly. His hands tighten around his bread. "But that's not why I helped you. I told you the truth—I think we'd make good allies."

"You hurt her. She died with the love of one less person. Nothing could justify what you did, and I wouldn't grieve if somebody slit your throat. That is, if I don't do it myself." Falan leans forward. "So why on earth would you ever trust me?"

Ronan swallows. She's suddenly aware of how close they are, only inches away from each other. The lantern's shadows make his black hair darker, his blue eyes brighter, his sculpted features sharper. "I trust you . . . because if somebody breaks down that door and comes crashing through, you stand a better chance of fighting them off with me alive." He finally takes a bite out of his piece of baguette without looking away.

He's right. It's the reason she stuck with him during the round. It's the reason she's in his room right now, and it makes her sick to her stomach. But in this tournament, she can't afford to be choosy. If Ronan trusts her, then there's no logical reason she shouldn't utilize this. She does know him inside out; she knows the pressure of his hands catching hers on the trapeze, the dips of his body as they soar through the air pressed together, all his strengths and weaknesses.

"All right," she finally says as he eats his last bite. "It's a deal."

Ronan nods curtly, back to his usual terse demeanor as he increases the distance between them. He doesn't bother to offer a handshake.

"We'll do shifts," Falan says. "I'll take the first watch."

She expects him to insist in that faux polite way of his, but he flops back onto the bed with a sigh, resting his head on his uninjured arm. It's only when Falan is certain he's asleep that she finally pulls out the note Bellamy gave her earlier.

It's written in English simple enough for many non-native speakers to understand, but Bellamy doesn't know that she's fluent in both French and English. However, she knows that *he* is. That night on the hotel roof flashes again in her mind. Bellamy, tipsily dancing near the roof's edge as if to challenge the world. Bellamy, crumpled against her when she yanked him to safety, his breath hot against her neck and his dark curls soft against her cheek. Bellamy, breaking the unspoken rule by pouring out bits and pieces of his past.

Perhaps she should have left him on the rooftop. Yet she stayed, listening as he told her how he lived in Marigot, a small town in Saint Martin, until he was about four and his father died of illness.

"I was glad when the bastard died," Bellamy said. "He and my grandfather treated my mother as they would a slave. In legal terms, they called it indentured. But to them, she was a slave, despite what Saint Martin's laws said."

And then his grandfather, against his mother's will, took him away from the West Indies to Marseille.

"The last time I saw her, Sunkara," Bellamy said quietly, "she wouldn't let me go. She cried so hard, squeezing me like I was her lifeline. I . . . I remember her eyes. They were brown, so brown. Not like mine. And then . . . nothing. I remember nothing else."

There wasn't anything Falan could say that would numb the pain of being dragged away from one's home, losing a loved one, especially at the hands of somebody who should not have had a say. Both of their homes were influenced by not just the French but many more colonizers, all with an entitlement trying to take what has never belonged to them.

So she said nothing. Instead, she took him by thc arm and began their journey back to the boardinghouse.

Falan forces herself to stop remembering, reading over Bellamy's note.

Tomorrow. Eight morning. Wait after the sweep. Top floor.

For what? She reads the message twice before popping the paper in her mouth and swallowing it.

As if in response, her stomach growls. The meager piece of bread she ate wasn't enough to satiate her, and she doesn't dare use up the rest of her water to ease her hunger. But this is nothing compared to the months before joining the Cirque. The months she and Lavanya were stuck on the streets of Paris.

The two of them stayed together throughout the ship journey, just as they had agreed on. As Lavanya promised, she supplied Falan readily with food, sparing her from continuous meals of hardtack, and Falan exercised her French fluency whenever needed. They continued this deal even after they reached Marseille and journeyed up to Paris.

Lavanya's company was strange. Most of their conversations were one-sided, with Lavanya doing all the talking, but she didn't seem to mind, indifferent to Falan's wariness. She appeared more than happy to blather on about how different France was from India, to express excitement over the colder weather and smoky air and horse-drawn carriages. Eventually Falan didn't mind either, although she never admitted it.

But their luck ran out upon reaching le Louvre. The Mirage Diamond was not there. The museum curators acted as if they had never heard of it before asking Falan and Lavanya to leave.

Even worse, Falan had run out of fare. Using the funds her father had sent her for the trip to sustain not only herself but Lavanya too left them utterly coinless. For hours, the two of them sat outside le Louvre, silently watching snow fall from the sky as it darkened. The chill was growing unbearable.

"Well, we're in trouble now, aren't we?" Lavanya finally said with a wry smile.

Falan said nothing. *Trouble* was not a word that properly described their current situation. They had no money, had no place to stay, and knew nobody in the entire city. They were on the road to starving or freezing to death, whichever came first.

"Seems I came to Paris for nothing," Lavanya muttered, her smile growing somber. For the first time, Falan saw a sadness behind the cheeky humor she always displayed.

"Why did you come here?" Falan asked quietly.

Lavanya blinked, surprised she had spoken. "I told you already. To see the Mirage Diamond."

"Why did you come here?" Falan asked again.

A long pause stretched between them. Then, softly, Lavanya said, "The Mirage Diamond is very beautiful, my thathayya used to tell me. He told me how it fit in his hand when he unearthed it in the mine. He told me how, even covered in dirt, it shone a different color from every angle." A beat. "He told me how it was taken from his grasp by a French missionary who said it would be sent to le Louvre, how he didn't even have a voice in the matter or any credit to his name for the discovery."

"Why did you come here?" Falan asked a third time.

"I came here . . . to steal it back." Lavanya tipped her head to the sky with a sigh, fingers curling in the snow.

"How stupid," Falan said callously. "What exactly was your plan? You know nobody here, you barely speak a word of French. Pickpocketing may work for a slice of quiche, but to pilfer a diamond is another thing altogether."

"I don't know," Lavanya admitted. "I just wanted to see if the diamond was here first. And perhaps traveling all this way without a proper plan was rather thoughtless of me." She paused. "But is that such a bad thing, Chelli? To be fueled purely by anger and hope? To want to take back something unrightfully stolen from your loved one? From your home?"

Falan studied the melancholy in her expression, her longing. Even her anger. What intrigued her the most was the fact that, in the end, Lavanya was doing this for somebody else. Even on the ship, she gave Falan first choice of all the stolen savory pies and éclairs. She was a thief, but there was never any malicious intent in what she did.

Nobody sane would sneak on a ship to France on the mere whim of wanting to steal a diamond.

For the first time in Falan's life, somebody truly fascinated her. Lavanya was like nobody she had ever met before. Perhaps that was why, instead of splitting ways after arriving in Paris and continuing to le Havre, she'd gone with Lavanya to le Louvre.

"No," Falan finally said. "But it appears neither of us will be achieving our goals because we'll be freezing to death tonight."

"Nonsense." Lavanya's smile returned. "I still need to track down that diamond, and your father is waiting for you in England."

And then Lavanya had pulled her up and off the streets, in search of somewhere warm for the night. Over the next few months, they often squatted in empty buildings, although some nights they were not so lucky and had to bear the chill outside. As the days went by, Lavanya taught her what she knew about scavenging on the streets.

Falan began to act on her own, sneaking into people's homes to steal goods. Lavanya stole only what others didn't want, or what could be easily replaced, but Falan despised that rule. They deserved fresh food as much as anybody. Despite her small frame and age, she never managed to amass any type of pity.

She knew why—pity wasn't spared for people like them, and it would never be. Not here.

And when it finally was, it arrived in the most cunning of forms.

It was mid-February 1891 when Falan awoke to a fever one morning after a night spent in an alley, her skin burning against the snowy ground. Within hours, she could barely remain conscious, her breathing hoarse and shallow. In and out of dreams, the world started to grow surreal. Flames danced at the ends of her fingertips. She heard her mother's voice. The snow was stardust. Strange, surreal, yet she could barely react to the same fear inside her that she'd felt when plagued with malaria back in India.

Then he appeared. A top hat of black. A red coat. Gold buttons. White-gloved hands. Fair skin and blond hair and shiny eyes. A mouth tugged into a practiced expression of sympathy.

Falan only realized this man was no hallucination when Lavanya responded to something he said. She wanted to close her eyes and drift off into oblivion, but each time she did, Lavanya's grip would tighten and snap her awake.

"I can help you," the man was saying to Lavanya in surprisingly fluent English. "You have something special inside you, ma chère. Your Affinity is a talent that will make you successful with my enhancement." He then spoke of a place called le Cirque des Ombres; he spoke of a game, how Lavanya could compete and change her life, win money and luxuries beyond her wildest dreams.

Even in her delirious haze, Falan didn't trust him. Nobody was this giving without an ulterior motive.

But Lavanya didn't point this out. Instead, she gripped Falan tighter. "Does this offer extend to her as well?" she asked.

The man's grin slipped a notch. He said something to Lavanya that Falan couldn't hear.

Whatever it was made Lavanya tighten her grip further. "I have two conditions. One, my . . . sister is part of this deal. She goes, and I go. Two, you will not convince her to sign a contract until she is older, as she is only twelve."

"I've signed people at that age before."

Lavanya remained stubborn. "Those are my terms. Only then will I go with you."

Falan wanted this man to tell her what her Affinity was. She wanted to say that she didn't want to go with him. But she was too weak to utter a word.

A dark look flitted across the man's handsome face, but then he said, "Come. I will carry the girl and see she's given care. We will get started on your contract meanwhile."

Falan barely felt it when he lifted her in his arms. She awoke in one of the hotel's rooms the next day, long after Lavanya had signed her contract, and learned the name of the mysterious man.

Jean-Pierre.

The ringmaster seemed too good to be true. Slowly, Falan got her strength back, ravenously eating the bowls of hot stew brought to her. A few days later, she and Lavanya moved into the boardinghouse, meeting Meera for the first time in their shared room.

Falan marveled at her. Brown skin so clear it rivaled the surface of water, black hair in thick waves that fell past her shoulders, long-lashed eyes. When Meera asked her name, Falan couldn't speak. She could barely breathe.

"A talker, isn't she?" Meera quipped.

"Don't worry. She gives everyone the silent treatment, including me," Lavanya said.

Falan's cheeks warmed as they both laughed.

She began her training on the trapeze like Lavanya despite no magical enhancement. For those few weeks, life seemed like it would be . . . safe.

Then Jean-Pierre's true colors began to show.

Past her anger and thirst for vengeance, it terrifies Falan how clever this man is. How he puts on a mask to the audience, a front to make himself seem so good-hearted and alluring, when to sign with him is to sign away one's freedom, one's spirit.

On the clock next to the lantern, it reads a quarter to four in the morning.

Ronan suddenly shakes himself awake, breathing hard, eyes dilated with panic. It's a look Falan knows all too well, one of the reasons she tries not to sleep at night. She wonders what exactly his mind tortured him with. His breathing slows as his eyes fall on her.

"Nightmare?" she says.

Ronan shudders. "I'll take watch now," he says as he stands, voice still rough with sleep.

Falan doesn't bother to argue. She gets off the chaise and sighs softly as her back hits the bed. This is no small bunk with a hard mattress. This is large enough for her to spread out and still have room, the sheets as soft and white as a cloud, warm from Ronan's body heat. They smell clean, despite the gore of the round. Earthy, like Ronan. It's something familiar and strangely comforting.

Falan expects the sudden emotion from thinking of Lavanya, as well as her stress from the round, to keep her up, but she's too tired. Too tired to think what news the morning holds, or that she took somebody's life, or that somebody could be outside the door right now trying to hurt her.

Instead, as she drifts off, she finds herself thinking of Marie-Lou, one of the first performers she ever met at the Cirque during a tour of the arena. The tightrope walker ambushed her in the dark hallway underneath the hotel and grabbed her arm, fingernails digging into her skin.

"Flee while you can, girl, before he makes you sign the contract," Marie-Lou whispered, eyes fraught with terror, face inches away. "You still have a chance. Run and do not return."

In response, Falan yanked her arm away and ignored her.

The next night, at the end of the Cirque's performance, Marie-Lou slipped from the tightrope during her act—and died.

XVIII

November 9, 1896

ARY CHEA HAS NEVER FELT SO TERRIFIED, APART from one prior night.

She sits huddled on her poor excuse for a bed, sheets wrapped tightly around her, jumping at every little noise she hears. Sounds seem to come from right outside her door, but Ary eventually realizes they're coming from the stories above. It would not be so bad if she had a weapon, or if she had somebody with her. But she has nobody.

Ary is no stranger to being alone, but she's become distant from it over the past seven months. Every day, she's had either Meera or Falan with her. They never let her go a day without a meal, they gave her advice to avoid inciting Jean-Pierre's wrath. In a situation like this, were the three of them together, Meera would be making some joke inappropriate for the circumstance and Falan would make a cutting remark in turn, provoking Ary to keep the peace.

Ary gasps softly as a bang echoes down the hall, and she hunches deeper into the chilly wall. She would do anything to hear one of Meera's jokes or Falan's callous remarks right now. She might have survived the first round, but barely. It was pure luck that she outran the Joker—Sylvestre, as she now knows. It was also pure luck that something else caught his attention and he left her alone. Ary doubts she will have such fortune in the next round.

A sudden knock at her door makes her jump. For a moment, Ary sits frozen, wondering if it was just an echo. But then the person knocks again, and Ary cautiously approaches the door, her heart slamming against her chest.

"Baby Bird," says a voice on the other side, "it's me."

Baby Bird. Ary's shoulders relax, but she remains on guard as she unlocks the door and opens it enough for Meera to slip inside. "What are you doing here?" she asks.

Meera stares back blankly. "What do you mean?"

"Why aren't you in your own room?" Ary says, feeling awkward because just seconds ago she was wishing Meera would come.

"Because you're here alone?" Meera says, still looking confused. "I stayed back to make sure nobody followed you to your room. Luckily, it seems neither of us are prime targets tonight." Without asking, Meera flops down in Ary's desk chair. "Falan had better be careful. The Lilies are trying to work out which room she's in. I can't believe she actually allied with Ronan."

Ary doesn't know much about Ronan, but she does know that Falan and Meera have never held high opinions of him. In the few times they've spoken, he was polite but detached. Not great, but better than her interactions with the other Lilies. "Did you run into them during the round?"

Meera pauses. "Yes, I did. They were already together by the time I came across them. Ary, listen." There is no laughter or trace of mirth in Meera's eyes. This is the most serious Ary has ever seen her. "You can't trust Falan. Not here. Allying with a Lily should have already tipped you off, but I know Falan well, and I know she will do anything to win. Even hurting you."

Ary thinks it over. Falan, for all her guarded persona and cold remarks, hasn't come across as a threat in her mind. She never even considered that Falan would harm her if it meant a win, because that doesn't seem like Falan. She may not have always shown it, but after seven months, Ary has learned that Falan's thoughtfulness comes through in her actions, not her words. She's callous, but always made sure Ary ate. Short-tempered, but took the blame for any of Ary's actions that she suspected would anger Jean-Pierre.

"I don't think she would hurt me, Meera," Ary finally says.

Meera shakes her head. "You've only known Falan for seven months. I've known her for five years. And tonight, I felt no surprise when she killed somebody right in front of me."

Shock presses the air from Ary's lungs. "Falan killed somebody?"

"Arthur. And she wasn't even the Joker. She could have run, but she chose to shove him right into Sylvestre's knife. She was the only one who killed somebody tonight without being forced to. And she showed no remorse."

Ary sits down on her bed. It shouldn't surprise her either, but it does. Falan killed somebody in a situation where she didn't have to, Lily or not.

But then, Ary imagines the wild desperation that might have overtaken Falan in the moment, the relief she must have felt with one more competitor out of the way. Ary can't help feeling glad herself and instantly feels shame, trying to push away that bubbling darkness inside her. She's here to survive, as they all are. And she can't blame Falan for doing what she had to.

But it also means Meera has a point. Falan can't be trusted. Nobody can. Ary glances at Meera, wondering if it's safe to sleep with her around. Her only consolation is the no killing rule between rounds and that having an ally might be good right now. Even if they have to kill each other at some point.

"Do you understand?" Meera says. "Channary, you can't trust her."

"I understand," Ary says with a nod. "After tonight, I certainly don't trust anybody."

XIX

November 9, 1896

BOIS DE BOULOGNE IS ABOUT AN HOUR'S WALK BACK to Quartier du Faubourg-du-Roule. Even though Bellamy has just finished his patrol shift in the Aviary, a meal at the bouillon awaits him, still open while the rest of Paris sleeps. Perhaps he should catch a few hours of rest instead, but he needs to be back at the Aviary at eight to meet with Falan, Lucien, and Jules.

He only hopes Falan gets some sleep tonight. He's still thinking about her as he reaches the bouillon and sits down with a bowl of stew. The stubborn light in her eyes despite her bruised body. The sudden shiver that raced up his spine when he passed her the note.

So damn stubborn, yet at that moment, she looked caught off guard by the touch of his hand.

The thought makes Bellamy smile. The girl who shoved somebody into a knife tonight is the same one who held her breath when his fingers brushed hers. It's amusing. But Falan has always been like this—willful, yet vulnerable in the simplest of ways.

Bellamy first met Falan a week after he joined le Palais Blanchet as a dealer. He had originally snuck in to steal something, but Monsieur Blanchet offered him a job as a dealer in his cercle, impressed by his dexterity. Bellamy decided to sit in on the Cirque's practice one morning and came across a petite, brown-skinned girl in the stands. She was dressed in a trapeze leotard and her long, dark hair was partly swirled up in two small buns like animal ears. But she was not practicing.

Despite becoming friendly with most people at the Cirque and the other cercle dealers, he had never seen her before.

"May I sit here?" he asked her.

She didn't say yes, but didn't protest when he sat down anyway. She chewed on something, and Bellamy caught a glimpse of what was in her hand.

Roasted chestnuts.

"Can I have one?" he asked her.

She finally turned to him. Her eyes were some of the darkest he'd ever seen, like pools of ink, her long lashes lined with black.

But she didn't speak or even shake her head. Nor did she offer him a chestnut. Instead, she silently turned back to the performance. She didn't say a thing throughout the entire practice, and when it finally ended, she left without even looking at him.

What a strange girl, Bellamy thought as he watched her walk away.

He found out later that night from the other dealers that she was the sister of a trapeze artist named Lavanya who signed a contract with Jean-Pierre about two years before. Bellamy knew from others that Lavanya was a popular person around the Cirque, but he had no idea she had a sister who looked to be the total opposite of her. Apparently nobody in the Cirque, except Lavanya, talked to her. When he asked why, people simply said she was unapproachable and barely responded to them if they tried speaking to her.

The next day, Bellamy walked into the hotel lobby to find Falan waiting for him. She stared at him for a moment as if contemplating something, before dropping an object in his hand. "I want you to teach me to gamble." Her voice was softer than he imagined, but direct.

When Bellamy looked at his palm, he saw that she had given him none other than a chestnut. He barely managed to hide a smile.

Chestnut seemed to be a perfect way to describe this girl: small stature, hard on the outside. "This is a nice gift, but I'll need more in return," he said.

So she offered to teach him to scale buildings and jump roofs.

Their agreement has worked well for the most part, growing from teaching each other to working together on cons. Somehow, she understands his thoughts during a plan without even having to ask, and he hers. And her impassive persona has grown from strange to amusing.

Bellamy's smile fades. But there are moments that have gone beyond deals. In particular, that night on the hotel rooftop a few months ago. He hadn't meant to drink so much. But the wine was one his grandfather loathed, cheap as anything, and he found himself not bothering with a glass at all. He guzzled mouthfuls, sarcastically toasting to his grandfather, knowing he would hate Bellamy drinking it on the anniversary of his death.

Here's to you, Grand-père, he'd thought, *wherever you burn in hell. I'll join you and my father there soon.*

Midway through the bottle, Falan interrupted and pulled him away from the roof. He remembers those ridiculously long eyelashes of hers. The quick beat of her heart against his own, far too fast. He remembers spilling out his past to her, unable to stop.

And then . . . she somehow got him back to the boardinghouse to sleep off the alcohol. He doesn't remember the details, but when he woke the next morning, Bellamy was too embarrassed to thank Falan, let alone mention it. Fortunately, she pretended like it never happened.

His bowl of stew finished, Bellamy gets up to leave. As he does, the three men sitting at the corner table shift just slightly in his direction. Bellamy pauses. All of them have the same look—tall, brawny, dressed in black coats with gold rings on their fingers. The one turned in his direction holds a newspaper in front of his face.

Gold rings. They must be Horrent's men. As if they are the only ones in the bouillon, Bellamy calmly says, "Does Monsieur Horrent not trust me to keep to my word?"

The newspaper falls, revealing Cadieux behind it. Somehow, in the light of the bouillon, he looks less intimidating than the night he beat Bellamy up in Horrent's office. "Not at all," he says, a wicked smile lacing his lips. "He warned you that we would be watching. And I look forward to dragging your corpse in front of him and reaping the rewards."

"Rewards?" Bellamy raises his eyebrows. "Oh, Cadieux, you're a lackey. Horrent will pay you mere scraps of the money I give him back."

Cadieux and the other two men stand up so harshly they nearly upset the drinks on the table. "You'd better be careful, Durand," Cadieux says. "You returning the money won't save you. At some point, Horrent will realize the cost of your life is worth far more than any debt you owe. And he will send me to take care of you at a moment you won't see coming."

"I'm absolutely terrified, especially now that you've warned me of Monsieur Horrent's agenda," Bellamy says with a mocking smile before walking away. "Say hello to him for me."

His smile drops the moment he walks through the bouillon doors. But he can't focus on Cadieux now—he has a game to win.

XX

November 9, 1896

THE ROOM IS UNNATURALLY QUIET WHEN FALAN wakes up the next morning, and the bed feels warmer than when she drifted off. She glances to her left to see Ronan lying next to her, fast asleep. After an initial jolt of surprise, annoyance seeps through her grogginess. He's supposed to be in the chaise, on guard. It's a miracle nobody attacked them during the night.

Falan is about to shove him awake, but she doesn't. For years, she never believed Lavanya when she said there was a soft side to Ronan. Looking at him now, Falan finally sees what she meant. There's a stark contrast in Ronan's demeanor while asleep. His lashes are longer than Falan realized, somehow darker than his inky hair. But what fascinates her most is his expression. It's the same vulnerable, relaxed look he has when he's on the trapeze, but there's a sense of control up in the air. Here, he's at anybody's mercy.

Instead of waking him, Falan slowly slides off the bed, her body aching. With each movement, her wounds flare up in teeth-gritting, head-pounding pain.

A small white envelope on the floor catches her attention; it could easily have been slid under the door. She barely takes a step toward it before Ronan, voice rough with sleep, says, "Leaving so soon?"

A glance at the clock tells her she still has an hour before she needs to meet Bellamy. "No," she says. "You fell asleep on watch." She doesn't ask why he was on the bed rather than the chaise.

"My apologies," he says quietly, sitting up. "I hope the bed made up for it."

It did, but she won't admit that to him. "Somebody left you a present," she says instead.

Ronan turns over and his eyes focus on the envelope lying on the ground. Instantly, he's on his feet. "When did this arrive?"

"You would know if you stayed awake," Falan says, and watches as Ronan opens the envelope and pulls out a piece of paper. His curious expression melts into a frown as he reads what's written on it. "What?"

Ronan hesitates. "It's written in French—"

"Which I can read," Falan says, snatching the paper. It's a letter from Jean-Pierre.

Salut, my dear competitor!

Congratulations once again on surviving round one in the Game of Oaths. This note is to let you know that there has been a slight change in the tournament.

Traditionally, meals have been delivered directly to competitors' rooms. However, the panel and I believe that this has made things far too easy. From today, food will be left every morning in the space where grants are given out. In order to receive your meals, you will have to collect them yourselves.

The only exceptions to this rule are the food items allotted through grants from bettors, which will be distributed accordingly each night.

We hope you see this change as we do—something to add more stakes to the Game of Oaths on a personal level for our players, increasing the excitement in the tournament.

Joue ta chance,

Jean-Pierre

Fury ripples through Falan as her fingers tighten around the letter. A rule change like this increases the chances of a Lily winning, as they are the most likely to receive grants. Even worse, the more times she sneaks out for food, the more chances her enemies have of figuring out which room is hers.

"If you run into any trouble, come to my room," Ronan says.

Falan nods slowly. Right. They're allies now. She doesn't have to face Sylvestre and the other Lilies by herself. "It would be nice if the grants alone sustained us."

"I suspect more will come in after this round," Ronan says. "The closer a bettor's chosen player gets to winning, the more desperate they will be to help. And the ones who have already lost will be looking to earn their money back by placing a new bet."

Although most of Ronan's assumptions can be gathered from common sense, it feels like he's speaking about this almost too knowledgeably. He sounds far too confident for Falan's comfort. "You truly think more people will bet on me as the competition goes on?" she asks.

"I'd be shocked if they didn't, after last night," Ronan says with a rather bitter smile. He's still judging her for Arthur's death. "They might not like you as a winner, but they won't pass up the chance to make money. So perhaps we will be sustained on grants."

Falan crosses her arms. "You're saying that like it's a bad thing."

"Not for us."

Silence lingers between them, their eyes still locked, each waiting for the other person to break the quiet.

"I should go," Falan finally says, thinking of a plausible excuse. "I've been meaning to check on Ary."

Ronan clears his throat, looking away awkwardly. "Of course. But if you want to clean yourself off first . . ." He gestures to the lavatory.

Falan's nails scrape at the dried blood still on her face. It's a generous offer. And she has the time to do so. "Thank you," she says, walking into the lavatory.

It's tiny, cramped, with only two buckets. One is empty, meant for waste, but the other is full of water, with a few towels next to it. Slowly, Falan unwraps the gauze around her palms, which did nothing to alleviate the pain. She sheds her coat and dress before pulling up her shirt to check her abdomen, finding it a horrifying mix of yellow, green, and purple. For a moment, she wonders if the physician misjudged that she doesn't have any internal bleeding. But no, she would have died in the middle of the night then.

Falan takes her time washing herself off, feeling cleaner the second the cool water hits her skin. She finally bathes the blood from her face and under her fingernails. It softens, wiping away in streaks of red. Falan stares down at the stained towel. Last night's events are something she thought she wouldn't dwell on, but an unwelcome feeling of discomfort now crashes through the barriers of her mind.

She took somebody's life. She purposefully shoved somebody into a blade and kept going until they reached a point of no return, something she can never take back.

But she had to kill Arthur. She was playing the Game how it should be played.

With a shudder, Falan throws the towel down. Her hands itch like they are still caked in blood, no matter how many times she scrapes her already washed skin. She needs to get out of here, focus on the next round.

When Falan exits the lavatory, Ronan is lying on the bed once more, eyes closed. However, he opens them when he hears her. "Done?"

Falan nods. A glance at the clock tells her it's time to go. Her gaze slides to her nearly empty water bottle sitting on the desk.

As she grabs it, it occurs to her that it could be a handy weapon, especially if broken.

"Thank you for the bread. And for allowing me to clean myself," Falan finally says, heading for the door. Her thanks runs deeper than that—it goes back to him offering for her to stay the night here.

But she can't be sure of anything, no matter what alliance they may have made. In the end, Ronan is a player, just like she is.

"See you tonight," Ronan says.

With a nod, Falan slips out the door, shutting it behind her. The chill of the hallway instantly washes over her and she shudders, not realizing how warm it had been in Ronan's room. Falan inches to the staircase at the end of the hallway. Going up two floors is risky, particularly passing the floor above. But with luck, the Lilies are still asleep.

It takes nearly ten minutes for Falan to reach the top floor. While her condition is better than last night, her abdomen still flares with pain each time she walks. She's in agony by the time she stumbles up the last step, spotting Bellamy waiting for her. "Why did you call me here?" she says through pants, glaring at him.

"You're late, Sunkara. I was beginning to get concerned something happened to you during the night. Alas, you're just unpunctual," Bellamy says playfully. But then he drops his voice. "I realized we needed a meeting place to discuss the plan for future rounds. Somewhere we wouldn't be spotted or disturbed. So, after a deliberation last night, our panelist friend offered just the place."

"Where is it?" Falan asks.

Bellamy walks to the dead end side of the hallway, and Falan keeps after him, curious. He knocks thrice on the wall, throwing Falan a secretive smile. A few seconds later, a section of the wall opens and Falan steps back.

Another door hidden by illusion. On the other side is Jules Devereux Blanchet, twirling a key on his finger. He doesn't look at her, but holds the door open for them, walking away as soon as Bellamy has grabbed it.

Bellamy gestures forward. "After you."

Falan steps inside to a long hallway. Bellamy closes the door and brushes past, leaving her to follow. A soft light glows at the end of the corridor, emanating from a room.

Once inside, however, the place reveals itself to be something more. Surrounding her are artifacts. Lots of them—on the walls, in display cases—in this room of white. A stone pot to her right, a shard of glass with an etched design in one corner, a clay mask on the wall. In another corner is a half-circle of plush brown couches, positioned for a view of the entire gallery. Jules has plopped down on one of the couches, where Lucien is seated as well.

"I see the two of you have been getting acquainted," Bellamy says.

Acquainted seems far from what they are. Lucien looks bored and irritable, Jules closed off and anxious. Both are sitting as far away from each other as they possibly can.

"What is this place?" Falan asks.

"Sunkara, we are standing in Monsieur Blanchet's privately owned gallery of treasures."

Falan walks forward, looking around at all the items protected by glass display cases, showcased on tall, rectangular pedestals several yards apart. They must be worth a fortune—and none of them seems native to France.

This is all stolen. It should come as no surprise to her, stolen valuables being auctioned off to wealthy Parisians at underground auctions. But it still angers her.

An object in the display case to her far right glints. Falan turns to face it.

It's a diamond.

Falan's blood runs cold. *It can't be.*

But in a gold-plated label in front of the display, it reads, MIRAGE DIAMOND.

Lavanya said this diamond was from the Kollur Mine, the same place the Hope Diamond and the Regent Diamond were found. Le Louvre didn't have it, and she never found out where it went.

All along, it was here, in the Aviary. And Lavanya never got to see it.

It's a beautiful diamond. It truly does look like a mirage, a celestial being trapped in the crystalline shape of a gem. Its colors shift with each angle. Pale purple, light blues and pinks, the slightest hints of silver and gold. It must be worth a fortune—and it belongs to India, to Lavanya's grandfather.

"These are all stolen," Falan finally says, directing her ire at Jules. "Why meet here of all places?"

"Quite the introduction," Bellamy says wryly. "Jules, in case you haven't caught on, *she's* the competitor you're helping. Meet Falan Sunkara. Sunkara, this is Jules Devereux Blanchet, as you know."

Falan ignores him, her steely glare still on Jules.

Jules winces, pocketing the key. "My father won't be coming down here this week due to the Game. He doesn't dare take the key with him to the hotel, and I know where he hides it, so we can meet here whenever we wish. We won't be disturbed, but you can't enter without me. Only I can see the door."

With one last glance at the diamond, Falan says, "Tell me what I need to know for the second round."

"The panel met this morning to decide the next game and came to a decision," Jules says as she and Bellamy walk over to the couches. Neither of them sit. "Jean-Pierre raised the prospect of introducing a brand-new game. He said the audience would love it, and that this year's tournament needed some more excitement, something the players wouldn't see coming."

"Even after that first round?" Bellamy says, but he can't hide the concern in his eyes.

Lucien doesn't say anything. He doesn't appear to be entirely present, staring absently into space, a quiet melancholy in his expression.

Sudden wariness strikes Falan. First the rule change about their food, now this new game. Has Jean-Pierre caught on to the fact that she's receiving help? From their interactions leading up to the tournament, it was clear he suspected her of planning to defy him in some way due to Lavanya's death, whether it was trying to escape herself or hurt him. Once he picked her for the tournament, he seemed relieved, triumphant.

But could he have put two and two together? Could he have realized that she *wanted* to be picked? Perhaps last night she seemed a little *too* ready for the Joker. Successfully killing a Lily must have heightened this. If that's the case, then this is Jean-Pierre's retaliation, his move in their own private game.

Something the players wouldn't see coming means something *she* wouldn't see coming.

"Keep going," Lucien finally speaks, breaking the silence.

"Jean-Pierre accepted suggestions for games," Jules says. "And my father's suggestion won the approval of the panel."

When Jules stops speaking, nervously fidgeting, Falan sighs impatiently. "Out with it."

He clears his throat. "It's called la Proie."

La Proie. The Prey.

Bellamy slumps onto the couch. "That can't be good," he mutters.

"Rules?" Falan finally sits along with Bellamy. The couches are as soft as Ronan's bed; she could fall asleep here, right now.

"My father took some inspiration from jouer à chat," Jules says.

"Chat?" Bellamy echoes, cocking his head. "As in, the children's game?"

"A lot like the children's game," Jules says. "Except with a guaranteed death."

The thought of another game with a guaranteed death, especially a game she can't prepare for, makes Falan's stomach turn.

"What is jouer à chat?" Lucien asks.

"You know, that children's game when one individual chases the rest to tap them," Jules says.

"I assume the consequences for getting tapped are far worse than becoming the new It," Falan says, leaning back on the couch.

"Each of the nine players has ten minutes as It, or the Hunter," Jules explains. "During their time as the Hunter, they must try to tap as many competitors as possible. When somebody is tapped, that player will be unable to move for the remainder of the current Hunter's time. The person who taps the fewest number of people by the end . . . will be killed."

"How?" Lucien asks.

"However the crowd chooses. Jean-Pierre said that would add to the excitement." Jules winces.

"Excitement. Like how he suddenly decided to make us risk exposure for our meals." The words taste bitter and chalky in Falan's mouth. She knows Jean-Pierre's strategy now. A game like chat seems like it would be boring to an audience, who look forward to games with illusion and displays of magic. But if it ends in a death, it'll rivet them.

"Did you discuss anything about the setting?" Bellamy asks.

Jules shakes his head. "Jean-Pierre told us to leave the aesthetics to him, that he would surprise us."

"As long as it's not another circus ground," Falan says.

"This game seems straightforward for the most part," Lucien says. "Tap as many people as you can or you're dead."

"I suppose," Jules says with an uneasy frown.

Lucien leans forward at once. "Are you keeping something from us?"

"No, I'm not!" Jules insists with so much vigor it only heightens Falan's interest. "I just . . . had a thought."

"How startling," Lucien mutters. Bellamy bursts out laughing.

Jules glares at Lucien, his cheeks flushed an angry red. "I'm sorry, did I do something to make you dislike me? Or is it just my mere presence?"

"Just your mere presence," Lucien says. "You're a panelist and Blanchet's son."

However, Lucien doesn't sound particularly malicious. If anything, his tone is far more tired than wary. Falan then remembers that Thomas, his replacement knife thrower, was one of the three who died in the first round. She wonders how close they were.

"I didn't *want* to be on the panel," Jules says, barely audible.

"Never mind that. What are you thinking?" Falan asks.

"I watched you last night," Jules says, tearing his furious eyes away from Lucien. "And you allied with one of the players. Ronan Allaire."

"And?"

"I think you should ally with him again for the next round."

"No," Lucien snaps at once. When the others raise eyebrows at his sudden sharp tone, he adds, "I wouldn't recommend allying at all."

"Did anybody work together in your Game?" Falan asks.

"A few, like the Lilies," Lucien says. "I kept to myself."

Falan suspects Jean-Pierre doesn't take kindly to alliances—that he sees them as a form of mutiny—but she also suspects the reason he doesn't ban them is because the audience enjoys seeing people team up, then turn on each other as the rounds progress. She wonders if Lucien initially planned to ally with Lavanya.

"That's going to be a bit hard. Ronan and I agreed to an alliance last night," Falan says calmly, but she might as well have said Sylvestre was her new ally, considering Lucien and Bellamy's reactions.

"Allaire of all people?" Lucien says in disgust.

His strong reaction seems so unlike him—for the first time, he almost seems to care. Even Jules, who doesn't know any of them well, says, "What's the matter with Ronan Allaire? You both did well working together in the previous round."

"Until he decides he no longer needs you," Lucien says, his brown eyes steely with anger.

Then it clicks. Lucien must have noticed the way Ronan treated Lavanya before her death. "I'm no fan of him either," Falan says. "But he's useful to me right now, so I'm enduring his company."

"The blood is gone from your face," Bellamy says suddenly. "How did you wash it off?" It sounds like he's challenging her to give an answer he already knows.

"We spent the night in the same room," Falan says. "In case either of us were attacked. And I didn't want anybody trailing me and finding my room."

"So you spent the night in *his* room," Bellamy says.

"What is your issue, Durand?" Falan snaps, turning to face him.

He's so close she has to tilt her head up to meet his eyes, which are full of derision. "You of all people should know the benefits that can be gained by using someone."

Bellamy's lips part like he's going to say something, but then he stops himself. A few more seconds of tense silence tick by between them before he scoffs softly, shaking his head. "You're correct, Sunkara. I'm all for using people like Allaire. Forget I said anything."

He turns away, leaving Falan puzzled. She gets Lucien's out-of-character reaction because of Lavanya, but Bellamy's makes no sense. The only reason he would despise Ronan is because of his status as a Lily. But Bellamy's annoyance was aimed at *her*, not him. His behavior is unexpectedly inane, and she doesn't know what to make of it.

Lucien clears his throat, cutting into the tension. "You still need a tactic to fall back on," he says, crossing his arms.

The room lapses into silence again. Falan stares at the Mirage Diamond, twinkling in its display case. Almost like it's winking at her. Her mind drifts back to last night's round, shoving Arthur into that knife's blade. But that wasn't supposed to happen according to the game. The Joker is the one who kills or is killed. Yet she wasn't punished for it because there were no rules against it.

Jules told them that the player with the lowest number of people tagged would be the one killed, decided by the audience. But he never said anything about sabotage in the game to make sure somebody else's score is lower.

As Lucien said the night before the Game, the tournament is all about loopholes.

"I think I know what to do," Falan finally says.

XXI

November 9, 1896

THE MEETING ENDS SOON AFTER. THE RISK OF rendezvousing is already too high. It's best not to drag it on and risk suspicion.

Falan is the first to leave the gallery, the others waiting to stagger their exits. She keeps her ears pricked for footsteps as she makes her way down the first flight of stairs. But the halls are empty. Falan does not hear or see anybody as she descends the next two flights of stairs. It could be a coincidence; they might have missed one another. But she wonders if, possibly, the Lilies might be afraid of her. It's nothing they would ever admit, but she's the only person other than Sylvestre who killed somebody last night. A Lily too—one of them.

Soft footsteps echo through the ground floor, and Falan's muscles tense. She creeps to the end of the hall, looking into the central space where they assemble before and after rounds. On the floor are eight bags. Food.

Falan sees two things instantly. First, that the Lilies have not been by yet, otherwise all the bags would be gone.

Second, Ary is currently grabbing a bag of her own.

"Ary." Falan steps out of the hallway just as Ary's fingers wrap around the top of a bag.

Ary freezes, her wide eyes fixing on Falan, before she grips the bag and runs.

"Ary, wait." Cursing, Falan follows her, grabbing two bags of food, one for Ronan. Although normally a swift runner, her injuries slow her pace, and Falan knows within seconds that she will not catch up with Ary.

But she can see which hall she goes into.

Ary disappears into the west hall, and the sound of a door slamming comes seconds later. Before Falan can feel even a sliver of triumph, somebody grabs her by the shoulder and spins her to face them so roughly she loses her footing.

In the meager lighting of the Aviary, Meera towers over her.

"Oh. You," Falan says, pushing herself up off the floor.

Meera briefly eyes the two bags in Falan's grip. For a long moment, the two of them stare at each other, the air thick with tension. "I'll get to the point," Meera finally says. "The second game is tonight. I know you have your . . . opinions of me after the first round, despite what you yourself did."

"What opinions?"

"You can't lie to me, Falan. I know you so well." Something like remorse flashes across Meera's face, but it disappears a second later. "You think low of me for leaving you to die in Sylvestre's hands. But you can't tell me that you wouldn't have done the same. You killed somebody in a position when you could have run."

"And you ran in a position when you could have helped get rid of a bastard," Falan says. "There is no point in comparing the two. I killed someone who attempted to kill me. You left a friend for dead. Both done for survival reasons. Get to your point."

Meera's face hardens, any lingering uneasiness gone. "Good to see you already understand. I can't afford any mercy in this game, and neither can you. It's best for both of us."

"Of course." Falan drops her voice, now soft. "And Ary? Would you leave her for dead like you left me?"

"We're not talking about Ary. We're talking about you and me."

"Of course," Falan says again. "No help, no hinder. We simply play the game."

Meera hesitates. She obviously has some qualms about the hinder part. "And if we are the last ones standing?"

"Like I said, play the game, Meera. That is our deal. Are we clear?"

A pause. "Clear."

Falan doesn't ask about Ary again. She doesn't want to know Meera's answer.

Preparation for round two is about the same as the previous night—after hours of waiting in their rooms, the competitors are led one by one to the center of the ground floor and blindfolded. Bellamy doesn't say a word, but Lucien gives her the subtlest of nods. Falan looks around at her competition just before the blindfold wraps over her eyes, wondering who will be the next to die. A fourth of them are already gone.

Like last time, Jean-Pierre instructs Lucien to hand out the grants to help aid competitors in the coming round. Falan isn't expecting anything, so her breath hitches in surprise when Lucien presses something folded and silky into her hand. She curls her fingers around the object, but she already knows what it is just by its touch.

An aerial ribbon.

Dismay pricks her. While it's better than nothing, it's not a weapon. An aerial ribbon against Sylvestre and his box of matches seems laughable. She slips it into her coat pocket, wondering how much this grant cost.

Soon after, the dealers come forward to hand each competitor a flask. Falan knows at once that Bellamy is the one approaching her;

she's practically memorized the way he walks. Careful, fleet-footed, like he's creeping up on somebody even in a casual gait. She takes the flask from him, the tips of her fingers brushing his, and drinks.

Falan expects his silence. But when she collapses, he catches her like last time and whispers, "Sunkara, I need you to make it out alive. For both our sakes."

Falan wants to ask what he means, but her mind is too lulled to form a coherent thought. Instead, she thinks of sunrise. Roof jumping. Lavanya burning her tongue while sipping a rare treat of hot chocolate at a café, the best in Paris. She thinks of slender fingers in her hair and small foxes.

Then nothing.

PART III

The Prey

"When those under contract use their Affinities, it's noted that they feel an intense burst of euphoria while having an infinite concentration on their gift. Strangely, however, one group of Affinities, whom we have named Abstractions, shows no mood change under the influence of contract magic. These individuals are still under study, as this is a very curious phenomenon."

—*Guillaume Gallien's Origins of the Arcane*; Ch. 5, p. 98 (1868)

1. Sylvestre - FIRE PERFORMER - King of Spades

2. Hugh - STRONGMAN - King of Hearts

3. Cyril - WEAPON DODGER - King of Diamonds

~~4. Thomas - KNIFE THROWER - Jack of Diamonds~~

5. Eliot - ESCAPIST - Jack of Spades

6. Ronan - TRAPEZE ARTIST - King of Clubs

~~7. Arthur - ACROBATIC BALANCER - Jack of Hearts~~

8. Collette - FIRE PERFORMER - Queen of Spades

~~9. Martin - CONTORTIONIST - Jack of Clubs~~

10. Meera - DEATH DANCER - Queen of Clubs

11. Falan - TRAPEZE ARTIST - Queen of Hearts

12. Channary - TIGHTROPE WALKER - Queen of Diamonds

XXII

November 10, 1896

FALAN AWAKENS IN A FOREST OF STAKES; THE WORLD around her resembles a stained glass window, made of shards. She blinks, her vision clearing to reveal the stakes are actually wooden stilts. The long, skinny poles have several footholds, like carved tree branches, and are lined with snow.

Falan reaches down and scoops up a handful of the white stuff—then immediately shakes it off. It's sharp and prickly, more like bluntly chopped ice than snow. If someone were to fall in it, it would act as the opposite of a cushion. Above her, an array of red and gold tightropes cross at varying heights from stilt to stilt, resembling a poorly knit net. Through the ropes, a patch is left intentionally empty so players can view the sky, barely lit by the setting sun. She can't see the hanging clock.

It's a place that resembles a winter forest of dead trees. A place that should be quiet, perhaps broken only by a creak of wind against the stilts. But instead, she hears applause and Jean-Pierre's voice as he explains to the waiting audience what the rules of the game are.

This time, Falan listens closely. It's as Jules said. Players get ten minutes each to chase and physically tap the other players, and the competitor who taps the fewest will die at the end. The audience chooses the method of death.

But there is something important Jules didn't tell her: At the end of each ten-minute interval, the paths of the stilt forest will switch, ensuring nobody has an unfair advantage at the start of each round. Falan clenches her jaw, knowing that means Jean-Pierre will shift the paths in such a way that she will hardly run into anybody during her turn.

Ninety minutes. *Joue ta chance.*

Just as in the first game, the sounds of the audience and music wash out, but this time they are replaced with the complete silence of the forest. Not even the rustle of wind against wood. The setting no longer soothes her. This is worse than the circus grounds. Here, there are no sounds at all. She's completely alone in this distorted forest of stilts.

For a moment, Falan simply stands there, wondering who the first Hunter will be. She guesses there will be no music this time to alert players of the Hunter's presence. Seconds later, a number and card face light up the sky overhead in gold. The number six and the King of Clubs symbol.

Ronan.

Falan wonders if Ronan will chase her if he sees her. They might be allies, but if the person with the lowest score will be killed at the end of this round, then one person could be the difference between life and a grisly fate. There is no room for small mercies.

As the minutes tick by, Falan is caught on whether to keep moving or stay where she is. Staying feels vulnerable, but if she moves, it increases the risk of bumping right into Ronan. At least here if she sees somebody coming, she can bolt. Her mind foolishly slides to her trapeze partner, wondering how many people he has caught by now, but she pushes the thought away.

Something flits through the stilts. Falan stiffens. She slips behind the nearest post, squinting to track the figure. It's Ronan, chasing after somebody, although she can't tell who. Falan watches with a strange fascination. She has never seen him run like this, so swift-footed. It's almost as graceful as it is terrifying.

But the most horrifying part is that she can't hear any footsteps.

She makes out faint panting as the chase continues, as well as a muttered curse, but no boots slapping against the ground or ice crunching. Through her limited vision, she catches Ronan break a foothold on a stilt as he runs right into it, barely acknowledging the impact. No sound of the wood snapping or hitting the snowbank below. She wouldn't have known had she not seen it with her own eyes.

What a strange place. The lack of sound gives the Hunters even more of an edge, for they will be able to sneak up on anybody with ease.

Ronan doesn't notice her. Falan just barely catches a glimpse of the person he's chasing. It's Meera. She's quick, but Ronan is quicker. He'll catch up to her soon enough.

Falan decides to head in the opposite direction, glad to have seen Ronan and Meera. But as she starts to walk, the deep toll of a bell echoes throughout the forest.

Time's up.

For a moment, nothing. Then, right before her eyes, the stilts start to shift. The tightropes above tangle. Falan shields her face as footholds scratch her. When she lifts her hands, the forest looks no different, but she knows better. She's sure that the Hunter is lurking somewhere nearby, courtesy of Jean-Pierre.

The sky above her lights up once more with a new number and symbol. The number two and the King of Hearts.

Hugh.

Falan lets herself relax, but not too much. Hugh may not be a fast runner, but he could still sneak up on her. As Falan stands beside one of the stilts, her hands resting on its smooth wood, it occurs to her that she can climb it. Her smaller stature has finally given her an advantage, as well as her experience on the trapeze and all those years scaling buildings when roof jumping.

Or . . .

She reaches into her pocket and pulls out the folded aerial ribbon, the color of mashed raspberries. It would be easier on her abdominal injury than climbing. Falan throws the ribbon in the air and it whips around one of the stilt's footholds. After wrapping the ribbon around her waist, she easily makes her way up the length of the stilt.

When Falan is a good ten feet above the ground, she stops on one of the footholds, not daring to go much higher. She may think she's safe up here, but this is Jean-Pierre's world. If needed, she can fall from a higher height safely, but she doesn't want to risk anything, even the chance of a sprained ankle.

Falan tucks herself close to the stilt, wrapping her arms around it. Many of the other competitors won't be able to climb up after her. If they do, she can take to the tightropes. When the bell's deep toll goes off once more, signifying the end of Hugh's ten minutes, Falan uses the ribbon to flip to the ground. She would stay up on the stilt if she could, but she doesn't want to take any chances with the shifting paths or the ropes in the air.

Falan perches on a foothold again during the next interval, which is Meera's, as well. Meera may not be physically as much of a threat as Sylvestre or any of the other Lilies, but Falan is no stranger to her cunning. If Meera sees her, she will chase her. Thankfully, Meera cannot climb. Staying up on the stilts is safe.

For now. Until Jean-Pierre thinks it's getting too easy for her.

To Falan's relief, Meera never comes across her, and she flips back down to the ground as the interval ends, stuffing the ribbon in her pocket. Like before, the stilts in front of her move, and she covers her face to protect it until the shaking stops.

When she takes her hands away, Falan freezes at the sight of Sylvestre, Eliot, and Collette no less than ten feet away.

In the twilight, Sylvestre looks just as ominous as he did back in the circus tents of the Joker. He grins at her knowingly and she only understands when she looks up at the sky, lit up with a new number and symbol.

The number one and the King of Spades. His symbol.

In her peripheral vision, Sylvestre puts a hand on Collette, then on Eliot, immediately ensuring that he has two people tagged.

Falan turns and runs. She doesn't hear Sylvestre's footsteps, but she can hear his panting breaths. She might be fast, but he's gaining on her, especially as she's slowed down by her wounded abdomen. In another minute or two, he will catch her.

Being fair to the players, aren't you? Falan thinks bitterly, nearly slipping on a patch of ice. She looks over her shoulder to gauge how far Sylvestre is. Far enough for her to climb up one of these stilts and wait out his interval. Falan doesn't bother to use the ribbon; her fingers are shaking as she scales the stilt, fear rushing through her. Mainly of Jean-Pierre suddenly making the stilt vanish so she falls right into Sylvestre's grasp.

"Sunkara!" Sylvestre roars up after her as he reaches the base of the stilt. "You coward!"

Falan doesn't bother with a response. She's rooted herself against a high foothold, looking up at the tangle of tightropes above. She's no tightrope walker like Ary, but she knows a thing or two about traveling through the air thanks to her trapeze training. Not to mention, she can use the aerial ribbon to carry her weight across each tightrope. What's important now is keeping Sylvestre's attention. If he wastes all his ten minutes on her, he will have tagged only two people, which might be detrimental.

But then Sylvestre smirks, shaking his head like she doesn't understand something. "Not coming down?" he says, pulling something out of his coat pocket.

His box of matches.

Sylvestre strikes a match and gathers the flame in one hand; it grows as he doubles it in his other hand. The Lily's eyes spark with the euphoria only a magic-enhanced Affinity can evoke, a hungry gleam dancing in the frosty blue of his irises.

Keeping him here doesn't seem like the best idea anymore. "You're willing to waste all ten minutes of your slot on me?" she says.

He scoffs. "You know nothing, Sunkara. I haven't wasted anything."

Sylvestre lifts his hand, readying the flame. She needs to move. She can't get down from the stilt. Using the tightropes to reach another stilt will take time she does not have.

Jump.

Stilts are far less steady than buildings, but she's jumped much farther distances between roofs. Her aerial ribbon can act as a safety net. As flames start to lick the wood, Falan wraps one end of the ribbon around her calf and throws the other end around the nearest stilt before leaping. She can barely think; desperation has overtaken every pore.

Jumpjumpjumpjumpjump—

"You can't run forever, Sunkara!" Sylvestre shouts.

His words startle her as she makes the next jump, and her fingers miss the foothold. Falan plummets through the air, arms still outstretched, when the aerial ribbon sharply tightens around her calf and breaks her fall. Even upside down, Sylvestre's triumphant expression shines clearly. Falan is about to flip back up when somebody pulls the ribbon first. She lifts herself up despite her aching abdomen, reaching for the nearest foothold.

Somebody's hands wrap around her wrists. Hands that have done this before. For a long moment, Falan hangs in the air, a once familiar place that now feels so foreign, blinking up at her savior.

Ronan pulls her up onto the foothold, eyeing her for injuries. "Are you all right?"

Before she can respond, the bell goes off, ending the round—and Sylvestre's chase. Falan turns to see his reaction, but it's too late. As the stilts shift, the foothold suddenly breaks beneath them. Falan automatically stretches her hand for Ronan to take, just as she's done many times before. His fingers wrap around hers and he grabs the aerial ribbon, the two of them dangling in the air.

Ronan pulls himself up onto a foothold, then her, and Falan sets her weight against the stilt's center to keep the foothold from breaking. Ronan darts forward as she nearly loses her balance, wrapping an arm around her to keep her from falling again. When the stilts finally stop moving, she harshly pushes him away.

He glares at her. "That's a nice thank-you for saving your life."

Before Falan can respond, the sky brightens and they both look up through the net of tightropes. The number eleven and the Queen of Hearts is splashed across its indigo surface. A new number and symbol.

Hers.

XXIII

November 10, 1896

THE FIRST THING FALAN SPOTS IS THE GOLDEN clock hanging overhead. Interesting. So only the Hunters can see it.

The second thing is a list of the Hunters so far and how many people they've tagged, marking the sky in scrawled calligraphy. Ronan is tied with Meera in the lead, both having caught three players. Hugh and Sylvestre both have two.

Falan locks eyes with Ronan. But he doesn't run. He stays where he is, watching her with a curious, knowing gaze. She slowly reaches her hand forward, unsure of whether to tap him. It feels like a strange way to repay him after he saved her life.

"It's all right," he says, wrapping his arms around the stilt to steady himself. "I'm in the lead. Your point count will not affect me."

That's all she needs. Falan touches his coat sleeve and Ronan stiffens, unable to move. He thought ahead by wrapping his arms around the stilt because it holds him in place, preventing him from falling off his foothold. After a moment's hesitation, she takes the aerial ribbon and secures it around Ronan's wrists.

"Falan, what are you doing?" he asks as she ties a knot.

"Showing my thanks," she says. "Make sure to give this back after the round is over."

Nine minutes left.

Falan scurries down the stilt with one last look at Ronan, forcing herself to focus. This is her game now. Everybody in this snow-covered forest of stilts is at her mercy. Even Sylvestre. Falan soundlessly moves through the forest, a new energy coursing through her. However, she stops when she spots something strange.

Cyril, the King of Diamonds, is tied to the base of a stilt. He doesn't seem to be struggling to get out of the binds, but when she approaches, he tenses. "Sylvestre and his allies," he says. "They cut one of the tightropes above to tie me up. They both have knives, Collette and Eliot. Grants."

The Lilies' plan is clear. Sabotage. If Cyril is tied up, he won't be able to tag anybody, resulting in the lowest score. It's the same tactic she devised before the round to use as a backup.

"Can you untie me?" Cyril asks desperately.

Falan hesitates for a moment before starting to undo the ropes. "Apologies," she says when her hand accidentally brushes his arm. Cyril's body goes rigid. "I'm the Hunter for this interval."

Her fingers move to one of the knots when a knife suddenly spirals toward her. Falan just manages to move her hand out of the way and the knife grazes Cyril's gut before landing in the snow. He curses loudly as Sylvestre, Collette, and Eliot all step out from behind nearby stilts.

"I was aiming for her heart," Collette says.

"I wouldn't do that," Eliot warns Falan as she raises her hands to the rope again. "He stays tied up."

Falan picks up the thrown knife instead, but Sylvestre is already taking out his box of matches. She pauses. As the Hunter, all she has to do is make contact with the Lilies and her problem is solved. But they are unpredictable and may have more weapons concealed. In a fight against three of them, she stands no chance.

Her eyes flicker up. The stilts are her strength.

Falan scales the stilt Cyril is tied to, the knife between her teeth. Her eyes dart to the hanging clock. Four minutes.

"She did this last time," she hears Sylvestre telling the others. "Hey, Sunkara, Allaire isn't here to catch you this time!"

She perches on a foothold and faces them. *Come close.*

Eliot is the first to approach the stilt. He looks at it, gauging if he can climb it, before saying, "Just set it on fire."

"We can't, you idiot," Sylvestre says, gesturing to a tied-up Cyril. "Besides, there's no chance she can jump to another stilt."

He's right. The nearest one is about thirteen feet away and the farthest distance she's ever jumped is ten. And that was with running momentum across a rooftop. But she doesn't want to flee.

As Collette and Sylvestre walk forward, joining Eliot, Falan makes the drop.

Her outstretched hands catch on the shoulders of both Eliot and Sylvestre, freezing them at once, before she tumbles onto the choppy snow. It feels as if she's rolled right onto a bed of stones. Falan winces as she pulls herself up on aching legs, holding the stolen knife in front of her.

Collette, who managed to avoid Falan's touch, surveys her from a few feet away.

Above them, the clock says there is two and a half minutes left. Enough time for Collette to hurt her, unless she makes the first move.

Falan lunges at her, but Collette somehow slams Falan's left hand against the stilt, her nails digging into the slit on Falan's palm that Sylvestre sliced yesterday. Collette is frozen, but Falan is the one who drops to her knees with a gasp. Fresh blood bubbles from the wound, spilling onto the snow below. She puts her hand against the snow, hoping it will relieve some of the pain, but the ice burns.

A few feet away, Sylvestre watches with a triumphant grin.

The bell goes off, echoing through the forest. Her time is up.

Falan barely manages to look up, her vision swimming, and sees she's been added to the scoreboard above Ronan's name. She is now in the lead with five people tagged. But there's still forty minutes left. She's not safe from death despite being at the top of the board.

The world around her starts to shift in preparation for a new interval, and Falan pulls herself to her feet, cradling her bloody hand. By the time she looks up, she is alone.

Chance, Cyril.

Above her, the sky lights up with a new Hunter's number and symbol. The number eight and the Queen of Spades. Collette.

That means they will keep hunting Falan. At least she still has the knife Collette threw at her. Her safest bet is to take to the ropes, but she doubts she can climb the stilts very well with her injured hand. However, if she can manage to, she could settle there for as long as possible.

Holding the knife between her teeth once more, Falan manages to hoist herself onto a lower foothold without much trouble. Her years on the trapeze have given her an edge, finishing shows with pulled muscles and broken bones.

However, when she reaches the third foothold about ten feet off the ground, it breaks. For a moment she's startled—she could not hear any sounds of the wood cracking. The next second she's free-falling through the air, curling into a tumble at the last moment. The rough snow cracks against her back, adding to the previous aches.

Falan stumbles to her feet, brushing snow off her clothes as she stares up at the stilt, then at the remains of the foothold. It should not have broken. It was far too thick.

Suspicious, Falan tries another stilt a few feet away. She makes it to the second foothold before it gives way. This time, she lands on her feet.

This is Jean-Pierre's doing.

Falan dares not try another stilt. It's clear Jean-Pierre intends for her to be on the ground so her enemies can reach her. She looks up at the clock, which has remained visible to her. A little less than seven minutes to go in this interval. She will not go looking for trouble. But she knows Jean-Pierre will have placed Collette somewhere nearby.

"Where are you?" Falan mutters.

Just as she utters the words, something moves behind a nearby stilt. She sees a thick lock of coppery hair, a pale hand curling around the wood, the corner of a red coat.

Perhaps if Collette had been there when Falan first joined the Cirque, she would have been too intimidated to speak to her because of her beauty. The long silky hair, the red lips, the clear green eyes. But Collette joined two and a half years ago, and by then, Falan knew there were more reasons to fear a person beyond their beauty. Their brains, for instance. Their skills. Their selfishness, superiority.

Collette steps out from behind the stilt. "Well, well, look who I happened upon."

There are five and a half minutes left for this interval. Fighting Collette is out of the question. There is no battle if Collette lays so much as a finger on her.

She has no choice but to run.

"I'll have to take my knife back," Collette says, eyeing the blade in Falan's hand. "The second I freeze you, I'll stab your heart with it."

Falan takes off. She nearly slips on a patch of slick ice, throwing her momentum forward to keep going. She can't hear how close Collette is, so she's forced to constantly look over her shoulder. With the threat of running right into somebody or tripping, Falan finds herself half stumbling, mind a whirl.

Not in a straight line, she tells herself.

She can't keep this up for thirty-five minutes. No matter who the Hunter is, the Lilies will be trying to kill her.

Collette starts getting desperate once the clock hits the three-minute mark. So does Falan. Running is torture at this point, and her wounds and aching muscles scream in pain. She glances back to see Collette speeding up, gaining on her. Falan's heart kicks. Time to change direction again.

Falan turns to her left and skids to a stop, nearly slipping on the snow. The odds of this are next to none. But there he is. Cyril, still tied to the stilt. His eyes widen when they lock with hers. Falan runs up to him, slipping the knife between the ropes to cut them.

"How far away is she?" Falan asks.

"Hurry," Cyril says raggedly, looking over her shoulder.

"Can you cut them yourself?" Falan asks as a rope finally rips.

"No. I'm frozen."

Falan quickens her movements, managing to cut three of the four loops before slipping away just as Collette approaches. She starts to run again, but a figure steps in front of her from behind a stilt, blocking her path. Sylvestre.

Impulsively, she starts to climb the stilt Cyril is tied to, eyes fixed on the tightropes above her. If she can reach them, she'll be safe. She hears Sylvestre struggling to climb after her. The top of the stilt is about fifteen feet in the air, shorter than most of the others, but there are at least two ropes crossing the space just below.

Falan is about to walk the tightrope when she spots Eliot on the other side, perched at the top of the connected stilt. A triumphant grin pulls his lips up, his knife ready to sever the rope.

It's a trap. One she so foolishly walked into.

Falan whirls around, about to climb down, but it's too late because Sylvestre has caught up. She freezes, just a moment of hesitation. But that's all he needs to send a blow across her face, knocking her off the stilt and plunging her into the darkness below.

XXIV

November 10, 1896

AFTER HIS DISTRACTED BEHAVIOR IN THE HONOR box the night before, Bellamy is now designated to the ticket booth. But it has proved to work in his favor. As soon as the last patron was admitted, Bellamy slipped unnoticed into the crowd and found a spot next to Lucien in the back row.

Falan was doing well and shone even brighter when she gathered the most points during her turn as the Hunter—until the Lilies led her into a trap.

Now Bellamy's heart races as he watches her fall from the stilt. One of the tightropes catches her, but she slides off before falling against another and hitting the ground below. The crowd breaks into whispers. Some are giddy, hoping for another elimination.

The man in front of Bellamy curses loudly. "I might as well throw my money in the Seine," he grumbles.

His friend next to him laughs. "You thought a little girl like her would stand a chance? How foolish."

Bellamy barely hears any of them, a ringing in his ears drowning out the world. His nails dig into his palms. "Sunkara, get up," he whispers.

But she doesn't.

The Lilies gather on the ground around her, where they begin arguing over who should check whether Falan is still alive—and, if she is, whether they should kill her now or wait until she regains consciousness—not even noticing when the stilts around them shift, removing Cyril from their sight, and a new symbol flashes overhead.

Eventually, Sylvestre is the one who checks. A scowl twists his mouth. "She's breathing. I'm certain she'll wake up in a few minutes." He grabs Collette's knife from Falan's uncurled hand.

"She'd better," Collette says, crossing her arms. "Otherwise, I'm sticking my knife in her chest and finishing the job."

Eliot scoffs. "Where's the fun in that? The audience came for a show, we might as well give them one."

"Cut one of the tightropes and tie her up," Sylvestre orders. He's still looking down at Falan. "She'll thrash like vermin when she wakes." When Eliot and Collette leave to cut down a tightrope, he brutally kicks Falan in the stomach. "I hope you felt that."

Bellamy doesn't realize he's standing, jaw clenched, until Lucien touches his arm. When he still doesn't sit, Lucien pulls him back down. "Durand, keep your head," he says in a low voice. "You don't want to attract attention."

Bellamy isn't sure how much it matters at this point. If Falan dies, then he's dead too. But the one thing he knows is that, game or not, he will kill Sylvestre if someone else doesn't kill him first.

Up in the honor box, Jules is watching not the round but the discontentment on his father's face. It puzzles him, for his father certainly holds no fondness for Falan.

"What's the matter?" he finally asks.

Blanchet laces his fingers together. "Monsieur Jean-Pierre promised to surprise us with his setting, but I can't help but feel rather disappointed."

It's then that Jules realizes that his father is not watching the round either. He's watching Jean-Pierre, who stands hidden away in a corner of the Chapiteau, unseen to everyone except those in the honor box. "You're not satisfied with the forest of stilts?" Jules asks.

"Are *you*?"

The question feels loaded; there doesn't seem to be a right answer. "Well, it was certainly a surprise to me," Jules finally says.

Blanchet scoffs but thankfully doesn't press. "He took my game—my vision—and turned it into something of his own." He raises a glass of wine to his lips for a drink. "That's unacceptable, don't you think?"

"Yes," Jules says at once, knowing the right answer this time.

Blanchet takes another sip of wine. "Only fools would dare oppose me. Monsieur Jean-Pierre proved to be one."

Jules's heart speeds up, thinking of how he's been feeding Falan information about the rounds, sneaking into his father's private gallery.

Fools indeed, him the biggest one of all.

XXV

November 10, 1896

ACCORDING TO LAVANYA, AN ENHANCED AFFINITY felt otherworldly. Falan could see it clearly in her shining, wide-eyed expression when on the trapeze, inhaling on her highest jump as if taking her first breath of air. Lavanya had never looked happier. She was ethereal, effortless, on top of the world. She was perfect, always so perfect.

It was something that breathed life into the dead-eyed performers for mere minutes.

It was something Falan craved, desperate to experience even a mere taste of it.

It'd been six months since Falan and Lavanya had joined the Cirque, but Falan still hadn't officially signed a contract with Jean-Pierre. She lived at the Cirque and trained, but something separated her from the others. Watching Lavanya on the trapeze released a dark hunger for the same kind of gift—the same kind of high—even if it meant signing a contract.

And she would have done so, had Lavanya repeatedly told her not to sign with Jean-Pierre.

"As soon as you save up enough money, you'll have the chance to go to your father," Lavanya had said. "You'll have nothing holding you back."

Falan doubted her father spared a thought toward her after all these months. She'd occasionally considered writing to him, to tell him where she was and why she never met up with him. But each time she'd tried, she could never find the right way to explain her circumstances. More so, she doubted he'd come looking for her if she did. It was not like they were particularly close even before he left India. He had probably forgotten altogether that he invited her to live with him. "What about you?" she asked instead. "You came all the way here for a diamond that you still have not found."

Lavanya shrugged. "Can't be helped. I have to finish my contract."

So Falan hadn't signed a contract, despite the hunger gnawing at her. But no matter how much training she put in, she would never reach Lavanya's skill. There was no point in comparing herself to somebody whose Affinity was enhanced by an Enchanteur's magic; it could not be matched.

Jean-Pierre, seeing her desire, started to coax her. Manipulate her. Tell her she could do great things if she signed with him. That he could easily kick her back out onto the street because she was not signed. Even that Lavanya was holding her back. The insatiable desire continued to gnaw at her for months, until one day it overwhelmed her entirely. Dark and wretched and greedy, the ugliest combination of her personal demons.

That night, nearly a year since she and Lavanya met Jean-Pierre on the icy streets, Falan sought the ringmaster out. Later, she stood in his office. A sheet of paper lay on the desk between them.

Jean-Pierre watched her carefully. "You know your Affinity, do you not?"

"Acrobatics, like my sister." Falan paused. "Is that correct?"

For a minute, Jean-Pierre said nothing. He stared at her like he was seeing right through her. Then he nodded. "Of course."

The first thing Falan is aware of is her pounding head. It feels like it has split in two. Her cheek is pressed up against ice, the taste of blood and snow in her mouth. The other side of her face is swollen, pulsing with pain, and she moans softly.

The second she shifts onto her back, the bottom of a boot is pressed against her stomach, right where her abdomen is injured. Falan's eyes flutter open to see the three Lilies standing above her in blurry silhouettes. The stilts around her sway, the tightropes crossing above in a kaleidoscope of gold and red.

"I told you she'd wake up before the round ended." The weight of the boot on her stomach increases.

Falan coughs, attempting to move her arms, only to realize they have been tied behind her back. Her legs are bound too with the same sturdy rope.

"Good, because a few minutes more and we couldn't have waited," Collette says.

"She's a lucky one. How on earth did she survive falling from the stilt?" Eliot says.

"Those two ropes broke her fall. A pity they didn't break her neck."

The tightropes. Falan doesn't recall hitting them on the way down, but she hardly remembers falling at all. The last thing she remembers is Sylvestre right behind her at the top of the stilt, a wild look of victory in his eyes. The look of a predator that has cornered its prey.

La Proie—living up to its name.

"It's worth it. Eliot was right; let's give them a show. The more entertaining we make her death, the more likely bettors will give us grants," Sylvestre says with a smile.

Perhaps if she hadn't killed Arthur, then Eliot and Collette would not be this eager for her death. Not like Sylvestre, who has always expressed a dangerous amount of hatred.

Or perhaps that's just the Game.

Falan's eyes drift to the scoreboard above. Eleven names are on the board so far—the only player missing is the King of Diamonds. Cyril. Which means this is the last interval and he is the Hunter.

Nine minutes on the clock.

"Pin her down," Sylvestre says. His murderous gaze sends fear penetrating through Falan's dizziness. "Let's give this round a grand finale."

Falan tries to sit up, but Sylvestre kicks her back down as Collette pins her shoulders and Eliot takes her legs. She's screaming, thrashing in their grip, bound hands curling futilely for Collette's knife. Sylvestre holds it up in front of her with a mocking grin.

"Looking for this?" He slaps her in the face before placing a hand over her mouth to muffle her shouts. "Shut up. You're hurting my ears."

A new type of wild panic, deep-rooted horror, bursts from within Falan when she realizes how trapped she is. How powerless.

Jean-Pierre's dark grin flashes in her mind, followed by the stinging memory of a slap. He has always tried to render her powerless. And she let herself get drawn in, fell prey to her own greed despite the many warnings beforehand, until she ultimately found herself trapped. A puppet on his string, just like all the other performers.

He must be watching right now, relishing the chance to witness her die. Relishing his victory against her.

Falan struggles more, this time strong enough that Eliot recoils in surprise. She kicks out at him, nearly catching him, but he grabs her bound legs again at the last second.

"Hold her properly!" Collette snaps at him. "She's barely five feet. She shouldn't be difficult to hold still!"

"How should we start this?" Sylvestre asks, dragging the tip of the knife from Falan's collar to her chest. "A simple stab through the heart is too quick. Perhaps I carve something into your skin." His smirk grows. "Yes, I think that would get the message across. A nice design, perhaps."

"Hurry up," Collette says impatiently. "We only have five minutes left."

Sylvestre pulls Falan's coat off her left arm and rips her shirt sleeve, tracing the knife down her bare shoulder. He stops a few times, as if he's going to stab her, but continues to drag the blade farther each time.

"Sunkara," Sylvestre says in a low voice, leaning close to her, "even as I watch the life leave your eyes, I want you to know that you deserve nothing better than to die on soiled, dirty snow, reflecting on your sins."

Falan realizes the knife has stopped again just before Sylvestre shoves it deep into her arm. Pain shrouds Falan's mind, pushing out any coherent thoughts, and she's screaming into his palm.

"That's it, petite fille, scream all you wish," Sylvestre says with a smile, his voice mockingly soothing. "It's music to my ears."

He drives the knife deeper, pulling it up her arm to lengthen the gash. Falan's screams dry to pitiful gasps, and her lungs burn for relief. Blood pools beneath her, a widening puddle of crimson on the snow.

But before Sylvestre can get any farther, Collette suddenly collapses, frozen. Sylvestre only has time to tilt his head up before he too freezes and falls over. Eliot moves back and Falan looks up with a shudder, breathing hard. Standing above them is Cyril, picking up the knife Sylvestre dropped.

Cyril slices through the ropes binding Falan's wrists and legs, careful not to touch her, before placing the knife in her lap. Although she cannot respond in her state, she understands what he just did. They are even now. She freed him from the stilt, and he just saved her from being tortured to death.

Before she can speak, the hairs on the back of her neck stand. Falan turns to see a seething Eliot throw his knife at them. She instinctively shields her face with her good arm, and Cyril, with his weaponry Affinity, effortlessly grabs the knife before it hits him.

With a frustrated growl, Eliot goes for Falan, spitting and snarling curses as he tackles her. A wave of white-hot pain hits her as her arm knocks against the ice. She gasps, immobilized, as Eliot rips Collette's knife from her grip.

Above, the clock shows three minutes left.

"Kill her, Eliot!" Sylvestre yells from his frozen spot on the ground. "Kill her!"

Eliot looms over her, about to strike, before something suddenly embeds in his stomach. He stops, looking down at his own knife sticking out of him, thrown by Cyril, who walks over with a satisfied smirk. "There's still time for her to kill all three of you," he says.

"Bastard," Eliot gasps, dropping to his knees and letting go of Collette's knife.

Cyril picks it up and brushes snow off the blade before holding it out to Falan. "Kill them before I do."

Falan stares at him for a moment. Then she takes the knife. Cyril saved her life again. To repay the debt, she needs to carry the burden of killing somebody.

But to her, it's not a burden. It's an opportunity.

Cyril suddenly shudders. His dark eyes go wide, and blood runs from his lips. When Falan pushes herself to her feet, she sees Eliot holding his knife in Cyril's back, careful not to make physical contact with him. Cyril collapses, coughing blood into the snow, and Eliot's furious gaze rests on Falan. There is nothing stopping him anymore.

Falan feels it bubbling up inside her, that same twisted, ugly hunger that once pushed her to sign with Jean-Pierre. Only now, it's to see somebody's corpse at her feet. Her bloodied arm burns with agony and fury.

So when Eliot stands and lunges at her, she brings the knife in front of her, aiming for his jugular. It's too late for him to stop. By the time he realizes what has happened, the blade is already deep in his throat.

The forest is silent except for Cyril's bloody gurgles. Sylvestre and Collette watch with wide, horrified eyes.

Eliot gasps, blood running from his lips. Falan stretches the moment, making sure he sees the complete lack of pity in her eyes before she yanks the knife out. Fresh blood splatters across her clothes as Eliot falls forward. Red stains the snow beneath them, joining the puddle already there. Falan uses her foot to nudge him onto his back, wanting the last thing he sees to be her. And then she stabs him again, right through the heart.

Falan looks up at the clock. Ten seconds left.

It's enough time to kill one more Lily, but, as during the previous round, her senses start to overstimulate. The smell of snow and soil and blood heighten along with everything she still feels. A hand over her mouth, a foot on her chest, rope around her hands and legs. Her own heart, beating so fast it might stop. Falan collapses next to a semiconscious Cyril, locking eyes with him.

"Why?" she manages to ask. They barely even know each other—yet he saved her life.

"You saved me first," Cyril says, as if reading her thoughts, then chuckles a little. "The weapons evader . . . felled by a weapon. Ironic." He pauses. "What's the use of saving each other if we have to kill each other later?"

It's rhetorical, but Falan says, "I don't know."

Another laugh, this one more of a sob. "They can't force me to be complicit if I'm dead."

Then, all at once, the forest disappears. The only thing left is Cyril lying next to her, tears running from his now dead eyes, the remains of a bitter smile on his lips.

XXVI

November 10, 1896

THE CACOPHONY OF THE AUDIENCE RUSHES BACK into Ary's ears. She keeps her eyes squeezed shut for longer than she should; facing the crowd somehow terrifies her more than the forest of stilts. At least during the round, nobody was targeting her in particular.

Ary finally opens her eyes when the spectators start jeering. Confused, she looks around, her stomach rolling at the sight of the corpses on the stage. Sylvestre and Collette are hovering over Eliot, begging him to wake up. Only yards away, Falan kneels by a motionless Cyril, but she's not looking at him. She doesn't seem to be looking at anything really.

"Ary." Somebody pulls her to her feet. Meera. "Are you all right?"

Ary nods, her gaze still on Falan. Ronan Allaire has walked over to her and is helping her to her feet, wrapping an arm around her waist when her knees buckle. It's then that Ary sees the amount of blood saturating Falan's sleeve, dripping onto the stage.

"It's a miracle she's still conscious," Meera says, having followed Ary's gaze, but doesn't sound sympathetic in the slightest.

Now that her mind is less tilted from the adjustment to reality, Ary's thoughts go back to the scoreboard. Her score was two, but it wasn't the only one. Has a tie ever happened before?

When the crowd's jeers grow louder, Jean-Pierre appears on the stage seemingly out of nowhere. "It appears we have a bit of a problem, my dear guests," he says. "I promised you that you would decide how to eliminate the player with the lowest score, but far too many performers have tied with a score of two."

"Kill them all!" one spectator yells, and Ary's stomach drops.

"No! That won't leave much for the next few games!" another refutes him.

The crowd's arguments layer over one another, creating such a racket that Ary has to restrain from putting her hands over her ears. They're closing in on her, all these masked figures, calling for blood simply for a few minutes of entertainment.

Jean-Pierre spreads his hand and a breeze washes over the audience, quieting them. "After speaking with the panel, we have come to a solution," he says. "We invite you to choose a way that gives all of the lowest-scoring competitors an equal chance of being eliminated."

The audience members call out several suggestions, but Ary hears one above all the rest, one that has her trembling. Meera's arm loops through hers.

"It seems we've reached a consensus," Jean-Pierre says with a grin. "La roulette russe shall be our decider!"

Ary can barely breathe. She watches as Jean-Pierre waves a hand and the scoreboard appears in front of them, this time without the deceased players. At the top is Falan with five points, followed by Ronan, Meera, and Collette with three. At the bottom are her, Sylvestre, and Hugh with two. Never did Ary think she'd be in the same position as Sylvestre. Neither did he, apparently, because his surprise nearly overshadows his anger.

The lights in the Chapiteau disappear, darkness enveloping the tent. A tug jolts in Ary's chest, the telltale pull of le Lien. She unhooks her arm from Meera's and walks forward tentatively, stopping when she no longer feels the pull. Spotlights suddenly beam down directly on Ary, Sylvestre, and Hugh.

“There is one bullet in my pistol’s chamber,” Jean-Pierre says from somewhere in front of them. “We’ll go in order of your playing numbers.”

Ary watches as Jean-Pierre stands in front of Sylvestre, aiming the pistol at his head. If Sylvestre is afraid, he doesn’t show it. When Jean-Pierre pulls the trigger, nothing comes out.

Silence. Then roaring cheers from Sylvestre’s bettors. The Lily grins in triumph, waving to the audience, who finally hushes when Jean-Pierre moves to Hugh.

Ary closes her eyes, unable to watch. For the first time, she’s wishing death upon somebody, and it sickens her. It isn’t in a malicious manner but a desperate one, which only makes her feel like more of a coward. She forces herself to calm down. She thinks of Meera. Falan. She thinks of them at a table at the bouillon, the only moments she’s felt safe for the past seven months. Meera laughing, glimpses of Falan’s rare smile, amused and wry yet somehow sad at the same time.

She thinks further back. She pretends she’s not here. That she never contracted herself to that French diplomat and came to France on the naive whim that she would eventually make connections, creating a better life for herself and her family. She’s back in Srok Khmer, enjoying her mother’s amok trei. Her mother, who has no clue where she is, that she’s fighting for her life right now, that—

A bang rips Ary out of her thoughts and she flinches, her eyes shooting open. Beside her, Hugh lies on the ground, blood running from the bullet wound in his head. Some of it flecks her boots. Soft lights illuminate the Chapiteau once more, and Ary barely remembers falling in line with the other remaining players. All she can think about is how brutally her thoughts were ripped from her. One moment, she could almost taste her mother's amok trei, the fish dissolving in her mouth.

The next moment, the blood of a corpse is on her shoes—and the sweet, gut-wrenching relief of living another day rushes through her.

Outside, the grounds are abuzz with conversation as the audience discuss highlights from the round. As he walks among the spectators, Lucien hears some points more than others. Disappointment and shock over Cyril and Hugh both dying. Anticipation for the battle between Sylvestre and Falan; it appears everybody wants to see those two duel in the finale, with Sylvestre as the winner. Tired, Lucien walks around to the back of the Chapiteau for a moment alone. But instead, he finds Jules there, taking deep breaths as if he might vomit.

"Drink too much wine?" Lucien says snidely.

Jules shoots him a glare over his shoulder. "Come to judge me?"

"On the contrary, I wish you'd brought me some. I'd have appreciated it."

Jules adjusts his coat. "We have nothing to discuss. Why are you here?"

Lucien tilts his face up to the night sky, just barely dotted with stars. "I wanted a moment alone. It appears I've been robbed of that."

"That makes two of us," Jules huffs.

In the dark of the night, with the moonlight sloppily spilling over the Chapiteau, it could be beautiful; the red stripes look almost black in the darkness, the white, gray. The world is devoid of color, an accurate reflection of his life. But there's this boy next to him with coiffed hair and strangely accusing eyes, like an accidental smear of paint across a finished canvas.

"Won't your father be looking for you?" Lucien asks, cutting into the silence.

"No."

The short answer surprises Lucien, but he doesn't pry. Instead, he takes note of the nauseous look on the boy's face and asks, "Do you still feel like vomiting?"

Jules shakes his head. "I can't tell if you're making fun of me or not," he admits after a pause.

"Why would I be making fun of you?"

"See, even now! You speak in that tone and I can't be certain!" Jules exclaims, pointing a finger at him.

In the night it's hard to tell, but Lucien swears the boy's cheeks go scarlet. The sight oddly threatens to bring on a smile. "I'm not making fun of you," he says honestly. "To make fun of one's reaction to anxieties is petty and underhanded."

"Oh." Jules looks rather surprised by this declaration.

"There are plenty of other things about you to make fun of," Lucien adds, unable to help himself, and Jules's cheeks flare once more. This time, Lucien can't stop the smile that tugs his lips up.

"I knew it. You *are* making fun of me," Jules moans, removing his spectacles to briefly rub his eyes.

"It's hard not to," Lucien admits.

When Jules turns to him, it is the first time he's truly seen the boy's eyes without his golden glasses around them. There's that flicker of ever-present fear, and Lucien suddenly finds himself wanting to rough up the boy—mess up his hair, rumple his clothes. Just to feel something more from him.

But to feel something from him is not important. The smile fades from Lucien's face. There is only one reason this boy is around—for information. Otherwise neither of them would dream of interacting with the other.

The medical tent is much emptier tonight. With only six players left, the competition has truly reached its halfway mark. A little earlier than Falan's liking, for there are still three more days to go. Three more games to fight through.

Falan doesn't realize she's drifting off, leaning against Ronan's shoulder, until he gently shakes her. "Falan," he says quietly, and her eyes blink open.

Her arm doesn't hurt anymore. But through her haze, she knows the blood loss is making her lightheaded. Falan's eyes flicker down to see blood has soaked into her seat's cushion. Her head once again falls against Ronan's shoulder, her eyes fluttering shut.

"Falan." He shakes her once more, trying to make her stay awake.

"What is the likelihood that I'll get a medical grant?" Falan asks.

She doesn't hear his response, caught in a place between consciousness and darkness. She still feels the curve of his shoulder against her cheek, his hand brushing against hers. Sometime later, she feels a shift. The shoulder she's resting against isn't quite as broad. When Falan's eyes finally open again, it's not Ronan next to her but Ary.

"What are you doing?" she asks. When Ary doesn't move, Falan pushes herself away. "Where's Ronan?"

"The physician called him," Ary says.

"If Ary hadn't rushed to support you, you would have pitched forward and smashed your head against the ground," Meera's callous voice says from a few chairs away.

"You would have liked that," Falan says coolly.

"I would."

"Both of you, stop," Ary says. Then suddenly, she starts laughing. When Falan and Meera stare in surprise, Ary laughs harder. She finally calms down after a minute. "I'm sorry, I didn't mean to laugh. It's just . . . been a while since I've done that."

For a moment, Meera looks remorseful. But then the physician slides the curtain open, and she goes to get checked as Ronan departs. On his way out, he stops by Falan and pulls the aerial ribbon out of his pocket. "Thank you for leaving this with me," he says. "That was . . . generous of you."

Not generous. Just a debt repaid. But Falan takes the ribbon back with a nod.

When the physician finally calls her, Falan stumbles to the table behind the curtain, already trying to think how she will survive with this wound. Her bruised abdomen is nothing compared to her bloody arm, which she can barely move.

But then the physician says, "You received quite a lot of medical grants tonight, Sunkara." He eyes her suspiciously, as if she must have somehow bewitched the audience. "Enough to cover all of your major wounds."

Perhaps he's expecting triumph, but Falan is just as shocked as he is. She anticipated that more of the audience would view her as a contender after killing not one but two Lilies, but she didn't expect them to buy any grants for her, let alone major ones. She strips off her coat, and the physician studies her mutilated arm.

"You're lucky," he says. "This might have been fatal if the knife had gone a few inches higher and nicked an artery."

He puts his hand on the wound and Falan watches. She's seen the physician heal injured performers after shows a handful of times over the past five years, but she's still fascinated. Manipulating the skin and muscle and blood vessels themselves, the physician uses his magic to knit the wound back together, both internally and externally. When he's finished, it looks like her arm was never injured; there isn't even a scar.

XXVII

November 10, 1896

BELLAMY STANDS OUTSIDE THE MEDICAL TENT, waiting for Falan so he can escort her back inside the Aviary. All he has to do is tell Falan to meet in the gallery tomorrow at the same time as before. And yet, he is barely thinking about that. When Falan exits the tent, Bellamy can see her swollen cheek in the meager light of the moon, bruised purple from Sylvestre's punch.

But her left arm looks fine. Completely healed. "A grant?" Bellamy asks in disbelief.

She nods. "It seems, after stabbing another Lily tonight, several people put forth money to heal my major wounds."

"So your wound from the beam hitting you yesterday . . ."

"Healed too." Despite this news, she seems indifferent. Hollow.

Something is off. Perhaps it's the look in her eyes, duller than usual. Or perhaps it's the way she's swaying just slightly like she's about to collapse. They don't speak as Bellamy leads her to the Aviary, until he opens the door and she stares blankly down the staircase.

Before Bellamy knows what he's doing, he's scooped her up into his arms and is carrying her down the stairs.

"Are you mad?" Falan says, but there's no real venom in her voice. "The other players and Jean-Pierre will see."

"See what? Me escorting you like I'm supposed to?" Bellamy says. Falan finally shoots him a glare. She looks so much more like her usual self that Bellamy is relieved. "I'll put you down once we reach the bottom corridor so nobody sees."

She huffs slightly but doesn't struggle. Instead, she curls deeper into his hold, her head against his chest. Bellamy hopes she doesn't hear how fast his heart is beating; it's like it has a mind of its own.

"Are you staying with Allaire again tonight?" he asks.

"Yes."

Bellamy can't help but feel annoyed. Ronan Allaire, of all people. He knows how much Falan despises Ronan. She's mentioned him unfavorably numerous times over the years, although it's never been clear to Bellamy why Falan hates Ronan specifically. He's always assumed it's because Ronan is a Lily, but it's odd that she would suddenly ally with him now.

Bellamy rolls his eyes. *I bet the bed in his room is half the reason why. It must be ten times better than the ones in the boardinghouse.*

Once they reach the ground floor, in the east hallway, Bellamy finally sets Falan down. When she sways, his arm curls around her slight figure. Falan gazes up at him, her brown eyes neither venomous nor faraway, and Bellamy's breath catches in his throat. For a moment, the two of them are frozen. It's only a second, but it's curiously long. Bellamy finally lets her go, clearing his throat.

"Gallery tomorrow. Same time," he mutters shortly before they walk down the hallway. Bellamy drops her off for the grant retrievals, noting the others' shock at seeing Falan's arm healed, and leaves. His shift time is set from three to four in the morning, so he's free to go to the bouillon for a late-night meal, maybe the boardinghouse for some sleep.

But he doesn't. Instead, Bellamy stops after the first staircase on the floor above, wondering which room is Ronan Allaire's. He must be the only one left on this floor; Sylvestre and Collette are above, while Falan, Meera, and Ary are on the floor below.

Don't do anything stupid, Bellamy tells himself. The smart thing would be to leave and come back in the morning to meet the others in the gallery.

Instead, Bellamy waits. He decides to stay put in the room in the east hall until the competitors return to their rooms, slipping inside. At once, he knows that this room is Ronan's. The bed is big enough for two people, and the room has its own lavatory, something only Lilies receive. Bellamy walks farther inside, running his hand on the white sheets atop the bed. He pictures Falan lying on the sheets, the same sheets Ronan lay on, and a strange feeling of malevolence washes over him.

The doorknob rattles and Bellamy swivels. The door opens and Falan walks in, Ronan shutting the door behind them and locking it. It seems Collette's knife is no longer in Falan's possession. Neither of them has any new grants.

Falan is the first to spot Bellamy and freezes.

Then Ronan sees him and jumps in surprise. "What the hell?"

"Durand, what are you doing here?" Falan asks.

That's a good question. One that Bellamy doesn't quite know the answer to. "I wasn't in the mood to walk to the boardinghouse and back before my patrol shift, so I figured I'd stay here," he says with that dangerously innocuous smile. "Did you not want company?"

"Durand," Falan says warningly.

Ronan raises an eyebrow. "Are you even allowed to stay here?"

"No rules against it," Bellamy lies. "It isn't as though I'm intervening in anything."

"Then go to one of the abandoned bedrooms," Ronan says, unmoved. "Not here."

"I came to check on her," Bellamy says without thinking. The words come so suddenly, he surprises himself.

Ronan scoffs. "Is that so?"

Bellamy looks at Falan. He's unsure of what he wants her to do, still unsure of what he's doing here. When she keeps quiet, not even looking at him, Bellamy turns to leave.

Slender fingers suddenly wrap around his wrist. "Don't." Falan's voice is barely audible. "Stay."

"Falan," Ronan says in surprise.

There's that hollow, faraway look on her face once more, her normally sharp eyes dull. "Are you sure?" Bellamy asks, stepping close to her. As close as they were back in the hallway, with his arm around her waist.

When she tilts her head up, Bellamy is thrown off guard. Falan's large, dark eyes gaze at him under long lashes. Curious, and exhausted. So very exhausted.

She nods and lets go of his wrist, stepping away. Bellamy clears his dry throat, his cheeks warm.

Ronan watches them, his face blank. "You can use the lavatory, if you need to wash off," he finally says to Falan, eyeing her blood-soaked outfit.

Unlike her clothes, his are clean. Too clean. Any dirt vanished with the illusion, and the only flaw in his outfit is a tear in his shirt sleeve. It makes Bellamy dislike him all the more.

Wordlessly, Falan walks into the connecting room and kneels in front of one of the two buckets, which is full of water. But to Bellamy's surprise, the only thing she washes are her hands, scrubbing dried blood off her skin.

"Sunkara," Bellamy says.

She doesn't answer, staring ahead blankly.

"Sunkara," Bellamy says again, gentler, and she looks back at him this time. "You should sleep."

"He's right. You took first watch last night. I'll take it this time," Ronan says.

"You fell asleep on your watch last night," Falan says as she joins them in the bedroom.

"I'll make sure he stays awake until I leave for my shift," Bellamy promises.

Oddly, Falan doesn't protest. "Wake me before you leave," she says, lying down on the bed.

"I will," Bellamy says, but he has no intention of it. He might as well return after his shift and stay awake the whole night if it means she gets a few more hours of rest.

Falan drifts off eventually, still restless. When he's sure she's asleep, Bellamy walks over and spreads the comforter over her.

Just watching tonight's round was brutal. Living it must have been an entirely different thing. He wonders how she felt shoving the knife into Eliot's throat. He wonders if she felt the same way he did the first time he killed somebody back in Marseille.

Yet the panic he experienced when she fell from the stilt, when Sylvestre was about to kill her, was overwhelming. Hearing her muffled scream as Sylvestre shoved the knife into her arm, as he tortured her. Bellamy can tell himself his fear was due to losing his shot at paying Horrent back, but he'd be lying.

Still, he's not ready to admit to himself that the thought of her dying scares him for reasons beyond not being able to pay off his debt. Falan Sunkara has never been a girl easy to care about.

"What's your relation to her?" Ronan asks quietly from the chaise, breaking the silence. "You're taking a large risk by being here."

Bellamy doesn't respond at first. He feels like he's caught somewhere between a dream and reality, where this night isn't really happening. He finally turns to look at Ronan, who is still waiting for his answer. "She's an associate and I wanted to check on her. That's it."

"You'd risk severe punishment from Blanchet or Jean-Pierre just to check on her? I don't believe it," Ronan says.

Bellamy speaks before he can think. "Why not? You wouldn't risk it for her?"

Ronan falters, suddenly looking unsure of himself. "That is not what I meant." A pause. "Do you . . . hold feelings for her? It's the only reason I can think of for you to take such a risk."

"Here's a question: Why are you helping her? I noticed you both aiding each other over the past two rounds," Bellamy says, ignoring Ronan's query. "She has mentioned you before and how you've acted toward her. You've never liked her."

Ronan rolls his eyes. "She's not particularly inviting, in case you haven't noticed."

Bellamy shrugs. He has a point there.

"I never said I didn't like her. It's . . . complicated. Everything is when it comes to her," Ronan says gruffly.

Bellamy lingers on that last sentence. It sounds far more layered than the simple frustrations of a grudging ally.

"But I'm looking out for her because I know her sister would want that," Ronan continues.

"If you're going to lie, you should practice more."

"I'm not lying." Ronan suddenly turns to look Bellamy in the eye. He appears oddly ashamed. "Why else would I want to help her?" His gaze drifts to Falan lying asleep on the bed, and he repeats in a whisper, as if talking to himself, "Why would I want to help her?"

That is the question indeed. Bellamy can usually tell when people are lying, and Ronan doesn't appear to be. Yet Bellamy doesn't quite believe him.

"I'll come back after my shift and keep watch," Bellamy says. "Just don't wake her."

"I wasn't planning on it," Ronan says softly, still looking at Falan.

No matter what he says, there's something off about Ronan's alliance with her. Perhaps Falan sees it. Perhaps this is an alliance she is planning to manipulate. As long as this ends with him getting his money and settling his debt with Monsieur Horrent, Bellamy isn't going to be the one to stop it.

But still, he thinks. *There's something about it.*

He just can't put his finger on why it makes him so uneasy.

XXVIII

November 10, 1896

THREE WEEKS AFTER FALAN SIGNED HER CONTRACT, Jean-Pierre hit her for the first time. He had called her to his office and told her she hadn't performed well during practice. She was getting sloppy. Lazy. Useless.

As he spoke, she felt the effects of his magic flowing in her veins. The magic that had promised to enhance her Affinity now made her a prisoner, felt like chains yanking through her body. Then his hand skidded across her face, sending her to the ground. She sat up, cupping her burning cheek, too shocked to do anything except blink at the space in front of her. Jean-Pierre told her to get out, and she did.

When Falan got back to the boardinghouse, Lavanya took one look at her and knew.

Falan had never seen the full extent of Lavanya's anger until that day. She'd shouted at Falan until her voice went hoarse. And then she could only smile bitterly and say, "You're now as powerless as the rest of us."

Powerless. That was the word to describe it. It was only after signing the contract that Falan knew what le Lien truly was, what she'd missed before when blinded by her greedy naiveté. Jean-Pierre claimed it was a bond, but it was a shackle. It never went away, yet she never got used to the feeling.

Even more, she never felt the ecstasy that Lavanya and any of the other performers felt. When she was on the trapeze, Falan didn't get the overwhelming burst of happiness she craved so desperately.

In fact, it resulted in the opposite—each time she took to the air, she was reminded of what she wanted so badly, leaving her hollow.

Something was wrong with her. Broken. That had to be the only explanation. Not even an Enchanteur's magic could get her to feel anything. Falan said nothing about it to anybody, not even Lavanya. She did not want them to see her as an outsider any more than she already was.

Three weeks before last year's Game of Oaths, Jean-Pierre called her to his study, angered beyond belief about something that she had nothing to do with. But he punished her for it anyway, with more than a few slaps. Stepped on her hand, fingers crunching beneath his boot. Yanked her hair back to keep her in place, a hold far more terrifying than his magic.

Falan somehow made the journey back to the boardinghouse after. She stumbled up the stairs. Entered her room. Stared absently into space. She had no more energy to move yet could not fall to her knees. She was a statue. Spots danced in her vision, fading in and out. She couldn't speak even when Lavanya rushed over and cupped her face in her hands, frantic words flowing over her head in a haze.

"Akka," Falan finally said hollowly, addressing Lavanya as a big sister for the first time. "I'm tired."

Lavanya led her to bed, the look in her eyes so ferocious it would have frightened Falan had she not been so fatigued. "He will pay for this," she vowed. "I swear to God, I will make him pay."

The very next morning, Lavanya told her that they would be leaving the Cirque.

Falan never asked Lavanya what her plan was, but she knew it involved severing the contracts. For the first time, she allowed herself to fully trust Lavanya to take care of things. But the pit of unease kept growing in Falan's stomach as the days went on. She then made a mistake: She decided to confide in somebody.

Three weeks later, Lavanya was picked for the Game of Oaths. Within two days, she was dead.

Falan wakes up surprisingly rested. She stares up at the ceiling, relishing the peace. Seems nobody attempted to attack them last night.

Her drowsy gaze falls on Ronan, currently asleep on the chaise, then trails to Bellamy, who is still here. He's awake, sitting on a corner of the bed, but his mind is elsewhere. Falan can see his face clearly, the lantern's light gilding and shadowing his brown skin like a painter's brush. His expression is a familiar one. She assumes he's like her—yearning for something else, a life somewhere away from le Palais Blanchet.

What time is it?

"Easy," Bellamy says quietly as she sits up in a rush. "We still have two hours."

"I told you to wake me when you left for your shift," Falan says, swinging her legs over the side of the bed. "Did you skip it?"

"No. I went and returned. And I let you rest because you were exhausted."

Falan remembers how she reached out for his wrist only hours before, asking him to stay. It's embarrassing how desperate she must have sounded. "You didn't get any sleep at all?" she asks.

Bellamy shakes his head. "I'll grab some when I have a moment today."

Falan glances down at the rumpled sheets, then up at the dark smudges of exhaustion under Bellamy's eyes. "Right now," she says. They still have two hours.

"No," he says at once.

"Now is the perfect time. It's also a fantastic way to irritate Ronan."

Bellamy smiles a little, far too wan to be amused. He clearly doesn't have the strength to argue. "Thirty minutes at most. All right?"

She nods.

"I mean it, Sunkara." He's scooted close to her now, as close as he was the night before. So near she can feel his body heat.

For a startling moment, Falan is frozen. It's terrifying; her body keeps her still, paralyzed, but her mind says one word over and over in a never-ending echo.

Closer.

She shudders lightly, pushing down the strange feeling. "Thirty minutes."

To her relief, Bellamy moves away and falls back on the bed, hitting the pillow with a sigh. "Thirty minutes," he repeats, his eyes fluttering shut.

In seconds, he's asleep.

Alone and awake, Falan starts planning her next steps. Jean-Pierre must already be thinking about how to get rid of her now that she has survived the first two rounds. She needs to begin making her moves outside the Chapiteau, starting with utilizing Bellamy. Falan's gaze trails down to the boy in question; she should be surprised by how soft, how vulnerable he looks when asleep, but she's seen it before.

When she sees him like this, it's hard to remember this is the same boy who outsmarts the wealthy, the same boy whose hands are so dexterous that it seems impossible that they aren't fueled by magic, the same boy who cheats and lies and is only helping her for money.

The same boy whose mere presence makes her heartbeat oddly erratic.

Falan faces away from him, clenching her jaw. It's irritating beyond belief. For that reason alone, she doesn't wake him up thirty minutes later. She doesn't wake him at all. Instead, when the clock strikes eight, Falan slips out of the room. With her major injuries healed, it only takes her a minute to reach the top floor, where she finds Lucien sitting against the wall. It appears Jules hasn't arrived yet, but Lucien looks like he prefers the solitude.

"You're early," she says, sitting next to him.

"No. They're just late," he says.

The two of them sit there in silence. If anybody were to cross them, it might look strange, but not suspicious. A previous winner and a current player. One might think he's offering her comfort.

"I wonder how Jules gets here without his father noticing," Falan says.

"Last time he took a fiacre."

It's odd to see Lucien this way, closed off and short answered. Only a year ago he was so different. Falan has seen the winners of the past Game of Oaths, none of them unscathed from their time in the tournament. But Lucien is different. The odds were stacked against him the whole time, with little support from the audience and his leg injury. Not to mention how he was treated when he won. On top of all of that, he lost Lavanya.

Lucien knows nothing of Falan's true intentions, but a part of her considers telling him. Perhaps he is the only one who might understand how she truly feels.

"You never told me who you want to find," Falan says instead. "The day we made our deal. The person worth the risk of your freedom."

Lucien looks over at her. "Her name is Fayette." He pauses. "She's my little sister."

Falan didn't know Lucien had a sister. All Falan knows is that Lucien's roots go back to Algeria. She doesn't know how long he's lived in France or where his family is. "You'll need to give me more information if I make it through the Game so I can pass it to Durand," she says. "Or better yet, talk to him directly. Tell him it's part of a deal we struck."

"He's under no obligation to listen to that," Lucien says.

"Believe me, he is."

Lucien looks at her. For the first time, she sees a trace of an emotion other than detachment. He's impressed. *"When,"* he says.

"When what?"

"*When* you make it through the Game, not if."

Before Falan can respond, the Aviary's door opens and somebody comes running down the stairs. Jules.

"You idiot," Falan snaps as he stops in front of them, doubled over. "Do you not know how to be discreet?"

"I thought . . . I was late," Jules pants, adjusting his glasses.

Lucien takes his time getting up, steadying his cane against the ground. "You are. But our dealer friend isn't here yet anyway."

Jules glares at him, his cheeks red with anger. "Well, how was I supposed to know that, exactly?"

"Magic?" Lucien says sarcastically.

Fear flashes across Jules's face. It disappears in a second when he realizes Lucien is not being serious, but the knife thrower is now looking at him quizzically. He didn't miss it.

"Durand's not coming," Falan says. "I'll fill him in later."

"No need for that," says a voice behind them. Falan swivels to see Bellamy walking up the stairs.

"What are you doing here?" she says. "From the way you were drooling all over the pillow, I assumed you were out cold."

Bellamy raises an eyebrow. "You thought you could leave without me noticing? Manners, Sunkara."

"What are they talking about?" Jules whispers to Lucien, who just shrugs and rolls his eyes.

Falan crosses her arms, sarcasm dripping from her voice as she says, "Fine. Mon chéri, Durand, I apologize profusely for trying to exclude you from this meeting in the hopes that you would gather a few more winks of sleep. Satisfied?"

"Completely," Bellamy says.

"Fantastic. Jules, open the damn door."

Entering the gallery this time feels different. Previously, Falan's surprise took up more space than anger. Now, fury is all she feels at the thought that Blanchet has all these stolen artifacts, especially the Mirage Diamond.

"Tonight's game will be a rather bloody one, I'm afraid," Jules says as they all sit down on the couches.

Bellamy scoffs. "Which one isn't?"

"My father and Jean-Pierre had a long argument about it," Jules says. He shudders as if recalling the fight. "My father didn't think this game would work as well with the small number of competitors left, whereas Jean-Pierre thought the audience would lean into the tension and violence. In the end, Jean-Pierre won over the rest of the panel. Tonight's game is the Impalement."

Nobody says anything. No droll remarks from Lucien or cheeky words from Bellamy. Falan, oddly, feels nothing at all. Perhaps because her fear has already been expended.

The Impalement is known as the deadliest game in the entire competition, one that has been played every Game of Oaths that Falan can recall. Always played with an even number of competitors, each player is given three knives and a partner. The pairs have an hour to find one of the target boards in the setting Jean-Pierre has conjured, and they each must take a turn strapping their partner to the target and throwing their three knives at the board.

Failure to hit the target with all three knives in the hour time limit results in death. If one of their knives hits their partner fatally, the thrower dies as well. Even more, the players are all put within proximity at the start of the round, generally inciting slaughters.

It's a brutal game. But Blanchet has a point. Having only six players might not result in as much bloodshed as Jean-Pierre intends.

"Remind me, we don't get to pick our partners, do we?" Falan says, breaking the silence.

Lucien shakes his head. "You won't know who they are before the round. The knives you're given will have symbols on them that match somebody else's set. It's up to you to figure out who at the start of the round."

Falan rolls her eyes. "Of course."

"Have you ever thrown a knife?" Lucien asks.

"I've stabbed with one," she says. "Does that count?"

This causes Bellamy to smile a little.

"One would think you are proud of that, by how you say it," Jules says to Falan.

Perhaps she is. When the Game started, Falan's only thought was to make it out alive. But remembering the rage she felt when Ronan prevented her from killing Sylvestre, and the feeling she experienced when she shoved a knife into Eliot's throat . . . it goes far beyond relief.

She feels satisfaction. Accomplishment.

Arthur and Eliot were trying to kill her. They would have slid a blade between her ribs without any guilt. On top of everything, to win means to avenge Lavanya. And if asked whether she would kill anybody for that goal, she would answer yes in a heartbeat.

"Come on." Lucien stands up with a sigh. "I need to prepare you for tonight's round." He glances at Bellamy and Jules. "You too."

"Me? Why?" Jules squeaks.

Lucien's lip finally quirks up in the driest manner. "To assist, of course."

XXIX

November 10, 1896

"THE FIRST THING TO KNOW ABOUT THE IMPALEment is that the key to winning is not being the fastest to complete the round's task but studying your partner," Lucien says as he hands Falan one of his knives.

The four of them are standing in Lucien's room in the winner's hall. Ronan's room looks simple compared to this one. It's a lot like the empty apartments Falan squatted in during her first months in Paris, with a bed, coffee table, and couch in the same room. He has a lavatory too, with a claw-foot tub for bathing. There's even a flowerpot beside the couch, comically bare of any actual plants.

There are also several targets on one side of the room. Falan wonders if they were put there because Lucien specifically requested them, especially since she notices multiple dents in the board. Perhaps he needs some way to blow off steam or to feel that burst of ecstasy that usually comes when using an enhanced Affinity.

"How do you mean?" Falan asks him.

"Know your partner inside out. Their strengths, their weaknesses. How they throw, their accuracy, their feelings toward you," Lucien says. "For a short time, they will become your ally. Your partner in this game could save your life or end it."

"You lost me," Jules says, confused.

"This game, like the others, is all about loopholes. Your partner may need to keep you alive on the target, but once the two of you are done and there's still time left in the hour, everyone is fair game. Not just your partner but any other competitor can kill you."

Falan thinks over who is left. Sylvestre and Collette would kill her in a heartbeat. Meera might work with her long enough to complete the game's task but could easily betray her. Same with Ronan. Ary seems to be the safest bet, but she's been unpredictable so far.

"What did you do last year?" Jules asks Lucien.

"You don't remember?" Bellamy says.

Jules fidgets, uncomfortable. "I try to erase the events of the tournaments from my mind. That, and I often felt ill and used that as an excuse to leave the Chapiteau."

"Well, to refresh your memory, my partner and I succeeded in completing the task—we found a target and successfully struck it without hitting each other." Lucien pauses. "But he attempted to kill me right after. I killed him first."

Jules looks like he regrets asking. "I didn't mean—"

"Throwing a knife isn't too hard," Lucien says to Falan, cutting Jules off. "The trickiest part is aim, which only comes with practice."

"I don't have much time to build up the skill," Falan says.

"Might we see an example?" Bellamy asks Lucien with a provoking grin.

"Of course. Panelist, can you stand there?" Lucien says, plucking another knife from his belt and gesturing to one of the targets.

"My name is Jules," he mutters indignantly, but does as Lucien says.

"Watch close," Lucien tells Falan before flipping the knife in his hand and throwing it, followed by two more.

"Are you sure you won't—" Jules screams as the knives hurtle at him, one skimming his right shoulder, the other his left elbow, and the third above his head. "You . . . you . . . lunatic!"

Bellamy is dying of laughter, slumped helplessly against the couch.

"Relax," Lucien says to Jules, who has genuine tears in his eyes. "I wouldn't have hit you." He eyes Bellamy, who is still laughing, and says, "Get up. Your turn."

Bellamy stops laughing at once. "I never agreed to this."

"If you can find humor in somebody else's fear, you can prove yourself unafraid of the same thing, yes?" Lucien says, raising his eyebrows.

Reluctantly, Bellamy takes Jules's place. "Satisfied?"

In response, Lucien throws a knife that comes so close to chopping Bellamy's ear off that even Falan tenses. Bellamy screams in surprise—much louder than Jules—as the blade shoots past him and sinks into the target.

"Not so loud," Falan says. "Someone could hear."

"He almost hit me!" Bellamy says.

"That was on purpose," Lucien says. "For laughing at him."

Bellamy huffs, brushing himself off. "I fail to see how this is helpful."

But it is. For Falan was studying Lucien and how he threw. She noticed how he held each knife by the blade, not the handle. How his good leg shifted forward and the opposing hand first bent back at the elbow, then swung forward. Each motion was quick, one fluid movement, but seeing it multiple times helped her get the image in her head.

"One more thing about the Impalement," Lucien suddenly says. "The setting will work with you or against you. Jean-Pierre will tamper with it in this game, stretching it beyond reality. The targets are hidden in the most unlikely of places. Not everything is as it seems."

"You're right," Falan agrees, although she has yet to see what exactly he means. "In the end, it's all an illusion."

Ary can't bear the hunger any longer. It's late afternoon—or so she guesses—and her stomach won't stop growling. With no grants, she has no choice but to brave the center of the floor once more for food. With fewer players left, it might be easier to get food without running into somebody.

But that also means it's only a matter of time before people turn their attention to her. Up until now, she's not been worth focusing on. But with only five other players, they'll surely kill her if they get the chance.

Even Falan and Meera.

The thought terrifies Ary, because she can't imagine herself killing either of them. She only hopes that somebody else does it for her.

Coward.

The word echoes in her head again. She shouldn't have even made it this far. Ary stands up from her bed and heads to the door. If she doesn't eat something, she will be at a disadvantage for tonight's round. She opens the door slowly, wincing at the echo it makes, before creeping down the corridor. Her months on the tightrope have made her silent when walking, able to balance herself on the tips of her toes.

In the middle of the opening sit six paper bags of food. So nobody has been here yet. Ary quickens her pace. She peeks out of the corridor, hearing and seeing no one, before darting forward. As her hands wrap around one of the bags, a strange feeling creeps over her. But it's too late because somebody grabs her from behind, throwing her backward. Ary's spine crashes against the stone wall edging the opening, the breath knocked out of her. Before she can get her bearings, the person grabs her by the hair and lifts her to her feet.

"I've got to say, your gift for going unnoticed has saved you," Collette says with a chuckle, still holding a fistful of Ary's short, dark locks. "You're a scared little mouse, and yet you're somehow still alive. It makes no sense that you've survived far longer than Arthur and Eliot. Even Cyril and Hugh were more worthy than you."

Ary wants to ask more worthy of what. But her voice fails her. The only thing she can do is stop herself from quivering.

"Barely a scratch on you." Collette hums. She no longer looks amused. "We might need to fix that."

Ary suddenly kicks out at her in a panic, her foot slamming into Collette's stomach. The surprise is enough—Collette tumbles on her back, giving Ary some time to run. She knows she can't go back to her room. Collette will follow her and, if they both survive tonight's round, will know her whereabouts. She needs to find one of the abandoned rooms and stay there.

Ary darts into the north hallway, making for the stairs. Collette's curses echo behind her, coming closer, and Ary hurries up the steps. As she reaches the top, she bumps right into someone. She nearly falls back, but the person grabs her by the shoulders to steady her. Falan's cool brown eyes are staring back at her, eyebrows raised questioningly, but realization crosses her face when she hears Collette coming.

"Help me," Ary whispers, ashamed of herself for sounding so desperate.

Falan grabs her by the arm and pulls her down the north corridor and to the center of the story. Unlike the ground floor, the center of this floor and the one above are open like a circular balcony, giving a perfect view of the space below. Falan continues toward the west hall, but she doesn't enter. She waits for Collette to come up the north stairs and down its hall. When the Lily sees Falan, her eyes light up. "You," she says, more of a snarl. "If *that one* is an annoyance, *you're* a parasite."

Falan doesn't say anything. She merely starts down the west corridor. Ary follows, puzzled. Collette's footsteps grow louder. When the Lily reaches the corridor, Falan starts to run, still dragging Ary with her, and suddenly stops right at the edge of the staircase. Collette reaches them at the same moment Falan holds her leg out. Collette doesn't have time to pause before she trips, tumbling down the stairs. She comes to a rest at the bottom, motionless.

Ary doesn't realize her hands are over her mouth until she lowers her arms. Her heart hammers against her chest. If they have killed a competitor—a Lily, no less—outside of the rounds, that's in direct violation of the rules. "Is she . . . dead?"

They glance down the stairs. "Unfortunately not," Falan says as Collette weakly pushes herself to her knees. "But she's not going to bother us for now."

Before Ary can breathe a sigh of relief, Falan starts down the corridor, taking the east set of stairs back to the ground floor. Ary hesitates before following her. She isn't quite sure how to feel now—she wasn't expecting Falan to help her after all Meera has said. She watches as Falan calmly takes a bag of food.

When Ary stands still, unsure of whether to go, Falan asks, "Are you just going to stand there like a statue or are you coming?"

Ary follows.

Falan's room is identical to hers but practically unused. The bed is still made, the chair still shoved under the desk. Most relieving, the suffocating smell of human waste doesn't reek from the bucket in the corner. Ary quietly sits in the wooden chair as Falan pulls out her bag's contents. It's the same as last time: old bread, a cut of hard cheese, and a small bottle of water.

"You should keep these," Falan says, holding up the glass bottle. "They make good weapons. Line your floor with them in case of any intruders."

"You didn't take a bag for Ronan?" Ary can't help asking.

"He can get his own." A pause. "Meera isn't with you?"

"She's sleeping," Ary says. "She claimed it was a good way to pass the day." She doesn't add that Meera is probably the only person who can comfortably sleep on this bed. They eat in silence for a bit until Ary says, "Thank you. For helping me."

Falan shrugs in response.

"I didn't expect you to," Ary admits. "I thought, well . . ."

"You thought I'd let her hurt you." When Ary nods, Falan says, "I don't blame you," and takes a bite of bread.

Despite her unbothered attitude, Ary feels the need to explain herself. "Meera told me—I mean, I heard about what happened to Arthur. How you killed him when he wasn't even the Joker. And I just thought that . . . that . . ."

"That I was willing to hurt anybody to win?" Falan says, and Ary flushes. "Arthur was trying to kill me, helping Sylvestre."

"Oh."

"Did Meera tell you that when Arthur had me in his grasp, knife to my throat, she ran? That she would have let me die?"

No. No, she didn't mention that.

"I assume Meera told you not to trust me," Falan says, her eyes burning with ire, "but she conveniently positioned herself as somebody trustworthy?"

"The only person I trust right now is myself," Ary says, crumpling the paper bag in her hands.

Falan doesn't respond. As they sit there, chewing on hard cheese and stale bread, it surprises Ary to recall that the last time they had a meal together was a mere week prior. It feels like a lifetime ago.

They were friends, even if Falan or Meera never used the word. They provided for one another, looked out for one another. And now here they are, three of six competitors about to fight again tonight. Ary's gaze strays to the wall. For once, she's not going to be the beam of sunlight among the storm clouds. She's not going to pretend it will be all right.

Everyone knows it won't be.

Falan doesn't speak for the rest of the meal and neither does Ary. But when Ary gets up to leave, Falan finally says, "Don't trust Meera, Ary." There's something strange about her tone; it's not quite anger, but something discomforting. "She betrays even those she cares about."

It's sadness, Ary realizes, leaving her more confused than before. The sadness stays with her even hours later when her assigned dealer comes to escort her. Even when she stands blindfolded, listening to the rules of the upcoming game, and once again is not granted any weapons. Even when she takes the flask her dealer gives her and drinks, tumbling into slumber.

Because it was the first time she has ever seen Falan so sorrowful. And that scares Ary more than the game itself.

PART IV

The Impalement

"Contracting has become increasingly important in French society. By these means, we can protect the civilized cultures of the planet; without it, we would have lost our already waning influence. Allowing legally certified Enchanteurs to exert control in this manner will ultimately ensure that the superior being of men can bring to fruition the powers that God has gifted them."

—*Guillaume Gallien's Origins of the Arcane*;
Ch. 7, p. 171 (1868)

1. Sylvestre - **FIRE PERFORMER** - King of Spades

~~2. Hugh STRONGMAN King of Hearts~~

~~3. Cyril WEAPON DODGER King of Diamonds~~

~~4. Thomas KNIFE THROWER Jack of Diamonds~~

~~5. Eliot ESCAPIST Jack of Spades~~

6. Ronan - **TRAPEZE ARTIST** - King of Clubs

~~7. Arthur ACROBATIC BALANCER Jack of Hearts~~

8. Collette - **FIRE PERFORMER** - Queen of Spades

~~9. Martin CONTORTIONIST Jack of Clubs~~

10. Meera - **DEATH DANCER** - Queen of Clubs

11. Falan - **TRAPEZE ARTIST** - Queen of Hearts

12. Channary - **TIGHTROPE WALKER** - Queen of Diamonds

XXX

November 11, 1896

FALAN WAKES UP TO BRITTLE BLADES OF GRASS tickling her face. She pushes herself up, looking around to see she's in the middle of a large field, the grass frosted with snow. Above her hangs the familiar golden clock. At first glance, the setting appears normal, a wintry field at night.

Yet something feels off about it. The sky is too purple, the grass too stenciled. Up until now, Jean-Pierre has made his settings feel like reality; this feels like she's caught in a waking dream.

It's then that Falan realizes she can't see any target boards, yet the field is open. The only other thing she notices is what looks like a lake somewhere on her right.

And the air is cold, so cold. Her breath appears in front of her in puffs of white.

It only gets colder by the round, she realizes. Jean-Pierre's voice echoes around her, explaining the rules to the audience.

"As soon as the bell goes off, the players are to find their partners," the ringmaster says. "I hope you have placed your bets wisely."

Falan gets to her feet, noticing the five other players spread out on the field in staggered spots. Nobody moves, each player's gaze darting defensively to the next person. Falan's hand brushes against something sharp, and she looks down to see that three knives have been hooked onto a belt somebody has tied around her. She yanks one from the belt, looking for a symbol.

Very faintly, she sees what looks like a clover etched in the hilt.

A hush falls over the audience as Jean-Pierre finishes explaining the rules, and then all external sound fades away. Silence fills the air. Falan stares straight ahead. The chill of the night packs tightly around her, but she does not flinch.

Everything is not as it seems, she reminds herself. *It's all an illusion.*

The bell goes off.

For a moment, nobody moves. Then, slowly, the players start to approach one another. Falan stays where she is. She can't see each person properly in the dim moonlight, but the size and height of their silhouettes is enough to guess. She recognizes Sylvestre and Collette together, who she assumes have been paired up. It's not hard to guess that they're more than pleased.

A footstep behind her makes Falan spin, knife out, and Ronan takes a step back. "It's me," he says quickly. "I came to check your symbol."

"What's yours?" she asks, not lowering the knife yet.

"A clover," he says.

Falan falters for a moment. She can't think why Jean-Pierre would pair her and Ronan together. "Show me," she says warily.

Without preamble, Ronan flips the knife in his hand and holds out the hilt. Just like her knives, it has a clover etched in the handle. When she shows him the clover on hers, he draws his knife back and says, "We need to go." Suddenly, his eyes widen as they fixate on something behind her. Ronan grabs her by the shoulders and pulls her out of the way just as a long, straight blade swings through the spot where she was just standing.

Stunned, Falan turns to see Collette with a longsword and a sinister grin. "The best grant I have ever received," she says before swinging the sword again, narrowly missing Falan's head as she throws herself back, falling onto the grass.

Falan rolls out of the way when Collette brings the longsword down, then stumbles to her feet and whips around to look for Ronan. Now she understands what Lucien meant about partners. She needs to protect Ronan, and he her. Without him alive to complete the game's task, she stands no chance.

A hand circles around Falan's wrist, and her eyes barely meet Ronan's as he pulls her away, breaking into a run. She doesn't know where they're going, but she knows Collette won't chase after them. She still needs to find a target of her own with Sylvestre, and time is ticking.

Don't stop.

Her breaths get sharper, shorter, as the heaviness beneath her feet builds; it's like the soles of her boots are sinking farther into the grass with each step. She finally collapses as they reach the lake, which she realizes is more of a small pond.

"There's fifty minutes left," Ronan says, looking up at the clock. He frowns, gazing at the horizon. "But I don't see a target anywhere."

Falan pants, still trying to catch her breath, her eyes fixed on the surface of the water. The more she stares at it, the stranger it appears. The liquid looks viscous and silvery like the moonlight, as if the pond is filled with mercury instead of water.

Jean-Pierre will tamper with the setting in this game, stretching it beyond reality. The targets are hidden in the most unlikely of places.

Falan edges closer to the pond, reaching her hand out. Is this what Lucien meant? "The pond isn't frozen," she says.

"So?" Ronan says.

"So why not? It's freezing right now." Falan's fingers brush the surface of the water. It feels as if she's touching sap. "I think this is part of the game."

"What are you talking about?" Ronan asks impatiently, crouching beside her.

"The targets aren't anywhere in plain sight. But this pond is here for seemingly no reason. Why would Jean-Pierre put this in the setting?" Falan says.

Ronan shoots her a flat look. "Maybe because he wanted to put in a bizarre-looking pond."

"Maybe." Falan scoops up a handful of the syrupy liquid. "But I doubt it."

If she's wrong, it will be impossible to get out of this pond. But Lucien's words once again ring in her head.

The targets are hidden in the most unlikely of places.

Before Ronan can protest, Falan grips his arm and jumps into the water, pulling him with her. He barely has the time to shout her name before the two of them hit the liquid, smoother than Falan expected. They slide right through it, down deep into its depths—

Falan's back hits a wooden floor. She opens her eyes and looks around in surprise as she sits up. Beside her, Ronan is also caught by their surroundings, too startled for anger.

"Where the hell are we?" he asks.

"It's . . . a room on a ship," Falan says softly as she stands. "The lower quarters."

It looks almost exactly like the quarters she stayed in when she traveled from India to France. Cramped, with soiled walls and a damp floor, debris scattered all over the ground. The smell of rotting wood and seaweed lingers in the air. There's a door to her right, one that neither of them entered through.

It's so similar to the one she stayed in that a shiver trails down her spine. It's like Jean-Pierre crawled into her mind for a reference to replicate. But it makes no sense. He would only know about this if Lavanya described it to him.

"Falan," Ronan says, breaking her out of her thoughts, and gestures to the opposing wall.

Against it is a target.

Unlike regular targets with alternating stripes, this one is white with six red circles serving as the aiming points for the knives. One under each arm, one on either side of each leg and one in between, and one above the head.

"Let's get this over with," Ronan says. The overhead clock isn't visible in this space, so there's no telling how much time they have left.

Yet neither of them makes the first move. Ronan looks down at the knife in his hand, continually flipping it. Falan eyes the target. If she goes first, she will have her pick of which spots to hit.

"I'll throw first," she says, breaking the silence. "If that's all right with you."

Tension flickers across Ronan's face, but he says, "Sure," and walks over to the target. Falan locks him in place with the metal straps, starting with one around each ankle and getting on tiptoe to fix the ones around his wrists. "Don't hit me," he adds.

With his face only inches away, she can see the mix of emotions flitting across his features. To her surprise, the one that surfaces the most is a sense of calm; he's placing his trust in her.

The key to winning is knowing your partner.

"I won't," Falan says.

These knives are a tad heavier than the one she used when practicing with Lucien, but she'll make do. The slit on her hand that she received during the first round stings, but it shouldn't be a hindrance now, when it counts.

There's no telling how skilled Ronan is with a knife, so the smart thing would be to take on the harder spots. Falan's gaze settles on the circle under Ronan's left arm.

Do it.

Falan grips the first knife tightly before throwing. It hits the circle clean in the center, sinking into the target. The practice paid off. A swell of triumph rises in her chest, but she forces it down as she picks up the second knife. Hitting one target is a good start, but she could undo herself with these next two turns.

Her grip tightens as she aims and throws at the circle between Ronan's legs. The blade misses this time, nearly skimming Ronan's left leg, and he yells, "I told you not to hit me!"

"I didn't," Falan snaps back, walking over to retrieve the knife. Her hands shaking slightly, she forces herself to calm down and tries again. This time, she hits the target.

One more to go. Falan's heartbeat quickens as she eyes the circle above Ronan's head. The riskiest one. Falan aims and throws. The knife sinks into the board and nearly cuts off a lock of Ronan's dark hair, causing him to flinch.

Falan walks over and opens the restraints around Ronan's wrists. "I told you I wouldn't hit you," she says.

He, however, is frowning at her. "You left me the easier targets."

"Yes."

Ronan crosses his arms. "You don't trust me."

"I don't trust your ability with a knife," Falan says. "A blade through my shin is better than one through my head."

"And yet you expected me to trust that you wouldn't hit *me* in the head," Ronan says.

His offended tone catches her attention, but she still says, "I know my own skills. I had to take matters into my own hands."

"It appears you always do," he says callously. "Get up on the target."

Without another word, Falan steps toward it, her body aching as she tries to reach the arm restraints. With a heavy sigh, Ronan strides over and lifts her up, instantly causing her to struggle in his hold. "What are you—"

"Hold still," he says quietly, far too close to her. "I've held you like this during many performances with no problems, Falan. Why is it such an issue now?"

Falan is about to say it's because she doesn't need his help, but the words die in her throat. Ronan may have held her many times, but he's never looked at her like this, with a shade of sadness in his blue eyes. He's never spoken to her like this, soft and somber. She doesn't know what to make of it. It's only when Ronan has backed away, having strapped her in, that Falan realizes she was unintentionally leaning toward him.

"Don't hit me," she finally says, throwing his words back at him. She looks at the unpunctured circles—one under her right arm, and one by either leg.

"I won't," he says, readying his first knife. He meets her gaze and nods reassuringly.

Ronan throws the knife.

XXXI

November 11, 1896

I DON'T UNDERSTAND WHY SHE ASKED ME TO DO THIS.

Bellamy sighs as he walks past the bouillon, toward le Palais Blanchet farther down the street. Although it was not meant to be a strategic move, it's convenient that his behavior in the honor box on the first night of the tournament got him bumped to the ticket booth. As soon as the last patron handed him their ticket tonight, Bellamy took off.

Normally, he would never be anywhere near the hotel during the Game of Oaths. But, at the end of their meeting in the gallery this morning, Falan asked him to do something during the round—break into the safe in Jean-Pierre's study and check inside for two things: the bearer bonds betted on each player in the Game, and the paper contracts for each Cirque performer.

Bellamy asked her why. She gave no reason, said nothing except to remind him that she's the key to his money.

"Do you want me to steal them?" he asked her.

She shook her head. "No. Don't touch them, don't meddle with them. Just confirm that the physical paper contracts and bearer bonds are in that safe. Can you do that for me?"

Bellamy had agreed at the time, but now he's puzzled. There's something else going on here, something she hasn't told him. He hadn't questioned her further, but he now wishes he had.

He wonders how the round is going, if any fatalities have occurred yet.

He wonders if she's among them.

No. She will make it out of the round alive. He refuses to think otherwise.

A shadow between the bouillon and the building next to it catches Bellamy's eye. He stops walking, wondering how long he's been tailed. More important, by whom.

"If you want to say something to me, don't be shy," Bellamy finally says calmly.

A few seconds later, the person steps out of the shadows. "Aren't you supposed to be at the Chapiteau, Durand?"

Cadieux. Bellamy turns to face Horrent's associate, who looks obnoxiously ominous in the absence of lamplight. "You're alone this time?"

"What are you doing here?" Cadieux asks again.

"The question is what are *you* doing here?" Bellamy steps closer to him, unfazed. "I thought we discussed this the last time you decided to stalk me. I'll have the money ready for Horrent like I promised."

"That arrogant smirk on your face will soon be wiped clean," Cadieux says, crossing his arms. "Like I told you last time, Monsieur Horrent is less interested in getting his money back and more interested in taking care of you. You've posed a problem for far too long. But you made a mistake targeting Monsieur Horrent and attempting to cheat him."

"We'll see once I get his money back to him," Bellamy says, but even he knows this has turned into an opportunity more valuable than three hundred thousand francs. Unlike the mondains Bellamy has previously targeted, Horrent is a tier above, with his extensive connections. Taking down a thief cheating the upper class will put many in his debt.

Cadieux suddenly grabs Bellamy by the shoulder. And for a moment, Bellamy sees his grandfather in front of him, looking at him with that same condescending smirk before punishment. "I forgot to tell you the best part. The next time I send my fist into your stomach, Monsieur Horrent won't tell me to stop."

Cadieux roughly lets him go, wiping his hands on his coat before walking off down the street. It's only after he disappears from sight that Bellamy shudders. For a moment, he feels that same terror he felt the night he fled Marseille, that desperate desire to run. Instead, he smooths down the wrinkles Cadieux's fingers left on his coat, turns, and heads for the hotel.

Jean-Pierre's office is on the ninth floor, a giant space that's the size of at least eight rooms at the boardinghouse. Bellamy expected a decrease in security due to the Game of Oaths, but it unnerves him how easy it is to walk up unnoticed, pick the lock, and sneak into the office. There must be some security measure put in place for any intruders. He braces himself when he enters the office, not sure what to expect, but there's nothing. Even when he walks farther in, nothing happens.

Bellamy gazes around the office, still skeptical, but finds himself admiring the room, lit by the glow of moonlight and a single oil lamp. The walls are practically made of windows, casting a view over the scope of Paris from a private balcony, with a large wooden trunk to the left. A crimson couch is on one side of the room, and a large desk on the other. The floor beneath him is so polished that Bellamy wonders if he should take off his shoes in fear of leaving traces of his presence.

When he's certain there isn't a trap waiting for him, Bellamy creeps closer to the safe sitting on the wooden shelf behind the desk. There's not much else there—a few books, a dying plant, a curved knife, and some unused paper. It looks like a type of safe he's cracked before. Just earlier this week, he was doing the same thing in Horrent's office. The thought of the old man makes his stomach twist.

Bellamy sets his attention on the safe's padlock. An ordinary lock is easy to pick or smash with a stolen tool, but this requires a combination. It will take him some time to figure it out. As he puts an ear to the lock and listens, turning the numbers ever so slowly, he's reminded of the first time he attempted to crack a padlock. It took hours to figure out the combination. He almost smashed the lock. Lucky he didn't. Messy jobs only mean getting caught.

First number: seven.

He was too careless last time. He wonders if Horrent knew that he was stealing from him and was lying in wait to catch him. Bellamy stiffens. Come to think of it, he did have to search for the statue that held his contract. It had been moved from the bottom shelf of the desk.

Second number: seven again.

Horrent must have been trying to set him up. Bellamy scoffs humorlessly. No wonder he let him go so easily. The only thing he can hope for now is that, when paying back the money, he can strike another deal with Horrent for his life. Ideally without that bastard Cadieux in the room.

Final number: five.

With a click, the padlock slides off the bolt and Bellamy grins. He carefully sets the lock on the ground and opens the door to the safe. The sight inside wipes away his triumphant smile. The bearer bonds are there. But there are no paper contracts.

Instead, the only other item is a gray pyramid-shaped stone.

Bellamy cocks his head, puzzled. Falan had definitely mentioned physical contracts, individual sheets of paper imbued with

Jean-Pierre's magic. Despite Falan's order not to touch anything, Bellamy carefully thumbs the bearer bonds without taking them out of the safe, checking to make sure the paper contracts aren't underneath. He notes the amount on each bond, tallying the total in his mind. It's a number that tempts him, that nearly convinces him to take just a couple of the bonds.

Even so, there are still no paper contracts. Knowing Jean-Pierre, this could be a trap itself. The lack of security and the still-lit oil lamp now make him even more uneasy. Bellamy shuts the door to the safe, snapping the padlock back on. Making sure he's left no evidence, he creeps back to the doorway, gazing around the room to make sure it's as it was.

Picture-perfect, dripping in luxury. When he walked in, it awed him. Now the sight sickens him.

Bellamy steps outside and relocks the door. As he sneaks back down the stairs, he can't get the strange feeling out of the pit of his stomach.

Something is wrong. Something is definitely wrong.

XXXII

November 11, 1896

FALAN SOON SEES THAT SHE WAS RIGHT TO TAKE ON the harder circles, for it appears she's finally found a weakness in Ronan.

His aim is abysmal.

He hits the spot next to her right leg fairly quickly, but it takes him several tries to hit the spot next to her left leg. On one attempt, the knife rips her black stockings, thankfully not cutting her skin. But it's the circle under her right arm that has her the most worried. A few inches to the left and the knife will sink deep into her chest.

Ronan seems to realize this too because his muscles are tense, and he's clenching his jaw. He throws the third knife before Falan can react. It whizzes past the side of her head, grazing her right cheek before sinking into the board.

Too high. He aimed far too high. Fresh blood traces her jaw, dripping down her chin.

Ronan immediately rushes over, yanking the knife from the board. "I'm sorry," he says. "I—"

"Go again," she says, trying to ignore the sting. The more time he wastes on apologizing, the less time they have to finish.

Ronan backs up, taking a breath as he grips the knife tightly. His gaze flickers to her once more before he throws it, this time hitting it right in the circle. The perfectly accurate result is so shocking that the two of them are silent for a moment, staring at each other, before Ronan strides over and frees her.

"I'm sorry," he says again as he sets her down on the ground.

"I told you not to hit me," she says flatly.

To her surprise, Ronan's cheeks pinken. She's never seen him blush before. "It was a graze. I already offered my apologies."

Falan averts her gaze, uneasy, and it strays to the door. "What do you think happens when we go through there?"

"I assume it will take us back to the field," Ronan says. "I think we should go through it. We can't see the clock from in here."

"Wait." Falan grabs his coat sleeve, stopping him. "Perhaps it's better if we stay here."

It pains her to say it, especially when this setting brings back raw memories, but going back out into the open field seems like a death wish.

Ronan shakes his head, turning to face her. "The others must have caught on by now that the targets are hidden in strange places. If one of your enemies saw us jump in the pond, they could easily corner us in these cramped quarters. We need to keep moving to avoid altercations."

"And go where?" she says. "If we don't find another hidden setting, we're in even more danger."

"Then . . . we return here," he says, stepping closer to her. "Is that all right?"

This is the first time Ronan has ever directly asked for her insight, as well as the first time he has looked interested in hearing it. Falan glances at the door once more before nodding. With a small smile, Ronan strides to the door and opens it. There is nothing on the other side; only an inky darkness awaits whoever walks through.

"I'll go first and tell you when I reach the other side," Ronan says.

Like the surface of the pond, the inkiness that lies on the other side of the threshold is viscous, sludgy. Ronan disappears into its depths. Falan waits to hear his voice, but there's only silence. It appears sound cannot travel through, and there is truly no telling what awaits on the other side. It's most likely the field again, as Ronan said.

Or it could be an entirely new kind of torture.

Falan braces herself, approaching the doorway steadily, when the hairs on the back of her neck suddenly rise. Intuitively, she whirls around, throwing herself back just in time to miss the flashing blade of a longsword.

Collette towers above her, all pale skin and coppery hair, a feral grin slashed across her red lips. "Ready for another go?" she sneers before bringing the sword down.

Falan rolls to the side at the last second, the sword chopping the floor inches from her head. "You found me," she says, stumbling to her feet. "Were you watching me?"

"At first I thought you had lost your mind when you jumped into the pond," Collette says. "But you just helped Sylvestre and me find a target sooner. And now that our task is over, we decided to split up and exterminate some competition before the round ends. I sought you out in particular."

"How thoughtful of you," Falan says drily, stepping toward the open door.

Before she can go through it, however, Collette's hand wraps around her wrist and throws her back. "You're not going anywhere."

Falan curses. She could try to pull out one of the knives from the target on the wall, but that might result in her disqualification. Her only chance is to run through that door. However, Collette predicts this—she tackles her, and they are both knocked to the ground by the force. The sharp debris on the floor pricks Falan's body. Before she can sit up, Collette is already on top of her, pinning her arms and legs.

"Unlike last time, I won't wait around for somebody to come to your aid," Collette pants. Long strands of hair fall past her face, tickling Falan's cheeks.

"Nobody aided me in killing Eliot," Falan says defiantly. "Or Arthur. I stabbed them both with my own hands."

Collette's face twists with anger. She slams Falan's head against the floor and rakes her fingernails across the right side of her face, leaving behind a set of deep scratches. "That's for throwing me down the stairs," the Lily snarls.

She scratched my eye, Falan realizes, her mind dizzy with shock as a searing pain burns her face. It's like a speckled black cloud has shifted over the right side of her vision, dappling parts of Collette's triumphant face.

Falan clumsily swipes at her, but Collette grabs her by the wrist and slams her arm down on the floor. "There's no escaping this time, unless you've miraculously been given a grant that I don't know about."

"Perhaps not her. But I have," says a voice suddenly from behind Collette.

Collette barely has time to turn around before something heavy hits the side of her head. She pitches off Falan onto the floor, knocked out. Falan looks up to see Ronan wielding a small but heavy blade, with an equally heavy hilt.

He spares no time in kneeling in front of Falan to check if she's all right. "How badly did she hurt you?" Ronan's gaze stops on her face. "Falan, your eye. What happened?"

Falan somehow rises to her feet along with him. "She scratched me. I . . . can't see properly out of it." She wants to ask Ronan about the grant, because he didn't tell her about it, but can't form the question with her cloudy mind.

"We need to go." Ronan heads for the door, but Falan stays where she is, still looking down at Collette, who's already starting to stir. She could kill her right now. Ronan has already gone through the door and isn't here to stop her.

Falan kneels and snatches the longsword from the Lily's hand, also taking the small knife from her belt for good measure. Collette's eyes open, first confused, then vicious when she sees Falan standing above her. "You little—"

"You know what tickles me?" Falan gazes down at her coolly. "This grant was given to you to help prolong your life." She pauses, lifting the longsword. "And yet, it has done the opposite."

Fear finally flashes across Collette's face as she realizes what Falan is saying, but Falan plunges the sword through her stomach before she can move. Collette screams, shattering her previous facade of smug confidence, and Falan yanks out the blade. Fresh blood splatters her outfit.

She knows how the audience must view her now. Every story needs a villain. That's her, someone who has just struck down a favorite character, relishing in somebody's agonizing death.

And yet, Falan is certain none of them thought the same when it was her on the floor, about to be stabbed. They were enjoying her pain just as much as Collette was.

Falan walks to the door still clutching the sword, Collette's breathy sobs the only noise in the room. But then the Lily whimpers softly, "It hurts." She sounds nothing like the sadistic creature pinning Falan to the floor only minutes earlier; now she sounds scared, pitiful.

Perhaps it would be merciful to end Collette's suffering. But Falan doesn't look back at the dying Lily as she finally crosses the threshold into inky darkness. For a moment, she is weightless, floating in a void. Then, in the blink of an eye, she finds herself beside the pond, where Ronan sits a few feet away. Falan pushes herself up, noticing his rather melancholic gaze on her.

He already knows what she has done.

"Spare me your judgment," she says.

"I didn't say anything," Ronan responds quietly.

"But you were about to." Falan clutches the sword close. Now that they're out of the room, it gives her time to process not just the surprise at his grant but what she felt when he saved her. "You came back for me."

"Of course I came back," he says as they get up. "You sound like you didn't expect it."

"I didn't."

"You thought I wouldn't care?"

Falan shrugs, suddenly feeling uneasy. She starts to walk away from the pond toward the field before he can continue to press her, looking up at the clock to see how much time is left. Eight minutes. Depending on who is still alive, they might be safer here on the field, as Ronan said earlier.

Ronan walks next to her in silence, but he keeps looking over at her. She refuses to acknowledge it, instead blinking rapidly to test if that will give full vision back to her right eye. Ronan suddenly puts an arm in front of her, halting her stride. His gaze is fixed on two people approaching them in the distance, partially obscured by fog. Falan doesn't need to be able to see them clearly to know it's Meera and Ary, but it's evident one of them is hurt. When they come closer, she sees Meera leaning on Ary, barely able to walk. Her stomach is bleeding far too heavily for a mere graze.

"You successfully found a target," Falan says, noting their empty belts. Her gaze goes to Ary, who looks guilty. "And you missed."

"Badly," Ronan adds unhelpfully, still staring at Meera's wound.

"Not your finest moment, Baby Bird," Meera says with a tight smile, and coughs. "It isn't looking too good for me."

"No, it isn't," Falan agrees. The wound might not be fatal, but it could easily become deadly if Meera isn't given a medical grant. Falan glances up at the clock overhead. Two minutes left. "I'm surprised you're able to move."

"Barely." Meera's legs shake, about to collapse.

Falan steps forward. "Don't waste your energy." She wraps her arm around Meera and pulls her gently from Ary's grip. "There is only ninety seconds to go. Sit."

"How did you find a target?" Ronan asks.

"It was quite honestly thanks to Meera's recklessness," Ary admits.

"I knew it would pay off one day," Meera says, her voice strained.

"You've always thought recklessness is something to be rewarded." Falan carefully lowers Meera until they're both on their knees.

"In this case, yes. I'm not predictable like you."

"It might have paid off in this instance," Falan says softly. Her right eye stings, but she refuses to avert her gaze. "But your carelessness will eventually come back to get you."

Meera rolls her eyes. "I'll probably be dead by then."

"You probably will."

Meera looks confused. Her lips part to ask a question, but Falan has already moved closer, embracing her. Meera freezes in shock; in all their time of knowing each other, Falan has never hugged her. Even Ary and Ronan stare in surprise.

To everyone watching, it looks like a tender moment. They don't see Falan's other hand between her and Meera's bodies, silently sliding Collette's stolen knife through Meera's wound. Meera gasps, trying to speak, but Falan pushes the blade in deeper.

"Five years," Falan whispers in her ear. "Five years of knowing you . . . when I really didn't know you at all."

Meera can only choke quietly. Her head slumps against Falan's shoulder; to anyone else, it looks like she's leaning into her embrace. Her shallow breaths warm Falan's neck.

"I guess you didn't know me either," Falan adds.

She draws the knife back, subtly wiping the blade's blood on her coat. Meera thinks she can predict her actions. She thinks she knows her, she thinks Falan just wants to win like the rest of them. But Falan's vengeance for Lavanya includes everyone who played a role in her death.

After all, somebody told Jean-Pierre of Lavanya's intentions to leave. And Falan confided in only one person.

She has known since last year that Meera was the one who tipped off Jean-Pierre about Lavanya's plan.

Falan lowers her embrace, but when Meera stays slumped on her shoulder, she nudges her as if confused. Ary's eyes widen and she drops to her knees, shaking Meera tentatively. "Meera? Meera?" A sob creeps into her voice. "Meera, wake up!"

"What happened?" Ronan asks, wary. "She was fine a minute ago."

"Blood loss," Falan says. "She might have passed out."

But she no longer feels Meera's breath on her neck. Ary's sobs and desperate calls grow louder as she pulls Meera into her arms. She doesn't let her go even as the round ends and the illusion disappears and the sound of the roaring crowd builds around them. A few feet away, Ronan's sharp eyes are on Falan.

Perhaps she should have found a more convincing way to make it look like an accident. The last thing she needs is inquiries about why she killed Meera. Falan looks up at the red-and-white spiraling Chapiteau ceiling, tuning out Jean-Pierre's booming voice. She wishes she felt something seeing Meera's corpse. Relief. Satisfaction. Justice.

But she feels nothing at all.

XXXIII

November 11, 1896

JACQUES ALAIN BLANCHET IN A SIMMERING RAGE isn't a new sight to Jules. He's seen his father angry nearly every day of his life. It's a frosty type of anger, with frigid glances and cutting words. It's something that terrifies Jules, despite how accustomed he is to it.

What *is* new is that his father's anger isn't aimed at him.

"I knew this game wasn't the right one to play," Blanchet says, practically breaking the flute of alcohol in his hand. He's drinking Chartreuse tonight, not wine, and his cheeks are flushed with indulgence. Also not an uncommon sight when he's angry. "That girl is causing far too many problems."

Jules's heart skips a beat. "Which girl?"

"Sunkara." Blanchet leans back in his seat. "After the first round, she proved to be a stronger contender than expected. It does not look good to our patrons that a girl of her standing has made it this far. That other one too, Channary Chea, is starting to pose an issue. Two of them making it so far is an anomaly."

"The audience won't be pleased," Jules says, playing his part with gusto. "But I think Channary has simply been lucky so far."

"I agree." His father swirls the Chartreuse in his glass. "The real danger is Sunkara. She will clearly do anything to win. And she might at this stage, something we cannot allow." Blanchet leans close and lowers his voice, already shielded by the drunken cacophony around them. "Which is why we are to take care of this problem tomorrow."

Jules stiffens. "What do you mean?"

"There's no way the girl has made it this far without help. Somebody on the inside is working against us." His father scoffs. "Look at her. She's smaller than the other players. Not at all appealing in looks or personality. Yet, despite all this, she's been doing exceedingly well. Too well, even with the aid of grants."

Jules's heartbeat patters away like rain on a rooftop. He needs to get out before he vomits in the honor box itself. But he can't leave without knowing his father's plan. He presses his lips together, not daring to speak.

"At the next panel meeting, I will propose that we make the Game's finale tomorrow." Blanchet smiles, a malicious glint in his icy blue eyes. "She will not expect this, and neither will those assisting her."

Jules nods, swallowing back bile. He manages to sit there through Jean-Pierre's parting words to the audience. When Jean-Pierre disappears with the performers, Jules finally gets up to leave. The moment he exits the honor box, Jules quickens his pace, ignoring the people staring. He desperately runs into the night and to the back of the Chapiteau, away from everybody, before he finally doubles over, his stomach's contents spewing from his lips. Jules gasps for breath, wishing for anything to rid the rancid taste in his mouth.

As he sits on his knees, wiping his mouth, he thinks over his father's words. He has to tell the others. But at this moment, Jules doesn't know what's worse: his father finding out about his Enchanteur abilities, or about him helping Falan.

Jules's hand instinctively goes to a still healing bruise on the side of his stomach. His father never strikes his face—people would take notice there. But everywhere else is at his mercy.

"I thought I might find you out here," says somebody behind

him. Jules whirls around in a panic, his stomach in agony with sharpened nerves, to see Lucien gazing down at him. "What's wrong this time?"

Jules swallows. "I . . . I need to speak with all of you now. It can't wait till morning."

"With all these people around, that's going to be quite hard."

"I can get into the Aviary unnoticed. I promise." Jules clears his throat, embarrassed. "And then . . ." He trails off. He doesn't have the key to the gallery with him.

Lucien holds out a hand. "Keep yourself hidden until the grant distribution is over, and then we'll meet in my room. I'll tell Durand."

"Aren't you concerned about getting caught?" Jules suddenly asks. Compared to him, Bellamy and Lucien seem so nonchalant about helping Falan. At first, Jules thought it was because the three of them were friends, but he dismissed that theory after their first meeting; if anything, the two look wary of Falan. Perhaps she's holding something over them, like she is him.

"Jean-Pierre can't do anything to me," Lucien says. "The eyes of the audience are on me, whether he likes it or not, and I have to be a picture-perfect winner. He may shackle me in other ways, but this week he can't touch me."

Jules isn't sure if Lucien is bluffing. But he takes Lucien's hand without saying anything. His grip is warm, his palm softer than Jules expected. He assumed it would be calloused from constantly throwing knives. "Go on ahead," Jules says. "I'll join you."

Lucien throws him a skeptical look. "You know, I never questioned it during your previous visits, but I had no idea panelists could see the Aviary door."

They can't, except for his father and Jean-Pierre. But Jules lies and says, "Yes, the panel has access."

Telling the truth would mean revealing that he can see it due to his Enchanteur abilities, that he can use magic to counter the illusion that hides the Aviary door. It's complicated, especially against an Enchanteur as powerful as Jean-Pierre, but it almost reminds Jules of solving a puzzle. The pieces fit only one way. Just the same with picking the parts of a still illusion that are a bit off, then putting the rest together.

Lucien disappears behind the bend of the Chapiteau, leaving Jules to sigh in exhaustion. He wishes he had Gallien's book with him. Teaching himself to control his magic so he doesn't slip up and reveal himself has been a trial, but even more daunting is actually using it.

An illusion is his best option—illusions, while the hardest type of magic to master, are also the most useful. He will be able to hide himself just like Jean-Pierre hides the Aviary door. Jules closes his eyes, summoning this strange energy inside him and focusing it on himself. He feels the magic shroud him like a cloak, until he becomes as invisible as the air.

And then the illusion disappears, like a candle flickering before going out. Jules curses. He needs to try again, to find a way to hold it long enough to hide in the Aviary.

Taking a breath, he tries again. When he feels the magic shroud him once more, he tightens his fists, like he's physically holding it over himself. To test the illusion, Jules walks among the meager number of lingering spectators. A triumphant grin spreads across his face as he walks right in front of patrons and nobody notices.

But he doesn't know how long he can keep up the illusion. Using magic to counter another illusion while trying to maintain one is too advanced for his knowledge. His only choice is to drop the invisibility illusion briefly to find the Aviary door and hope nobody notices.

Bellamy arrives at Bois de Boulogne far later than he anticipated. The path is a familiar but long one. By the time he arrives, the round is over and there are only a handful of patrons left.

As Bellamy tries to catch his breath, a hand latches on his shoulder. He spins at once and Lucien rears back, nearly tripping but righting himself with his cane in time. "What's the matter with you?" he asks.

"Falan?" Bellamy says, voice rough.

Lucien raises his eyebrows. "You didn't watch the round?"

"Falan?" Bellamy says again, this time more urgent.

"She's alive," Lucien says, but there's something odd about his tone.

Regardless, those two words inject some relief into Bellamy, and he sighs softly. "Good."

"Where have you been?" Lucien asks.

"Nothing. I mean, just . . . running around. Errands for Blanchet."

"Is that so?" Disbelief flickers in Lucien's eyes, but instead of pressing, he says, "I've been trying to find you. Something is going on. We need to meet—tonight."

XXXIV

November 11, 1896

JULES SHIVERS AS HE WAITS IN THE NORTH HALLWAY on the second floor of the Aviary. Hiding in the gallery was not an option and he wouldn't be able to hear when the grant distribution was finished. And lingering outside the winner's hallway is too big of a risk in case the illusion over him wears off, so he's kept himself hidden in the corridor instead, unseen by the dealers and performers as they came into the Aviary.

Jules listens as the grant distribution goes on below, but it's brief. A few minutes later, he hears Jean-Pierre and Lucien somewhere above him; he hadn't heard them use the stairs. After Jean-Pierre's voice fades, Jules moves. He runs up the staircase to the top floor, where he finds Lucien standing by himself outside the winner's hall. Jules waits until Lucien enters before willing his magic to disappear. Hoping it has worked, he knocks on the door to the winner's hallway. "It's . . . me," Jules whispers awkwardly.

Lucien opens the door a few seconds later. "Get in," he says, and he closes the door behind Jules. "How did you get in the Aviary unnoticed?"

Jules, who slides to the ground with his back against the door, tenses. "I, uh, ran inside before anyone saw me," he lies. His stomach gurgles.

Lucien says nothing but sits next to him, setting his cane down beside him. Something about him seems off, troubled.

"Everything all right?" Jules asks.

Lucien nods rather absently. "That girl Falan stabbed at the end of the round . . . they've been roommates for five years."

"What do you mean stabbed?" Jules asks, confused. "She died of blood loss."

Lucien laughs humorlessly. "That's how Falan wanted it to appear. But I saw the knife. She killed her."

"Why . . . why would she act like she didn't?" Jules asks, still puzzled.

Lucien shrugs. "Perhaps she didn't want Channary or Ronan to know. Channary was their other roommate—perhaps she was close to Meera."

A new sort of fear creeps over Jules. To know somebody for five years and then suddenly murder them is frightening. It means Falan can betray anybody without remorse.

What if she reveals his secret regardless of how much he's helped her?

After a while, Jules hears footsteps approaching. Before Lucien can stop him, Jules stands and dares to open one of the double doors a crack. His eyes widen when he sees it's not Falan or Bellamy but Ronan Allaire. He gets just a glimpse of Ronan's gaze turning his way before he slams the door shut, his heart pounding.

"What did you do? Who was that?" Lucien furiously whispers.

"Ronan," Jules says, sinking down next to him once more.

"And he saw you?"

"I don't know!"

The two of them listen for his footsteps to move on and fade, but they don't, which only makes the bile in Jules's throat rise higher.

"Why isn't he leaving?" Lucien murmurs, still listening.

Before Jules can respond, more footsteps echo outside. He

exchanges a look with Lucien, who presses his ear to the door and listens. There's a bout of silence, thick with tension.

"Allaire, what are you doing up here?" It's Bellamy, cool and unbothered.

"I should be asking you that." Ronan's voice, on the other hand, sounds the opposite.

"I'm leaving, and she's seeing me out. Is that breaking any rules?"

Silence.

"I thought so. Now, what are you doing up here?" Bellamy asks.

"Making sure you leave," Ronan says.

A third voice speaks, so impassive it can only be Falan's. "And how is that your business?"

"I wasn't talking to you," Ronan snaps. "I'll speak to you later. And as long as you're here, dealer, you might want to check behind that door. I saw somebody behind it who certainly was not Lucien Trichet."

Jules's heart drops.

"I don't have access to that door," Bellamy says. "And you must have been seeing things. Only Jean-Pierre and Lucien can go into the winner's hall."

Ronan doesn't speak for a few seconds more. But then he finally says, "Come to my room once he leaves, Falan. And if you walk in with him in tow, this alliance is over."

To Jules's relief, he hears heavy footsteps storming off and fading. He sighs. "A miracle, truly."

Lucien, however, is frowning. "Why did he leave so easily?" he mutters, talking to himself more than Jules. "The stubborn bastard would usually argue more."

A sudden knock on the door causes Jules to nearly leap out of his skin. Even Lucien flinches. "It's us," says Falan.

Lucien and Jules stand before the latter opens the door, peering out cautiously. Falan looks bruised, bloody, a patch now over her wounded eye.

Bellamy raises his eyebrows at the sight of Jules, impressed. "How did you get into the Aviary unnoticed?"

"I ran," Jules says, using the same weak lie he told Lucien. Bellamy knows about his magic and might even suspect he used it, but he's not about to talk about it in front of Lucien.

"What important thing did you want to talk to us about?" Bellamy asks.

Lucien opens his mouth to speak, but his eyes fix on something behind them and he freezes. Jules, also noticing, pales. Falan and Bellamy turn around.

Player twelve, Channary—Ary, as some of the players call her—Chea, is standing a few feet away, staring right at them with large eyes. "What's going on?" she asks when none of them speaks.

"What are you doing here?" Falan finally says.

"I came to find you," Ary says to Falan, looking uncharacteristically resentful. "And I heard voices up here, so I assumed it was you and Ronan. But . . . what is all this?"

"That's what I'd like to know," says another cold voice. Ronan steps into view, and Jules's stomach churns; Lucien's instinct had been right. Ronan only feigned leaving. "I knew you were lying to me. What is Monsieur Blanchet's son doing down here?"

"You're not at liberty to ask questions like that," Lucien says, stepping in before Jules can trip over his own tongue.

"I can, actually, because I'm seeing a lot of broken rules," Ronan snaps.

For a long, silent minute, all of them are staring—no, glaring—at one another. "You killed Meera," Ary finally says, tears welling up in her eyes. "I saw you."

Falan shrugs, not bothering to deny it. "I was playing the game. She and I agreed that we would play to win, that we would neither help nor hinder each other."

"You pretended she died from blood loss!" Ary yells, surprising everyone. "She kept telling me not to trust you, and she was right!"

"I never said she was wrong about me," Falan says. "I simply told you not to trust her."

"And you aren't showing an ounce of remorse," Ronan adds coldly.

Bellamy raises an eyebrow. "Sunkara, I didn't think you had it in you to kill your roommate of all people."

Lucien narrows his eyes at him. "You weren't there to witness it. Where did you run off to during the round, Durand?"

Jules looks at Lucien, confused. He had no idea Bellamy was gone during the round.

"I don't understand," Ary says. "Why are you all talking to each other? You barely know each other."

Falan and Bellamy exchange another one of their glances. It appears the two of them are the only ones here who aren't confused about anything. Suddenly both are shoving everyone into the winner's hall, causing Lucien and Jules to stumble back.

"Hey!" Ronan says. "What the—"

"Open your room door, Lucien," Falan instructs.

"This has gone too far," Lucien mutters, but obliges. Jules stumbles into Lucien's room with the rest of them, and Lucien sharply closes the door behind them. He leans against it, heaving a sigh, then sets his cool glare on Falan. "Now, tell us what we're missing." He glances at Ronan and Ary. "We'll get to you two in a minute."

The room lapses into silence, waiting for Falan's explanation.

"Did you do it?" Falan finally asks Bellamy.

"Yes," he says.

"And?"

"And the bearer bonds were in the safe. But there were no physical paper contracts. Just a gray stone. Pyramid-shaped."

Falan is the one frowning now. "No, that can't be right. He keeps his contracts in his safe."

"Well, they weren't there," Bellamy says, uncharacteristically sharp. "Just a stone. Or are you questioning my judgment now?"

"Excuse me for interrupting, which I'm not sorry about at all," Ronan says acidly, "but what the hell are you both talking about?"

Bellamy looks over at Falan to explain. But she's lost in thought.

"Well, Sunkara?" Bellamy finally says. He seems nothing like the carefree boy Jules has seen this whole time; he appears restless, agitated about something.

Instead of answering, Falan walks over to Jules and drags him away from the others to the far side of the room. "What is it?" he asks, puzzled.

She whispers behind a cupped hand, "Is it possible to transfer contract magic from one object to another?"

Of all questions, Jules was not expecting this one. Then it clicks. Bellamy mentioned a safe, contracts, and bearer bonds. His eyes widen. "You broke into Jean-Pierre's—"

"Just tell me," she cuts in.

"Well . . . yes," Jules says, recalling all that he's learned about Enchanteur abilities. "An Enchanteur can transfer contract magic from one object to another. Can even put multiple contracts within the same object."

Falan nods, somewhat distracted, before asking, "I've been wondering something else. As an Enchanteur, you can see other people's Affinities." She pauses. "What is Jean-Pierre's?"

It's funny she asked, because Jules can see hers right now. He wonders why Jean-Pierre let her join the Cirque in the first place with an Affinity like this.

"The same as yours," he finally says.

Falan's lips part in surprise. But before she can speak, the others are walking over. The nearby lamp's light illuminates their grim expressions.

"Bellamy told us what you had him do," Lucien says. "What is wrong with you?"

"I didn't know you were so loose with secrets," Falan says to Bellamy.

"Technically, I didn't tell them. They guessed," he says. "Although it does pique my interest why you're so concerned about the Cirque performers' contracts."

Ronan, who has been quiet, suddenly curses under his breath.

"What is it?" Ary asks.

But Ronan strides toward Falan. "How did I not see it earlier? I know exactly what you're doing. You're using everybody around you for your own personal gain. I doubt they know what you're really doing."

"They're helping me survive," she says, but he shakes his head.

"Perhaps, but it seems you didn't tell them a crucial part." His blue eyes are steely, resolute. "You're trying to avenge Lavanya."

XXXV

November 11, 1896

FALAN SHOULDN'T BE SURPRISED THAT RONAN eventually caught on to her plan. Despite how he treated Lavanya during her final few weeks, it's undeniable that he cared for her. Unlike Lucien, however, Ronan has always viewed Falan unfavorably. Her conducting an act of revenge is unsurprising only for him.

She could deny the accusation. But everyone knows that she asked Bellamy to check Jean-Pierre's safe for the contracts. There's no simple lie she can concoct to refute Ronan.

"Lavanya," Ary finally says, breaking the silence. "I've heard that name before. Meera told me about her. She was . . ." She trails off, casting a chastened look at Falan.

Falan never mentioned Lavanya around Ary, and Ary never gave any inclination she knew about her. But Meera must have told Ary not mention her around Falan.

"Wasn't Lavanya the name of one of the players who died during the first round in last year's tournament?" Jules asks uncertainly.

"Yes, she was in the Game of Oaths last year," Ronan says before anybody else can speak. A pause. "She was also Falan's older sister and my previous trapeze partner."

"Oh."

"What are you planning? To destroy all the contracts? To destroy his cert? Steal his money? Or all of that?" Ronan presses, stepping closer to Falan.

She says nothing.

Ronan huffs a bitter laugh. “I don’t know how you and Lavanya were sisters because you are nothing alike.”

If only they knew. “This again,” Falan finally says. “I thought the comparisons would stop after she died.”

“Her death was a casualty,” Lucien says, but doesn’t sound so sure of himself. “I saw it.”

“You’re planning to destroy all the contracts, aren’t you? And you weren’t going to say anything to anybody?” Ronan says.

Falan’s hands curl under her oversize coat sleeves. Her heart sparks with anger. “Of course you would be upset. Try living at the boardinghouse and you might have a different opinion.”

Ronan shakes his head. “Don’t tell me this is for Lavanya. This is for you.”

“And you’re telling me this isn’t for you?” Falan says, the spark growing to a flame. “You’re pretending to give a damn about everybody else, but you’re the one with a room to yourself and food in your stomach each day. You’re a Lily. You don’t know what it’s like for the rest of us.”

“You think I don’t know?” Ronan snaps. He’s inches away, so close Falan has to tilt her head up to meet his eyes. “Let me tell you that—”

Jules suddenly runs for the nearby flowerpot and vomits, stopping the conversation. His cheeks redden as he wipes his mouth, trying to take in a few shuddering breaths.

“Feeling sick?” Ronan says callously. “Why are you still here? Aren’t you just dying to go report all of this to Papa?”

“Shut up, Allaire,” Lucien practically snarls, and surprise flickers across both Ronan’s and Jules’s faces at the defense.

“What I want to know is how you planned to destroy the contracts,” Bellamy says. Unlike everyone else, he doesn’t sound irate, merely intrigued. "I'm sure you weren't planning on storming Jean-Pierre's office after your win."

"I would have asked you to do it for me without providing an explanation," Falan finally admits.

Bellamy laughs, but there's something derisive about it. "So you would have used me again? I must applaud you, Sunkara. I knew you were manipulative, but your extent impresses me."

"Let's not pretend you're not manipulative yourself," Falan points out, suddenly furious at him. Lucien has his sister at stake. Jules, his secret. But Bellamy has nothing to lose. For him, it's about money. Just money. "You're helping me for the sake of your own greed. I simply tried to exploit it."

"How noble."

His careless attitude further stokes the flame of anger burning Falan. It engulfs her whole, forcing the words up her throat before she can stop them. "Her death was not a casualty."

Everyone pauses.

"What?" Ronan says.

"Lavanya's death was not a casualty," Falan repeats. "Jean-Pierre deliberately murdered her. It was premeditated. And if I have to make him and everyone else involved in this sick game pay for it, no matter the price, I will."

"What do you mean?" Lucien asks, voice strained. "She fell during the first round."

"It wasn't because of the Game alone," Falan spits out. "Jean-Pierre set her up."

"I—I don't understand—"

"She wanted to run from the Cirque." The flames are dying now, turning to smoke and sorrow. "She had a plan to sever both of our contracts. But Jean-Pierre found out and he made sure she was picked for the Game of Oaths. The rung broke when she was climbing down from the beam in the first round, but he used le Lien to distract her so she couldn't grab the ladder—I saw it. She fell. And nobody questioned it."

Ary clasps her hands over her mouth. "Oh my God."

Bellamy no longer has that mocking smile on his lips. He takes a step toward Falan, about to say something, then thinks better of it and backs away.

"So you kept this to yourself the whole time?" Lucien says quietly, lower than a whisper. He suddenly seems far younger than his nineteen years of age.

"Yes. And I was going to finish what she started."

All of them, finally, are rendered speechless.

Lucien turns away, still trembling. It's hard to gauge what he's feeling—sorrow because Lavanya's death was premeditated, guilt at surviving the tournament when she didn't, anger at Falan for not telling him, or betrayal because Lavanya planned to run off without telling him.

"All of you, get out of my room," he finally says.

Falan refuses to feel guilty. If she had told any of them beforehand, they would have tried to stop her. They would have looked at her like they're looking at her now.

She storms from the room, slamming the door behind her, unable to stop her hands from shaking as she walks to the mahogany doors at the end of the hall. Falan finds she cannot turn the handle.

Stop, she wants to tell her fingers. *Stop so I can leave.*

But her hands continue to tremble, even as she slides to the floor with her back against the wall, every other part of her unable to move.

XXXVI

November 11, 1896

LUCIEN CAN'T BREATHE. HE BARELY REGISTERS THE sound of the door closing as the others exit soon after Falan's departure. His mind is a hurricane.

This entire year, he believed a lie. And the worst part is that Falan knew.

Something brushes his arm and Lucien immediately pulls a knife from his belt, but a familiar voice yelps. "It's just me!"

Oh.

"I thought I told you to leave," Lucien says, shoving the knife back in his belt.

"You knew her well, didn't you? Falan's sister?" Jules says.

Lucien whirls, about to tell Jules that it's none of his business and to get out, but he turns so suddenly that his cane falls out from beneath him, sending him onto his knees. A wave of pain snakes up Lucien's left leg at the impact and he grits his teeth. Jules watches, looking unsure of himself. When he finally bends down to help, Lucien harshly shoves him back, panting.

He doesn't need anybody's help.

Cautiously, Jules sits down next to him. "Are you . . . in pain?" he asks slowly, as if he's still unsure of whether to keep his mouth shut.

"I'm always in pain. It's only the degree that differs." Lucien eyes Jules incredulously. "Aren't you afraid of dirtying those clothes of yours?"

"It's a black coat and trousers. Dirt won't show up on them. And your floor is pretty clean anyway," Jules says so seriously that it tickles Lucien. He chuckles tiredly, more sardonic than amused. "What? Why are you laughing?"

"No reason. Why are you still here? What do you want?"

Jules shrugs, but it's unconvincing.

Lucien sighs heavily. "You want to say something, so say it."

Jules's hands curl into fists. "If my father finds out about this failed plan, I'm as dead as the rest of you. He's already suspicious. He was talking to me earlier about how he suspects Falan has been receiving help."

"Of course he's suspicious," Lucien says, unfazed. "If your father was talking to you about it, that means he was testing *you*." When Jules stiffens, Lucien adds, "You look like you're going to vomit again."

"I might."

"Well, the flowerpot is right there for your convenience."

"I don't do it on purpose, you know," Jules says. "This is just one of the many things that make me a burden."

"You're not a burden," Lucien says so plainly he surprises even himself.

"Tell that to my father," Jules mumbles.

Lucien shoots him a sideways glance. For the first time, he sees Jules differently. He notices the way Jules hugs his body, as if to shield himself, the sallowness of his tanned skin. He is no hotelier's son. He's a boy who has been frightened his whole life, protecting himself at every opportunity.

"What else did your father tell you?" Lucien asks.

Tension leaks out of Jules's muscles, as if he expected Lucien to question him further about his relationship with Blanchet. "Now that you have brought it up, I see he might have been trying to trap me. He told me some vital information regarding tomorrow and now . . . I'm not sure what to do. I suppose I need to wait for the final verdict at tomorrow morning's panel meeting. However, if Falan and the others seem prepared, then he'll know I told them." He adds quietly, "But when one is blackmailed into doing something, they become desperate."

Lucien has figured out Jules's secret by now—he's known it since that second day outside the gallery, when Jules flinched at the word *magic*. And he's certain that's how Jules managed to get into the Aviary unseen. No wonder the boy hugs himself close, like he's physically trying to conceal his abilities.

"There are other reasons for desperation," Lucien says softly.

"Why did you agree to help Falan, if you don't mind me asking?" Jules says. "I know that your contract ends as soon as the tournament is over. Why did you risk it?"

Fayette. That is the first word that pops into Lucien's mind.

You're her big brother. It's your duty to take care of her, his father always said. When Lucien woke up a few weeks later to find her gone, he'd never been more terrified.

I knew of a household with four children looking for a housekeeper, said the master of the house when Lucien asked. *I thought the girl was perfect and offered her contract.*

That very night, he kicked Lucien out onto the street, declaring him a burden. With Lucien's father dead, he was under no obligation to look after his son.

It's been six years. But Lucien intends to keep to what his father asked of him.

And then there's his other promise. To Lavanya.

"We made a deal. I asked Falan for something, she agreed, so I decided it was worth it," Lucien says vaguely. "Now tell me the information your father told you."

"The final round is tomorrow," Jules says, voice barely a whisper, and Lucien stiffens. "My father is going to propose it to the panel. He wants to do this to throw Falan off, in case she has anything planned."

Lucien curses. "This *is* a trap."

"You're still going to tell Falan?" When Lucien nods, Jules says, "But I thought—"

"I have a lot of issues with her at the moment. And I have lost my trust in her," he says. "But I'm not about to watch her die."

Aside from the need to find Fayette, Lucien is doing this for Lavanya. Perhaps she was going to run away without telling him, but she was still Lavanya. And he still loved her. And he still promised her that he would look after Falan.

"If I get picked for the Game of Oaths and die, keep an eye on her. Make sure Jean-Pierre doesn't corner her ever again," Lavanya had said right before the Reckoning last year, during a meal.

"Nothing is going to hap—"

"Lucien." She wrapped her warm hands around his, her large eyes glossy with tears, and he froze. "Promise me you'll watch out for her."

Around them, the bouillon continued to move. But the two of them stayed in place, his hands in hers.

"I promise," he finally said.

And then he had tried to break the heavy air, assuring her she wouldn't be picked and that everything would be all right. How wrong he'd been.

Lucien can't blame her for trying to run. People join the Cirque out of desperation, realizing their mistake far too late. He remembers the night he joined. It was a few weeks after he was kicked out onto the streets. He didn't know where to go, what to do. Nobody would acknowledge him or talk to him, much less help him.

One night, it started to snow. When Lucien finally collapsed on a street corner, he didn't bother getting back up.

I'll just lie here, he'd thought, closing his eyes, *just for a little while.*

He didn't remember losing consciousness. But when Lucien woke up, he found himself lying on a plush red couch. A fire crackled merrily in the fireplace across from him. A man stood nearby, donning a red coat and black top hat. He smiled when Lucien pushed himself up, walking from behind the desk on the opposite side of the room.

"Glad to see you have woken, mon cher. Tea?" He held a cup out to Lucien who, overwhelmed and confused, took it.

I'm dreaming, he told himself. *That or I'm dead.*

"Who are you?" Lucien asked after taking a sip from the steaming cup. Warmth washed through his chilled body as the tea pooled in his stomach. He shuddered, then took another sip.

The man's shiny eyes gleamed. "You may call me Jean-Pierre. I don't normally sign people of your age, but you display a gift that may prove useful to both of us."

That was the night Lucien learned about le Cirque des Ombres and le Palais Blanchet. At the end of the night, he ended up signing a contract with Jean-Pierre, who claimed he had an Affinity for weaponry. Now he would have not acted quite as rashly. But Lucien was only a child at the time, starving and cold and lonely. It's all part of the ringmaster's plan: Charm those desperate enough and trap them.

If what Falan said is true—that Lavanya's death was not due to the chance of the Game, that she was deliberately targeted and murdered—then Lucien wants Jean-Pierre to suffer for it. But it's how far Falan is willing to go that scares him.

"How much money do you think is in that safe?" Lucien asks Jules.

"A lot."

"Thank you for that insightful guess," Lucien says sarcastically, and Jules blushes. Despite himself, Lucien tries not to smile. The boy blushes a lot, and he can't help but find it amusing.

"There is only one person who knows the amount, and that's the dealer," Jules says. "He's the one to ask."

"If there is enough in that safe, it might solve this conflict." Lucien pauses. "And I was just teasing you, you know. You are insightful."

Jules smiles. His cheeks redden further and his gaze dips to the ground. Lucien wonders when the last time he got a compliment was. But then Jules suddenly tenses. "My father. I need to get home before he becomes suspicious." He stands up, still embarrassed, and offers a hand.

Lucien brushes him off. "If I wanted your help, I would have asked for it." He pauses. "You shouldn't accept outstretched hands at every opportunity. It makes people see you as weak. Like you need to rely on them, and . . ." He trails off, afraid he's said too much.

Of all things, Jules laughs, surprising Lucien. It sounds so unburdened and mirthful, so vastly different from his usual self. "Whoever thinks you are weak is in for a surprise," Jules says, still laughing. "You have a set of knives hanging from your belt at this moment that you can throw with controlled accuracy. You survived the Game of Oaths. You are the last person I will ever think of as weak."

Lucien's eyes trail down to Jules's hand, still outstretched, before finally taking it. As Jules helps him to his feet, Lucien takes another good look at the boy. Who is Jules Devereux Blanchet really? For the first time in a while, he wants to know more about somebody's past.

He notices Jules is still holding his free hand. Jules, realizing at the same time, lets go. "Sorry," he mumbles, turning away.

Lucien is glad for that, because Jules can't see his smile. "You should hurry. You don't want to give your father any more reason to suspect you."

"All right," Jules says. "All I ask is that you be careful how you relay the information I gave you. If my father finds out . . ."

"Don't worry. We'll find a way to ensure you aren't implicated." Lucien pauses. "Jules."

"Yes?" The boy's hazel eyes are round with surprise; this is the first time Lucien has called him by his name.

"Just so you know, your secret is safe with me."

"Oh?" Jules cocks his head before realization paints across his face. Then fear, soaked in gratitude. *"Oh."*

XXXVII

November 11, 1896

FALAN CAN'T GO BACK TO HER ROOM JUST YET. SHE still sits in the winner's hallway, knowing the bottom floor will be empty except for her and Ary. With only four players left in the game, the Aviary feels hollow, full of empty tunnels and old ghosts.

Ary said nothing when she left earlier.

As for Ronan, he snarled, "This alliance between us is over. You're on your own from now on," before heading to his own floor.

Falan didn't stop him.

Jules finally departed Lucien's room sometime later, surprised to see her still in the hallway. However, he didn't say anything when he walked through the door.

Only Bellamy hasn't left. The two of them sit side by side on the floor for a long time in silence. "You aren't going to go?" she finally says.

Bellamy shakes his head. "You're abominable, you know that?" Normally it would be banter from his lips, but now it sounds like he truly means it. "The last thing we needed was Allaire getting involved."

"If I could have prevented it, don't you think I would?" Falan says.

Bellamy sighs. "Sunkara, the only reason I haven't abandoned you is because if you die . . . so do I."

"That's rather dramatic, isn't it?"

But there's no trace of a joke on Bellamy's face. "There's something I didn't tell you." A beat. "Remember I said I met a client the night we made our deal? I owe him. Three hundred thousand francs.

He's a rather prominent figure. And if I don't pay off those three hundred thousand francs by the week's end, then . . ."

"Idiot," Falan snaps, realizing now why Bellamy is so desperate for her to win. All this time she thought his greed had just increased. "Who did you target?"

"A man named Horrent," Bellamy says, and Falan shoots him a pitiless look. Monsieur Horrent is one of the most powerful men in Paris with a large connection of underground networks that nobody dares question. One of the richest too.

"Did you really think you could outsmart Horrent?" she says. Past her irritation, she can't help but feel a swell of concern.

"I've outsmarted a lot of people," Bellamy says softly, stretching his legs in front of him. "I've had to."

His melancholic expression quiets her. Falan has often thought about how the two of them have had to change over the years, going from naive to smart enough to keep themselves alive. But it was only after Lavanya's death did she realize that they were never really children at all.

That night on the hotel roof flashes once more in her mind. Bellamy, drunk, dangerously close to the roof's edge. She'd pulled him back. His hair against her cheek, breath against her neck. How he'd poured out details about his past. About his mother, bits from Saint Martin. Growing up in Marseille after his grandfather took him away from the West Indies. The cruel things his grandfather said, how he tried to shape Bellamy into a "proper French boy." How his grandfather had tried to suppress the parts of his mother's heritage that she had passed on to him, as if he could hide his darker skin or different facial features, even the freckles on his nose and cheeks. The last time he and his grandfather had spoken—how they had fought.

"It was an accident," Bellamy had said, his voice shaking with a barely veiled sob. "I pushed him, just to get him away from me . . . but he fell and his head hit the corner of the table and . . ." He'd trailed off, gulping another mouthful of wine. He hadn't needed to finish. Falan knew.

More of the night flashes in her mind. Leading him down the stairs. Stumbling through the darkened streets with Bellamy slumped against her. In his room at the boardinghouse, where he'd violently puked into a pail, coughing as tears streamed down his cheeks. Falan hadn't been sure if they were due to the sting of the alcohol or sobs, but she hadn't asked.

And then what he'd said. Something she's tried to forget but just can't, no matter how many times she shoves it in the corner of her mind.

"I think you care about me," Bellamy had slurred as he tumbled onto his mattress. "I think you care about me, and you won't admit it."

"Go to sleep." Falan had tossed a blanket over him. "The next time you drink a stupid amount of alcohol, do it three feet from your bed."

"Sunkara." Bellamy's unfocused eyes had met hers. "You may not care about me, but I care about you. I do. I know we just use each other, or we're supposed to . . . but, for some reason, I care whether you end up cheated or dead. I don't mind if you keep using me." He'd laughed, short and humorless. "Pathetic of me, isn't it?"

Falan hadn't had any reason to stay, especially since he drifted off a few seconds later. But his roommates hadn't been there, so she'd stayed the whole night to make sure he didn't choke on his own vomit, then left early that morning.

For a night she remembers so vividly, Bellamy probably remembers nothing of it. But for Falan, it was the night that he went from Durand, her associate, to Bellamy, the boy who hid his sorrow behind a smile. The boy who cared for her, who called himself pathetic for it. He became somebody she didn't quite know what to do with.

"Unfortunately, obtaining the money seems to be the least of my problems now," Bellamy says, bringing Falan back to the present. When she cocks her head, he adds, "It seems Monsieur Horrent is more interested in making an example out of me than getting back what I stole from him. He's been having his associate Cadieux follow me around."

"A power play," she guesses, and he nods.

"Many would be in his debt if he took care of me. It's an opportunity too large to pass up."

"Fantastic," Falan mutters. "And I assume that Cadieux is the one who gave you those lovely bruises a few nights ago?"

Bellamy finally grins. Laughs ruefully and says, "The one and only."

They sit there like the world isn't closing in on them, like there aren't powerful, connected, monstrous men who want them dead, who would toast to the sight of their corpses at their feet. The tips of Bellamy's fingers barely touch hers, and Falan can't help but wonder what would happen if she moved hers closer, whether she would feel the same warmth he has in his smile.

"I must ask you something," Bellamy says quietly, breaking the silence. "If you've been plotting against Jean-Pierre for the past year, why did you not attempt to kill him? The contracts would have been automatically severed, and you would have gotten your vengeance."

Falan is silent for a full minute. "If I had made an attempt on his life right after Lavanya died, it wouldn't have worked, because he was waiting for it. But attempting something while in this game—something impossible—was meant to catch him off guard. Unfortunately, it appears he's realized." She pauses. "And . . . simply killing him would be far too quick. I don't want him to merely die. I want him to suffer, to watch his world crumble around him. And I want to revel in it."

Something flickers in Bellamy's gray eyes. "Then we'll watch it crumble."

They've spent years successfully conning plenty of wealthy, arrogant, privileged men. They can con a few more, burn their worlds down, and lounge on the ashes.

"Check on Lucien for me," Falan says as she finally stands up to leave. "Make sure he hasn't completely fallen apart."

Bellamy glances at Lucien's door. "I need to ask him the time. My shift should be coming up soon." He smiles wryly. "Not ready to talk to him yourself?"

She doesn't respond. She starts to walk out the door before suddenly stopping. "Durand?"

"Yes?"

"Those bearer bonds in the safe . . . did you see how much they're worth?"

Falan's journey back to her room is slow. The corridors seem to grow colder with each descending flight of stairs, and she wonders if she will run into Ary sometime before tomorrow's round. Perhaps not. Ary has made it clear what she thinks of her now.

The thought of going back to her cold, empty room is withering, so Falan ends up sitting on the east staircase. There are too many thoughts tumbling through her mind. For one, the lack of contracts in Jean-Pierre's safe. Jules said that contract magic could be moved from one object to another, but why would Jean-Pierre do such a thing? Putting all the contracts in one object is too risky.

Her mind strays to something else that Jules said: Jean-Pierre's Affinity is the same as hers. Something else that doesn't make sense. His Affinity can't be acrobatics. Not unless . . .

Falan's breath catches in her throat. Jean-Pierre lied to her about *her* Affinity. But why? What do the two of them share?

After about a half hour of mulling, Falan finally makes her way to her room, closing the door behind her. She hasn't spent a night here during her entire time in the Aviary. Tonight will go by without any hope of sleep. She will have to keep watch in case Sylvestre finds her room.

What she doesn't expect to find is him already in there, grinning venomously at her.

XXXVIII

November 11, 1896

ARY STANDS IN FRONT OF LUCIEN'S DOOR. IT STARES back at her, waiting. Perhaps she should just go back to her room. But after the initial wave of resentment toward Falan swept away, it only left her puzzled and wanting answers.

She has no clue where Bellamy is. Blanchet's son is out of the question. Ronan, aside from being as clueless as she was, might come up with his own conclusions.

That leaves Lucien. Taking a breath, Ary knocks on the door.

A jolt of surprise hits her when Lucien actually opens it. "Durand, I told you, I'm—" He stops when he sees it's her. "How did you get into the hallway? Did Bellamy let you in?"

"No. I didn't know he was still here. But the hallway door was unlocked, so I assume he didn't lock it when he left," Ary says, wringing her hands.

"Oh. Well, he was just here pestering me," Lucien says. "I thought I'd have a moment's peace but . . . regardless, what are you doing here?"

"I need answers," Ary says, awkward but determined. "I just need somebody to give me a grasp of everything. I believe I deserve that."

"Yes, I suppose so," Lucien says rather dryly. "Why not go to Falan?"

"I'm not going to Falan for anything," Ary snaps, sudden venom lilting her voice. Her eyes grow hot with the threat of tears. "She betrayed Meera. She betrayed *me*. But I see no reason for you to lie to me."

Lucien studies her. Then he says, "Lock the hallway door before you come in."

Falan should have guessed that Sylvestre would use this opportunity to track down her room. With the player count down to only four, many of the room doors are unlocked. A smarter choice would have been to spend the night in the room of a deceased competitor.

But it's too late. Because here he is, mere feet away.

"That's right. You look scared. When it's simply the two of us facing off against each other, you stand no chance against me, Sunkara." His grin turns to a sneer. "I may not be able to kill you now, but I swear once I'm through with you, you will be begging for death."

Physically, she's at a disadvantage. He has a foot in height and at least a hundred pounds on her. But if she can escape, she can run upstairs to an empty room and batten down the door so he can't get in.

The row of glass bottles next to her bed wink at her in the lantern's dim light. There's one on the table just within reach. Falan grabs the bottle just as Sylvestre charges at her. She smashes it against his head as he slams her against the wall. He shakes off glass fragments, undeterred, and throws her against the row of bottles by the bed.

Glass shatters against her back, the sting of shards caught deep in her skin. She barely has time to take a breath before Sylvestre grips her hair and yanks her to her feet so she's forced to look up. "I'm doing what I should have done in round one," he growls.

Falan spits at his eye and Sylvestre curses, hands going to his face, giving her the chance to run out the door and down the hall to the stairs. Her limbs shake, the shards of glass digging deeper into her back with each step, but she quickens her pace at the sound of Sylvestre's footsteps.

The world around her is dark, the tunnellike halls are a maze. With the patch over her right eye, her blocked peripheral vision tilts her balance off, causing her to constantly bump into the walls of the corridor. It's like she's in another illusion, like there's an audience watching her right now.

See how she runs, she practically hears them say. *Watch her scurry like the prey she is.*

Falan barely makes it to the top of the stairs when Sylvestre grabs her from behind and throws her against the ground. The glass in her back sinks deeper into her skin and she gasps, scarcely daring to breathe.

"You should have died a long time ago," he snarls, then kicks her hard in the stomach. "In the gutters of Paris like the savage you are."

With shaking arms, she pushes herself up and glares at him. "You're . . . the one kicking me . . . yet *I'm* the savage?"

Sylvestre's face scrunches with fury and he delivers another kick, knocking her back on the ground. The world swims, tilting in and out of focus like before an illusion ends. Falan's arms feel like lead, too heavy to lift. When Sylvestre kicks her abdomen again, something foul spills from her lips. She can't tell whether it's her stomach's contents or blood.

"Not so tough now, are you?" Sylvestre says. His voice sounds like it's coming from the other end of the corridor. "Without anyone around to help you, you stand no chance against me."

"Then I'll . . . see you in . . . hell," Falan manages to cough out.

Sylvestre bares his teeth, and Falan knows she can't protect herself from the next blow. His boot makes contact with her temple, and a loud ringing envelops her hearing. She slumps, her eyelids so heavy she can barely keep them open. Sylvestre kneels and pins down her arms, and that deep-rooted panic floods through Falan, enough that she struggles in her sluggish daze.

"Don't bother," he says viciously, voice muffled through her fading consciousness. "This is what you get for killing Arthur and Eliot. I'm sure you killed Collette too. And I'll be damned if I let people like you win for a second year in a row."

People like you. People who don't belong in Paris. People who Sylvestre will always see as other, who he dehumanizes, who he thinks he has always been superior to and always will be.

Falan waits for the next blow, but it doesn't come. Through the loud ringing in her ears, she barely hears a shout of pain. She catches other voices through the haze. Familiar, but her mind is too fuzzy to place them.

Then she's floating. The chill of the ground disappears, and her limbs hang loose in the air. Someone is cradling her, their arms strong yet gentle.

Very faintly, she sees Lavanya's face behind her eyelids. A ghostly smile, mocking and melancholic. Then her voice, somber and soft. *You really thought you could win? Chelli, you should have known better. You should have learned from my mistakes.*

A different voice calls her name. Not Lavanya. This voice is deeper, rougher. She's gently shaken by whoever is holding her. Somebody's chest presses against her cheek.

"Falan, open your eyes!"

She manages to, just for the sake of quieting whoever is yelling. Familiar blue eyes meet her blurry gaze, rich with anger.

Ronan.

She wants to ask what he's doing here. But instead, her head slumps against Ronan's chest again, no matter how much he shakes her. Desperation overcomes the anger in his voice.

"Falan, stay awake. Stay with—"

She doesn't remember anything afterward except darkness.

XXXIX

November 11, 1896

AS A DEALER, BELLAMY KNOWS THAT HIS ROLE should be limited when it comes to the players. Even if he is secretly aiding Falan, his demeanor with her should be distant, cool. He just needs to treat her as he always does—as a business partner.

All of this vanishes from his mind when he sees Sylvestre attacking her.

Just a few minutes ago, he was down by her room, wanting to assure her that Lucien was all right. But Bellamy arrived to find her door open and the room empty, the floor littered with shattered glass.

What happened here?

He turned around to see Ronan coming down the hallway.

"What are you doing here?" Ronan demanded.

"I'm the dealer doing this hour's sweep. What are *you* doing here? You said the alliance was over."

Ronan opened his mouth to answer, but a sudden thump echoed from the story above them. The two looked up, listening for more. Through the ceiling, Bellamy could barely hear thrashing. People fighting. A look of realization spread across Ronan's face, and he bolted for the stairs. Bellamy, after grabbing a long shard of glass from the bedroom floor, followed.

Now his heartbeat rushes in his ears as he has Sylvestre against the ground, holding the shard's jagged tip against his chest. "I should shove this into your heart," Bellamy snarls. "Tell me why I shouldn't."

Sylvestre flashes a bloody smile. "You're a dealer, aren't you, Durand? Attacking a player has got to be a breach in the rules."

"So is killing one," Bellamy says. His mind is a bit clearer now, looking for how to salvage his impulsive action. Behind them, he hears Ronan desperately urging Falan to stay awake. Bellamy gets to his feet, sending Sylvestre one last glare. "You know the rules. Save the bloodshed for the next round. Attempt to murder her again tonight and I'll be relaying this information to Jean-Pierre."

Sylvestre slowly rises and departs, wiping blood from his scowling mouth.

"Durand!" Ronan calls, drawing his attention.

Bellamy hurries over to Ronan, who holds Falan in his arms. He can't tear his eyes away from her. She's small, so small. Her head is slumped against Ronan's chest, her long black hair matted with blood. The only thing that separates her from a corpse is the faint rise and fall of her chest.

"Damn it, Sunkara." Bellamy's voice cracks on her name, more of a plea than anything else.

"She can't go back to her room," Ronan says. "Not like this."

It doesn't matter where she stays. It isn't safe in any player's room.

Unless . . .

"Lucien's room," Bellamy says. "She'll be safe there."

For a moment, he thinks Ronan will express discomfort over breaking the rules again. But Ronan surprises him by heading for the staircase. Bellamy passes him on the way up, reaching the winner's hall first. He could have sworn he left the door unlocked, but picking a lock is second nature to him. However, with his racing heart and trembling hands, it takes him longer than usual. He's still working on it when Ronan catches up.

"Hurry up," he snaps.

The lock clicks, and Bellamy pushes the door open. "Getting her to his room faster won't wake her up sooner," he says as Ronan strides past him and knocks on Lucien's door.

Before Ronan can retort, Lucien opens the door. He looks irritated, but whatever insult he was going to say dies in his throat when he sees Falan. He blinks. "Shit."

"Indeed," Bellamy says with a heavy sigh.

Somebody peers around Lucien in the doorway. It's Ary. Her horrified gaze fixes on Falan. "What happened to her?" she whispers.

"Let us in and we'll tell you."

Silence cloaks the room. After Bellamy and Ronan have filled Lucien and Ary in on what happened, there seems to be nothing else to talk about. The others lounge on the couch, but Bellamy sits on a chair beside the bed. Falan's been set on her side for now; Ary was able to get out the visible pieces of glass from her back, but there are most likely more embedded in her skin.

"I wonder what she dreams about," Ary suddenly says, breaking the silence.

"You think she dreams?" Bellamy asks, intrigued.

"She barely sleeps. But when she does . . ." The tightrope walker tilts her head, looking at Falan curiously. "She looks different, doesn't she?"

She's right. Falan seems younger, like the girl he first met in the audience eating roasted chestnuts. A lock of black hair falls across her face, and Bellamy resists the urge to smooth it back behind her ear. If he does, he'll continue to stare at her. He might let his fingers brush her bruised skin and study the rare softness in her features.

The length of her eyelashes, the curve of her cheek, the bow of her parted lips.

"She probably dreams about her sister," Lucien says, drawing his attention back. "It's the only reason she would look this sad."

The room goes quiet again for a few seconds.

"You told Ary everything?" Bellamy asks Lucien.

"*I* sought him out," Ary says. "I just needed clarity about what was going on."

Bellamy can't help cracking a wry smile at Lucien. "Did you also tell her about how Sunkara convinced you? She has a . . . way with words." Although he should be wary of her manipulation, Bellamy can't help but admire her cunning. Falan Sunkara will do anything to get what she wants.

"More like threats and deals," Lucien mutters.

"Of course, any potential alliance with her is out of the question since she killed Meera," Ary says. "Who knows when she was planning to betray me?"

"I doubt she was," Ronan speaks for the first time. He's sitting with his arms crossed, deep in thought. "I'm not denying that the girl can be . . . trying. And selfish. And arrogant—"

"Please, keep going," Bellamy says dryly.

"But she has a reason for everything she does," Ronan continues, ignoring him.

"That is true," Ary says softly. "But she stabbed Meera so ruthlessly and Meera herself looked surprised, like she wanted to say something, and we'll never know what it is."

"Perhaps, 'oh shit'?" Bellamy says.

Silence. He locks eyes with Lucien. Then suddenly, the two of them start laughing. It's a horrible thing to laugh at, yet they can't stop.

“Oh, we’re going to hell for this,” Lucien says.

“How awful, because we’re probably going to be dead by the week’s end,” Bellamy points out, and they both howl with fresh laughter.

“You’re despicable,” Ronan says with a glare.

Lucien forces himself to take deep breaths. “I apologize. That was incredibly inappropriate of us.”

Ary is looking at them with a strange expression, as if fascinated. But then she glances over at Falan and says, “My only question is . . . What now?”

Bellamy sighs, sobering. He doesn’t see a way out of this except to run. But this time, he will not.

“I don’t know,” he finally says.

He turns back to Falan and rests his head on his arms. It’s odd how even after all she’s done, he’s still scared for her. Somehow, this willful, callous, perplexing girl has always fascinated him, ever since the day they met. It puzzles him, because it doesn’t feel like fleeting moments of attraction he’s had to others before. A coy whisper from a girl, or a wink from a boy.

With her, she’s simply there and he doesn’t question it, like the steady beat of a heart against somebody’s chest. Like the assurance of a shadow in the sunlight. And yet he recalls moments she has rendered him speechless with how unpredictable she can be.

She’s a paradox.

He doesn’t understand. Perhaps it will continue to remain a mystery to him—fascinating, just like Falan Sunkara herself.

XL

November 11, 1896

IT SNOWED THE MORNING OF LAVANYA'S MURDER. Bits of white fell from the sky like slivers of stardust, blocking out the dawn. Falan sat on the top bunk in her room at the boardinghouse, looking out the window as Lavanya readied herself to be taken to the Aviary.

She expected Lavanya to look as nervous as she felt. But to her surprise, Lavanya seemed calm, even anticipative. It was unnerving to watch. Perhaps it was a defensive tactic to keep herself from breaking down.

"You're coming to watch, aren't you?" Lavanya asked, finally breaking the silence.

Falan slid down from the top bunk. "Yes."

Lavanya cupped Falan's face in her hands. She didn't say a word, just stared at Falan as if studying every part of her face. Sadness finally twinkled in her eyes. "Sometimes I wonder what would have happened had you never met me on that ship," Lavanya said softly. "Whether we'd be here, where we are."

Falan stared up in silence, thrown by the sorrow in her voice.

Lavanya closed her eyes, resting her forehead against Falan's for a moment. "I'm sorry for it all." Tears slid down her face, dripping between them. "I think you would have been better off if you had never met me, Falan."

Falan had never heard Lavanya call her by her name. Nor did she know what to make of what Lavanya said. But before she could consider a response, Erwin arrived and Lavanya was whisked away to the Aviary.

The Game of Oaths started off that night as it always did, with Jean-Pierre announcing the chosen game to the spectators. Falan stood behind the back row of the audience to remain unseen, looking down at the stage. This was a new game devised by Jean-Pierre called Cross. It was rare in not involving an illusion for the setting, and instead consisted of a balance beam that started about ten feet high and rose two feet more after each turn. After about three turns, it was at a height high enough to kill.

For a tightrope walker, this game was a cinch. Lavanya's expertise on the trapeze would help as well. But then Jean-Pierre announced the competitors would go in their chosen order. The feeling of dread crept back into Falan's stomach. At number ten, Lavanya would be one of the last at one of the highest altitudes. Strangely, Lavanya looked bemused at the announcement, as if not expecting it. She suddenly glanced up and spotted Falan—as if sensing her gaze—and smiled. She mouthed something at her.

Tenir fermement, petite renarde.

Hold tight, little fox.

The beam was about thirty feet off the ground, nearly level with the front row audience seats, by the time it was Lavanya's turn. Two competitors had already fallen. Falan could see the body of one on the ground, bones bent in awkward shapes no living figure could imitate. The other was Lucien, who had landed with a wet crunch on his left leg but miraculously escaped with his life.

Falan's fingernails dug into her palms as Lavanya climbed up to the beam. Sixteen feet. Just sixteen feet to walk.

Lavanya began. She walked with a grace that told the spectators she was used to being so high above the ground. The audience broke into whispers as Lavanya reached the center of the beam, but Falan barely noticed. Halfway there.

When Lavanya was about three-quarters through, Falan's gaze momentarily strayed to Jean-Pierre. Something about the way his lips curled up, in not quite a sneer but not quite a smirk, had Falan on edge. So she was very much relieved when Lavanya made it to the other end of the beam.

The audience clapped and Lavanya smiled, her eyes lingering on Falan. Falan finally allowed her shoulders to relax, although the pit of dread in her stomach still hadn't disappeared. Her eyes fell on Jean-Pierre once more. This time he was definitely smirking. Falan's head whipped back to Lavanya as she started to climb down the ladder.

Falan stepped forward at the same time the rung broke beneath Lavanya's foot. She saw the exact moment Lavanya's face turned to one of surprise, then pain as her hands instinctively went to her chest. The same pain Falan knew all too well, when Jean-Pierre pulled le Lien. Too late for her to grab the ladder, Lavanya plummeted to the ground thirty feet below.

A sickening crack echoed through the Chapiteau as she hit the stage.

The entire room was silent. Falan was frozen in place, staring down at Lavanya's still body. *She's going to get up. Any second. Her eyes are open, that means she's looking up at me.*

But Lavanya continued to lie there, her expression still frozen into one of alarm. The audience broke into hushed conversation.

No one except the competitors or Jean-Pierre were allowed on the stage during a game, but Falan found her way down there, pushing past those who tried to hold her back. She ran onto the stage, and

Jean-Pierre made no effort to restrain her. If he was surprised to see her there, he did not show it.

For the first time in her life, Falan wept for somebody. She buried her face in the crook of Lavanya's broken neck, tears soaking her hair. She screamed through her sobs, a feral, voice-ripping, desperate noise that echoed throughout the Chapiteau. She cradled her sister, rocking back and forth, wanting to beg, but no words would spill from her lips.

Don't leave me, she wanted to say. *Don't leave me here by myself.*

A gentle hand settled on her shoulder, as if to comfort her. It was when Falan tilted her tearstained face up and stared into Jean-Pierre's shiny eyes, a practiced expression of sympathy masking his satisfaction, that she realized her pleas would never solve anything.

She would never see Lavanya again, dead or alive. They cremated her body, sprinkling her ashes on a corner of Cimetière de Passy like all the Game's fallen players.

She is nothing but a memory now.

The first thing Falan registers is an ache all over, but most of all on her back. She shifts only slightly, but it sends a burst of pain across her abdomen. Panting for breath, she manages to open her heavy eyelids.

She's in Lucien's room. Ary, Lucien, and Ronan are all on the couch, asleep. And in a chair only a few feet away is Bellamy. He rests his head on his arms at the edge of the bed, his soft snores muffled.

Falan removes the patch over her eye and blinks a few times, noticing her vision is still not quite clear, the black spots dappling her view. Either her eye still needs more time to heal, or Collette has damaged it for good. It's a thought that should alarm her and perhaps will later.

Right now, all Falan thinks is that she's glad she killed the Lily in the end.

Gritting her teeth, Falan pushes herself up, fighting through the pain. The movement rouses Bellamy, who groans softly. His eyes then widen and he sits up, moving closer. "Easy," he says. "You shouldn't be sitting up yet."

"I'm fine," she insists.

A pause. "No, Falan, you aren't fucking fine."

The hardness in his tone coupled with his callous words surprises her into stillness. She looks up into his smoky eyes, which are dark with anger. This is the first time he's called her by her first name. He said it so roughly that his voice cracked, like a curse instead of a title. She then realizes he's more scared than angry.

"I am fine. I have to be," she says, barely audible. Her limbs shake, struggling to hold herself up, and Bellamy's gaze softens. She leans back, propping herself against the headboard with the pillow. "What happened to Sylvestre?"

Bellamy tiredly runs a hand through his already mussed hair. "He ran off. Bastard. He nearly killed you."

"He's done it, because there's no chance I can make it through the next round," Falan says, wincing as a sharp pain flares up in her back. "Not like this."

"Come on." Bellamy smiles wanly. "You always have a trick up your sleeve. Don't tell me you're out."

"Perhaps." Her gaze shifts to the others, who are still asleep. "But perhaps not."

His smile fades. "You always have a reason for what you do. So what was the reason behind Meera's death?" Bellamy lowers his voice. "You enlisted my help in this plan, so that means you need to explain your decisions, even if you think I am too dim-witted to understand."

"Since when did you become so self-deprecating?" Falan says. "My secrecy has nothing to do with your wit. I merely wanted to spare you a few details."

Bellamy's eyebrows furrow. "Why? What did Meera do?"

Falan's lips part to speak. Instead, she winces in pain. Bellamy instantly tenses, alarm in his eyes, but she shakes her head. "I'm fine," she says.

"Do me a favor and stop saying that." Bellamy gets up and disappears into the connecting lavatory. He returns a few minutes later, carrying a bucket full of water and a washcloth.

Falan has managed to move to the edge of the bed, her bones on fire with each motion. Setting the bucket down beside him, Bellamy moves his chair forward and dips the cloth in water. He pauses, hesitant, watching for her reaction.

She should tell him to stop. That she can clean her wounds herself. He's waiting now, ready for her to take the cloth from him. But she doesn't, despite her tense body. It's not fear she feels, at least not the type she experiences in life-threatening situations. This is something strange, a hunger that intrigues her as much as alarms her.

Because, just like in Ronan's room yesterday morning, she wants him to come closer.

"Is this all right?" he finally asks, voice low.

Falan nods.

Slowly, as if trying not to startle her, Bellamy brings the cloth to her bruised temple. Although the cloth is chilled from the water, her skin burns when it makes contact. Drops of water trickle down her face, plastering stray strands of hair to her cheek.

"Better?" he asks softly. The cloth slides down to her jawline, gently wiping the blood away from her face.

She nods again, her breath hitching.

"The cuts on your back might still have glass in them. I can check for you."

Every part of her is urging her to back away; this is too intimate for her liking. He's merely checking her wounds. He's being kind, because that's the person he is deep down, unlike her. Falan slowly slides the straps of her dress off and turns away from him, unbuttoning her shirt and letting it fall. She hugs the dress close to her chest, despising how naked she feels. How vulnerable.

Like a fallen angel ripped of its wings, she has tumbled into darkness, bearing the scars on her back to a soul foolish enough to witness.

Bellamy works carefully, extracting bits of glass from her cuts. He treats her as if she is something delicate, his fingers as nimble and dexterous as she knows them to be. She's watched them all these years—shuffling his deck of cards when he's anxious, swiping a coin—but never knew how gentle they would feel against her skin. He doesn't talk, waiting for her to speak when she is ready.

"A year ago, when Lavanya planned to escape, I confided my worries in somebody I thought I could trust," Falan finally says, her voice quiet. "Turns out I could not."

"Meera?"

"She was the only person I told. Soon after, Lavanya was picked for the Game of Oaths." Hesitantly, Falan looks over her shoulder as Bellamy dips the cloth back into the bucket. "I don't believe in coincidence."

"No," he agrees. "I don't either."

"And . . ." Falan suddenly feels much too vulnerable. This is personal to her, something he doesn't need to know about. But still, she speaks. "If I hadn't told Meera—if I had kept it secret like Lavanya told me to—then Jean-Pierre would not have found out. Lavanya would still be alive."

"You don't know that," Bellamy says. "Jean-Pierre might have found out one way or another and orchestrated her death. He already knows about you."

"I know. He's known about my intentions for a long time, perhaps since after Lavanya's death last year. And I thought I was outsmarting him in our little game," Falan says, pulling away. She doesn't care if he hasn't finished cleaning her wounds. Her walls are going back up, shutting him out. "But he's been three steps ahead of me the entire time."

"Sunkara—" Bellamy tries anyway, but it's too late. She's closed herself off.

"And that is a mistake I cannot forgive myself for. Not unless I win."

XLI

November 11, 1896

FALAN CLEANS THE REST OF HER WOUNDS HERSELF. She can barely look at Bellamy. He doesn't say anything, but he doesn't move from the bedside. Her arms are in bad shape from shielding herself from Sylvestre, but it's nothing compared to the horrifying state of her torso. Unfortunately, the only thing she can do for now is hope none of her vital organs have been damaged.

Just as she finishes adjusting her clothing, she hears a gasp from the couch. "You're . . . all right." Ary sits up, looking at her with wide eyes.

Falan isn't sure what to expect, but she doesn't anticipate it when Ary suddenly starts crying, waking the other two. Lucien snaps awake, gripping one of his knives, while Ronan blinks blearily. Falan wants to get out of this bed. None of them should dare look at her with pity.

But the only emotion in Ary's dark eyes is sadness as she comes over to sit down next to Falan. "I was so scared," she says. "I—I told myself I hated you for what you did to Meera. But when Bellamy carried you into the room and I saw how hurt you were . . ."

"Don't waste your tears on me," Falan says callously. "There are more pressing matters to cry about."

"I see Sylvestre hasn't knocked the impertinence from you, even if he managed to bruise everything else," Ronan says from the couch. "Still as rude as ever."

"And you're still as haughty as ever. If you'd arrived minutes earlier, I'd be in better shape than I am now. And why were you seeking me out? You told me our alliance had been severed." Falan stiffens. "Did you come to my room to harm me?"

"What? No," Ronan says at once. "I was . . . worried. I knew Sylvestre would most likely be coming after you." He pauses. "And to take back what I said. About our alliance."

"Really?" Falan says, skeptical.

"Sylvestre is still around. He poses a threat to all of us," Ronan says. "But if you both agree to this alliance until he's out of the way, then I will."

Ary throws a hesitant look at Falan.

But Falan says, "Deal." She doesn't need to think much about it. Ronan is feeling the hunger to survive, but he will aim his efforts at Sylvestre before pulling anything on her or Ary. She might as well use that.

"All right. Then I agree as well," Ary says, although she still seems dubious.

With some prompting from Bellamy, Falan tells them all what she told him, about how Meera went behind her back and told Jean-Pierre of Lavanya's plan. The only thing she doesn't speak of is her guilt. It's something she should not have even told Bellamy, and it angers her that she so witlessly confided in him.

"I knew there was a reason," Ronan says when Falan finally finishes, looking far too pleased with himself for her liking.

"I didn't think Meera could do such a thing." Ary frowns, looking conflicted. "I always knew you to be ruthless, Falan. But you cared about her. I know you did." She pauses. "Or perhaps I don't know you at all."

"Perhaps you don't," Falan says.

Only Lucien has not spoken, deep in thought.

"What is it?" Bellamy asks him.

Lucien finally locks eyes with Falan and says, "I might have some vital information about tomorrow. It's what Jules wanted to talk to us about. But before I tell you, I think I have a solution to this conflict."

"Do tell," Falan says.

Lucien frowns at her derisive tone, but he says, "Regardless of your other motives, at the end of this, I propose we split the money among everybody in the Cirque. And the cercle dealers."

"Funny. I was about to offer the same solution," Falan says.

Lucien blinks, unable to hide his surprise. "You were?"

"Durand told me how much was in the safe—one hundred million francs in bearer bonds. It's not just the betted money; it's all of Jean-Pierre's cash assets. It's enough for everybody."

"And you will keep to this deal?" Lucien says skeptically.

"I chanced losing you once and realized the impact," Falan says. "It was foolish, and I won't risk it again. Especially since you're withholding information from me right now."

"I'm serious. I don't take well to traitors."

"Neither do I."

Lucien finally smiles wryly, but it fades quickly. He leans forward, lacing his fingers together. "Jules relayed this to me earlier tonight: His father is ensuring the final round is tomorrow, not Friday."

Ronan swears. Falan's heart plummets. With her injuries, she doesn't know how she will compete, let alone win.

"Jules didn't mention this earlier," Bellamy points out.

"Jules is afraid of telling anybody," Lucien says. "His father is trying to trap him. I don't know about Jean-Pierre, but Blanchet suspects Falan is receiving help and has grown suspicious of Jules. I'm sure he's relayed this to Jean-Pierre too."

“So if I act prepared, they’ll know that he’s helping me,” Falan says, and curses. “It’s a lose-lose situation.”

“Precisely,” Lucien says grimly.

“So what do we do?” Ary asks.

They need more information. With that, they might have enough to craft a plan for tomorrow night. But Jules isn’t here, nor will he know what the fourth game is until the morning.

Right now, they can only wait.

XLII

November 11, 1896

WALKING THROUGH PARIS AT NIGHT IS NOTHING like Jules expected it to be. Somehow, he thought the vibrant essence of the city would carry through the darkness, like a new world would awaken when the other went to sleep.

But here, in the outskirts, there isn't much of anything but trees. There is no company except for the moon and its light. Nevertheless, something about the air here feels cleaner, less stuffy, and the walk back to his place is one that allows Jules to clear his head, come up with excuses to tell his father in case he's questioned about his late arrival. Most ideally, his father will be asleep by the time he returns.

The Blanchet mansion is three stories high, with an iron gate painted gold around the property. The gravel in front of the house is meant for their personal carriage, but to Jules's surprise, he sees not one carriage but two parked near the walkway.

Who could be visiting at this time? he wonders as he walks through the gate. Jules goes to look through the mansion's drawing room window, where his father entertains guests, but the dark fuchsia silken curtains are pulled shut. He has no choice but to go in.

Once inside, Jules walks through the foyer. From the open drawing room door nearby, he hears two male voices talking quietly, as well as the clink of teacups on saucers. Tentatively, Jules steps toward the door to see his father sitting across from another man. The visitor is dressed sharply. His black dress coat has no wrinkles, and his silver hair is combed back so smoothly it looks slicked.

He looks like the type to frequent le Palais Blanchet's cercle.

"Jules, it's late." No greeting or warmth. Blanchet's voice is smooth, detached. "Where have you been?"

"I couldn't sleep and decided to go for a walk, get some fresh air," Jules says, his stomach twisting. He shifts his gaze to the man in the other chair, waiting to be introduced.

But Blanchet doesn't. It's the man who puts down his teacup and says, "You must be Jacques's son, is that right?" He stands, extending a hand. "I am Louis Horrent, an . . . old friend of your father."

Jules senses the weight behind those words but shakes Horrent's hand anyway. It's strangely rough; he expected such a polished-looking man to have smooth palms. "Enchanté. I'm sorry to interrupt your conversation. I must retire for the night."

With a polite nod, Jules leaves the room. But he stops in the foyer outside, wondering why this man is here. It's past four in the morning. It's entirely possible he could be an old friend of his father's, but he's never seen Horrent before. Still, it's best not to be lurking here, especially when his father is already suspicious of him.

Jules is about to walk to the staircase up to his room when a name in their conversation catches his attention. Durand. He stops, creeping back to the wall, and flattens his back against it.

"So you see, Monsieur, your dealer has done this to many respected members of the upper class, including me," Horrent is saying. "So I came to speak to you about this predicament. Earlier tonight, my associate Cadieux found him about to go into your hotel. Was he supposed to be there?"

"No," Blanchet says, and Jules's heart skips a beat. "But I have suspected him of some other issue that has been troubling me."

"I don't wish to pry," Horrent says, playing nice. "I merely came to bring the issue to your attention and see if we can work something out."

"And I appreciate that," Blanchet says, a tad too cordially. "It seems the boy might be looking to cheat me too. My associate Jean-Pierre suspected something amiss in his office in the hotel after returning from the Game's events earlier. It seems his safe has been broken into, although nothing appears to have been taken. It's no coincidence if Cadieux spotted Bellamy at my hotel."

Bile rises in Jules's throat. This is not good.

"If the thief hadn't stolen from me, I would applaud him," Horrent says with a short laugh, puzzling Jules.

His father laughs in turn. "What compels you to say that?"

"Come now, Monsieur Blanchet. Jean-Pierre's hold over Paris is getting a bit dangerous, wouldn't you say? It's overshadowing yours."

"I can keep him in check, thank you." Blanchet's voice is cold, but there's something else too. Insecurity. Jules has heard the irate remarks from his father about Jean-Pierre before. Their partnership has only become more and more tumultuous over the years.

But Jules didn't think that other powerful men in Paris also held no fondness toward Jean-Pierre.

After a short silence, Horrent asks, "So what do you propose we do?"

"If Bellamy is planning on stealing anything from the safe, then tomorrow night will be when he strikes." Blanchet pauses. "Taking care of the issue is simple. Have Cadieux ready and waiting in the office."

"And then?"

Jules quivers, awaiting his father's answer.

Blanchet's voice comes, cold and resolute. "Kill the thief."

Jules bites back a gasp. This is going far beyond the constraints of the Game. There are larger things at play here, things that he feels naively unaware of. Things that the others need to know as soon as the round's details are finalized tomorrow morning.

Having heard what he needs, Jules escapes to his room.

XLIII

November 11, 1896

FALAN SOON FINDS HERSELF ALONE WITH LUCIEN. Bellamy left first, stating he needed to let the next dealer on patrol know about the fight. "He'll see the blood on the ground and will ask questions. I'll tell him I stopped the fight and that you're staying in Ronan's room right now, in case he wonders where you are," Bellamy said.

It's unlikely the dealer will question him any further. As several dealers have made their own agreements with Bellamy before, they know a thing or two about looking the other way.

Ary and Ronan wanted to stay longer, but Lucien persuaded them not to risk it. Instead, he told them to meet on the top floor tomorrow morning at eight o'clock.

Falan knows she needs to go too. But she stays curled up on Lucien's bed even after the other two leave, her knees tucked up to her chin. Lucien watches her from the couch. He doesn't push her to speak, nor does he tell her to hurry up and go. She's not sure what he's waiting for.

Finally, she says, "Lavanya never told you anything she planned, did she?"

After a beat, Lucien shakes his head. "Nothing. I had no clue she was intending to run until you told me tonight." He pauses. "The only thing she did was make me promise to look out for you in case something happened to her. It was right before the tournament."

This is a surprise to Falan. "You and I have talked not more than five times in the past year before this week."

"Because you didn't need my protection." He almost laughs. "You were already making money by gambling and knew Erwin's bribes. You didn't need anybody to teach you because you were paying attention the entire time." His wry smile fades. "Then again, perhaps I should have kept a closer eye on you. Then I would have seen what you were planning all along."

"No, you would not have," Falan says quietly. "Because you thought her death was an unfortunate casualty, just like everybody else. The only person who could have seen me coming was Jean-Pierre." She pauses. "And Meera."

"Yes." His voice is hollow. Accepting. "You astound me. You want to avenge Lavanya, but you want to burn down the world around you while doing so."

He's not wrong. There's a difference between not caring about destruction and relishing it. What's more alarming is that Falan isn't ashamed of admitting to herself that she's the latter.

"You've been angry for so long," Lucien says, as if reading her mind. "And it's not just because of Lavanya's death."

Falan's hands curl into fists, her fingernails pressing into her already bloody palms. "They see us as . . . less than animals. They think the only thing we're good for is killing each other and ourselves for their entertainment, despite how much they've done to us, our families, our homes." Each word is filled with resentment, hatred, a fuel that burns hotter than coals. It nearly consumes her whole.

Lucien is quiet for a minute. Then he says, "I know. Fuck them all."

Just solidarity from somebody also angered and exhausted. Somebody who knows that resistance often requires being brutal.

That the world is an unforgiving place to those it doesn't favor—sometimes you must fight fire with fire.

"What do you plan to do after your contract is severed?" Lucien asks eventually.

Falan almost tells him that it's none of his concern. But this is not like the guilt she confessed to Bellamy. "If I don't die tomorrow night, then I plan to go to England to see somebody."

"Your father." When she looks at him in surprise, he says, "Lavanya told me long back."

"She broke the unspoken rule." Something else that doesn't quite surprise Falan. Lavanya could never keep her mouth shut. Falan pauses, lingering over the thought of her father. "He might not be there anymore. It's been more than five years. He probably thinks I'm dead. Or *he* might be."

Lucien rolls his eyes. "You're far too bleak for somebody who gambles."

"Gambling is a mind game." She shifts on the bed, and Falan bites down on her lip as every muscle in her body burns. "Any insight as to how the next day will play out?"

Lucien watches her with pity. "Anaïs will visit you and the others a few hours before the final round. She'll get you cleaned up, give you fresh clothes, make you good as new for the audience."

It's a mocking reward for the finalists. Falan looks down at her bloodstained, marred clothes, knowing a clean outfit will not change the unloveliness donning it.

Without realizing it, Falan falls asleep on Lucien's bed, waking up to find the comforter carelessly thrown over her. Her eyes stray to the couch, where Lucien still sits. He's staring into space, absently drumming the arm of the couch. Falan finds herself watching the rhythm of his fingers, caught by the warmth of the comforter.

As if sensing her stare, Lucien turns in her direction. "You're up," he says.

"Why didn't you wake me?" she asks.

"Because you were exhausted and—"

White-hot pain suddenly flares all over Falan's body as she shifts, and she gasps.

"—I knew the pain of your injuries would kick in," Lucien finishes.

Gritting her teeth, Falan pushes herself up, hating how Lucien is watching her. She breathes out a curse, tossing the comforter off her. "What time is it?"

"Half past seven," he says, glancing at the grandfather clock. "We need to be at the gallery in a half hour."

"Assuming Jules even shows up," Falan says, her voice tight as she slowly gets to her feet. Perhaps if she walks a bit, she'll grow desensitized to the pain, although it's wishful thinking. So is the thought that the pain will ease in the meager hours before tonight's round.

"He'll be there," Lucien says.

"You said his father was growing suspicious of him." Falan dares to take a step. "He might not come if he thinks he's being watched."

"His fear of something else might overshadow that," Lucien says snidely. "I know you know what he's hiding too. I knew from the moment his expression changed when I merely said the word *magic*."

She doesn't respond, quickening her pace and grimacing at her too-stiff legs.

"Don't overdo it," Lucien says. "You'll end up stressing those injuries even more."

"If I were not in such bad shape, I might stand a chance."

"Of winning?"

"Of killing Sylvestre myself."

The thought of Sylvestre still alive boils her blood. She would give anything to go back to the first round and shove his tourné knife deep into his throat. But should the same situation happen tonight, Ronan will not stop her. Not at this stage of the Game.

By the time she and Lucien arrive at the gallery, the others are already there, and Jules is unlocking the door that none of them can see. It looks as if the key is sinking right into the wall.

"Good morning," Bellamy says, annoyingly blithe. "You all look like death."

"Makes sense, considering I almost died a few hours ago," Falan says.

"Something I would not like to be reminded of." Bellamy's tone is light, but he's shuffling his deck of cards, something Falan knows he does when he's anxious. His gaze flickers to Lucien. "You look like you slept on the floor."

"Since you seem intent on commenting on everybody else's appearance, want to know what you look like?" Lucien says irritably. "Because I'll gladly tell you—"

"All right," Ary cuts in. "I think we can acknowledge everybody is tired and miserable. Except Bellamy."

"Oh, he is too," Falan says. "That's why he's making gibes. He's trying to brighten his own mood at our expense."

"That is the definition of selfish," Ronan mutters.

Bellamy grins roguishly, tucking the card deck away. "Don't act like anybody here is a saint. We've all done things that the angels would scold us for."

Ronan scowls. "What did *I* do?"

"Be annoying," Bellamy says.

"Be a jerk," Lucien says.

Falan averts her gaze. *Shun Lavanya.*

Ary starts to laugh, but it dies at Ronan's glare. Sheepishly, she says, "I don't understand what we're doing here . . ." She trails off as Jules opens the secret door to the gallery. Oddly, he walks inside without looking at them, leaving Bellamy to hold the door open.

A walk down the hallway later, everyone is settled on the ring of couches in the gallery. Ary and Ronan are both looking around the room, as awed and appalled as Falan was her first time in here.

Ronan notices the display case with the Mirage Diamond and realization washes over his face. "That diamond," he says quietly to Falan. "Lavanya mentioned it before."

Falan doesn't want to get into this now, particularly with Ronan. Luckily her attention is caught by Jules, who is staring at Falan with wide eyes. "What happened to you?" he asks.

It's almost a relief to see his horrified expression over the melancholic one. He looks more like the Jules she's used to. "Sylvestre nearly killed me," she says.

Jules blinks. "You almost died?"

"Forget that. Tell us what you know about the next game."

Jules looks at the others, appalled. "She almost *died.*"

Bellamy shrugs, amused. "So she did. You might too if you don't start talking."

Jules glances again at Falan's bruises, then says, "It's the Garden."

The others exchange knowing looks. All except Ary, who asks, "What's the Garden?"

"It's something that will be a long shot to win," Lucien says bluntly.

Bellamy scoffs. "Thanks for that description. It's pretty straightforward: You'll all be put into a garden with different paths and many clearings where the paths meet. In one of the clearings is a prize; it's usually something like a jewel. Something that symbolizes a win. Whoever takes it first is the winner."

"Popular game for the finale," Falan adds.

Before Jules can ask how they know, Bellamy says, "Lucien filled us in. Is it confirmed that tonight will be the final round?"

"Yes," Jules says quietly. "And to avoid any backlash at the shorter length of the tournament, any surviving runners-up will be touted around for a day, brought to a party the next night—and then killed in front of the audience. 'A rather theatrical end to the show,' as Jean-Pierre put it."

Ary cringes. "It sounds gruesome."

Falan sits still, trying not to disturb her wounds, thinking. Lucien is right. It will be a long shot to win. She will not be able to move quickly, and Sylvestre will be on her tail. Not to mention it's guaranteed the Garden will be littered with other obstacles, beautifully dangerous from its flowers to its hidden creatures.

"Not only do we have to figure out how the three of you will survive that, we need to be wary of breaking into Jean-Pierre's safe tonight," Bellamy says.

Jules suddenly goes pale. "You're *what*?"

"We came to a decision last night," Lucien says. "We're aiding Falan with her plan. But that means splitting the money among the Cirque performers and cercle dealers."

"No, you can't," Jules says at once. "Last night, when I came home, there was a man talking to my father. A man named Horrent."

At the name, Falan casts a sharp look at Bellamy, who stiffens in shock. "This man—Horrent—was talking to your father?" he asks.

Jules nods. "He was talking to my father about . . . I don't know, how you've cheated people in the upper class, and how he wants to put a stop to it. And my father mentioned that Jean-Pierre knows somebody broke into his safe."

Now Falan is the one stiffening. "He knows?"

"He could tell his safe was tampered with," Jules says. "And since Bellamy didn't take anything, they know you were merely assessing and are planning on stealing the contents tonight."

"This is just what we need," Lucien says sarcastically.

"Wait. That's not everything." Jules now looks sick. "They mentioned Horrent's associate—a man named Cadieux—who has been following Bellamy. He's going to be waiting in Jean-Pierre's office when you break in tonight. And . . . he's going to kill you."

The room lapses into horrified silence. Falan stares straight ahead at the Mirage Diamond, twinkling in its display case. Not quite as bright now, due to the patch over her eye. She should have foreseen this. Bellamy even mentioned earlier that Cadieux had been following him, that this goes beyond money for Horrent.

"At least we know we're not the only ones opposing Jean-Pierre," Jules adds suddenly.

"What do you mean? He and your father were fighting again?" Lucien asks.

"No, not exactly. It just appeared that Horrent wasn't particularly fond of him either."

Lucien rolls his eyes. "Even some government officials despise the man."

Bellamy laughs. "Well, it's no surprise to me that Horrent doesn't like him. When one powerful man is threatened by another, he'll do anything to keep the other out of the way."

Falan nearly comments that Jean-Pierre would keep anyone out of his way, powerful or not. She was wondering when Jean-Pierre's next countermove was going to come. Like her, he's now gone beyond the confines of the Game. No wonder it seemed Bellamy had no issue getting into Jean-Pierre's safe.

The ringmaster *wanted* somebody to come. He expected it. He might have not known who, but now thanks to Horrent, he will certainly know it's Bellamy.

It's her move. And she needs to strike accordingly.

"Go ahead with the plan tonight," she finally says, shocking everyone. "Durand, I want you and Lucien to go to Jean-Pierre's office and steal the contents of his safe."

"Falan, have you lost your mind?" Ronan snaps.

"Not at all," she says. "Our advantage now is that we know what they have planned. They don't know how much we know."

"They might." Ronan shoots a poisonous look at Jules. "How do we know *this one* won't go telling his father everything we're discussing?"

"Quite frankly, the only person I'm not comfortable with around here is *you*," Lucien cuts in coolly.

"Me, the person competing in a deadly game?" Ronan snaps back. "Not the son of one of the Game's owners?"

"I don't know what Lavanya ever saw in you," Lucien mutters, so quietly that Falan can barely hear him. But she catches it, and so does Ronan.

For a moment, it seems like he's going to speak, his lips parting. But then a guilty look suddenly wipes over Ronan's face and he closes his mouth, sinking back into the couch.

"So, Cadieux?" Bellamy says, cutting the tense silence short. "Whether we're prepared or not, he's going to be a problem."

And then it hits her. The solution. A ghost of a smile brushes over Falan's lips. The threads of a beautiful plan form in her mind, her final gambit against Jean-Pierre. "There is a way to defeat them all and get what we want. And Cadieux is the very starting point of that plan." She nearly laughs at her own answer. "You have to kill him."

"Kill him?" Bellamy raises his eyebrows.

Falan nods, self-assured. "There's no other choice. You cannot merely knock him out. You cannot let him go. You must kill him. Otherwise, we've already lost."

"If we kill Cadieux, Horrent will only come after us," Lucien points out.

"Do you trust me?" Falan says.

The five others exchange glances. "That's a bit of an ask after all you've done," Ronan says. "It's a lot to overlook."

Falan doesn't put up an argument or defense. She knows that if she pushes it, takes the decision away from them, she will lose them. And she can't afford that.

"Do what I tell you, and you'll get out of this alive," is the only thing she says.

Another shared glance between the others, this one of consensus. Right now, Falan is their best chance. Ronan is the only one who looks unconvinced.

"How can you promise that?" he asks.

"Hear me out and then decide," Falan says.

Ronan stares at the wall, his lips pressed together stubbornly. But when they all look at him, he finally sighs, giving in.

"All right," he says. "Tell us what you want us to do."

XLIV

November 11, 1896

FALAN SITS ON THE WEST STAIRCASE, LONG AFTER the meeting in the gallery. After she had finished telling them the plan—and getting Ronan's approval—she asked for Jules to stay back as the others left the gallery. He obliged, confused, until she explained that she needed to ask another favor.

As per her request, Jules attempted to use magic to heal the wounds Sylvestre inflicted on her. His skill was nowhere near that of the Cirque's physician, but he was able to ease her pain and unintentionally prove he has more control of his magic than he realizes.

As he healed her, Falan lightly questioned him about a few more things. He answered patiently and with uncharacteristic calm, but he was surprised at her train of thought. It was only after he agreed with her that they finally left the gallery.

Falan considers this as she lifts the patch from her eye, testing her sight again. But it's still dappled with black.

Footsteps sound behind her as she puts the patch back over her eye and somebody sits down next to her. Ronan. He sighs, gazing down the steps, and says softly, "I wish she'd gotten to see it. The diamond."

"We can wish all we want," Falan says icily. "That won't change anything."

"I'm sorry."

Those words are like bait hanging in front of her. Falan should resist it. But she turns to him and says, "Sorry for what? For the fact that Lavanya will never see that diamond or for how you treated her before her death?"

Ronan blinks, clearly taken aback. But when Falan stares him down for an answer, his expression turns remorseful. "I—"

"You stopped talking to her. You shunned her—wouldn't even look in her direction." The rage, the confusion, the sorrow, every mixed emotion that Falan has kept bottled up for a year is finally pouring out. "She died knowing you thought of her as less than nothing."

"No, I adored Lavanya," Ronan says at once. "When she died, I was furious at myself for treating her as I did."

"That's the problem. You only felt remorse because she died," Falan says. "If not? Would you have gone on ignoring her?"

"I'd like to say I wouldn't," Ronan says quietly but somehow sounds unsure.

"Then why? Why did you treat her like that?"

He takes a deep breath. "A few weeks before Lavanya was picked for the Game, she . . . confessed something to me. Feelings that I wanted to avoid because I didn't feel the same about her. Not like she wanted me to." A beat. "Not when you were there."

It's Falan's turn to be taken aback. "What are you talking about?"

Ronan shrugs, dropping his gaze. "I don't know. I still don't. All I know is I couldn't feel for her what she felt for me. And every time I've seen you the past year, you've reminded me of her, forcing me to face my own guilt. Both for how I treated her and for how I felt for you." He's skirting with his words, being vague. "It's something I hoped I would never have to admit to you."

"I don't understand," Falan says.

Ronan smiles, but something about it is melancholic. He stands up, dusting off his trousers. "My apologies, disregard what I said. I'll see you tonight." He walks down the staircase and disappears from sight.

Falan stays on the steps, her puzzled mind trying to work out what just happened. Ronan has never been particularly nice to her, but his scorn has only increased ever since Lavanya's death. He says it's because she reminds him of his guilt, so how does this talk of feelings for her come in? Their conversations have been civil at best, most of their time spent arguing. It makes her uncomfortable, especially since Ronan confirmed Lavanya felt something romantic for him.

It's best to forget it, like he said. It's not worth thinking about because it will never be brought up again.

Ary joins Falan on the staircase, causing her thoughts of Ronan to vanish. It's almost comical, this revolving cast of people who want to speak to her. The two of them sit in silence, but it's clear Ary is bursting to ask a question.

"What was she like?" Ary finally says.

Falan says nothing.

"Your sister, I mean." When Falan still doesn't respond, Ary shakes her head in apology. "Never mind. I'm sorry, I—"

"I was nothing like her, if that's what you are wondering," Falan says. "She was determined. Ambitious. Brave, taking on challenges that scared her for my sake. Kind, helping others when she didn't have to. Likable. She knew how to bring life to a room, make everybody adore her."

Ary doesn't speak, but Falan can imagine her eyes filled with tears, the apologies ready on her lips.

"She inherently trusted nobody but herself," Falan continues. "At the same time, she took on gambles she couldn't have won. She was spontaneous. Reckless. Excessively hopeful, to a point where it made her careless. Naive." A beat. "Stupid."

Ary's breath hitches.

"She might have smiled a great amount, but I don't think she was truly happy."

Because of me. Because I came up to the deck that day on the ship and you happened to be there. Because I ran out of fare and we had to stay in Paris. Because you signed with Jean-Pierre to save me. Because I was your biggest burden. You said you thought I might be better off if I never met you, but it's the other way around.

I hurt you the most, Akka.

"Falan," Ary whispers.

Falan clenches her jaw, anticipating what Ary is going to say. She doesn't need apologies. She doesn't need somebody to tell her that Lavanya was adored, that she's missed, that she loved Falan.

But Ary surprises her by saying, "You're right. You sound nothing like her at all." Her eyes are full of tears. But she doesn't let them fall. "You think you know me, but you don't."

"I do know one thing. You're scared," Falan says pitilessly. "And that's something you can't afford."

"How can I not be? I don't want to die."

"You won't. Only the deserving ones will."

But Lavanya's voice in the back of her head continues to speak.

You're the cause of everything that led to my death, Falan. Perhaps you're the most deserving of all.

Anaïs comes by later, just as Lucien said would happen. When Falan opens her door, the tailor's expression twists with repulsion. "You don't look the greatest, do you?"

"Looks haven't been high on my priority list the past few days," Falan bites back, but the objects behind Anaïs, suspended in the air by magic, are a welcome sight. A large bucket of clean water. A bar of sweet-scented soap. A washcloth. Fresh clothes and gauze for her wounds. A comb.

"Congratulations," Anaïs says dryly. "You're a finalist."

"Finalist?" Falan says, pretending she doesn't know. "There are still two more rounds to go."

Anaïs grins. "There's been a change. The final round has been moved up to tonight." Clearly she's relishing dropping this information on her.

"Why?" Falan asks.

Anaïs's smirk drops at Falan's flat tone, but she doesn't seem to suspect anything. It seems Falan's usually indifferent attitude has finally paid off. "How should I know? Perhaps Jean-Pierre thought there were too few players left to stretch across two rounds. I'll be waiting outside. Let me know when you're finished."

She slams the door behind her, leaving Falan to bathe in peace. She takes her time, even as the water goes from tepid to cool. Her hair softens as she scrubs blood from her long black locks, and she uses the washcloth Anaïs supplied to scour dirt and sweat from her skin. She mocked it only hours before, but this truly is a reward.

When Falan is finished, she notices Anaïs has set a new outfit on her bed, which is exactly like the old but clean and untorn. She wraps fresh gauze around her wounds and dresses quickly. However, when she opens the door to tell Anaïs she's finished, Falan's heart drops.

Jean-Pierre looks down at her, shiny eyes gleaming, his lips curled into a sinister smile.

XLV

November 11, 1896

IF HE HAD THE CHOICE, JULES WOULD GO TO THE telegraph office. It would be much easier getting a message to the police, and easier to remain anonymous. But at this time of night, a letter will have to do. It might work better anyhow. Going into the office and conversing with the worker there would put his identity at risk. An errand boy paid an extra sum to drop the letter off at the station will not remember his face.

With the Blanchet mansion empty and the final game hours away, Jules settles down in front of his father's typewriter. He wipes his sweaty palms on his trousers, gathering himself before starting the first sentence.

"Dear Monsieur, I'm staying at le Palais Blanchet, and I'd like to report something suspicious."

"Sunkara, what a surprise it is that you've made it to the finale," Jean-Pierre says, blocking the doorway. "And what an honor too, of course."

Lucien never mentioned that Jean-Pierre would be dropping by. This visit has to be unprecedented. "Where is Anaïs?" Falan asks, finding her tongue.

"I dismissed her. I decided this year I would personally congratulate each finalist. I assume Anaïs has told you that tonight's round will be our last for this year," he says. With a wave of his hand, the objects Anaïs gave her all pile into the bucket. "I commend you for making it this far. Many thought you wouldn't, but I didn't feel so absolute. You've proved to be quite the contender."

Falan doesn't thank him.

"I also came by because I was curious to know how each finalist was feeling," he continues, ignoring her chilly stare. "You seem . . . on edge."

She remains silent.

"This year's Game of Oaths has certainly been a fierce one, well fought by you all. But sadly, all games must come to an end." Jean-Pierre pauses. "Enjoy your last few hours before the finale."

Falan tenses, about to step back, but he grabs her wrist.

"As I said, all games must come to an end. Remember that, Sunkara," he says, fingernails digging into her skin. "And all games have a winner."

His eyes are glaring now, despite his smile, and she reads his expression clearly. He's no longer talking about the Game of Oaths.

"You're right," she says coolly. "And I don't intend to lose."

Jean-Pierre's eyes narrow. But he lets go of her wrist with a flourish, walking away down the hall, the bucketful of items floating behind him.

Night falls. Falan imagines snow drifting against the wind, like the night Lavanya died. She smooths her outfit. Redoes her hair.

All done, petite renarde. Lavanya's voice mocks her from her memories.

This time, Falan is ready for the knock on her door. However, when she opens it to greet Bellamy, her gaze slides to the flask in his hand. "No lineup tonight, you're going straight into the game," he says.

This is it. The last time.

"Everything will be fine," Bellamy whispers. He doesn't mention grants, leading her to assume she's not getting any tonight. His smoky eyes are steady. Determined.

Only the deserving ones will die.

For the first time, Falan sees Bellamy as she takes the flask and drinks. Her eyelids grow heavy. The flask slips from her loose grasp. She falls forward into Bellamy's waiting arms, one final dance of soporific apprehension. His fingers brush back the hair from her face, his palm warming the small of her back. She thinks of his tenderness last night as he cleaned her wounds, the care of his fingers, the softness of his gaze.

If she dies tonight, this will be her last memory of him.

"Chance, Sunkara," he whispers.

And then her knees buckle and she drops into the darkness.

PART V

The Garden

"Such arcane power always holds a price.
What it is, however, we simply do not know yet."

—*Guillaume Gallien's Origins of the Arcane*;
Ch. 10, p. 203 (1868)

1. Sylvestre - FIRE PERFORMER - King of Spades

~~2. Hugh STRONGMAN King of Hearts~~

~~3. Cyril WEAPON DODGER King of Diamonds~~

~~4. Thomas KNIFE THROWER Jack of Diamonds~~

~~5. Eliot ESCAPIST Jack of Spades~~

6. Ronan - TRAPEZE ARTIST - King of Clubs

~~7. Arthur ACROBATIC BALANCER Jack of Hearts~~

~~8. Collette FIRE PERFORMER Queen of Spades~~

~~9. Martin CONTORTIONIST Jack of Clubs~~

~~10. Meera DEATH DANCER Queen of Clubs~~

11. Falan - TRAPEZE ARTIST - Queen of Hearts

12. Channary - TIGHTROPE WALKER - Queen of Diamonds

XLVI

November 12, 1896

FOR THE FIRST TIME IN THE GAME OF OATHS, FALAN wakes up to silence. There is no sound of a crowd or Jean-Pierre's voice.

The world around her is ethereal, shrouded in darkness and mist. She's lying on frosted grass, surrounded by rosebushes dusted with white snow. The roses themselves stand out against silvery ivy. Everything is pale and delicate with winter in the Garden, except for the bright red of the roses.

There is no clock overhead, no countdown ticking. This is the finale, and the spectators are to relish it until a winner finally finds the prize in one of the many clearings. A quick ending is never satisfactory.

With difficulty, Falan pushes herself to her feet. There are four different paths surrounding her, each opening framed by archways made of intricately twisted branches. She suspects Jean-Pierre has no intention of ever letting her reach the clearing with the prize. But she must play her part.

She finds herself staring at a nearby rosebush. The petals look like hearts, velvety soft. However, what grabs her attention more are the thorns on each stem, as big as her hand, sharp enough to slice through skin. For a moment, she considers snapping one off as a weapon. But there's no telling what will happen if she does.

Falan shakes her head, focusing on the paths. There's no method to work out which is the correct one, so she chooses the one straight ahead of her. The mist oddly seems to light the way, as if the fog itself is composed of delicate dewdrops of light woven together in translucent clouds. Even though Jules partially healed her wounds, she still cannot run without her body aching. But she can walk at a brisk enough pace.

The crimson roses continue to line the path, whispering for Falan to pluck them. The murmurs trace across her skin like the tendrils of a breeze, sending chills up her body. Each time the whispers start to take hold, the sight of the thorns keeps her in check.

Walking farther, Falan suspects the other three have been placed nearer to the prize. Or, in Sylvestre's case, on paths that will eventually cross hers.

As if on cue, she hears a noise behind her. The creak of vines twisting, thorns gnashing together like teeth. Falan whirls to see the path behind her closing in, the vines tangling together, itching to wrap around her and promising nothing good if they do.

On instinct, Falan runs. Pain chokes her as she pumps her legs, fighting to reach the next clearing. One hand clutches her stinging abdomen. She won't be able to run much longer.

The vines will stop when I run into Sylvestre, she realizes. *The spectators are hungry for blood.*

"Come on, Sylvestre," she says through her ragged breathing as she nears the end of the path. "I'm ready."

Falan enters the clearing up ahead, then throws herself back as a fireball skids in front of her face. Sylvestre stands mere feet away. Behind her, the path is empty, like the pursuing vines were never there.

Sylvestre lifts his hands, a fireball dancing in each one, casting ominous shadows across his face. He is at an advantage here. But just because she's hurt doesn't mean she's forgone her skills.

Like the night before, it is the two of them against each other. But, Falan realizes, Sylvestre was always meant to be her final opponent. And they both know only one of them will walk out of this garden alive.

Jules's main job is to keep his father in the honor box. It's perhaps the simplest job compared to the others, yet he's trying to stop his hands from shaking. There is no reason his father would leave the honor box tonight. Spectators are watching with full attention, breath held, fingers clenched. Even the patrons in the honor box are no longer drinking so heavily.

"Anxious?" Blanchet asks Jules as he sits next to him.

Jules manages a small smile. "A finale is always nerve-wracking," he says. On the stage below, Falan and Sylvestre face off, a duel everyone has been waiting for.

"You seem rather ill." His father sounds concerned, but Jules knows it's a thin veil for the unpleasant emotion underneath. A cold sweat sends a shiver up his spine.

"I wouldn't want to miss this," Jules insists, but his stomach gurgles rather loudly in protest.

"No, no." Blanchet rests a cold, falsely comforting hand on his shoulder. "I know how high-stress situations tend to indispose you."

His father states the truth, but it's still bitter to hear aloud. It's all the more frustrating because it's something Jules can't control, and that makes him feel weaker. Blanchet's hand tightens around his shoulder, more brisk than comforting, and he nearly pushes Jules out of the honor box after a quick word to the others. Jules's pace quickens as bile suddenly races up his throat. He's practically running by the time he reaches the exit of the Chapiteau and slips outside, falling to his knees and doubling over. He can feel his father watching him as he coughs, his arms trembling, the world swaying before his eyes.

"Better?" Blanchet asks, his tone about as warm as a snowstorm.

Jules knows the correct answer isn't a yes. He dips his head, eyes on the dark blades of grass below. His spectacles slide down his nose. "I'm sorry for embarrassing you," he says quietly.

"It wouldn't be the first time," Blanchet says. "But lately you've been more anxious than usual. Any particular reason?"

Jules freezes for a moment. "It is my first time on the panel. It's a stressful position with little rest."

"Especially the way you've been running around," Blanchet says, but it doesn't sound like praise. "In fact, you never explained where you were last night."

"I told you, I went for a walk." Jules pushes himself to his feet, adjusting his spectacles. "I think I'm well enough now to go back inside."

"No, let's stay out here for a bit. The fresh air will do you good," Blanchet insists.

"I wouldn't want to miss Sylvestre and Falan's final fight," Jules says.

But Blanchet doesn't move. "I can't imagine why you, complaining about a lack of rest, would want to go out for a walk at four in the morning. So tell me the real reason."

"I couldn't sl—"

"And don't think of lying to me, garçon. Remember what happens when you lie."

Jules's stomach gurgles once more, but he's emptied all its contents; there's nothing left. It burns, a pain that reaches his chest. "I know what happens when I lie," he finally says, eyes dropping to the ground. "But I couldn't sleep, really."

Jules feels the punch before he sees it. Right in his stomach, below his ribs. He crumples to his knees with a gasp, limbs quivering. "Did you really think I would be fooled with such a weak untruth?" his father says.

"What untruth?" Jules manages to ask.

"You're far more trouble than you're worth." He viciously slaps Jules across the face, sending his spectacles skidding across the grass. Jules blinks in shock, stars spinning in front of his eyes. Automatically, he touches his cheek, which is already starting to swell. His father never hits him in the face; he always attacks places covered by clothes so people won't see the bruises.

"You know what happens when you lie to me, yet you still do," Blanchet snarls. "You think I didn't know you were lurking outside the door during my conversation with Monsieur Horrent?"

"What do you think you know?" Jules asks through deep breaths, picking up his spectacles but not putting them on yet.

Surprise flickers across Blanchet's face; about now is when Jules generally breaks. But then anger twists his expression and he grabs a fistful of Jules's collar. "I noticed yesterday morning the key to my gallery was missing. Do you have any explanation for that?"

"No."

Blanchet hits him again, and Jules bites back a cry of pain. "You could have made me proud. You could have been the son I always wanted. What you *are* is the unfortunate result of a mistake that I've had to bear for eighteen years. If I had not taken pity on you, you would be living on the streets as the beggar you deserve to be."

Jules tries to remain strong as his father continues to beat him. He demands that he confess to helping Falan, tells him he should be grateful for a roof over his head, that he is as useless as his dead mother. That it's because of him that Jules got half the looks of a proper man. Eventually, the tears start to flow, and Jules isn't sure whether the remarks or the blows cut more. He stops when he gets another slap for crying.

Blanchet is getting visibly more frustrated with each hit. Jules isn't sure how much more he can endure. But when his father pulls out a blade, Jules's eyes widen. "It seems you need a little more convincing," Blanchet says in a smooth voice. "If I were not so angry, I would commend you for your resilience."

Before Jules can run, his father grabs him by the neck, forcing him to stay on his knees. "What are you doing?" Jules asks, voice trembling.

"We'll start with the fingernails. Then the fingers."

Horror floods Jules as his father grabs his arm, forcing his hand in place. "Stop!" Jules shouts when the blade is inches from the tip of his index finger. He's sobbing despite knowing tears will result in another slap, unable to take it anymore.

"You know how to make this stop," Blanchet says calmly.

Jules stubbornly shakes his head, but when his father moves the blade forward again, he finally breaks. "All right! I aided Falan Sunkara. I admit it!"

Blanchet's ice-blue eyes gleam. "Was Bellamy Durand aiding her as well?"

Jules nods rapidly.

Blanchet sighs, bringing the blade to Jules's face, purposefully brushing over the bruises purpling Jules's skin. "I'm disappointed in you," he says. If Jules weren't so terrified, he'd laugh at Blanchet attempting to act as a concerned father. "I should kill you along with those other offenders. But . . . if you cooperate, you get a choice."

He lets Jules go and Jules takes in a deep breath, fingers digging below the grass into the dirt. "A choice?" he asks hoarsely.

“If you help put an end to whatever scheme they have planned, I might forgive you for your unpalatable betrayal,” Blanchet says, and Jules’s breath hitches. “So? Will you choose the side of the winners? Or do you wish to die among the others like the spineless coward you are?”

Jules’s fists clench the blades of grass beneath him. His father is right. He is a spineless coward. He always has been. “I’ll help you,” Jules whispers. He barely feels the pain of the hits anymore; all he can think of is the others when they find out. “Just don’t kill me.”

“Good boy.” His father pats his head like he would a dog. “You made the right choice.”

XLVII

November 12, 1896

DESPITE ALL SHE'S BEEN THROUGH, ARY STILL DEEMS her first performance on the tightrope as the most terrifying night of her life. Even more terrifying than the night Jean-Pierre found her.

"I don't want to go to the brothel!" she yelled desperately at him when he walked over to her, shocked at her own viciousness. But after several previous attempts from slimy men during her six nights on the streets, citing appeal in her "exotic looks," she couldn't think of any other reason he would approach her.

After a bout of surprised silence, Jean-Pierre chuckled and said, "On se calme, ma chère. I'm not from a brothel." And then he told her about the Cirque and its possibilities.

In a couple of hours, Ary had already signed a contract. After allowing her to fill up on stew and bread, Jean-Pierre directed her to a room at the boardinghouse. When she walked in, two girls were already there. Both were Indian; one welcomed Ary with a teasing smile while the other surveyed her with cool, impassive eyes. They both showed Ary around the arena the next day, made sure she had enough to eat at breakfast. After only a week of training, Jean-Pierre put Ary in her first show.

Magic injected euphoria through Ary's veins when she took to the tightrope, feeding off her acrobatics Affinity, but somehow it only heightened her terror. Like her heart was about to give out from the sheer amount of ecstasy she felt. So high above the audience, dancing on air, it was a long way down to a grisly death, stopped only by Jean-Pierre's Enchanteur abilities. Acrobatics may have been her Affinity, but it was the magic that reached inside her and brought it forth, making her superhumanly adept at the skill.

It's a long way down, she told herself while waiting in the rafters. *I will not fall.*

And she didn't. But that didn't stop her from feeling like she was going to. That first night on the tightrope, Ary was asked to do the impossible. And nothing scared her more than that.

Now she's used to the impossible. The Garden around her isn't real, but it's her reality. A prettier reality than the past few rounds, but more menacing than all of them put together. Despite the danger, Ary finds herself drawing closer to the rose-covered vines, eyeing the large thorns, wanting to pluck one off just to see how it feels.

Ary suddenly realizes her hand is reaching up to do just that and she backs away. The thorns could be poisoned; it's best to keep on the path and look for the clearing with the object. Ary wonders what it could be. She can't help wondering, ridiculously enough, whether the winner keeps the object.

A shadow suddenly flits in the corner of her eye and Ary stiffens, whirling around. The path behind her is empty, although a tangle of faint whispers in the air makes her shiver. It could be an illusion. It could also be Sylvestre, wanting to finish her off before going after Falan.

The whispers, still unintelligible, grow louder. Ary runs. She doesn't get more than two steps before someone grabs her. Ary screams, a desperate shriek of pure fear that nearly rips her throat, struggling as the person's arm wraps around her neck to choke her. She gasps for air, unsure if this is part of the Garden or if this is real. It feels so real; her lungs burning, her eyes bulging, the acceleration of her heartbeat. But everything here feels real, until it isn't. Her mind grows fuzzier as she goes limp in the person's grasp. She weakly attempts another struggle, but it's pitiful. Her feet slide out from under her.

"I'm sorry," the person says, barely audible yet somehow familiar. "It'll be over soon."

Just like she feared that first night on the tightrope, Ary slips and drops in a never-ending fall into darkness.

XLVIII

November 12, 1896

FOR A MINUTE, FALAN AND SYLVESTRE SURVEY EACH other, a dangerous silence thick in the air as they wordlessly challenge the other to attack first.

Sylvestre finally throws a fireball at her, which she dodges by darting to the side. When he throws the second one, it nearly hits her shoulder, the cinders singing a few locks of her hair. She swipes at it before a fire sets to her coat, raking her fingers through the strands.

Sylvestre laughs, a grating sound that echoes throughout the clearing. "What's the matter, Sunkara? Tired tonight?"

Falan doesn't answer. She's studying him, watching for a weak spot. With the right side of her vision blocked, it makes the task harder, but a day with the eye patch has made her quicker to adapt.

"I was considering making this fast. Showing a little mercy," Sylvestre says, whipping out a blade. A grant. "But the audience demands a good show. A finale. And I can't argue with that."

There's a slim chance of besting him in a physical fight, especially with her injuries. But the thought of running from him makes her stomach roll—until an idea comes to mind.

Falan slowly steps forward, as if she's about to meet Sylvestre's challenge, before suddenly running into the pathway to her right. With a laugh, Sylvestre chases after her. Her body aches as she races down the path; Sylvestre could easily catch up to her. But he won't. He's enjoying the chase too much, and that's precisely what she's counting on.

She knows Jean-Pierre will use a method to drive her back, forcing her to face Sylvestre when the audience gets tired of watching them run. Sure enough, the path ahead starts to close with a mess of thorns and roses. Behind her, Sylvestre huffs triumphantly, speeding up. Falan reaches into her pocket, pulls out her aerial ribbon, and ties it around her wrist. She eyes the snarl of burrs at the top of the bush, predicting it should be strong enough.

This is just like any other performance, she tells herself.

Falan looks back to see Sylvestre's smile drop as he realizes what she's about to do. She throws the ribbon up, catching it on the burrs, and climbs the ribbon just as Sylvestre reaches her. But she doesn't climb to the top like he expects. Instead, she uses the ribbon to flip herself backward over Sylvestre, as naturally as any trapeze artist, and rides the momentum to slam into him. Sylvestre sprawls forward, right into the thorny mass of roses, and screams.

The aerial ribbon rips, sending Falan onto the ground. A wave of dizziness washes over her along with pain from the impact, and she looks down to see one of the thorns embedded in her scraped leg. With a wince, she pulls it out, but it's nothing compared to Sylvestre. He has them all over his bleeding body.

This is her chance. Strike while he's incapacitated. Falan gets to her feet and grips the thorn, readying to slit his throat, when a scream in the distance grabs her attention. The scream of a girl.

Ary.

Falan snaps back to Sylvestre, but it's too late. She's knocked to the ground as he tackles her, the thorn slipping from her hand. Sylvestre places a knee on her throat to hold her down, striking another match. Falan's fingers stretch, frantically searching for the thorn, as Sylvestre brings the fire closer to her face.

"At least now you'll join your sister," he snarls. "She deserved to die like the bitch she was."

At the last second, Falan's fingers find the thorn and she swipes her outstretched hand into Sylvestre's. The impact slaps his fire-bearing hand right into his face. Sylvestre screams, batting at the flames, but the few seconds of distraction is all she needs to send him onto his back.

In a single motion, she sends the thorn down into Sylvestre's throat, piercing clean through his skin. She doesn't stop after she pulls it out, sending it back down for a second strike. It's not enough. A third. A fourth, a fifth, until she loses count and she's covered in as much blood as he is. She doesn't cease even long after he's stopped moving, even as her arms ache, even as her voice cracks as she screams out all the rage she's held the past five years. Rage for everything he has said and done, down to his last ugly words about Lavanya.

Then, all at once, she stops.

Exhaustion overcomes her and she lowers the thorn. She doesn't dare let go, in case he somehow survived. The world swims, either with tears or dizziness. She's on her knees, fingernails digging into the grass beneath her, her mind begging her to get up.

Get up. She has to get up.

Somehow, even through her daze, it occurs to her to take the matches from him. Falan plucks the bloodstained box of matches out of Sylvestre's hand before sluggishly pulling herself to her feet, her legs shaking. She steps over Sylvestre's mutilated corpse, waiting to see if it rises. Evil always gains a second wind when one finally drops their guard.

But it seems his has already been used, for even as she keeps looking over her shoulder, he doesn't move. There are no signs of life in his body. Perhaps she should feel triumphant, even relieved. However, all she feels is exhaustion. She wants to close her eyes and let her aching body drop, give it what it's begging for. But she continues to stumble through the nearest passage, unable to keep track of where she's going.

Her head is dense, saturated with fogginess. The world around her lags like she's been drugged.

The thorns. They must have some sort of poison.

This is Jean-Pierre's chance to finish her off. She's dazed and wounded, the thorn's poison working its effects on her. She tries to think what he must be planning, but her thoughts keep melting into each other. Falan lifts her heavy head to see a clearing coming up.

I can collapse there.

She barely manages to pull herself into the open space, only to run right into somebody. They steady her at once, supporting her as her knees buckle, and she looks up into concerned blue eyes.

"Falan," Ronan says.

XLIX

November 12, 1896

BELLAMY HAS NEVER SEEN LE PALAIS BLANCHET'S lobby so bare. He has also never been so grateful for it. He would have normally preferred going on a job like this by himself, but having Lucien with him is beneficial.

"I should have taught you how to pick a lock," Bellamy says as Lucien steps into the elevator. "It would have been helpful if you opened the door by the time I climbed the stairs."

"I'm helpful in other ways." With his free hand, Lucien plucks a knife from his belt and twirls it effortlessly between his fingers. "Let me remind you that there is a person up there waiting to hurt us, and I'm good with a blade."

"I'm not so bad with weapons either," Bellamy says, closing the elevator door.

"If you insist." Through the gridded door, Lucien does not look convinced at all. "Now, send me up."

"Believing in someone works wonders, you know," Bellamy says half-jokingly and starts to work the elevator's large crank, pulling the rope on top of the car.

Bellamy waits a minute after he stops the car on the ninth floor, giving Lucien time to step out, before lowering it back down carefully. As soon as he does, he bolts for the staircase. By the time he reaches Lucien, he's standing in front of Jean-Pierre's office door at the end of the hall.

"Did you run into any trouble?" Bellamy asks, panting.

Lucien shakes his head. "No. Cadieux must be waiting inside the office. Did they really send only one man to stop us?"

"Cadieux is good at his job," Bellamy says, remembering the beating he got from him last time. "He's . . . it's difficult to explain. You'll see soon enough. It will be hard to fight him, let alone do what Falan wants us to."

"He's lost the element of surprise," Lucien points out. "That will work in our favor."

"Perhaps," Bellamy says, but he's doubtful. Cadieux doesn't need it. He kneels to pick the lock on the door. "Give me your thinnest knife."

Lucien scoffs but hands it to him.

A few seconds later, Bellamy leans back as the lock clicks. "Told you I'm not bad with weapons."

"Congratulations," Lucien says dryly, taking back his knife. "I'll be sure to call you if I ever get locked out of my room."

It's ironic how Lucien thinks Bellamy and Falan are alike, given that Bellamy thinks that Lucien is more like Falan than the two of them realize. Both dry, skeptical, and too smart for their own good. But Lucien is not selfish, nor does he let his temper control him. Not like Falan. She focuses only on getting what she wants, not the consequences for it.

It's something Bellamy can't help but admire her for, although it's also something that will continue to land her in danger. The memory of her in Ronan's arms after Sylvestre nearly beat her to death flashes in his mind, and Bellamy's smile fades.

"You're thinking about Falan," Lucien says, watching him. He still hasn't opened the door.

Without answering, Bellamy gestures for him to go on, and Lucien obliges.

The first thing Bellamy notices is that several oil lamps in Jean-Pierre's office are lit, unlike last time when only one was left burning. Lucien walks in first, ready with a knife. As Bellamy walks in after him, his eyes sweep the room.

It looks exactly how it was the night before. A red couch on the far right, a wood-and-glass table in front of it, and a wall of windows behind leading to the private balcony. A large wooden trunk sits next to the windows. On the left is the large desk, a wall of shelves behind it with the same objects—a few books, paper, a curved knife, the dying plant. The safe is still on the shelf, ready to be cracked and emptied.

Then Lucien's gaze focuses on something behind Bellamy.

Bellamy doesn't wait for him to shout a warning before ducking. Above him, a fist swings at air as Lucien throws a knife. Cadieux growls as the blade sinks into his left arm, then yanks it out and tosses it back. Lucien just barely manages to avoid the knife by throwing himself backward, but overshoots and falls onto the floor, his cane rolling out of reach.

"You again," Bellamy says, rolling his eyes. "Stalking me, as usual."

"Stealing from a more successful man, as usual," Cadieux shoots back.

Bellamy whips his gaze around, scouring the area for a weapon. But Lucien yells, "The safe!" He grunts as he pushes himself up on his elbows. "Bellamy!"

Bellamy runs for the safe, but Cadieux tackles him before he can reach it, straddling him. "I told you. I follow, gather information, and bring it back to Horrent. He's not interested in your little debt anymore." Cadieux pins Bellamy's arms by the wrists and his lips split into a sinister grin. "And like I said before, he's not going to stop me this time."

Before Cadieux can do anything, something pierces his arm, thrown from the other side of the room. Cadieux turns to face Lucien, who is still on the ground, and that's all the time Bellamy needs. He throws Cadieux off, gets to his feet, and runs. Cadieux makes to follow, but Lucien throws another knife at him, drawing his attention.

"Don't perish before I finish checking, please!" Bellamy says as he reaches the safe.

To his surprise, Lucien laughs. "That's the first time I've heard you use that word."

"Perish?"

"Please!"

Bellamy grins. He quickly scrolls through the padlock until he lines up the three correct numbers, unlocks it, and throws open the safe door.

He stops.

"What's the holdup?" Lucien's struggling voice asks behind him. "Bellamy!"

As if in a daze, Bellamy reaches inside and pulls out the bearer bonds. They are all there, the same amount as last night. He thumbs through them quickly to make sure. But there is no sign of the gray pyramid-shaped stone.

"The stone isn't in here," Bellamy finally says, dislodging the shock blocking his throat.

"What?" Lucien shouts, followed by a crash.

"The object holding all the contract magic . . . it's not in the safe." He turns to see Lucien has somehow gotten Cadieux on the floor, both throwing punches at each other. The table in front of the couch is broken, its legs collapsed beneath it, and Lucien has a bloody gash on his right cheek.

Cadieux grins. "It's already been moved, thief. You'll never find it."

Bellamy clutches the bonds tighter. Part of him wants to stay and search for the stone, not wanting to leave Lucien alone with Cadieux. The other part is telling him to run and hide the bonds where Falan told him to.

As if reading his mind, Lucien says, "Go."

Bellamy hesitates. "And leave you?"

"I can handle this bastard myself." Lucien says, eyeing Cadieux getting up.

"Where do you think you're going?" Cadieux demands, turning in Bellamy's direction, but Lucien throws himself forward and grabs Cadieux's ankles.

"Go!" Lucien yells desperately, making Bellamy's decision for him.

As a parting gift, Bellamy winks at Cadieux mockingly before he turns and sprints from the room.

L

November 12, 1896

FOR A MINUTE, FALAN STUDIES RONAN, MAKING SURE he's real and not an illusion from Jean-Pierre or brought on by the thorn's poison. In this garden, she cannot trust anything. Her gaze flickers to every part of him, from his dark hair all the way down to his scuffed boots.

"It's me," Ronan says.

"Prove it," she says, unconvinced.

"The morning before the Reckoning, you attempted to grab onto me with one hand when flipping from the trapeze during practice." He raises an eyebrow. "If I hadn't caught you, we wouldn't be having this conversation."

She scowls, pushing herself away. Her unsteady legs shake. "I believe you. Now . . . wipe that smug look off your face. Have . . . have you seen Ary?"

Ronan shakes his head. "No, but I heard her scream."

Falan stiffens. "You . . . heard her?"

"I didn't see her. I haven't seen anybody until now." He eyes the fresh blood on her dress.

Unable to stay on her feet any longer, Falan collapses to her knees. "Don't . . . touch the thorns," she says.

"Poison?" Ronan kneels next to her. Falan nods. "We can rest here to see if you get better or worse. There's no use in you roaming the paths half-conscious."

Falan nods again, too disoriented to argue, but keeps her guard up. The audience will grow bored if there is no action soon, and this is the perfect time for Jean-Pierre to unleash something upon them.

"Sylvestre's dead," she says. It's hard to talk or think through her fuzzy mind, but perhaps if their conversation rivets the audience enough, it will give time for a bit of the poison to wear off.

"You killed him?"

The surprise in his voice makes her glare at him. "You think that I'm . . . incapable of defending myself?"

Ronan shakes his head. "That is not what I said. I was just concerned about the amount of grants he might have been given compared to you."

"That . . . didn't matter in the end." She remembers the bloody mess of a corpse after she was finished with him. No matter what he had been given, how many people bet on him, she still won. Again, she waits to feel triumph or relief, but experiences nothing except her own exhaustion, aching body, and disoriented mind.

Ronan suddenly holds a finger to his lips. His gaze is focused down the passage beyond one of the archways, deep into the mist, from which a light fluttering sound emanates. Falan looks in the same direction, puzzled, and something small flies out of the mist and into the clearing.

A butterfly. Fitting, in a garden of pretty flowers.

It's beautiful, velvety wings the color of ice and sage and ink, fluttering around them. Falan doesn't trust it. Yet all she wants to do is hold her hand out so the butterfly can perch on her finger. She gets to her feet along with Ronan, who is also mesmerized by the creature.

Falan shakes her head, now a bit less heavy. They cannot trust anything in this garden. She backs away as more butterflies emerge from the mist into the clearing, a whole kaleidoscope of them. It is enchanting. It is terrifying.

"Allaire," she says.

He doesn't move, staring at the butterflies approaching.

"Allaire," she says again, voice on edge.

The first butterfly lands on his shoulder and crawls closer to his neck. A row of sharp teeth glints in the mist's light, bared to bite.

"Ronan!" Falan throws herself forward and smacks the butterfly off his shoulder before it can sink its teeth in, yanking him back by his sleeve.

Ronan blinks, dazed. "What?" he asks, still out of it, and she gestures farther down the path. The flock of butterflies now looks like a storm of vicious teeth and sharp wings. "Oh."

Falan runs through the nearest archway and into the passage, Ronan with her. Only a few seconds in and she knows she's in trouble. She's too weak, from both the thorn's poison and her wounds. The butterflies and their teeth are seconds from reaching her when Falan remembers the box of matches in her pocket. With shaking fingers, she pulls out a handful of matches and strikes them.

A screeching sound fills the air as she holds the fire up toward the swarm of deadly butterflies, some rearing back and others bursting into flame. She's fascinated by how they wither into dust, once here and then not. Falan throws down the matches, nearly eaten down to their cores, and strikes more.

"Where did you get that?" Ronan asks, hurrying back to her.

"Sylvestre. Looks like he was useful for something after all. Thanks for your help."

Ronan has the decency to look embarrassed. But he takes the matches from her and lights some of his own, which deters the butterflies further. "I wonder why they don't like fire."

A butterfly crumbles to ash, answering his question.

It's getting harder for Falan to figure out Jean-Pierre's game. He sent these vicious butterflies her way for a reason. Is it to hint that Ary came across the same creatures? Her scream appeared to be real, especially since Ronan heard it as well.

She can roam the Garden searching for Ary, but that might send her and Ronan into more danger. The more they delay, the more susceptible they are. And the audience will grow bored, which might cause Jean-Pierre to unleash another type of horror on them.

Falan's teeth sink into her lip. By now Bellamy and Lucien must have retrieved the stone and the bearer bonds from Jean-Pierre's safe. Which means it's time for this round to end.

The butterflies had to have meant something else, something unrelated to Ary. Last time she came across an obstacle, it was to guide her closer to Sylvestre. If the butterflies came from the other direction, then that means she's currently heading toward the prize. And since Ronan is now with her, Jean-Pierre has no choice but to let her reach it.

"You take the lead," she says as Ronan burns up the last of the sharp-toothed butterflies. Luckily, because she only has one match left.

Ronan's eyebrows shoot up. "Why?"

"Because you will lead us to the prize," she says. "Whichever way you choose is the right way."

Something changes in his face, an unreadable expression flashing across his features. But then it hardens and he starts to walk, going at a pace Falan can keep up with. The desperation-fueled energy has leached out of her, leaving her tired and pained once again.

"I'll be glad when this is all over," Ronan says quietly as they go down a new path.

She nods, too saturated with pain to speak. It's not over until the bearer bonds are cashed and split. Until Bellamy is out of immediate danger with Horrent. Until she finally avenges Lavanya.

At the next clearing, Ronan chooses to go right this time, and she follows.

The Game of Oaths is only the beginning of the end. But Falan thinks of what will come after that. Perhaps going to find her father. He might not even be in England after all this time, and she isn't sure she wants to see him. After spending five years at the Cirque, she might not be able to adapt to a quiet life, reacquaint with somebody she hasn't seen in nearly ten years.

But perhaps that's what she needs. Somewhere calm with the only family she has left.

Ronan suddenly stops walking. "Do you hear that?"

Falan listens closely, ears straining for any sounds, when she hears it. No, not hears. Feels. "Yes," she says quietly.

It's almost like a throbbing, a pulse. She can feel the faint vibrations. It doesn't scare her, oddly. It soothes her. It tells her that she should find its source.

They quicken their pace down the path. No dangers have plagued them in a while, which raises her guard. But Falan's increasing heartbeat tells her they are supposed to go this way. The rhythm only gets louder, the foggy mist brightening as they approach the next clearing, like it's shrouding something waiting to be found. It thickens until she can barely see a foot in front of her.

"Falan." Ronan's voice through the mist sounds awed. Triumphant.

Heart pumping, she pushes her stinging body forward. She arrives on the other side of the mist into the clearing. And in the center stands a table with a box on it. The world is dark around the table, as if a spotlight is shining down on it.

They have reached the right clearing. The one with the prize. The second either of them takes it, the Game of Oaths will finally end.

Ronan suddenly grabs Falan by the shoulders, sweeping her into a quick hug before she can react. He leans back only a few inches, cupping her face with one hand. His eyes are blown with excitement, that rush she sees when he's up on the trapeze . . . and desire. For a single, terrifying moment, Falan thinks he's about to kiss her, about to give this audience that certain une cerise sur le gâteau for this finale.

A sudden pressure around her shoulder blade makes her stop. Seconds later, a burst of pain races through her body. Falan gasps, falling to her knees. Something drips onto the ground, dark and red.

Blood.

It's only when she reaches up and touches her shoulder that she feels the hilt of a blade peeking through her shirt.

And Ronan is the one holding the knife.

LI

November 12, 1896

DURING LUCIEN'S EARLY DAYS OF THROWING PRACtice, sometimes he'd hold a knife incorrectly and accidentally slit his palms. The first time he cut himself, he cried, like most people would. Over time, he got used to it, barely flinching at the sting. The immunity grew the more skilled he became.

But the man in front of him seems to have some kind of superhuman shield, plucking each blade thrown out of his skin and tossing it aside with ease. And he doesn't show any pain when doing so, just grim satisfaction in Lucien's astonishment. No wonder Blanchet felt the need to send only one man.

"I wasn't expecting another person," Cadieux says after he easily catches Lucien's eighth knife and throws it aside. The two of them are still on the ground; Lucien made it a priority to keep him there for a better aim, but Cadieux stayed as if to humor him.

"Disappointed?" Lucien says, pressed up against the back of the couch behind him. The floor is sharp and icy against his knees, dull pain emanating from the left one.

Cadieux shakes his head. "Durand would have been easy to take care of; he's a runner, a swindler. Not a fighter. Not a killer. But you . . . you're different. Even with that leg of yours, you're a threat."

"Thanks, the cane makes for a good weapon too," Lucien says sardonically. "Although I see it doesn't matter. You don't feel pain."

"I used to. But I trained myself, perhaps you know the same. If one of your knives cut you, I doubt you'd flinch."

He's right. He wouldn't. But Lucien says, "I feel pain. I'm not like you."

Cadieux chuckles. "You like to be underestimated. It used to bother you, but now you treat it like an advantage. But unlike other opponents you might have faced, I'm not fooled so easily."

"You and I are not alike," Lucien snaps, despising Cadieux for what he's insinuating. There's something unnerving about this man's eyes. Unfeeling even beyond the sensation of pain.

Cadieux attacks first, shooting his fist out. Lucien angles his body out of the way. He manages to push himself to his feet by putting his weight on the arm of the couch, readying another blade in his free hand. He's down to two, the other eight scattered around the room. Lucien throws himself back over the couch as Cadieux picks up one of his knives and hurls it at him. The blade skims Lucien's already injured cheek and he curses.

"I think we are alike," Cadieux says with relish, grabbing Lucien by the collar and holding him against the curve of the couch's backrest.

"You don't know me. How can you say that?" Lucien says.

"You don't know me either. How can you say we aren't?"

Lucien could choose any eloquent phrase from a variety of things he's heard the French say over the years in response to irritating behavior. But all he says is, "Go to hell."

"You try not to let your anger consume you, yet you can't help yourself," Cadieux says tauntingly. Condescendingly. "I used to be like that too. Until I learned to turn it to pleasure. Before, I would have hurt you out of anger. Now I take satisfaction in your reaction, in your weakened state."

"In other words, you're a madman," Lucien spits out.

"Not a madman. A revolutionary. What would the world be like if more people thought like I did? Turning anger to pleasure means fewer wars, less conflict."

Lucien stares at him with alarm, more wary of this man's perspective than his combat skills. *He really is insane.* Using the moment, he leans against the couch to lift his good leg and kicks Cadieux in the stomach, sending him backward. "Did you feel pleasure from that?" he asks, gripping the couch to stay standing, and is rewarded when Cadieux growls. "It seems your emotions are only in check when convenient for you. You aren't in control at all."

Before Cadieux can retaliate, Lucien lets go of the couch and sends his last two knives at him in one fluid motion, falling onto the floor once more. Not to kill; lightweight throwing knives are rarely fatal. But as he watches Cadieux pull the knives out of his shoulder and thigh, it occurs to him that the one thing that Cadieux has specifically trained himself to do is his weakness.

The curved knife on Jean-Pierre's shelf catches Lucien's eye. *Find anything that can be used as a weapon to kill him,* Falan said earlier in the gallery. *But I wouldn't be surprised if Jean-Pierre has an actual weapon in the office.*

It's an obvious choice, but one that Cadieux might see coming. Then again, killing him with an ordinary object might suggest something unplanned or in self-defense. Lucien casts a desperate glance at his cane a few yards away, one of his knives lying next to it. There's no chance he will reach the shelf first without the aid of the cane.

Unfortunately, Cadieux knows this too, because he walks over to the cane just as Lucien starts to crawl to it. But this is precisely what Lucien was hoping for. Because as Cadieux bends over to pick up the cane and prepare to gloat, Lucien grabs the knife lying nearby and slashes the back of Cadieux's heels.

Cadieux doesn't feel the cuts at first. Confusion flashes across his face, then realization as he collapses, unable to walk. "What did you do?" he snarls.

Lucien grabs his cane from Cadieux's loosened grip, taking his time to get to his feet. "That's the thing about pain," he says. "It may hurt, but it's quite useful too."

Cadieux curses, attempting to stand, then collapses immediately.

"Don't bother to move. You may not feel the effect of the cut, but your nerves do," Lucien says. Cadieux grabs the cane, about to attempt to trip him, but Lucien sees it coming. He kicks Cadieux in the temple with his good leg, causing him to loosen his grip. Lucien seizes the opportunity, pulling the cane back and righting his balance.

"What do you get out of this?" Cadieux asks as Lucien walks over to the shelf and takes the curved knife, careful to grab a piece of paper off the shelf and wrap it around the hilt first. "I understand Durand, but Horrent doesn't know who you are. Why are you involving yourself?"

"You don't understand. I'm *too* involved," Lucien says, walking back over to him. It's clear Cadieux knows little of what is actually going on. "I do apologize, although you may not deserve it. Unlike yourself, I'm not somebody who enjoys murder."

"I don't need your pity," Cadieux says.

"I think you do. Having a knife slash your throat isn't a pleasant feeling."

Before Cadieux can respond, Lucien balances his weight on his right leg, takes his cane, and swings it toward Cadieux's head. As soon as it strikes him in the temple, the light in Cadieux's eyes dims and he goes still. Lucien sighs. Cadieux may not feel pain, but Lucien has to carry the burden of killing him. Because, as twisted as he is, Cadieux was right. Bellamy is not a killer.

But I am, Lucien thinks, recalling all he did in the previous Game of Oaths. *Whether to survive or not, I killed all the same.*

He didn't knock Cadieux unconscious out of pity. He did it so he wouldn't have to see the life fade from his eyes once the blade bit into his jugular. A selfish reason, not one of kindness. Lucien kneels, barely wincing at the ever present throb in his left knee, brandishing the knife. He tries to tell himself Cadieux doesn't deserve an ounce of pity or kindness. But it makes no difference, all the same.

Lucien slashes the knife across Cadieux's throat. He gurgles, blood bubbling from his neck. His head lolls to the side and stays there. Lucien doesn't need to check whether he's dead; it's a feeling, an emptiness in the void of the room. He stands, careful to move before any blood gets on his cane or shoes.

With the task finished, Lucien looks around the room for an inconspicuous place. *Now, to hide this.*

LII

November 12, 1896

"I KNOW YOU DON'T UNDERSTAND." RONAN HOLDS the hilt of the knife tighter, stroking Falan's hair with his other hand. "And I know you'll hate me for this."

Falan can only gasp in pain, her mind a muddle. This shouldn't be happening. She tries to find a trace of something in Ronan's eyes. Anything to hold on to, to indicate that this is a part of a plan he came up with on his own.

But the only thing she sees is remorse. Remorse means that this is true, that Ronan has betrayed her, disregarding everyone and everything they've planned.

She tries to speak, but her throat is blocked with something acrid and sticky. Blood. Or bile. Perhaps both. An involuntary whimper comes out of her mouth, as pitiful as a dying animal.

"Shh . . ." Ronan strokes her hair again, and she shudders. "I'm so sorry for this, believe me, Falan."

"Why?" Falan gasps.

"It's a flesh wound; it's not fatal," Ronan says, ignoring her question. "I made sure of that."

Falan finally finds the energy to glare. "I'm ever so grateful. Perhaps you can tell me why you shoved a knife through me in the first place." She lurches forward but gasps when pain shocks her body.

"You shouldn't move," Ronan says, standing up. "Don't worry; it will all be over soon."

"Ronan!" Falan yells as he starts to walk to the prize. Gritting her teeth, she wraps her fingers around the hilt. If she pulls the knife out, she could end up bleeding herself dry. But she can't fight him with the hilt sticking out of her like this.

Falan yanks the blade out and a wave of pain drowns her, so intense she nearly passes out, but she dizzily pushes herself up to see Ronan at the box. Using all her strength, Falan throws the knife. The blade sinks into Ronan's lower back and he collapses to his knees with a grunt. As he pulls the blade out, Falan runs forward and tackles him.

The two of them hit the ground, sending up a cloud of snowy dust around them. The knife clatters from his grip and out of sight, lost in the mist. Falan lies on top of Ronan, futilely hoping her body weight will keep him down, but he easily pushes her off.

"Why?" she asks again, grabbing him with her good arm. "Did you want to win so badly?"

"Yes," he says. Just one word.

Ronan stands again, but Falan throws herself forward and bites his ankle as he grabs the box. With a shout of pain, Ronan collapses, the box tumbling from his grip. It spins a few feet away and opens, the object inside rolling off its silk pillow onto the ground. At the sight of it, both Falan and Ronan freeze.

It's not a jewel or a precious metal. It's a stone.

Gray, shaped like a pyramid. The stone holding all the contracts.

Ronan's face goes pale. He pushes himself up, but Falan yanks him back down, using the force to propel herself forward. His hands grab her around the waist, pulling her back. A delirious urge to laugh suddenly bubbles up her throat. If she weren't so desperate or in such agony from the knife wound, this would be comical. She can imagine how it looks from the crowd's perspective: two children grappling over a toy they don't want to share.

Falan grabs Ronan by the collar, climbing atop him. Her hair falls over her face as she lowers her lips to his ear, whispering, "If you think winning will save you from death, think again, because I will make sure you cease breathing."

Ronan rolls her over, straddling her. Falan gasps as her bloodied shoulder hits the ground. Ronan looks up, as if considering the audience, then leans close to her. "I don't think so." His voice is cool, trying to bring back that forced politeness, but it quivers too much to be genuine. He's afraid of her, and he knows she knows it.

Falan bites his wrist so hard her teeth draw blood. Ronan curses, clutching his arm in pain, giving her the chance to slip from beneath him.

"Falan!" Ronan is the one yelling after her now as she crawls forward, dragging herself on her knees and good arm, her stabbed shoulder screaming in pain with each motion. Her heart speeds up when she's about a foot away from the stone.

Almost there.

Cold fingers suddenly wrap around her ankles, dragging her back. Falan stretches her good arm out as she wriggles to shake Ronan off, her fingers just wisps away from making contact with the stone. Her other hand digs into the dirt for grip, but it's not strong enough. Falan's quick breaths grow shallow. This isn't working. Ronan will overpower her before she can reach the stone.

The last match.

Fumbling for the box, Falan pulls it from her pocket, her trembling fingers failing to light the match on the first two tries. Her urgency grows when Ronan lets go of her ankles, grabbing her by the waist. Just as he starts to lift her, the match catches fire and Falan shoves it in his face.

Ronan drops her, more startled than injured. Had she hit the ground, Falan would have been immobilized by pain. But she's ready for the reaction and lands on her poised toes, propelling her jump. The world moves in slow motion as she lands and wraps her fingers around the stone.

Overcome by the excruciating impact, Falan slumps, blacking out. She regains consciousness a minute later to see the world around her distorting, the illusion ending. The Garden tilts in saturated colors, the taste of blood and smoke and snow thick in her mouth, the scents of copper and stone and mist penetrating her nose. Ronan sits a few feet away, unburned but defeated all the same, looking up at the Chapiteau's spiraling top. The sounds of the crowd slowly increase to a roar, and Falan achingly pushes herself up, shoving the stone in her pocket.

Jean-Pierre appears on stage as the illusion dissolves, walking over to Falan. He pulls her to her feet by her good arm, his hand tight around her wrist. Beneath the showmanship, she sees anger glittering in his eyes.

They both understand that he cannot do anything to her at this moment.

Jean-Pierre, still holding Falan by the wrist, raises her arm high. "Ladies and gentlemen, our winner of the forty-fifth Game of Oaths—player number eleven, the Queen of Hearts, Falan Sunkara!"

The crowd applauds, simply because it's the right thing to do. No matter the winner, the finale enraptured them, although Falan senses the aftermath will be nothing but hostile. People won't be happy about another boarder winning after Lucien, except perhaps those who bet on her. But it doesn't matter, at least not for now.

"Thank you very much for your attendance this year; I hope you have enjoyed our show," Jean-Pierre says to the audience. "At the moment, our winner needs time to recover. She will be at the celebratory dinner tomorrow night along with our runners-up, Ronan Allaire and Channary Chea."

At the mention of the runners up, the crowd's applause increases. Killing them off is at least a consolation prize after another boarder winner. Falan looks around, trying to find Ary, but she can't due to Jean-Pierre's stony grip.

"I will see you tomorrow night to officially finish off this year's Game of Oaths. Thank you, and good night!"

With his free hand, Jean-Pierre throws a bunch of lights in the air. They explode like golden fireworks, sparks raining down toward the audience below. The audience gasps in wonder as the sparks in the air swirl in a mesmerizing spiral until they combine into a giant ball mimicking the sun itself. Then the light explodes, and the Chapiteau falls into darkness.

Falan tenses, head whipping around, when Jean-Pierre's hand around her wrist pulls her toward him. "You may have won this game, Sunkara, but you certainly haven't won ours," says his cool snarl of a voice.

Before Falan can respond, a wet cloth is pushed over her nose and mouth. She struggles, managing to spit out a curse, but Jean-Pierre keeps the cloth firmly pressed over her face.

A couple of seconds later, the world is as quiet as it is dark.

LIII

November 12, 1896

BY THE TIME BELLAMY RETURNS, LUCIEN HAS already hidden Cadieux's body and the bloody knife, and rifled through all of the drawers in Jean-Pierre's desk. He's found nothing so far. No stone or any other eye-catching object.

When Bellamy enters the room, he looks around. "Where did you hide him?"

"Where do you think?" Lucien tilts his head toward the wooden trunk near the window. The floor is still mostly clean except for the smashed glass table, the blood swept up except in places one would forget, such as under the couch. But lugging the body into the trunk by himself was Lucien's real challenge.

"You could have waited for me. I would have helped." Bellamy walks over to the trunk and opens it, studying the body inside. "Are you certain you killed him?"

"Dead as a doornail. Do you want to continue checking?" Lucien says testily.

Bellamy raises an eyebrow. "Is that wonderfully biting sarcasm of yours a result of stress?"

It is, but Lucien doesn't bother to respond.

"I only ask because I'm impressed," Bellamy says. "If I'm being honest, I was concerned we wouldn't take care of him by the night's end."

Lucien silently agrees. After one battle with Cadieux, it's clear the kind of fighter he was. Although egotistical and something of a madman, he was still calculated, trained. To end up besting him in their duel was something close to a miracle. The fight has left Lucien exhausted, aching in a way he hasn't since last year's Game of Oaths.

Bellamy crouches in front of the trunk. It almost looks like he's saying a prayer for the dead man, but Lucien knows otherwise. He can't see Bellamy's face from his position behind the desk, but he imagines the triumphant smile on the thief's face.

"If you're finished inspecting Cadieux's corpse, you could do me a favor and gather my knives," Lucien says, cutting into the silence.

To Lucien's relief, Bellamy closes the trunk and obliges without a flippant comment. "I wouldn't bother still looking for the stone here," he says. "Cadieux mentioned it was moved, remember?"

Lucien sighs in frustration, trying to think of any other place it could be. "Blanchet's office?"

Bellamy sets the gathered knives on the desk. "He might have moved it to a different building entirely."

"You think?" Lucien asks as he starts to slide his knives back into his belt one by one, already feeling more secure. He wishes Jules were here. Knowing his father, he might guess accurately where the stone has been moved. Probably somewhere nobody can access, including them.

Lucien's eyes widen. *The gallery.*

"What?" Bellamy asks. "You know where it is?"

"If it's where I think, we're in trouble," Lucien says, toying with one of his knives. "I predict the gallery."

With a curse, Bellamy starts toward the door. "We need to leave."

"Durand—" Lucien starts.

"There's no point in wasting another second here. Time is ticking," Bellamy says as he starts to walk out the door into the hall. "But why would they take the time to move the stone but not the bonds—"

He suddenly stops talking. Lucien tenses, listening for any sounds in the hallway. A few seconds later Bellamy walks back in, followed by a smirking Monsieur Blanchet, who holds a pistol behind him.

"Well, well," he says triumphantly. "What have we here?"

Lucien, however, is focused on the person just coming through the door. Jules, bruised and beaten, holding himself uncertainly. Lucien's stomach drops when he realizes Jules is unrestrained, standing next to his father.

No.

"Jules." Lucien's voice involuntarily cracks. "Tell me you didn't."

"Oh, but he did," Blanchet says before Jules can speak. He throws an arm around Jules's shoulders. Jules flinches slightly at the touch but doesn't step away. "My son proved himself tonight."

Bellamy glances back at Lucien. Even the usually facetious thief can't hide the alarm in his eyes. If Jules told Blanchet everything, then their plan is ruined.

"Was assisting Falan Sunkara worth this?" Blanchet asks, leveling the pistol at Lucien now. He glances around the room.

"Looking for Cadieux?" Bellamy says before Lucien can speak. "We cut him a deal."

"A deal?" Blanchet says skeptically.

Lucien jumps on the lie. "It took much negotiation, as you can see," he says dryly, looking at the broken coffee table. "But it was enough to make him back off."

Blanchet narrows his eyes at them, clearly miffed. A muscle ticks in his jaw. "Jules. Get Trichet. I'm sure even you will be able to handle him."

Tentatively, Jules walks over to Lucien, whose anger is starting to swallow his shock. He knows he could end Jules's life in a single fluid motion. But with the pistol ready to fire, it's too much of a risk. Lucien is surprised to feel more hurt than angered.

"I'm sorry," Jules whispers as he holds Lucien's wrists with one hand and takes his knives with the other. "I tried to stand strong, but . . ."

"I should have expected it from you," Lucien says coolly, finally finding his sardonic tongue. He sounds unbothered, hoping his words cut Jules. He's satisfied when the boy flinches. Another part of him is awash with shame; he wonders how much Jules must have endured before finally breaking. But then he thinks of the consequences Jules will avoid that the rest of them won't, and it's enough to bring his anger back.

"It's quite laughable, really, how you expected to get away with this," Blanchet says. "Of course, the real problem is that wretched trapeze artist. The girl will get what's coming to her, exactly as an instigator like her deserves."

Bellamy's expression suddenly chills. "Where is she?" he asks, voice dipped in ice.

"Really, Durand, as one of my employees, I expected better from you," Blanchet says, ignoring his question. "More decorum."

"The irony of you preaching about decorum amuses me," Bellamy says with a goading smirk, although his eyes are dark with rage, "considering you're holding a gun to my head. Seems very . . . boorish of you."

Blanchet's triumphant expression grows cold. He suddenly strikes the butt of the pistol across Bellamy's face, knocking him to the floor. "So disrespectful," he chides.

Lucien lurches forward only to be held back. "Don't," Jules says in a low voice.

Bellamy groans, attempting to push himself up, but then slumps unconscious. The hotelier nudges his prone figure with his shoe and sighs as if inconvenienced. "Great, now I must be the one to lug him down to the carriage." His pistol still at the ready, he leans down and throws Bellamy over his shoulder. "Jules, get that one. It's time to make sure this is a mistake that will not happen again."

That one? Lucien rolls his eyes despite the situation. He shoots Jules a flat glare as he's pushed forward. "I may have killed him, but his blood is on your hands," he tells Jules quietly, referring to Cadieux.

His words must have done their job, because Jules stops walking even as Lucien follows Blanchet into the hallway. He pauses, waiting for Jules to come out, wondering if he should attempt to overpower him now that Blanchet's back is turned. But without his knives, Lucien stands much less of a chance.

Then Jules finally walks out into the hall, looking like he might vomit once more, and takes Lucien by the arm, cutting off any hope of freedom at all.

LIV

November 12, 1896

FALAN WAKES TO HER HANDS TIED BEHIND HER BACK and a pounding skull. Something twinkles in her blurry vision as she raises her head and forces her heavy eyelids open. The object forms into something solid as her vision slowly focuses, her mind still cloudy.

It's the Mirage Diamond.

Falan stares at it, half dazed, before realizing she's in Blanchet's gallery. And she's not the only one.

"Up from your nap?" Lucien says, but there's no humor in his voice. His knives and cane are against the opposite wall, too far to reach. To his right is Ary, who is also tied up. She stares into space, her eyes glazed with tears and despondency.

"Where's . . ." Falan turns to her left to see Bellamy tied up like they are, but unconscious.

"We were caught in Jean-Pierre's office after taking care of Cadieux. Jules told his father everything. Blanchet came in and held us at gunpoint. He knocked Bellamy out because the fool couldn't keep his mouth shut." Lucien drops his gaze. "We got the bearer bonds out, but we couldn't find the stone holding all the contracts. I'm sorry, Falan."

"Don't be. I have the stone." She feels it pressing into her bound arm through her coat pocket, the sharp tip poking her wrist.

"What?" His eyes flick back up in surprise. "How?"

"It was the object in the Garden," she says. "You never would have found it."

"So you won?"

Falan nods. Realizing that she officially won the Game of Oaths is oddly disappointing. This moment was supposed to be a triumphant one. But remembering what happened between her and Ronan sours it. "Jules wasn't the only one who betrayed us," she says. "Allaire stabbed me in the Garden."

Lucien's eyes widen. "He stabbed you?"

Falan nods. "Clean through the shoulder. I won by a sliver." But it's only when she struggles against the ropes binding her hands that she realizes there is no pain. "It looks like they healed the wound." Despite this, she's still trapped.

Bellamy taught her how to escape restraints, but it will take her a while. He, on the other hand, could escape these ropes in less than a minute. But he shows no sign of waking up.

Steps echo in the hallway. Blanchet walks into the gallery, followed by a timid Jules. "Finally awake?" Blanchet kneels in front of Falan, retrieving a pistol from his belt. He presses it against her cheek, and she resists a shudder at its icy touch. "That's unfortunate for you. If you stayed unconscious, you wouldn't have felt the bullet yet to enter your skull."

"Quite an impressive collection you have here," she says. "How does it feel knowing none of this belongs to you?"

"Oh, but it does, ma chère." He digs the pistol's mouth deeper into her skin. "I am the one who paid for them. And that means I own them."

The entitlement of this man is laughable. Because he handed over money in an illegal auction, he thinks he owns these stolen valuables? They have never belonged to him.

Blanchet, visibly irritated that he couldn't get a reaction from her, draws back the pistol and stands.

"We should pat them down," Jules says, hesitating before speaking. "I already took Lucien's knives, but we don't know what hidden weapons they may have."

Blanchet nods in approval. "Go ahead. They can't harm you like this."

Hesitantly, Jules walks over to Lucien, taking his time despite Lucien's glare. For a moment, after he's finished, he lingers. But then he moves on to Ary and Falan. It's with Bellamy, who's still unconscious, that Jules finally finds something. "Should I hold on to this?" Jules asks his father as he pulls Bellamy's card deck out of his pocket.

Blanchet nods. "It's best to leave them with nothing." As Jules settles on the couches at the other end of the gallery, card deck in hand, Blanchet focuses his attention on Ary. "A shame you all chose to involve yourselves in this. Chea, you had a chance of being this year's champion. You could have won your freedom."

Ary bristles and looks away, but her face shines with tears.

"And you, Trichet. You already won last year. Your contract would have ended tonight. Of course, there is no hope of that now."

Lucien glares defiantly at him, also wordless.

Falan glances at Bellamy again, willing him to wake up as Blanchet approaches him. "Such a waste of an employee." He tuts, moving in front of him, and strokes Bellamy's bruised cheek with his thumb. "Piètre garçon."

"Don't touch him," Falan snarls.

"I can do whatever I like," he says, but lets go of Bellamy roughly as Jean-Pierre walks into the gallery. Bellamy moans, eyelashes fluttering, but doesn't wake up. Blanchet rises to his feet, visibly irritated. "At last. You kept us waiting."

“My apologies,” Jean-Pierre says. “I was preparing to relish this, the moment where she realizes that she stood no chance in outsmarting me. Just like that sister of hers.”

“Lavanya did nothing to you,” Falan says.

“Is that so?” Jean-Pierre says mockingly. He kneels in front of her, too far to lunge at him, and smirks. “You never wondered how I found out about her plan to run?”

“I know somebody sold her out,” Falan says, not liking the tone of his voice. “And I paid them back accordingly.”

The ringmaster’s eyes gleam. “And who was that?”

“You know who it was,” Falan says.

“Oh, I do. But I don’t think you do.” His grin is childishly gleeful, like he’s sucking every bit of enjoyment he can from her confusion.

“What are you saying?” Falan dares to ask, her stomach tightening with dread.

Jean-Pierre doesn’t speak. He stands up as another set of footsteps echoes in the hallway, moving to the side to let the incoming person take the attention.

Ronan walks into the room.

Falan can only stare. After what he did in the Garden, she thought her opinion of Ronan couldn’t drop any lower. But she was wrong. Because what he did wasn’t a spontaneous, desperate attempt fueled by fear. He’s walking free, unrestrained. And there can be only one reason for that.

Ronan’s gaze flickers to each of them. His hard expression softens to an apologetic one when he looks at Ary, then Lucien, Bellamy, and finally Falan. Guilt flares in his eyes. Even Jules looks startled.

“I’m sorry,” Ronan says.

“No, you’re not,” Lucien says, voice soaked in anger.

Falan narrows her eyes. “Once a Lily, always a Lily, isn’t that right?”

"Falan," Ronan says, crouching in front of her. She wishes they were back in the Garden again, with the match in her hand. She would have made sure to set him aflame.

"You're the one who told Jean-Pierre about Lavanya's plan to run? Is that why you couldn't look her in the eye before her death, instead of that shit you told me about her confessing feelings for you?" A fresh wave of anger washes over her, and she struggles against her binds. "You let me kill Meera knowing you were the one the knife should have gone through?"

"Falan," he says again, looking desperate.

"Stop saying my name. Make sense of what you did in the Garden. The entire time before, you protected me in situations where you could have let me die. Was that a ploy to get my guard down, to allow me to believe I could trust you?"

"Tell her, Allaire," Jean-Pierre says from behind. "Tell her how as soon as her sister told you she was planning to run away from the Cirque, you came to me and spilled every last detail."

Rage overcomes Falan and she manages to knee Ronan in the stomach, knocking him onto his back. She throws herself forward, sending all her weight on him. Suddenly she's unable to breathe, her lungs straining for air. Falan gasps and collapses on Ronan's chest. Above her, Jean-Pierre's expression is tight, his fists clenched.

Le Lien.

Ronan easily sits up, gripping her shoulders hard. "Her death was not my intention," he says, eyes pleading. "I did it for her own safety."

"You were the one who got her killed," Falan says hoarsely, thrashing in his grip. The feel of his fingers sends her skin crawling.

"If you stop struggling, I'll remove my hands," Ronan says, and lowers his voice so only she can hear. "I didn't mean for her to die. I thought Jean-Pierre would stop her if he knew. I didn't think . . ."

"You deserve to rot in hell. You're just like them, pretending to be so self-righteous when you're all more worthless than the dirt scuffing my shoes." She chokes once more, le Lien subduing her.

"That's enough out of you," Jean-Pierre says.

"Why even pretend to help us?" Lucien asks. "You already knew what Falan was doing."

"I . . . I thought it wouldn't last," Ronan says haltingly, casting an anxious glance at Jean-Pierre. "I never intended to help her at all, but I . . . I couldn't help myself. I thought she would—"

"You wanted to assuage your own guilt." Falan laughs bitterly. "You thought I would die eventually, but you could tell yourself you helped me anyway, so you aren't all bad."

"I kept you alive, didn't I?" Ronan says, but drops his gaze in shame.

"For you, not for me. It was never for me, nor was it for Lavanya. It was all about you." Her laugh dies to pure venom. "You attacked Ary in the Garden too, didn't you?"

"I kept it as painless as I could," he says, as if that makes it any better. "I just needed her subdued."

Falan looks at Ary. "So when you screamed . . ."

Ary lowers her gaze and finally speaks, voice soft and cracked. "He caught me and knocked me out. I didn't know it was him; I couldn't tell what was real or not in the Garden."

"I had to protect myself from going back to the streets." The hard, obstinate look returns to Ronan's face.

"What are you talking about?" Falan snaps.

He throws a hesitant glance back at Jean-Pierre, who gestures for him to go on.

"They won't be making it out of here alive regardless," the ringmaster says. "The look on her face is an opportunity I cannot pass up."

Ronan faces Falan again and has the audacity to look guilty. "I asked Jean-Pierre for something in exchange for giving him the information about Lavanya." He takes a breath. "In exchange for my information about Lavanya's plans last year, and for keeping an eye on you after her death . . . Jean-Pierre rigged this year's competition for me. I was set to win, to get the life I have always wanted. But your plan of destroying the Cirque would have never worked, and I was not about to go down with you. The winner's rewards meant for me would have vanished. I had to stop you."

Falan can hardly breathe. All this time, she considered Sylvestre the last enemy she'd have to face. The one she truly had to beat.

But it was Ronan all along. It has always been Ronan.

"Jean-Pierre, what is this?" Blanchet cuts in. His face is red with anger and shock. "You didn't speak a word of this to me."

"Apologies, mon ami," Jean-Pierre says, but doesn't sound remorseful at all.

Blanchet's eyes narrow. "The Cirque may belong to you, but do not forget who popularized it. Do not forget that your circus is still part of my hotel, and these patrons are my associates. Not yours."

"I was doing this for the good of the Cirque, which benefits us both," Jean-Pierre says, attempting to placate.

"Taking such decisions into your own hands without my father's approval feels like an abuse of power," Jules pipes up from the couch. "Allowing patrons to bet thousands of francs on a rigged game is something that could destroy you both if the secret gets out."

Jean-Pierre aims a vicious look at him, hands raised threateningly, before glancing at an irate Blanchet and thinking better of it.

"I can't believe this," Lucien mutters.

"I can," another voice croaks. Bellamy. An unexpected rush

of relief washes through Falan at seeing him conscious. He shakes his head to wake himself, looking at Ronan with unfocused eyes. "I never trusted him."

One of the unspoken rules the boarders have is to never sell one another out, to never act as informants for Jean-Pierre or Blanchet about broken rules. But Ronan is not a boarder. He is a Lily, and that treatment was enough to drive him to a selfish type of desperation. Enough for him to betray them all to make sure that the Cirque stays standing.

Perhaps if he hadn't been involved in Lavanya's murder, some small part of Falan might have tried to see Ronan's point of view. For Ronan, while he has been treated better than the rest of them, is still treated like somebody who doesn't belong in Paris, without the privilege that Sylvestre or Arthur or even Collette had. For Lavanya's sake, perhaps Falan would have tried to muster some mercy.

But he *was* involved in Lavanya's murder. She died because of him. All this time, Falan thought Meera was the one who betrayed her, and Ronan allowed her to think that. Allowed her to send a blade through the wrong person.

For that, he doesn't deserve her mercy.

"At least Jules had the intention to help us," Lucien mutters, and Jules flinches. "But you . . . you never intended to from the very start."

"What you are is a liar. And a coward." Falan's eyes bore into Ronan. "And I'll make sure you rot in hell, just like the rest of those bastards."

A hint of sadness flickers across Ronan's face before being replaced with that self-righteous look of his that she despises. He crosses his arms. "Sorry, but you can't move. Your hands are still tied."

Falan smiles darkly. "Are they?"

The ropes around her wrists drop and Falan lunges forward, hands going to Ronan's throat. She digs her nails into the soft flesh of his neck so hard she draws blood. Behind him, Jean-Pierre's hands rise to tighten le Lien, but she's quicker. She rolls off Ronan, grabbing the pyramid-shaped stone from her pocket.

"Falan, no!" Ronan shouts.

But it's too late because she has already smashed the stone against the floor, destroying it—and all of Jean-Pierre's contracts.

LV

November 12, 1896

FALAN PICKS UP THE SHARDS OF STONE AND SLAMS them repeatedly against the formerly pristine floor for good measure. But the stone is gone forever, shattered beyond repair.

Her triumph lasts for approximately five seconds before Jean-Pierre's soft laughter breaks the air. He shakes his head, like she's a child who doesn't understand a joke. And then he holds out a hand, curling his fingers into a fist. Falan gasps for air.

"You really think I would be so foolish to put such an object in the Game? To allow you to destroy it so easily?" he says as she collapses.

"I don't understand," Ary says.

Lucien swallows. "He transferred the magic again."

"Correct." The Enchanteur releases le Lien, allowing Falan to breathe once more. "The question now is: Where did I transfer it?"

He's looking at something to the side, and Falan follows his gaze.

No.

"More than a year ago, I transferred the contract magic to this—the beautiful Mirage Diamond."

Falan turns to ask Ronan if he knew about this, but he looks as shocked as she is. In fact, everyone in the room looks shocked, including Blanchet. It appears Jean-Pierre kept another decision from him. From the couch, Jules is staring at the diamond, clutching Bellamy's card deck.

"You transferred the magic to the diamond a year ago, yet you kept the papers in your safe this whole time as a decoy," Falan says, getting to her feet. "But the second decoy—the stone—was for me to find, wasn't it? This game you've been playing with me didn't start last week. It started an entire year ago."

"And what an exciting game it has been, to see your strategy skills against mine," Jean-Pierre says with a satisfied smile. "You may not be a performer, Sunkara, but to see your mind at work has been . . . entertaining."

Falan looks at Jean-Pierre steadily. The Game of Oaths may have held twelve contenders, but the entire match was centered around her. Jean-Pierre plotted everything simply to see if she could escape his plan, or if she would fall right into all of his predictions. He has planned this since the day of Lavanya's murder. This past year, the two of them have been playing a cat-and-mouse game, matching wits.

"You must have had quite a fascination with my mind to risk keeping me around for so long," Falan finally says.

Jean-Pierre laughs. "You don't understand, do you? This is the most rewarding part—telling you what you truly are."

Falan stares at him blankly. What is she missing?

"Physical and artistic Affinities are too varied to be categorized, but they are straightforward," Jean-Pierre says. "Things like weaponry. Acrobatics. Singing. Fine arts. But those with a mental Affinity are different. There are infinite routes as to how we can tap into the abilities of our minds once boosted by magic—through strategy, creating and solving enigmas; but there is only one term for people like us."

"Abstractions," Jules suddenly cuts in. "But . . . they're incredibly rare."

"You're looking at two right now," Jean-Pierre says.

Falan's blood chills. Suddenly, she's thinking of when she asked Jules what Jean-Pierre's Affinity was.

The same as yours.

Now she understands. This is why she didn't get any better on the trapeze after signing with Jean-Pierre. Why she didn't feel the burst of ecstasy every other performer did when using their Affinities.

She is no performer. She never has been.

The entire year, she has been Jean-Pierre's little experiment. He watched her to see what her Affinity could do with the help of magic.

"You wanted to see my Affinity at work," Falan finally says. "You were studying me just as much as I studied you."

"I wanted to see what you could do, as I cannot fuel my own Affinity with my own magic. Unfortunately, the results were disappointing."

Falan has no clue if her Affinity was ever boosted by magic. If not for Jules's earlier affirmation, she would have suspected Jean-Pierre of lying. But if she is an Abstraction, then that means she has a higher probability of outsmarting him, experiment or not. And that is something that nobody else at the Cirque has accomplished until now.

Slowly, Falan walks over to the display case holding the Mirage Diamond. It's an artifact from her home. The only thing left of Lavanya's dreams. But that precious diamond also holds the key to their freedom. She brushes the glass of the case.

"You wouldn't dare," Jean-Pierre says.

Falan glances back at him before knocking the display case stand over. The glass shatters against the floor, the diamond glittering among the shards. Just as Falan is about to pick it up, Jean-Pierre grabs her by the collar. Falan struggles against his grip, but he curls his other hand, pulling le Lien, and she gasps helplessly.

"You are irrepressible," he hisses. "If a dog can't be trained, they must be put down."

"Don't!" Lucien shouts.

"Jean-Pierre, stop!" Ary yells desperately.

Jules looks away, shielding his view. Even Ronan looks alarmed now. Only Falan spots Bellamy, free of his restraints, eyeing the diamond on the floor.

"Have you forgotten what real magic can do?" Jean-Pierre's voice grows lower, almost a demonic growl by the last word.

In response, Falan spits in his face.

Jean-Pierre's expression tightens. "I should have just left you to die in the gutter that night."

With a snarl, he pushes her back onto the floor. Flames pierce her skin, burning her from inside out. She feels the fire melting her bones, her organs—

And then disappear all at once.

"You aren't immune to my illusions, Abstraction or not," Jean-Pierre says. From her ringing ears, Falan realizes she was screaming. She's curled up on the ground, panting for breath. Jean-Pierre kneels in front of her. "Let me show you what else I can do."

The ringmaster grabs her by the hand and curls his fingers around her thumb. As easily as he would a twig, he snaps it off. Her hand begins to crumble into shards like the glass case, finger by finger, then her arm. The crumbled bits float through the air before disappearing, as if her very existence is fading from reality. The pain is unimaginable, like her bones are rotating inside her. The crumbling cracks across her stomach and chest, and the taste of blood fills her mouth.

Jean-Pierre watches with gleaming eyes, the same eyes that looked on as Lavanya fell from the ladder to her death.

“The diamond!” A voice cuts through Falan’s agony, startling Jean-Pierre, and the illusion vanishes.

“What?” Jean-Pierre snaps, clearly angered at being disrupted. He throws Falan against the wall, where she slumps.

Falan’s back aches and the taste of blood still sours her mouth, but her body is whole once again, no cracks or fragmented pieces. Still, she flexes her unscathed hand to assure herself, her face sheened with sweat.

“The diamond is gone,” Jules says. “I can’t see it anywhere.”

Jean-Pierre shoots to his feet, fury twisting his features as he scours the floor to find nothing but glass. His eyes fix on Bellamy, noticing the fallen ropes. “You. Your restraints.”

As Jean-Pierre stalks toward Bellamy, Jules says something quietly to his father. Lucien and Ary exchange glances at what he said, but Falan can barely move, let alone focus her hearing.

“Wait,” Blanchet says as Jean-Pierre yanks Bellamy to his feet. “I own the thief. It is my choice how to handle him.”

“He has the diamond with my contracts, so this is my decision,” Jean-Pierre says.

Blanchet slowly walks toward Jean-Pierre, a dangerously calm look on his face, and yanks Bellamy away from him. The hotelier roughly rifles through Bellamy’s pockets before finally finding what he’s looking for. “This diamond belongs to me. The diamond which you neglected to ask prior permission before transferring your contracts.”

Jean-Pierre clenches his teeth. “Fine. I’ll move them from the diamond once I’m finished here, starting with taking care of *her*.” Falan is lifted off the ground by her collar.

“You can’t kill her,” Jules blurts out.

“Jules!” Blanchet snaps. “What do you think you’re saying?”

"No, he's right," Lucien says. "She won the Game of Oaths and needs to attend the upcoming celebration dinner party. And after that, the spectators will be looking out for her presence. If you kill her, people will wonder what happened."

"I'll just tell them she cheated," Jean-Pierre says. "Her win is void."

"But that would mean revealing somebody on your own panel went behind your back." Lucien casts a meaningful look at Jules, and he bristles, uncomfortable.

"Best case, they'll demand refunds," Falan adds, her voice cracked. "Worst case, you'll get an even larger backlash than the one last year—one that would result in you losing your reputation, your audience, and your money." Despite her pain, she takes delight in how Blanchet's face pales.

The hotelier frowns, deep in thought. Finally he says, "Jean-Pierre . . . the points they have brought up are making a lot of sense. For the sake of our audience and our reputation, we can't kill her right away."

"She is more dangerous alive than dead!" Jean-Pierre hisses, tightening his grip on Falan's collar. "Do you think keeping her—or any of these vermin—alive is wise when they risk spilling something that could destroy us?"

"Nobody would take our word for it," Bellamy points out. "We would say anything to make you look bad in their eyes."

"And if the secret of the rigging did get out . . . it isn't my father's fault," Jules adds. "Why should he take the blame for your mistakes?"

The air in the room turns tense at Jules's remark. A sudden gleam flits across Blanchet's eyes, and he squares his shoulders; Falan can practically see the wheels in his mind turning. "My son has a point again, monsieur. In fact, you have been absolutely insolent recently.

Influencing the panel about games despite my decisions, using my property as your own. You may think of us as business associates, but don't forget you work under *my* hotel. Everything and everybody in this room truly belong to *me*."

For a moment, Jean-Pierre stares blankly at him. Then a smile curves his lips. Falan looks up at him through her haze, tensing. With one hand, he throws Falan at Ronan, who wraps his arms around her to restrain her. Her stomach sickens at his touch, but she dares not struggle. Not yet.

The ringmaster's eyes are fixed solely on Blanchet. He chuckles lowly. "You might think I work for you, mon ami, but you are forgetting who has the true power here."

Blanchet senses the danger, for he releases Bellamy and reaches for the pistol in his belt, but it's too late because Jean-Pierre has already sent him flying back.

LVI

November 12, 1896

BLANCHET HITS THE WALL BEHIND HIM SO HARD IT cracks. Falan watches from Ronan's arms as Bellamy takes the opportunity to run over to Lucien and Ary, undoing their restraints before grabbing Lucien's cane and knives for him. She's surprised when Ronan doesn't yell a warning.

Jean-Pierre towers over Blanchet, who is frozen with shock. "The only reason I have kept you alive this whole time is for what you could offer me," the ringmaster says, his tone icily calm. "So if I want to kill the damn girl, I'm going to kill her. D'accord?"

Blanchet laughs humorlessly. "Do you truly think you can survive this city without me? Once our patrons find out you have rigged the Game, then—"

"They will never trust you again either, Monsieur," Jean-Pierre points out, plucking the diamond from Blanchet's grasp. "You're the one who partnered with me, as you keep reminding us."

Blanchet's face reddens with fury. But he does nothing.

"Your job now is to sit here quietly," Jean-Pierre continues. "And keep your son in check. If he shows any sign of revealing what happened tonight, he won't be exempt."

Blanchet doesn't answer, but from the look on his face, it's clear he doesn't care if Jean-Pierre does anything to Jules. At this point, Jules is a liability for him.

Time is running out.

Falan seizes the opportunity to struggle against Ronan again.

He is caught by surprise, and the momentum pulls them both to the ground, allowing her to break from his grip. Ronan curses, but Bellamy is already at her side, lifting her to her feet with an arm around her waist.

At the noise, Jean-Pierre straightens and turns back to the others. His smile momentarily drops when he sees all of them freed, Lucien's knives back in hand. "You truly insist on making things as difficult as you can for me. If an Abstraction was not immune to my illusions, what makes you think any of you are?"

In response, Lucien throws two knives at Jean-Pierre.

The ringmaster blinks, pulling the blades out of his arm and torso, before his face twists with fury. A moment later, Lucien gasps, falling to his knees as if somebody struck him. But it's the look of terror in his wide eyes that sends a shudder down Falan's spine.

"What are you doing to him?" Ary asks, trembling. "What—"

She stops talking too as Jean-Pierre focuses his gaze on her. Just like Lucien, her eyes widen as if she's seeing something monstrous, as if she's living her worst nightmare. She screams, the scream of somebody being stabbed by a thousand knives, and drops to the ground, sobbing and clutching her stomach.

"You see, Sunkara, illusions are the most complex magic," Jean-Pierre says calmly over Ary's sobs. "I can make an illusion visible to everyone in the world if I choose. I can also make it visible to one person. Right now, that girl is being eaten alive by her own organs. And she feels the pain of every bite." He glances at Lucien, who lies motionless on the ground, staring at nothing. "And him? His bones are turning to water inside him right now."

Bellamy's grip around Falan's waist tightens, her anchor against any illusion Jean-Pierre might throw her way. But when the ringmaster's eyes go to him, Falan is the one who tenses.

"Jean-Pierre," she says before he can do anything to Bellamy. "If you kill us, you'll never know where your bearer bonds are hidden."

"You left them in the safe on purpose, to keep us occupied. If the safe had been empty, we would have left before Cadieux could try to kill us," Bellamy says.

"Why do you think I haven't killed you yet?" Jean-Pierre says. "I'm merely having some fun before you take me to the bonds."

"And what if we refuse?" Bellamy dares to ask.

Jean-Pierre smirks. With a glint of the ringmaster's eyes, Bellamy gasps as if choking. His hands go to his throat and his fingernails scrape into his skin, drawing blood. Falan's breath hitches when she realizes Bellamy is going to claw his throat out if not stopped.

"You've made your point," Falan says quickly.

"Vraiment, Sunkara?" Jean-Pierre says mockingly. "I expected you to let him suffer for a few minutes more before giving in."

"I wasn't finished. We'll take you to the bonds, if you spare our lives," Falan says. "You will get your money back, your reputation will remain intact, and you will never see any of us again."

"No," he says at once. "You are far more valuable to me as an example."

"Then you'll never know where the bonds are," Falan says. "You'll kill us and they will remain hidden forever."

Jean-Pierre looks at Bellamy, who is still gasping and scraping at his throat. "So you're willing to gamble his life?"

"Durand." Falan tries to grab Bellamy's wrists, but he's too strong. "It's an illusion. Snap out of it, Bellamy. Look at me."

"He doesn't know it's an illusion, ma chère." The smug smile is back on Jean-Pierre's face. "He sees someone in front of him right now, choking him. He feels it. And he will keep clawing to get the person's hands off his throat."

"Fuck you," Falan spits at him. "You're asking me to choose whether he dies now or a little later."

"The decision lies with you."

Blood is now pooling into Bellamy's shirt. A few minutes more and the damage could be irreversible. Falan's hands curl into fists. But finally she says, "We'll take you. Just stop this."

"As you wish." Jean-Pierre's muscles slack and his intense gaze drops, releasing his illusions over Lucien, Ary, and Bellamy, who all take in deep gasps of air. "You and the thief, come with me. Allaire!"

Ronan, who has been watching guiltily, says, "Yes?"

"Keep an eye on the other two." Jean-Pierre stalks over to Falan and grabs her and Bellamy, who stumbles into her. Falan steadies him. "Blanchet! Come. Have your son watch the thief."

Silently, Blanchet stands up as Jules walks over to Bellamy, taking his arm. Jules's gaze flickers to Falan and then he lowers it.

Without protest, Falan walks out of the gallery.

Falan finds it ironic that her only time riding in carriages has been as a prisoner. First when she was taken from the boardinghouse to the Aviary, and now when she's on her way to the hotel. Bellamy and Jules sit on either side of her, Blanchet and Jean-Pierre across from them. The ride is silent except for the sound of horse hooves on the road and the creak of wheels grinding over cobblestones. The palpable ire between Jean-Pierre and Blanchet only adds to the air of unease, but Falan welcomes it.

For once, Bellamy doesn't break the quiet with a flippant remark. Instead, he stares out the window of the carriage at the darkened buildings. Jules too is looking out. Falan understands the appeal of Paris in the dead of the night; while devoid of lights, there's a quiet that can never exist during any other time. Even at dawn, the city is restless, as if waiting for its citizens to awaken and explore what it has to offer.

Le Palais Blanchet is the only building on the street that is still lit up, a gold and white beacon in the night. But the quiet of Paris fades as they get closer to the hotel, which has several wagons parked around the front as well as a crowd of people. A large majority are policemen, as well as some detectives, but hotel residents are among the crowd. Both Jean-Pierre and Blanchet go rigid at the sight.

As soon as the carriage stops and the driver opens the door, Jean-Pierre hisses, "Stay here," to Falan and Bellamy and hurries onto the street, followed by Blanchet.

They don't listen. Bellamy steps out, quietly wrapping his hands around Falan's waist and lifting her down to the street. Her muscles tighten at his touch, especially when he lowers her to the ground. Falan walks after Jean-Pierre and Blanchet, who have been stopped by one of the policemen.

"This is my hotel!" Blanchet is yelling.

The policeman looks at him strangely. "*Your* hotel? And you might be?"

"Jacques Alain Blanchet." He holds out his hand to shake, which the policeman does not take. Before he can inquire further, Jules, who has caught up with them, leans over and whispers something in Blanchet's ear.

"What is happening here?" Jean-Pierre demands.

The policeman looks him up and down, studying his attire. "You must be Monsieur Jean-Pierre Allard, yes?"

The ringmaster tips his hat in response. "What can I do for you?"

"We were about to go looking for you; you've made our job much easier. We received a message earlier tonight about a disturbance on the ninth floor of this building," the policeman says. "Will you please come with us?"

"You might inform me what is going on before asking me that," Jean-Pierre says with thinly veiled patience.

The policeman crosses his arms. "A body was found hidden in your office, Monsieur Jean-Pierre. A man by the name of Xavier Cadieux."

"Cadieux . . . I've heard that name before," Jules says, looking up at the sky as if to think.

Panic flits across Blanchet's face, gone as quickly as it came. "In my hotel? Without my knowledge?" he says indignantly.

"We already have a warrant issued for your arrest," the policeman says to Jean-Pierre. "Won't you come with me, sir?"

"A warrant?" Jean-Pierre repeats. "On what grounds?"

"The evidence found in your office was quite incriminating. At the moment we can't say anything, but we will need you to come with us."

"This is absurd." Jean-Pierre turns to Blanchet, about to ask for his defense, but any words die in his throat. Falan notes the triumphant look on Blanchet's face, the realization that this is a golden moment.

"Now that I remember, you *did* mention a meeting with Monsieur Cadieux earlier tonight," Blanchet says, and looks at him with faux horror. "You were unavailable all night, Jean-Pierre. You . . . you couldn't have . . ."

"Monsieur Blanchet!" Fury ripples across Jean-Pierre's face. "You're lying!"

The officer raises an eyebrow. "Please stay here, both of you." He calls over another policeman to keep an eye on them as he goes to talk with someone.

Jean-Pierre uses the moment to whirl around to face Falan. "What have you done?" he snarls.

Falan says nothing. But slowly a small smile tugs up her lips, so subtle only Jean-Pierre sees it. In the corner of her eye, she sees Jules nearby talking to another officer, trying not to vomit, but it's an expression she catches simply because she's looking for it. To most others, he looks nonchalant, curious.

Jules's letter to the police was the start, masquerading as an anonymous concerned hotel guest the hours before the Game started. He reported alarming noises from the floor above, shouts, sounds of a fight. Then all the pieces of a hastily hidden crime—blood cleaned up, but not in forgettable places; smashed furniture; a bloody curved knife hidden under the cushions of a couch. All enough for the police to look around and find a body in the trunk. The body of an associate to one of Paris's most powerful men.

A powerful man who is threatened by Jean-Pierre and would gladly take the chance to get rid of him.

Falan merely needed a reason to bring Jean-Pierre back to the hotel with Blanchet so they could be greeted by the police. So she stretched their time in the gallery—she made him think he was winning, she let him hurt her. She gave him no reason to suspect anything. And finally agreed to hand over the bearer bonds.

The key to success was Blanchet. Jean-Pierre might have been able to escape incarceration by using him as an alibi. But with both Blanchet and Horrent ready to throw him to the wolves—and with the rumored government officials already concerned about Jean-Pierre's growing range of power—the ringmaster won't be escaping his fate.

And now he will pay the price for everything he's done.

"I will make you regret this," Jean-Pierre says quietly. "You are still bound to me. You are still my puppet."

Falan's smile only grows.

Before he can say anything else, two officers walk up to him and grab him by the arms. Falan watches as they lead Jean-Pierre away into the crowd.

This is only the start. He'll be watching his life slowly crumble around him without any way to stop it, rotting in prison, his own wrongdoings undoing him. That will agonize him far more than a quick knife to the heart ever could.

Bellamy, who has been standing next to her, says quietly, "So it's over?"

Falan's gaze flickers over to Blanchet. "Almost."

She watches as two police officers now walk over to Blanchet, asking him to come with them. He goes willingly, perhaps thinking that they need his statement against Jean-Pierre, but Falan knows better. By the time the hotelier realizes what they've done, it will be too late for him.

Jules walks back over to Falan and Bellamy with a nod. It's over now.

"Good to have you join us," she says to Bellamy's surprise. "What did you tell him?"

"Exactly what you told me to. The bruises my father so viciously inflicted on my face earlier made it all the easier," Jules says quietly. He then holds out Bellamy's card deck to him. "I believe this belongs to you."

Slowly, Bellamy takes the card deck back and tucks it away, his surprised gaze flitting between them. "So . . . you two . . ."

"It's always good to have an ace up your sleeve. You taught me that, Durand," Falan says. By now, Blanchet has been shoved into a carriage, carted down the street after Jean-Pierre. Falan starts to walk into the shadows of the building, the other two slipping along with her. Here they can remain unheard, unnoticed, yet still watch the show.

Jules aims his glare at Bellamy. "You thought I would betray you? I've never been so offended."

"In my defense, you let your father hit me across the face with a pistol," Bellamy says with an eye roll. "What did she tell you to say?"

This time, Jules doesn't bother hiding his nauseous look. "As reported to the officers, I have no clue where my father was tonight either. He's been having tensions with his longtime business partner, Jean-Pierre. Something about a diamond, the diamond in Jean-Pierre's pocket right now. Something my father threatened—I mean, made me promise not to talk about."

"And did you take care of everything in Jean-Pierre's office?" Falan asks.

Jules nods. "Lucien slashed Cadieux's ankles, which I had to heal to avoid suspicion. But I made sure there was no room for theory."

"And now?" Bellamy asks, beginning to grin.

Falan looks up at the sky. The moon tonight, somehow, shines brighter than any night the past year. "Now they do the work themselves."

With Jean-Pierre still smarting against Blanchet, he will try to make the hotelier take the fall. But with the diamond in Jean-Pierre's pocket, Blanchet will try to shift more charges on the ringmaster. Snarling wolves caught in a never-ending war, fangs frothing for power, unable to catch the little fox that brought about their downfall.

"They'll destroy each other," Bellamy says.

Falan nods. The three of them stand in the shadows, gazing out at the City of Lights. Perhaps she was wrong; a new city wakes up at night after all. It still is not a city that glitters for them, but it's a place Falan finds herself drawn to, far more than Paris in the daylight.

Clair de lune indeed.

And the wolves will continue to howl at the moon, while the fox slips unnoticed into the night.

LVII

November 12, 1986

LE PALAIS BLANCHET'S BALLROOM IS ALL SET FOR THE Game of Oaths concluding dinner party.

The floors have been scrubbed, shined to perfection. The gold curtains have been dusted. The chef's prepped ingredients sit waiting to be used. Bottles of champagne in crates are stacked in the kitchen's cooling room.

Night falls. Not a single guest appears.

The floors stay spotless. The curtains, still freshly dusted, remain drawn. The culinary ingredients continue to wait. The champagne bottles stay lined in their crates. The hotel's regular staff, unlinked to the cercle or Cirque, go home.

Nobody mentions the missed dinner that night. Nobody mentions Jean-Pierre or Jacques Alain Blanchet. Nobody talks about the Game of Oaths. Nobody speaks of le Palais Blanchet or le Cirque des Ombres.

It is as if it was a dream, as quick to melt into the shadows it was named after, disappearing like the illusion Jean-Pierre always said it was.

LVIII

November 13, 1896

ARY DOESN'T REMEMBER THE LAST TIME SHE SLEPT in so late. When she wakes up, it's dark outside, revealing an entire day has passed. For a moment, she forgets where she is, believing she's back at the boardinghouse. But the boardinghouse doesn't have beds like this, with comfortable sheets and soft mattresses. Jules's mansion, on the other hand, has far too many rooms like this.

Ary sits up in bed and looks out the window at the sky with its sewn stars and waning moon. It reminds her of a quilt she once saw in Paris's marketplace, one she so badly wanted but would never be able to afford. She swings her feet over the bed and winces when her toes touch the icy floor, but she gets up anyway. Even deep into the night, the mansion feels awake; she can hear the stirrings of other people somewhere on the floor below her.

Ary steps into the hallway to see light glowing from the end leading to the foyer. She creeps forward, all the way down the stairs to the kitchen, where she finds Bellamy, Lucien, and Jules all at the table, wolfing down as much food as humanly possible.

The three of them stop eating for a moment and Jules smiles at her. "Finally awake?"

Ary smiles back at him. She's still confused as to most of what happened the night before, but when Falan and Bellamy returned to the gallery, they came back with Jules and without Jean-Pierre or Blanchet. The only thing she gathered was that Jules had not really betrayed them, that it was something he and Falan had planned the entire time without telling the rest of them. At some point during the discussion, she realized Ronan was gone. But she didn't point it out. Nobody did. Perhaps they all noticed, but nobody wanted to acknowledge it.

The rest is a blur, but perhaps it's a blessing not to relive those feelings of confusion and utter exhaustion.

Right now, all she feels is hunger. At the sight of the feast, Ary's stomach growls. "Where's Falan?" she asks, noticing she's missing from the table.

Lucien shrugs, too focused on his food to care. "I don't know."

"And that doesn't concern you?"

Lucien shrugs again. Ary slides into a seat between Bellamy and Lucien, taking in roast chicken, savory hand pies, buttery brioche, pommes fondantes, a block of Brie with crackers, a trio of jams, even a platter of profiteroles. "Where did all this come from?" she asks.

"Cook," Jules says through a mouthful of potato.

It takes Ary a minute to realize the Blanchet mansion has its own cook, that there is someone here who prepares meals several times a day. She takes a pie, the flaky pastry crumbling on her fingers, and sinks her teeth into it. The tentative bite turns ravenous and before she knows it, Ary is wolfing down food as quickly as the boys.

Ary's on her third helping of chicken and potatoes and her fourth pie when Falan walks through the kitchen door. She smells like the winter night itself, like snow and wind.

Bellamy shudders when she seats herself next to him. "You let in a draft, Sunkara."

In response, she takes one of his crackers and eats it.

"Where have you been?" Ary asks.

"Retrieving our compensation," Falan says. Instantly everyone at the table stops eating.

“Were the bearer bonds still there?” Bellamy asks.

“On the roof, right where you hid them. Of course, I couldn’t pass through the hotel’s front door, so I scaled the building.” She pauses. “I stopped by the boardinghouse as well. I told Erwin to keep the remaining performers and dealers there for a month without charge. The bonds need to be liquidated and divided before I pay each person accordingly.”

Bellamy snorts. “And Erwin offered to do this out of the goodness of his heart?”

“No, but a generous cut from the total sum did the trick.”

“Ideally the whispers about the Game and Jean-Pierre will die down in a month, and I’ll be able to cash the bonds unsuspected,” Jules says.

Ary doesn’t say it, but she isn’t certain the whispers about the Game of Oaths or Jean-Pierre will die in a month’s span. She doubts Falan believes it either, judging by the jaded look in her dark eyes. The Game of Oaths, while underground, was a large part of Paris. A reminder of the Sortilège Riots. To have it ripped away from the citizens—along with Le Cirque des Ombres altogether—without any official reason will set off a string of speculations, of people seeking answers as to why an Enchanteur so powerful could be jailed, people looking to defend Jean-Pierre and Blanchet.

It might even lead people on their trail. People who might figure out what really happened last night.

“I don’t have a month,” Bellamy says. “My deadline is tonight.”

“I know.” From her coat, Falan takes out a stack of papers folded in half and places it in front of Bellamy. “Three hundred thousand francs across six bonds. All Horrent has to do is exchange them.”

Bellamy’s shoulders slump as he takes the papers and tucks them away. Relief softens his gray eyes, a seriousness that looks unnatural.

"Our only issue now is the contracts," Lucien says with a soft sigh. "If only we had been able to snatch the diamond from Jean-Pierre."

The sinking feeling in Ary's stomach deepens. "We're still linked to him. And if the diamond was taken from him during interrogation and locked in a safe somewhere, then we always will be." Her voice chokes on the last sentence; it's a future unimaginable, one she hadn't even considered until Lucien reminded her of it.

"Oh, we have the contracts," Falan says.

Everyone freezes except Jules, who has started eating once more. Even Bellamy looks taken aback. "What?" he says.

"We have control of Jean-Pierre's contracts," Falan says again. She seems to be relishing the stunned look on their faces. "I spoke to Jules privately after our meeting in the gallery before the final round, and I asked him whether it was possible for an Enchanteur to control another Enchanteur's contract magic," she says. "And he said yes."

"How did you convince him?" Lucien asks, starting to smile in his astonishment.

Jules makes a noise of protest around a mouthful of chicken. Ary can't quite make out what he says, but it sounds a lot like, "I'm not that difficult to convince."

"You saw Jean-Pierre's actions coming," Ary says. It isn't a question. After finding out Falan is an Abstraction, nothing is a shock anymore.

"I suspected Jean-Pierre would try something," Falan says. "The moment I saw the stone in the final round, it confirmed Jean-Pierre had transferred the contract magic again. I also knew that Jean-Pierre loves to gloat; if he moved the contract magic to another object, he would physically show it just to add salt in our wounds. Fortunately, that gave Jules a chance to transfer the contract magic. The one thing

Jean-Pierre and Monsieur Blanchet—and even Monsieur Horrent—didn't see coming was the presence of another Enchanteur."

"Jules truly was our secret weapon," Bellamy says with a grin, causing Jules to blush. "So where did you end up transferring the contract magic to?"

Falan gestures at Bellamy's coat. "Check your pocket."

Bemused, Bellamy puts his hand inside, a look of realization washing over him as he pulls out a deck of cards. "Here?"

She nods. "I know you always carry them, so I told Jules to direct the magic to the card deck when he took it from you in the gallery."

"So I am holding all the Cirque's contracts right here in my hands?" Bellamy says in disbelief. "And if I destroy this card set, I will destroy every single bond that Jean-Pierre made?"

"That is correct." A ghost of a smile finally breezes across Falan's lips. "We have control, Durand. I've won. *We've* won."

Hearing it said aloud sends a burst of euphoria through Ary, one that causes a beam to brighten her face. Once that deck of cards is destroyed, once she has her share of the bonds, her future is open.

She can go back to Srok Khmer. Back to her mother.

Lucien laughs, a sound of pure relief, and Ary can't help but join in. She can't stop even as they continue to eat, thinking only of all the possibilities.

Baby Bird, it's time to spread your wings and fly.

LIX

November 13, 1896

BELLAMY REACHES HORRENT'S OFFICE TEN MINUTES before midnight. The window is open, ready for him to slip through. Monsieur Horrent stands at the other end of the room, staring at nothing in particular. The room is empty of any associates now, the moon's light barely spilling into the study. But the broken statue is still there on the bottom shelf of the desk, a reminder of Bellamy's last deal. He remains perched on the windowsill, bearer bonds in hand.

Horrent's low voice cuts through the dark. "I lost somebody who was not only an associate but a dear friend of mine." He pauses. "Murdered by the famed ringmaster Jean-Pierre. The evidence was found all over his office. Jacques Alain Blanchet is rumored to be involved as well. My shock was uncontainable when the police showed up at my door to hand deliver the news to me."

"My condolences," Bellamy says, but they both know that Bellamy despised Cadieux.

They both know what truly happened last night.

But they both also know that there is no way for Horrent to prove it without implicating himself. If he tells anybody that he made a deal with Blanchet and knew Cadieux would be in Jean-Pierre's office, it will only drag him into the spotlight of the general public's attention, something a man like him cannot afford. Bellamy wonders what lie Horrent came up with to implicate Jean-Pierre, what concocted motive for killing Cadieux.

Horrent finally turns around and Bellamy is surprised to see he truly does look saddened; the creases in his face are deeper, the shade of blue in his eyes more aged. "Do you have what you promised me?"

In response, Bellamy sets the papers down on the desk.

Horrent walks over and checks the bearer bonds, making sure the total adds up to the owed amount, before tucking them away in the pocket of his coat. Bellamy assumes they're done, but then Horrent says, "So I assume that you will slide by unaffected as I mourn?"

"I already offered my condolences," Bellamy says.

"Hm." Horrent now gazes out the window at the slumbering city. "And how is the little trapeze artist? Did she relish watching the ringmaster and hotelier get arrested? Did she pride herself on outwitting the police? Myself?" He pauses. "Did you?"

"I don't know what you're talking about," Bellamy says.

"One day, Blanchet or Jean-Pierre will say something that will make the police think twice. Make them realize something else happened that night, that the people they should have arrested were right in front of them." Horrent finally looks directly at Bellamy. "And when they do, I will drink to your incarceration."

Although he keeps his face straight, a shudder trails down Bellamy's spine. What Horrent is saying could happen. But it might never.

Bellamy jumps back on the windowsill. "Au revoir, Monsieur Horrent. Hopefully this is the last time we cross paths."

"Indeed," he says, but there's a dangerous gleam in his eyes that suggests he hopes otherwise.

With a parting nod, Bellamy escapes out the window.

Despite it being the middle of the night, Lucien can't sleep. He stands on the balcony in his chosen room at the Blanchet mansion, looking out at the darkened garden, the quiet song of a robin warbling from somewhere nearby.

Oddly, Lucien finds himself thinking about Ronan, of all people. He's been thinking about him a lot over the past few days. He should despise Ronan all the more after what he did. Yet, when he thinks about him, all Lucien feels is pity for Lavanya. This was the boy she had once loved. Somebody who ultimately chose to betray her.

I wonder how Lavanya would have reacted to all this, Lucien thinks. Not well. She may have held feelings for Ronan, but Lavanya loved her sister more than anybody. If she found out that Ronan stabbed her, Lavanya would have stabbed Ronan in turn. The thought causes a fleeting smile to drift across Lucien's face.

It has taken Lucien more time than he likes to admit to accept that he has been holding some unacknowledged anger toward Lavanya as well. For always seeking Ronan out, for planning to run away without so much as a goodbye. It makes him wonder if he meant as much to her as she did to him.

But then he remembers how the two of them broke the Cirque's unspoken rule, pouring out their pasts to each other over time. At the Cirque, that was the most vulnerable you could get with somebody. Finding out bits and pieces of who a person used to be by accident was one thing; to have somebody willingly speak to you about where they came from, how they ended up in the Cirque, what they wanted for the future despite its bleakness, was something far deeper than a romantic confession.

A soft cough sounds from behind him. Lucien looks over his shoulder to see Jules. "I knocked on the bedroom door before coming in," Jules says haltingly.

Lucien gestures for him to come outside, and Jules joins him on the balcony. Lucien isn't quite sure how to speak to Jules. He can't pinpoint exactly why. It isn't anger or disappointment; Jules did what was necessary to help them. But still, something is blocking Lucien from looking him in the eyes, from speaking to him in a light, carefree manner. Even from teasing him like he used to.

"What are you still doing awake?" Lucien eventually asks.

"I came to tell you something." Jules pauses, uncertain. "I know you asked Bellamy to use his underground contacts to search for your sister, but I was able to speed up the process a bit by dipping into the few assets I do have."

Lucien's eyes widen. He finally faces Jules. "What?"

Jules shrugs awkwardly. "I was able to send out some scouts. And I think I already have a lead on where your sister might be."

Lucien's bones are suddenly weak. "Where?"

"Toulouse. I'm going to ask Bellamy and his contacts to look into it more."

"How . . . how do you know it's her for certain?" He almost doesn't want to ask, but he has to be sure.

"We don't. But based on the information you gave, it's likely." Jules pulls a folded paper out of his pocket and hands it to Lucien. "She's a girl of sixteen working as a housekeeper for the Laurent family," Jules says as Lucien skims the meager contents of the paper, written in hastily scrawled French. "The Laurent family used to live in Paris until four years ago, when they moved to Toulouse.

The family is made up of Monsieur Laurent, his wife, and four children."

Working for a family with four children. Lucien can barely breathe. The possibility that it's her—that Fayette is out there and he will be able to find her—is almost too much.

"Thank you, Jules." Lucien hands the paper back to him. Jules nods, his cheeks slightly pink. And Lucien suddenly feels that inability to look Jules in the eye again.

It's fear, he realizes. The fear that he will get close to Jules just like he did Lavanya, only to be ripped away. Jules is nothing like Lavanya, yet Lucien is beginning to feel the same rough staccato of his heart that he felt with Lavanya. And he can't stop it, no matter how much he doesn't want to let anybody else in.

"It must be a curious privilege," Jules suddenly says.

Lucien shoots him a sidelong glance. "What is?"

"Being sought for." A soft, somber smile tugs at Jules's lips as he tilts his head up to the wind, letting it ruffle his dark locks. "My mother is dead, my father disowned me, I have no siblings. Nobody would go searching for me if I disappeared one morning. To be sought for . . . what a precious thing."

"I would search for you," Lucien says before he can stop himself.

Jules's hazel eyes go wide in disbelief. It takes him a minute, but Lucien's words finally roll through his brain and his gaze flickers to the ground.

"Still blushing at everything, I see," Lucien can't help adding, hoping Jules won't notice his own blush in the dark.

He expects Jules to shoot back a defensive remark. But he doesn't. He continues to look at the floor, his fingers curling and uncurling around the cuffs of his coat. After a long minute he says, quiet and awkward, "I would search for you too, you know."

Lucien is about to turn his face away, but it's too late—Jules is already looking at him. He must see his flustered expression, because Jules is the one smiling now. But he doesn't point it out. Instead, he looks up at the star-speckled sky, taking a deep breath of night air.

"It's a beautiful night, isn't it?" Jules says, exhaling.

"Yes." Lucien nods, then clears his throat. As the sweet notes of the robin's song continue to fill the air, a small smile spreads across his own face. "It is a beautiful night."

LX

November 15, 1896

LAVANYA'S ASHES LIE AT THE VERY CORNER OF Cimetière de Passy's northern side. There is no marker, yet the dirt has always looked different here, looser than the packed earth around it.

It feels like a lifetime since Falan was last here. Her eyes stray to the stone slabs on which she held the game of poker, Meera on her right. The right side of her vision is still speckled with black, but she stares for a moment longer, caught by the winter sun pouring over the graves in its beautifully morbid way.

Perhaps she isn't as immune to the view as she thought.

Falan kneels in front of Lavanya's grave. Yet she doesn't know what to say.

Bellamy stands a few feet away, giving her privacy. She didn't ask him to come, but here he is anyway, having followed her out of the house this morning. His eyes are on the rising sun, but the faraway look he usually has when staring at the horizon is gone. He's alert, like he's keeping watch of her presence.

There's so much she wants to tell Lavanya. She wants to tell her that she won the Game of Oaths, that she cheated Jean-Pierre and lived. She wants to tell her how much Lucien misses her. She wants to tell her that, for the first time in a long time, she might trust somebody as much as she trusted her.

But there's so much Falan doesn't want to say as well. She doesn't want to say that she's the reason Meera is dead. She doesn't want to say that, despite winning, she feels like she's still lost in some ways.

Meera never told Jean-Pierre anything—she was innocent the whole time. It was Ronan all along, Ronan who Lavanya confided in. Ronan who went running to Jean-Pierre. And yet, it was Meera who Falan stabbed, a mistake she can never take back.

Despite her anger, she doesn't want to tell Lavanya that Ronan betrayed both of them in the end. Last Falan saw him was outside the hotel when she snuck back in to get the remaining bearer bonds. She was taking one last look at le Palais Blanchet, and it felt as it did the morning of Le Jour de L'Élu: empty, devoid of life.

And then he'd come. Even without looking, she'd known it was him. She knows him by his presence, down to the way he breathes. And she hates it. She hates that she knows him so well; she wants to unlearn it all, to unravel her mind and pick out any lingering facts about him.

"You have no business being here," Falan had said coolly.

Ronan hadn't spoken for a long minute. But then he'd stepped toward her, only inches away. Seeing him so close had reminded her of their proximity as they had knelt on the ground of the maze, his knife above her chest. His eyes had looked just like they had then. "I just wanted to tell you . . . I'm sorry."

"You needn't have come here to tell me that," she had said.

"Did you see my betrayal coming?" he'd asked.

Falan had wanted to look away. She hadn't wanted to see those blue eyes, the eyes of a boy Lavanya loved so much. "No," she'd finally said. "And yet, all the same, I wasn't surprised."

A pause. "I'm lying low for now. I don't want to be spotted by any spectators still sour about the ending of the tournament. But if you ever need to find me . . . I'll be at Lavanya's favorite café every Sunday morning. You know which one."

She had. The best hot chocolate in all of Paris.

Falan had wanted to tell Ronan that she would never need to seek him out. Instead she'd asked, "Was any of it real?"

It took him a moment to understand the question, his blue eyes flickering. "If I could take it back, I don't know if I would."

He could have been talking about plenty of things. Telling Jean-Pierre about their plan. Telling Jean-Pierre about Lavanya's. His feelings. All of it.

But as she told him before, wishing does not change anything.

"Look at that," Bellamy suddenly says, breaking her out of her thoughts. She hadn't even noticed him come over. "In winter, it still blooms."

Poking up from the dirt is a single blade of grass, a fresh tip of green in a sea of dark brown.

Falan's fingers brush the dirt, skimming the top of the blade. It's the first time anything has grown here in the past year. To see something grow now, in the middle of winter, when the dirt has a frozen layer of topsoil, is an anomaly.

"She would have liked this. Something new birthing in the dead of winter." Falan pauses. "I hate it. I want to yank it. It's just a reminder that life is continuing without her."

"At least you aren't denying it," Bellamy says. She hears amusement in his voice.

"What's tickling you?" she asks.

A soft smile flickers across his lips. It almost looks fond. "You never change, Sunkara. No matter who you are and what you've done, you're still as prickly as a thornbush. You're like that blade of grass—there is no reason it should be growing. And yet it does out of sheer stubbornness."

"Tell me why that's a bad thing."

"I didn't say it was."

Falan doesn't know what to say to that.

Bellamy's smile grows. But then he sobers and, after a bout of hesitation, says, "Back in the gallery, when Jean-Pierre was torturing you, you never gave in. Yet . . . when he started hurting us, you did. Was that planned?"

Falan finally turns to look at him, standing up. "Plan or not, I had no intention of letting Jean-Pierre hurt you." The words are difficult to say. She's awash with that strange thrill again when she realizes how close they are. The one when her lungs can't seem to find air, yet she's curious what will happen if she inches closer, if she looks at him a little longer.

Bellamy's gray eyes flicker, the color of a morning haze. The dawn's light falls upon his face as he looks down at her with that emotion she is unable to grasp. It's one she wants to cease, for it makes her feel vulnerable. It makes her want to get close enough to count the faded freckles dusting his nose and cheeks.

His lips part like he wants to say something. But before he can, Falan takes a step back and says, "We should go."

"You've finished?" Bellamy asks, making sure.

"Yes." Falan glances down at the grave with its single blade of grass. Lavanya's grave finally has a marker. "I've finished." A breeze rushes by, blowing her hair and cooling her cheeks. As they begin to walk away, Falan pulls the deck of cards from her pocket. She finally holds the foundation of Jean-Pierre's power in the palm of her hand.

She can unleash a series of destructive acts on his life, starting with this card deck.

And yet, she still hasn't destroyed it.

It's then that she sees Bellamy is staring at her. And the questioning look on his face is one she wants to avoid. Yet she speaks.

"I know it's stupid," she says. "I haven't broken it because I keep thinking about what Jean-Pierre said about my Affinity. And I keep wondering why I never felt any euphoria even after knowing what I am, clinging on to the hope that I would feel it once before breaking the contract. But I never will. Because, according to Gallien's book, Abstractions don't feel it. They can't."

"You still won, Sunkara. It's up to you when you tip the first domino."

He's right. But she shouldn't wait—every member of the Cirque is still bound to Jean-Pierre. "I have lots to do here," she says, trying to change the subject. "I need to make sure the bonds are cashed and divided evenly among the performers and dealers, to make sure my deals are seen through." She pauses. "But you could be anywhere except here."

"Not quite yet," he says with a wry grin. "You currently have me completing that favor for Lucien. So it looks like you're stuck with me for a while."

Stuck with him. Falan shoves the card deck in her pocket. She feels more relief than she expected, knowing Bellamy will continue to be here.

"Good," she says.

They walk out of the graveyard and down the dimly lit streets of Paris in silence. His hand brushes against hers as they walk. First wisps, then streaks of warmth tracing her knuckles. Falan's heart skips a beat. The brushes grow longer, until the back of his hand continues to linger against hers. Slowly, carefully, Bellamy's fingers slide into hers and they interlace, an unexpected thrill shooting a shiver up Falan's spine.

The only other time Falan has felt a thrill like this is when flitting across the rooftops of Paris. It brings her back to that night from months ago. She sends a quick sidelong look at Bellamy, wondering if he's remembered all along and, like her, hasn't said anything.

“Do you recall a specific night on the hotel rooftop?” Falan asks quietly. “I found you drunk.”

A beat. Then he smiles rather sheepishly. “Yes. I remember you listening to me as I told you about my past. I don’t remember much else after that.”

“You don’t recall me taking you back to the boardinghouse? And . . . what you said before you fell asleep?”

“What did I say?” he asks.

A sudden sense of desperation washes over Falan, achingly embarrassing. She’s been clinging to this memory for months and he doesn’t even remember.

“Sunkara, what did I say?” Bellamy asks again, stopping. She stops too, pulling her hand from his but facing him all the same. The tree above them creates dappled shadows on Bellamy’s skin, dimming the parts not glowing with the rising sun’s light.

“It’s nothing,” she says. But when he continues to wait patiently, the words come tumbling out of her mouth, awkward and halting. “When I brought you back to your room at the boardinghouse, before you fell asleep, you admitted that . . . you care about me, not just as somebody you make deals with.”

“Is that so?” His tone is light, but a small smile plays on his lips. “And what did you do?”

Falan’s flat glare returns. “I stayed to make sure you didn’t choke on your own vomit in your sleep.”

“You stayed?” His eyebrows shoot up in surprise. “All night?”

Suddenly that feeling of desperation is back. “A small price to pay to keep a thief around at my disposal,” she says, but Bellamy’s knowing smile only grows. “Like I said, it’s nothing. You make deals with lots of people anyhow. And I’m sure you irritate them too.”

"No. I leave that only for you." It feels like he's laughing at her now.

"I shouldn't have said anything. The next time you get drunk, don't expect—"

"Falan." He gently cups her face in his hands, his smoky eyes filled with adoration. "From the day I met you, you've always intrigued me. Fascinated me."

She shivers lightly. And then she feels it again, that hunger to be closer, even if she doesn't quite understand it or herself yet.

"I've always been drawn back to you. Only you, Falan." Bellamy continues to cup her face. The wind blows past them gently, brushing her hair back, but he tucks a lock behind her ear anyway. "It's always been you."

It's always been you.

A rush of euphoria suddenly washes through Falan. It's real. And she knows when Bellamy cups her face again, when he holds her hand again, even when he shoots her that irritatingly confident smile, she will feel something real.

Slowly, Falan pulls the deck of cards out of her pocket and Bellamy's hands lower from her face. His gaze drops to the card deck, then back up to her eyes. "Now?" he asks.

She nods. "I'm ready." She pulls out a box of matches she's been carrying for this reason, unable to light the flame until now. Bellamy strikes the match for her, handing her the fire, and Falan puts it to the corner of the bound card deck.

They watch as the fire burns through each of the fifty-two cards, eats through each symbol, each waxy corner, until they're nothing but ash. She lets it fall into the snow below, mingling with the dirt.

And then, a sudden pull yanks around her chest before disappearing all at once. A startled laugh spills from her lips. It's over. The link between Jean-Pierre and his performers is no more.

She won. She won. She won.

"It's done," she says.

Bellamy grins. "The world is your oyster now, Sunkara."

Falan tilts her head up to the sky as the wind rakes through her hair, relishing its display of the rising dawn.

The world is her oyster, because she gambled her luck—and won.

The threads cut all at once.

Jean-Pierre feels it. His fingers dig into the stony prison wall as he takes in a deep breath. It doesn't hurt necessarily, but it surprises.

She's done it. Jean-Pierre doesn't know how, but he knows it's her. Somehow she has cut all his contracts, breaking the bonds of all the Cirque performers.

He should never have picked Falan Sunkara off the streets that winter day so many years ago. From the moment he met her, the moment he saw her Affinity, he knew the girl would bring trouble. But he thought it would be fascinating to see an Affinity like hers at work, an Affinity like his.

The Enchanteur clicks his teeth in frustration. He should be able to get out of this prison. These walls can't hold him. But the people watching him—Enchanteurs as advanced with magic as he is—are difficult people to get past. Jean-Pierre knows best that revenge must come from a place nobody would suspect. And nobody would suspect a man behind bars to be the cause of new chaos in the city.

But not yet. He must allow himself to play the long game once more.

Still, Jean-Pierre finds himself wary. To have a chess partner like Sunkara, to find himself bested, leaves him cautious as well as vengeful.

But perhaps there will be somebody in the city waiting to cross paths with Sunkara and her allies and attempt to take them down. Yes, let somebody else do the work for him. It will turn into a new kind of show, different from the Game of Oaths, but just as impactful.

A new type of circus will rise to entertain the masses of the city, complete with glittering masks and illusions and beautiful lies. It always does, like a wrathful phoenix born anew from its ashes, no matter who wins and who loses, who is an entertainer and who is a spectator, who has power and who lacks it.

For the people demand a show, and there are always those waiting to dance into the spotlight.

Acknowledgments

IN THE PROCESS OF CREATING THIS NOVEL, I LEARNED that while my name might be the only one on the cover, it takes an entire ~~village~~ city to publish a book. Like Falan, I could not have achieved my goal without the help of a brilliant, criminally talented team of individuals who deserve thanks.

To my literary agent, Catherine Cho—you took a chance on a very anxious college student and believed in me and my books from day one. Thank you for being my advocate in this industry, for being there during every step of the debut process and more, and for cheerleading all my story ideas. I'm so privileged to have you in my corner. Thank you also to the Paper Literary team, especially Melissa Pimentel for your insightful early editorial notes.

To my editors, Emily McDonnell, Miriam Newman, and Lindsay Warren—there aren't words to describe how grateful I am for the passion, guidance, and time that you have all spent helping me bring Falan and the ensemble to life. Thank you for your boundless encouragement and intelligent visions to make *The Game of Oaths* shine.

To my copyeditors, Maggie Deslaurier and Julia Gaviria, and to my proofreaders, Martha Dwyer and Sarah Chaffee Paris—thank you for catching the inconsistencies and littlest of details to make this story as perfect as can be.

To my cover artist, Micaela Alcaino—thank you for giving me the most gorgeous cover. I still find myself staring at it to admire it.

To my designers, Faith Leung, Lissi Erwin, and Larsson McSwain—thank you for making sure this book turned out so beautifully, inside and out. I'm in awe of what you can do.

To my illustrator, Tomislav Tomić—it's been one of my dreams to have a map in my book. Thank you for bringing to life what this alternate magical 1890s Paris looks like.

To my marketing and publicity champions, Dana Eger and Maggie Salko, and Aaliyah Riaz and Courtney Jefferies—thank you for making sure the world knows about *The Game of Oaths*. You are the reason this book is on somebody's shelf.

To the foreign rights team, Lara Armstrong, Karen Coeman, and Gianluca DiCristofaro Alfaro—thank you for helping *The Game of Oaths* find a home in different countries.

To everybody at Candlewick Press and Walker Books, with special thanks to Pete Matthews for your management in copy, Poppy David and Sarah Parker for handling production control, Maria Middleton for overseeing art direction, and Natalie Bricker for your editorial assistance and for checking the French terms—your efforts were key in the creation of *The Game of Oaths*. The enthusiasm and drive you've shown for this book is something that has made this experience so special. Thank you for all your hard work.

To Dr. Donna Hope and Amy Smith—thank you for your thoughtful insights in making sure I wrote the ensemble cast as respectfully and authentically as possible.

To Ann Sei Lin, D. L. Taylor, and Brooke Archer—thanks for taking the time to read this book and provide such kind blurbs. It truly means a lot.

To this book's first reader, aka my writing soulmate, Kate—honestly, what would I do without you, the love of my life? You are one of my best friends. I still can't believe I got the honor of being a bridesmaid at your wedding. Thanks so much for your words of encouragement that expand far past this book, for getting all my SpongeBob references, for sending me unhinged TikToks, and for being my number one fan and cheerleader.

To the Writer Youngins—I truly could not have done this without you all, and I'm so humbled to cheer you all on your writing journeys. Thanks for reading my many drafts, for the chaotic messages and voice chats (and Alex's lovely planned writing days), for hearing my unhinged rambles, for the inside jokes, for becoming some of my closest friends. I still can't believe I got to meet and travel with some of you (including a flat tire on the side of the road in Ireland with Brooke and Kate, which was quite an experience, as was the spider cottage oof). We made memories I will never forget, and I hope to continue making more. You all helped me not only blossom as a writer, but as a person. I love you all, Pocket Friends Club (shout-out to Nathalie for that adorable name)!

To the VS server—you're all so cool and talented, and I can't wait to fill my shelves with more of your books. Thanks for the endless support (and for answering my random questions when I pop in). Also, thanks, Clare, for your profound industry wisdom. CL, thanks for reading my work—I always smile when I remember your excitement over my characters. Scarlett, thanks for your immense support. Emma, thanks for our chats; I always look forward to yapping for hours.

To my best friend, Kriya—no matter where we are, whether just down the street from each other or across the country, we pick up conversations right where we left off. Thanks for being my blab partner about all sorts of things past books (but also books!).

To my sister, Nikhita—you're probably the whole reason I became a writer in the first place. If it wasn't for you introducing me to a certain online writing website one fateful day, I probably wouldn't be on this path. Thanks for being my first fan, for listening to my stories, no matter how weird, and for the giant Pokémon plushies.

To my amma and dad—thanks for all the warm meals, for allowing me to explore my creativity, for bearing with me during my angsty days, for buying me a vast number of books during my childhood and taking me on library trips, and for proudly telling everyone you know I'm getting published. I wouldn't be able to do this without your support.

To the rest of my family and friends—thanks for all the love. Your excitement and interest in my publishing journey are immensely appreciated, and I'm so grateful.

To my online readers—you were my first audience back when I was a teenager and used to post my stories one chapter at a time after a long day at school. Thanks for tuning in and asking for updates. I'll never forget how your encouraging comments made me certain I wanted to write professionally one day.

To you, the person reading this right now, and to anybody else who has ever supported me during my journey to publication—thank you for picking this book up.

And finally, to my younger self—through the anxieties, lack of self-confidence, and lowest of days, thank you for persevering toward your dreams and not giving up; we made it.

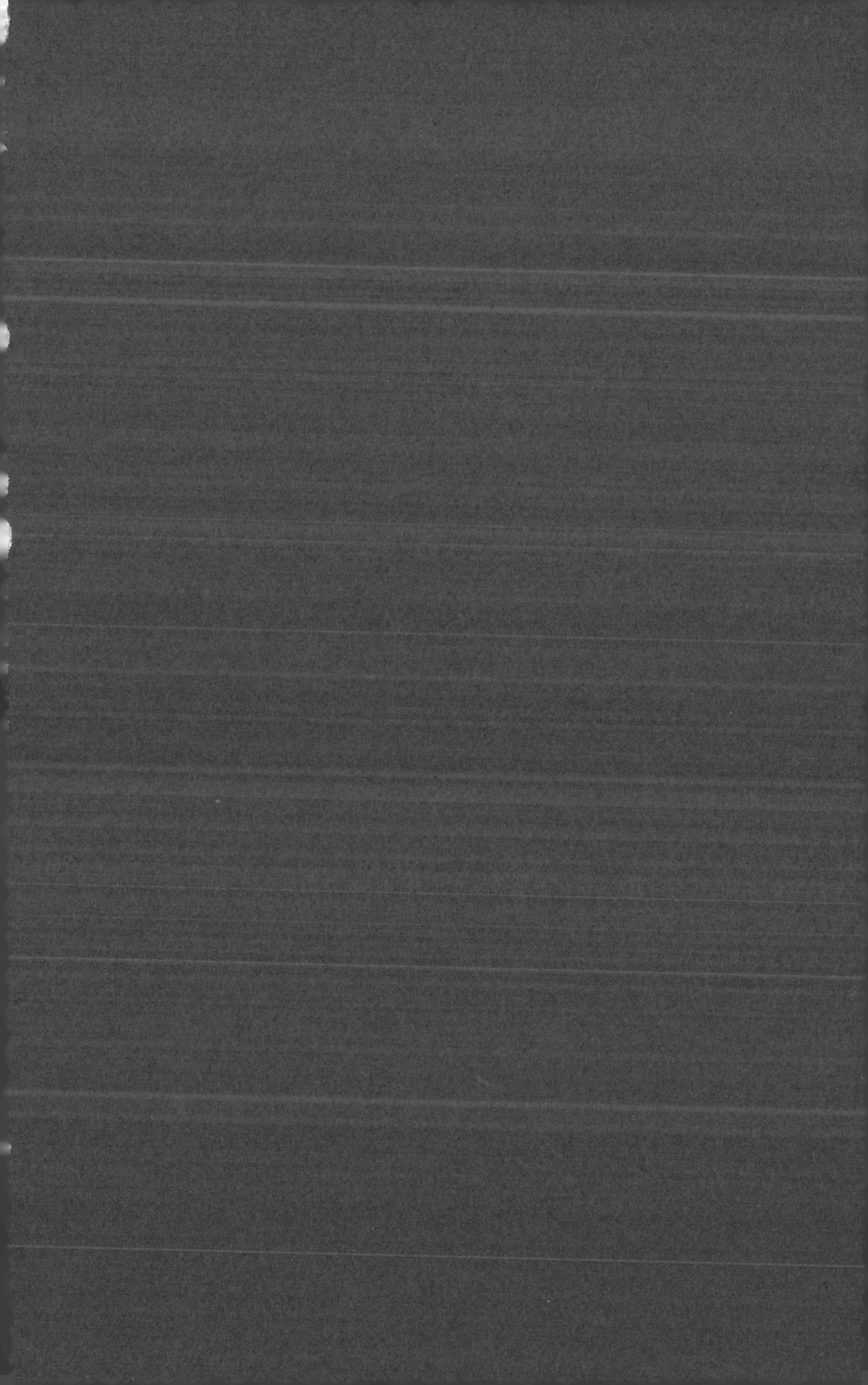